Flowers for Victoria

BY

SUNNI JEFFERS

RIVER
OAK

PUBLISHING

RiverOak Publishing

2nd Printing

Flowers for Victoria
ISBN 1-58919-965-0
46-613-00000
Copyright © 2002 by Naomi "Sunni" Jeffers

The characters and events in this book are fictional, and any resemblance to actual persons or events is coincidental.

Published by RiverOak Publishing
P.O. Box 700143
Tulsa, Oklahoma 74170-0143

DEDICATION

To my beloved husband, Jim, who believes in me and encourages me through every word and revision.

To Maggie Osborne, who opened the doors of my imagination and gave me the tools. And to my precious Lord, who gently called me to yield all, including my writing, to Him.

DULLED FROM CONSTANT MOPPING, the decorative speckles in the room's institutional-gray linoleum tile floor had all but disappeared. Stark white walls reeked of acrid disinfectant. Breaching the room's sterile atmosphere, one solitary item—a shiny, blue cardboard kaleidoscope filled with bits of colored glass—lay on a bedside table otherwise devoid of any objects that might attract germs or dust.

In the middle of the iron post hospital bed, a skinny four-year-old girl clutched a Raggedy Ann doll with red yarn braids. The girl also had braids, only dark brown, like the big brown eyes that stared out of her pale, thin face. Yet, where the doll wore a bright red embroidered grin, the child's mouth drew down on the left, drawing the paralyzed right side of her face into a distorted mask. Her lower lip trembled.

With her free hand, the girl pressed a buzzer over and over. No one responded. She tried to be patient, but she couldn't wait any longer.

"Nurse! Nurse! I have to go potty," she called in frantic, raspy syllables, reaching out to someone, anyone. But no one responded. Every utterance stabbed her throat and threatened to strangle her breath as well. After a few tries, she gave up.

To the distraught child, the bed appeared to be a mile off the ground. Still, she wiggled her legs over the side of the bed and slid to the floor. Her feet hit the cold surface, and her knees buckled. Grabbing the mattress, she clung to the bed until her breathing steadied. Steps faltering, she crossed the cold tiles to the bathroom. Her right side dragged. The short distance—fifteen feet at the most—seemed endless to the weakened child, but she made it. She had nearly accomplished the return trip back to her bed when an ancient, prune-faced nurse arrived.

"Lordy, child, what are you doing out of bed?" the nurse demanded. "You're not supposed to get up. You've been told that before."

"I had to go potty." The girl sniffed, tears pooling in her eyes. She didn't want this nurse. She wanted the pretty nurse who liked children.

"You're supposed to ring the buzzer and wait for someone to come help you."

"I did," she wailed. "I rang and rang, and nobody came."

"You didn't wait very long." The woman scooped the child up and deposited her on the bed.

Examining the fever-parched skin and pain-filled eyes of the sick girl, the nurse steeled herself against emotions that would render her ineffectual. She remembered the days, not so long ago, when the run-down, old Children's Hospital had overflowed with fragile young victims of the polio epidemic. She had watched pitiful little bodies die because they were too weak to breathe—children so paralyzed, they were better off dead. The worst had passed, thanks to Dr. Salk, but there were still cases, like this child. Some people blamed the vaccine. "You're not the only patient here, you know," she said gruffly. The harshness in her voice transmitted to the child, who didn't understand.

"I-I'm s-sorry." The weak voice shook. A tear spilled over and scorched a path down the child's cheek. "I didn't want to wet the bed again."

"A bed can be changed." The nurse picked up one thin wrist, automatically counting the pulse as she listened to the child's labored breathing. Tsk-tsking, she shook a warning finger at her patient. "You stay in this bed no matter what, young lady. And no more yelling. I promise I won't get mad if you wet the bed, but if you get up again, I'll have to put you in one of those big iron lungs out there."

"No!" Shaking her head furiously, the girl shrank back against the pillow. She'd seen the terrifying machines when a man dressed all in white had wheeled her into the hospital. His shoes had squeaked as he'd pushed the gurney past rooms where the big machines wheezed like old men. He had told her mommy the machines pumped air in and out. Even her mommy had looked scared and had squeezed her hand and said everything would be all right. But Mommy wasn't here now. "I won't go!"

she rasped, jutting out a quivering chin in defiance. Her fearful eyes filled her whole face.

The square-framed nurse planted her hands on her hips and leaned toward the child, who cowered in response. "If you don't rest and behave, that's where you'll end up."

"I'll kick and scream," the little girl threatened. Her feeble voice told the real story. The child didn't have the power or the stamina to kick or scream.

Stoically, the nurse stared at the child, then nodded. "You've got spirit, Little One," she said almost to herself. "If you fight the right battle, you might make it." She placed a hand on the child's head. Lines etched the old woman's face. Her eyes mirrored the pain around her, but her voice held soft steel. "You could be a real soldier, but you have to be brave."

Fevered brown eyes stared back. A glimmer of hope took hold of the old nurse, but she suppressed it. She had her own heart to protect. If this child's will was strong enough . . . but even that might not be enough.

"All right, I'm going to tell you a secret. If you listen real hard, you just might win. But you have to fight the real enemy. You think I'm a dragon, don't you?"

The eyes stared, unblinking, but watchful.

"I'm not. I'm on your side. Sometimes soldiers have to do things that are hard, that they don't like. Things like staying in bed and doing what the general says. That's me—I'm the general. The enemy is sneaky, and you can't see it, cause it's hiding inside your body."

If possible, the eyes grew wider. The child's chin trembled.

"Don't be afraid. The enemy likes to scare little children, like you. Now, imagine those nasty, wiggly germs inside of you. Can you see them? They make your throat sore and your arms and legs hurt. They make you tired and weak. But I have a magic flower."

The nurse held out her hand, fingers together like they were wrapped around something. "It's invisible. You can't see it, but it's real, and the enemy is afraid of its magic power. You can have it."

For a tense moment, the child stared, doubt clear in the crinkled lines on her forehead. Finally, hesitantly, she reached out and took the imaginary flower, clenching it tight.

"Good. Now, each time a germ tries to get you, banish it. Just wave the magic flower. And, if it doesn't want to go, close your eyes and concentrate hard. Pretend you're kicking and screaming at it until you scare it away. But not out loud. Just in your mind."

The little chin stopped trembling. The nurse smiled.

"You're going to be a top-notch soldier. And remember, you might not like me much, child, but I'm here to help you battle those ugly germs. Me and the doctor and the other nurses. Do you understand?"

The child gave a little nod of her head.

"Good. Let us help you get well by doing what you're told. But I warn you. If you don't, I won't have a choice. I'll have to carry you out there kickin' and screamin'."

The girl's skin turned ghost-white. Burning pain radiated from her eyes. She gnawed on her lower lip, trying to hold back tears. She wanted to go home. Like a frightened, cornered animal, she wanted to fight. But her throat hurt and her eyes burned. She tried waving the magic flower. She knew it wasn't real, but she liked to pretend, except her hand didn't want to lift up.

Maybe if she shut her eyes and imagined her room at home, her doll house and her little blue and white tea set, and the new puppy with the wet nose and lots of soft, shaggy fur . . . Maybe if she imagined hard enough, the magic flower would transport her to her own bed. She curled up against the stiff white sheets and closed her eyes.

Flowers for Victoria

THE BOUQUET NEARLY filled the doorway. Victoria Halstead stifled a groan. "Could you hold, please?" she said into the phone and punched a button, sending a frustrated construction site boss into telephone limbo. "Not more roses!"

Victoria's secretary peered around the huge bouquet. "But they're so beautiful!" She beamed as if she were delivering a sweepstakes prize. "Where shall I put them?"

"How about the trash."

Janice's eyes widened as if she couldn't believe what her boss said. Victoria relented, but not without a resigned sigh. "Put them with the others, then stay a minute, please." Rubbing the tension in her neck, she leaned back in her leather executive chair and watched her secretary place the flowers next to three equally large bouquets. Victoria winced as she pressed on a particularly tight knot. The tension headaches hit with more frequency lately. The neck spasms never completely went away.

Releasing the hold button, Victoria completed her call, then turned to her secretary. "This office looks like a flower shop."

Janice's *"Oh, yes,"* sounded like a swoon, her wide-eyed curiosity obvious. "What I wouldn't give for an admirer like this. Sixteen dozen roses in one week!"

Victoria's laugh held no humor. "Admirer? Unlikely. A bribe, maybe. Janice, I'm expecting a fax from Montana. Purchase order problem. And have someone take these . . . " she said, with a sweep of her arm towards the roses, " . . . to the women's shelter. Someone might as well enjoy them. Pick one for yourself first."

Janice hesitated a moment. "Are you sure?"

"Yes. Please, take one."

"Okay, then." She chose the deep pink bouquet. "Thanks." Still looking perplexed, Janice took the bouquet and left the office. Victoria knew her secretary was dying to find out who sent the roses. Victoria knew *who,* but the *why* left her puzzled. She eyed the large bouquets lined in front of the floor-to-ceiling window, a breathtaking picture.

Four distinct layers. Four contrasting textures. That had to be a coincidence. Victoria couldn't help but admire the layout. Graceful hundred-year-old red stone and marble buildings commingled with brick, glass and steel skyscrapers, making a cosmopolitan layer of rectangles and squares beneath the peaked magnificence of the Rocky Mountains. Above the clean, precise layers, a clear, pure blue sky spread in unmarred perfection. Beneath, the heart-stopping color and intricate detail of one hundred and forty four roses.

The artist in her longed to grab a paintbrush. The executive in her felt annoyed by the distraction. The woman in her wanted to scream.

She finally had worked Matt Halstead out of her system. How dare he intrude now. She stared at the roses, puzzled. The first bouquet of four dozen white roses had come Monday. The card read, *White flags of surrender. I was wrong once, and it was a doozy.* The note alluded to an old lawyer's joke—"Once, I thought I was wrong, but I found out I was mistaken." The card was signed, *Matt.* Typical. Never *sincerely,* or *respectfully,* or any endearment. Just, *Matt.*

Tuesday, the yellow roses arrived. Again, four dozen. *The sun doesn't shine in Boston.* Signed, *Matt.* Of course, Colorado had an abundance of sunshine, but what did that have to do with her?

Wednesday, four dozen deep pink. *For what's missing.—Matt.*

Today, Peace roses. Delicate yellow tipped with pink, her favorite. Maybe she'd keep those. Matt had planted a bush for her on Mother's Day the first year in their dream house. She had transplanted the rose bush when she moved, but it hadn't survived the first winter. Like their marriage, the roots froze, killing the plant. No, on second thought, they definitely had to go. She didn't need to resurrect those memories.

Absentmindedly, she rubbed the back of her neck and made a mental note to get a massage.

She turned to the paperwork but couldn't concentrate. With a sigh, she took the card off the new arrival. Unable to resist, she leaned down to smell the gorgeous blooms. The faint hothouse scent mocked the real thing. Disgusted, she returned to her chair and swiveled away from the flowers. Opening the small florist envelope, she removed the card.

"The roses speak for themselves." Signed, *Matt.* The barrage of flowers made no sense, but Matt loved strategy, so there had to be an angle. Apology, sunshine, something missing, peace. Why would he send her those messages, after all this time? What did he want? The roses had her stumped, which irritated her. She had no patience with things she couldn't understand and fix right away. She'd rarely beaten Matt at chess.

Saturday morning, Victoria donned her rubber gloves. With her housekeeper gone on vacation, she tackled the cleaning of her bathroom. Monday through Friday she had teetered on a budget tightrope between project managers and clients, architects and marketing. Crisis management had colored her life for so long, putting on gloves and facing a dirty sink was almost a relief. Here in the bathroom, water spots on the faucet presented her biggest challenge.

Constricting her nostrils against the pungent fumes, she wiped her stinging eyes on the sleeve of her tee-shirt, careful to keep her rubber-gloved hands away from her face. Her youngest daughter, Jessica, poked her head around the bathroom doorway.

"Phew-y! That stuff stinks. Why don't you get some of that lemon-smelling cleaner?"

"Mrs. Green says anything this strong has to be killing germs. Who am I to argue?"

"Your hair is sticking straight up. You look pretty cool with a spike, Mom. It'd be totally awesome if you dyed it purple. You could do purple mascara, too, like Tina."

"Tina can do 'awesome' and look good." Turning to the mirror, Victoria laughed. "Goodness, I'm a mess!" She tilted her head one way, then the other. No makeup, her chin-length, straight hair sticking out in damp tendrils, a tee shirt proclaiming "Life is a Mountain" and ragged cutoff jeans, she looked like a mop lady in a cartoon. "Purple, you think? I can just imagine the reaction at work."

"Mrs. Clean goes punk." Jessica grinned, and Victoria almost hugged her, then remembered the caustic cleaner all over her gloves.

"I can see it now. One look at me and security would escort me out of the building."

"Yeah, that'd be great! Then you could take me camping."

Victoria's smile faded. She tried not to let work rob her of time with her daughters, but the job required after-hour meetings and study. With Mrs. Green gone, their "together" time seemed to be spent cleaning house. The usual guilt crowded at her mind. She'd much rather be doing something fun with the girls, but they were busy, too. Mandy had her own activities and a job. Jessica spent a lot of time with her friends. Like today. Her daughter would take off, leaving her alone. Yes, she'd brought work home, but only because the girls had plans. She turned to Jessica. "Is your room clean? And the den?"

"Just about."

"I want your chores finished before you go. Put away your laundry too."

"Sure, Mom." Jessica flashed a cheeky grin that promised nothing, then bounced her way down the hall, bobbing her head in time to the song she belted out in her undeveloped soprano voice. Victoria wondered how the fourteen year old ever accomplished anything. Jessica's temperament was totally opposite that of her older sister, Mandy, who set goals and never swerved once she made up her mind. Victoria could relate to that, but Jessica just bubbled and flitted her way through life, always cheerful, rarely serious.

The doorbell rang, followed by an excited shriek. Victoria grinned and shook her head. Must be Becky. Jessica was going with her best friend to a slumber party. Was the time that late, already? And still a lot of cleaning to do.

"Mom." Jessica poked her head into the bathroom. "Guess who . . . "

"Did you finish the laundry?" Victoria asked, determined not to get stuck folding and putting the girls' clothes away again.

"Mom," Jessica repeated. "Dad's here."

Victoria's head shot up to mirror level. The image of her ex-husband, holding a large bouquet of red roses, watched her from the doorway. She froze. Matt? Here?

"Dad's moving back to Denver. Isn't that great? Now we can see him all the time, not just for holidays. And I won't have to go to Boston this summer. Way cool!"

Forcing a smile, Victoria turned to face them. "Hello Matt. I didn't realize you were in town."

A quick twinkle lit his eyes, a half-smile, a familiar expression that stirred up old, unwanted emotions. Victoria blinked. The memory faded. His expression looked uncomfortable.

"Hello, Victoria. Sorry I didn't call, but I wanted to surprise you—" he looked down at Jessica and winked, "—and the girls." Jessica hugged him around the waist and grinned up at him adoringly.

Victoria's mouth dried up as his smooth, rich voice rippled through her. He looked up and caught her gaze. Warm hazel eyes flecked with gold. She'd forgotten the gold, like tiny flickers of candlelight. Suddenly dizzy, she grabbed the counter. Must be the ammonia fumes. "You certainly succeeded," she said, pushing hair back away from her eyes. "When?"

"Immediately. I arrived this morning. I'm meeting a Realtor later today to look at houses."

"You can stay here while you look, can't he, Mom?"

"I don't think . . ."

"That's not . . ." Victoria and Matt spoke simultaneously.

"I appreciate the offer, but I already have reservations at a hotel."

"But Dad, you don't want to stay at a hotel."

"As a matter of fact, I do." Matt ruffled Jessica's hair affectionately. "I want to be close to my new office until I get settled. You can visit me there. I'm right downtown."

"Yeah, that'd be great."

As father and daughter talked, Victoria stood in stunned silence, rubbing her crossed arms with her hands. How could he just walk into her house—*her house*—after what he'd done.

Taking a deliberate breath, she forced herself to calm down. The past, and Matt's betrayal, no longer had the power to hurt her. At first, she'd wanted to hate him. Soon, however, her innate practicality kicked in. Negative emotions were self-defeating, so she'd worked hard at indifference and turned her energy toward lofty goals. Success had long since defused her anger and taken the edge off her hurt.

Victoria had not seen Matt in five years. Though they'd spoken regularly when he called to ask if Mandy and Jessica needed anything, their conversations had never gone beyond polite. After the girl's first visit with him in Boston, they'd gone on and on about Dad this, and Dad that, not to her, but to their friends within her hearing. Victoria had reached her maximum level of pain tolerance and had yelled at the girls that she never wanted to hear about him again. She had seen their hurt expressions, but they'd been careful not to talk about him in front of her again.

They had visited their father regularly. Matt's love for his daughters brought him to the forefront of her thoughts too often, wondering how he was, what he was doing. She had expected him to marry the woman who had caused their divorce, but that hadn't happened. The younger woman had left Matt for a younger man. Her defection had almost made

Victoria believe in justice. Since then, as far as she knew, he had not been involved in a serious relationship.

Seeing him now, unprepared, shocked her. She steeled her heart against the charm she had helped him cultivate. The doorbell rang again and Jessica disappeared, leaving them alone.

"Why are you here, Matt?" Her voice held an edge sharp enough to cut bone. He didn't even have the grace to wince.

"I wanted to see you."

"No, I mean, why are you moving back to Denver?"

A grin lit his face like a peacock unfurling his tail feathers. "You're looking at the newest partner of Stone and Halverson."

"The law firm? You quit Global Data?"

"Yup."

"But your pension, your seniority . . . "

"Gave them up. I've accumulated a healthy retirement portfolio. The rest was more a ball and chain than a benefit. I should have quit a long time ago, instead of . . . well, I just should have. I feel great—best I've felt in years."

"That's quite a coup. They've never taken on an outside partner before. Congratulations."

"Thank you. Oh." He handed her the roses. "These are for you."

"More roses?" Beautiful, deep red velvet buds. She put her head down and sniffed them, an automatic reflex since she didn't expect them to smell any stronger than the bouquets at the office. These had a spicy-sweet, heady scent—unmistakable, even over the cleaning fumes. "Why all the flowers?" she asked, setting them on the counter

"A peace offering. I want to bury the past." The regret in his smile pricked her heart.

He looked good. Single life suited him, she thought, not particularly pleased with the observation. His soft, bookish looks had matured, replaced by a leanness, which defined his features and gave him a distinguished, sophisticated air. No dark-rimmed glasses. He must have switched to contacts. The faintest hint of silver added a sheen to his light brown hair. His office physique had been honed away. His clothes fit—very nicely, in fact. And he finally had his dream job, the dream he'd traded for a wife and child twenty-four years ago when she'd gotten pregnant, and he was still attending law school. The reminder of his sacrifice made her uncomfortable, but then, Jessica returned, trailed by a friend.

"This is my dad," she said, beaming. "Dad, this is Becky, my best friend."

Matt acknowledged the introduction as Jessica rushed on. "We're going skating before the slumber party. I finished all my laundry, Mom. Gotta run. Call me tomorrow, Dad, okay?"

"Sure, Cookie." The hug and kiss he gave his daughter reminded Victoria of when she'd been included in his affection. How sad to know that life had to change—people had to change. Yet she didn't want to go back to the person she'd been five years before.

As Matt followed Jessica to the door, Victoria grabbed a towel and wiped the moisture off her face. The voices were cut off as the front door slammed. At first she thought Matt had left, but she heard him humming as he returned. She put down the towel and tried to look composed.

"You didn't issue any instructions," he said. "I told her to behave and all." When Victoria frowned, he shrugged. "It seemed the fatherly thing to do."

Victoria resented him barging back into her life. She forced a smile. "She's heard the rules so many times, they're permanently imprinted in her mind. Seriously, the girls seldom give me any reason to worry."

"I know. You've done a great job with them. I wish . . . "

Whatever he had meant to say, he seemed to forget. He stared at her, embarrassing her. Stripping off the rubber gloves, she dropped them in the sink. A hint of a grin turned up his mouth, a look that conjured up a memory of a steamy bathroom when they'd been young and in love. She blushed and hoped he wouldn't notice. He did. She wiped her hands on her shorts. The movement drew his focus.

As his gaze swept over her, she stepped back and crossed her arms. She hadn't felt so vulnerable in a long time. Pushing past him, she went into the open den. A deep breath slowed her racing heartbeat.

Following her, he looked around the family room. Victoria tried to imagine his thoughts. He stopped in front of a picture of an ancient Indian woman.

"I can't look at that picture without feeling humbled," he said. "The hardships of an entire race of people are etched in the lines of her face and the sorrow in her eyes, yet you captured her fierce pride. I think it's the best picture you ever did. Many times I wished I'd taken it with me, but I didn't deserve it."

Victoria didn't know how to respond. She had created the detailed black and white pencil drawing as a gift for him on their tenth anniversary. He loved western history and had been speechless when she'd unveiled his gift. However, for him to keep the picture, after he betrayed their vows, would have seemed a sacrilege. He stared at the picture for a minute longer, then turned, and surveyed the room.

Victoria followed his gaze as he looked at the well-used family hangout with its worn, overstuffed sofa and love seat. She felt defensive about the clutter.

"Nice place," he commented. "I didn't expect the house to be quite this large."

"I got a super deal." She shrugged. "The market had taken off, and I couldn't afford a decent house. Tina steered me to this one. One of her customers lived out here and mentioned there were still some deals to be made. This was a repossession that sat on the market a long time, probably because the house wasn't finished. I got lucky." Now why did she tell him that, she wondered. She was proud of her house. Why did she feel a need to apologize for her good fortune?

"Lucky? I don't think so. You've always had an eye for a good investment, just as you have an eye for art. When developers started building this community, the remoteness created a major problem. Your intuition paid off. Roxburough has turned into a beautiful community. Do you still golf?"

"Occasionally." While his praise pleased her, anything he said made her wary. For what purpose did he show up at her door? And why the interest in her recreational habits? "I don't get to play as often as I'd like," she added. "I don't have much free time."

"Maybe we could play a round someday."

"Maybe," she responded, noncommittal.

He wandered over to a card table that held a half-finished jigsaw puzzle. She followed him as if needing to guard her possessions. He looked down at the table. After a few seconds, he picked up a piece and fit it into place.

"You could always do that," Victoria said. "I used to get so frustrated. I could stare at the same piece for an hour and not see where it went."

He turned to her with a wry smile, which faded as he gazed at her. "You haven't changed a bit, except for your hair." He reached up to where her hair had fallen forward and scrunched a handful, then dropped his hand like he'd been burned. His face reddened. "It's nice," he said. "Makes your eyes look big."

Big, as in shock, Victoria thought. *He hates my short hair. He always threatened to shave his head if I ever cut my hair.* She moved to stand by the glass doors that opened onto a deck overlooking Denver and the golf course. "You've changed a lot," she said.

"Yes. I finally grew up. These have been hard years, Victoria."

"Hard, ha! You don't know hard," she spat at him before she could stop the words from spilling out. A twinge of pain crossed his features. *For him, or for me?* she wondered.

Whatever his thoughts, he didn't comment. Instead, he asked, "When will Amanda be home?"

"She's going out with Tony after work. I doubt she'll be in until midnight."

"Tony? A new boyfriend?"

"Yes." Victoria smiled. "She met him at church. They've been dating several months."

He shook his head. "Doesn't seem like she should be old enough to date."

"She's almost eighteen, Matt."

"I know. And just graduated from high school." Matt shook his head. "I wanted to be there, but I couldn't leave work then. I've missed so much." He looked around the room again at the signs of teenage life—a fashion magazine, a hair clip, a sweatshirt tossed over the back of a chair. Picking up a pop can, he wiggled it, then set it down. He tapped the can top, then stopped and looked at her. "Have dinner with me tonight?"

"Why?"

"I want to talk to you. I've missed you."

"Sure you have. What do you really want, Matt?"

"I have so much to tell you. So much has happened to me since I left. Please, come out with me and let me explain. I want another chance. I want us to be a family again."

His declaration stunned her. She tugged her hands loose and stepped aside, out of his reach. A chill made her rub her hands up and down her arms. "Surely you don't expect to waltz back into my life as if you'd never left!"

"I wish I could erase the past, but I can't. I made a terrible mistake." He reached toward her, palms up, an imploring gesture. She moved to stand behind a chair. As he dropped his hands, his shoulders slumped. "I have no excuse, but I never stopped loving you. I am so sorry."

His eyes, staring at her, were bleak, the golden flecks all but gone as they beseeched her to believe him. His voice broke, as if he spoke with great emotion. She couldn't doubt his sincerity.

"Victoria, I sinned against you and against God. I . . . I asked Jesus to forgive me, even though I don't deserve it. I hope you can forgive me too."

"Jesus has forgiven you?" That hit her stomach like a swallow of vinegar. "How convenient. No more guilt. Life must be just about as sweet as all those roses you've been sending me. You've got religion and a partnership. What a great combination. As I recall, Global Data recommended their executives join a church to help build corporate image, or perhaps political image. Of course, you were too busy, except on holidays, or when the girls were in a Sunday school program, so I came alone." She laughed mirthlessly. She had performed a good many functions to help enhance Matt's career, although she had originally started attending church after she'd miscarried their first baby. Then, church had been a haven—a false haven.

"Victoria, I know you are a Christian. I hoped you'd understand."

"Oh, I understand all right. You need the image for your new position. 'Matt Halstead—an honest lawyer, husband, and father.'" She paused as a new thought struck her. "That would make a great political slogan. Do you have political aspirations, Matt? Well, I certainly can't help you with your good Christian image. I quit going to church after you left."

Thinking about the church brought a bitter taste to her mouth. "Silly me, I thought God was supposed to give me strength and comfort. I had been faithful. I'd prayed—oh, how I prayed. And my 'Christian' friends? They were supposed to give me support and understanding. What a joke. While we were married, whether you came to church or not, I was accepted. When you left, two of the deacons came to the house to pray with me and give me 'spiritual guidance,' as they put it. They told me to be a submissive wife and move to Boston, regardless of the fact that you didn't want me. When I refused, they suggested that I quit teaching Sunday school and give myself time to seek God's will." The acid drip began, hitting her stomach like a hot cinders. "I think they were afraid our divorce might be contagious. And God? He didn't hear me." A sob welled up in her throat. She forced it back down. The church's rejection on top of Matt's betrayal had plunged her to the bottom of despair. For months she'd wondered what terrible sin she had committed to deserve such punishment. Life had forced her to forge ahead, for the girls' sake, and she'd buried all that grief like so much garbage. Now she realized the past had not disintegrated, and unearthing it released the painful memories.

Matt winced. " I hate what I did and how I hurt you. Jesus loves us so much, He paid the penalty for our sins, even though we're not worthy— and me least of all. That is grace. But God doesn't fix our mistakes, and I can't undo what I did. I want a chance to repair some of that hurt. As far as those church people, what they did is terrible, and they will be held accountable for their actions. But you were wrong to think I didn't want you. I wanted you to need me."

"Why? So you could reject me again, like you did for Melissa? Ah, but then your lady friend dumped you, didn't she? So what's the matter, Matt? No other prospects?" she asked, inwardly cringing at the venom in her voice, but unable to contain the distress his presence inflicted upon her. Wounds she thought had healed were breaking open again, thanks to him. Not that he'd said anything terrible, but she suspected his motives. Image had always been important to Matt. Mr. Nice-Guy. Was it important enough for him to want her back? Nothing had changed as far as she could see, except that she was five years older—and successful in her own right. That had to be the key.

The muscles in his jaw grew rigid. "There hasn't been a woman since . . . since Melissa. Victoria, is there someone else in your life?"

"No. Not that my relationships are any of your business. Of course, that means I'm available, and I would be an asset, even if I don't go to church. I enjoy a modest reputation around town, and I'm acquainted with a lot of influential people. Naturally, you know that. And we have a new crowd of movers and shakers since you left. I could introduce you around. Besides, running into each other at functions might be uncomfortable. An ex-wife, one you deserted, would be a blot on your sterling character."

"That's an unfair exaggeration, even for the old me, but I can't blame you for feeling that way. All I ask is a chance. Give us a chance. Let me prove I still love you. Let me prove I've changed. Come have dinner with me."

"No, Matt," she said, shaking her head sadly. "I don't think so. Not tonight. It's been a tough week. I plan to sit in the hot tub and relax. I'm not up to an evening of analysis."

"We won't rehash the past."

"But we would."

"Victoria. I'm not going to go away. I made that mistake. I won't repeat it."

"No?"

"No. Tell the girls I'll call them tomorrow night."

"All right." Victoria walked him to the door. When she shut the door behind him, she sagged against the door jam for support.

⁂

"I really blew it, Lord," Matt said aloud as he drove the rental car back to downtown Denver. "I knew better than to think this is going to be easy. I had my strategy all worked out. First the roses, then I'd take her out somewhere nice and quiet, and I'd explain and ask her forgiveness. Maybe I overdid the roses. Maybe . . . " Matt turned onto the highway headed north along the foothills. He hit his brakes to avoid a deer that darted out in front of him and ran across the highway.

"Truth is, I know You want our marriage to work, so I thought she'd be more receptive. Pretty arrogant of me, wasn't it?" Matt shook his head. His throat felt tight. The optimism that had carried him from Boston to Denver to Victoria's house had become a lead weight. "Lord, You really have Your work cut out with me. I'm a slow learner, but I know You have a plan for me—for all of us. Show me what to do. Father, protect Tori and the girls." He relinquished his future and his family to the Lord and tried to let his anxieties go, but they were entwined around his heart, and he had to struggle to cut the strings.

⁂

Victoria was headed for the hot tub when the phone rang. She took a step, intending to ignore it, then changed her mind. Mandy or Jessica might be calling. She grabbed the receiver on the third ring.

"Hello."

"Hi. How goes the war?"

Swallowing a groan, Victoria said, "Oh, you know—same old stuff." She didn't want Tina to discover Matt had been there. She'd find out sooner or later, but Victoria preferred later. Tina had been her best friend since they'd worked together on a cancer fundraising drive ten years earlier. Her friendship was absolute, but she had a tiny blind spot concerning Matt. Not that Tina defended him, but she'd told Victoria more than once that he would come back some day. Right now Victoria did not want to rehash the morning.

"Yes. So-o-o . . . what's up? And why are you home on a Saturday night?"

"I'm always home on Saturday night."

"I know. That's the problem. Which is why I called. I have this gorgeous cousin—six feet tall, blond, forty-two, a widower with a really sweet teenage son, an impressive stock portfolio, a beach house in Maui—this guy's perfect for you, and he wants to meet you. We'll double. Take in a concert at the Botanic Gardens. I'll supply the picnic."

"Can't. I'm busy."

"How do you know? I didn't say when."

"No blind dates, Tina. I'm just not interested." They'd been down this road before. Often. Tina didn't know when to quit.

"The word is interest*ing* with an i-n-g. You are not interesting," Tina repeated, putting the emphasis on the ending. " As in dull—as in hermit, or is that hermitess? Whatever, it describes you. Victoria, Matt's been gone for years. You need to get a life."

"Thank you very much, Doctor. I don't need a man to make life *'inter-esting.'* I am perfectly happy with my own company."

"You are not happy. You work fifty hours a week, then you take work home. When you aren't working, your whole life revolves around Mandy and Jessica."

"What's wrong with that? I am their mother."

A frustrated sigh huffed in Victoria's ear. "Mandy is about to leave the nest. Jessica isn't far behind."

Victoria resisted hanging up. They'd been down this route numerous times, and besides, she was getting cold.

"I saw that."

"What?"

"I saw you roll your eyes and make a face."

"You did not." Victoria smiled. Sometimes she thought Tina knew her too well.

"I didn't have to. The point is, you have nothing in your life but your girls and your job. No personal life. No fun. No romance. Have you looked in a mirror lately? You're turning into an old maid."

"That is not true!"

"Last time I saw you, you had on sensible shoes, a plain navy blue pants suit, and no eye-shadow. No perfume, either."

"I don't work in a beauty salon. And some people are sensitive to perfume. I'm being considerate."

"You're being dull. You need some magic in your life, like a knight in shining armor to ride into your life and carry you off."

Victoria couldn't help laughing. She pictured some hunk picking her up, throwing her over a horse's back, and riding off into the sunset. "I can just see it now. He'd probably have to drag me, and he'd end up with a hernia. And then what? The picture ends. Happily-ever-after has to come from inside, not some man. You, of all people, know that."

"Low blow. And mighty lonely. All I'm saying is, let your hair down a little. Go out and have some fun."

"In case you haven't noticed, there aren't any knights riding around downtown Denver. If there were, they'd get arrested for letting their horses make messes on the street."

"There are good men out there, but your ice maiden routine keeps them away. No respectable knight is going to breach the castle walls if the princess is wearing a suit of armor. Take a chance! You don't have to get into a serious relationship. Just drop the shields and smile a little. Relax and be available."

"You make me sound like I have one foot in the grave. I'm perfectly happy. Honest."

"You're perfectly chicken. And I dare you to come out of the hen house."

"Tina, I know you mean well. Quit worrying about me. I'm fine. And I'm going in the hot tub now. I'll see you later."

I'm fine, she repeated to herself as she hung up the phone. So, why did she feel like crying? Rubbing her eyes with the sleeve of her terry cloth robe, Victoria stepped out onto her secluded deck. The dark solitude hugged her like a dear friend, silent, accepting, requiring nothing of her. Not like Tina, nagging at her. In all fairness, Tina was her dearest friend, but she always wanted Victoria to do or be something more. Here, in the dark, sheltered by tall potted plants and the giant red rock formations that flanked both sides of the house, she could be herself. Accessible only through her second-story bedroom, the deck overlooked a magnificent view of the park below and the brilliantly lit city beyond, but no one could see her.

As she stepped into the hot tub, she sucked in a breath. Slowly easing into the steaming hot whirlpool, she sat back against the pulsating jets. Liquid silk bubbled and swirled around her, kneading tight muscles, easing strung nerves. Leaning her head back against a foam pillow, she gazed at the stars, searching until she spotted the Big Dipper and Orion's Belt. Like anchors, riding the heavens as they had since time began, the constellations were always waiting for her, a constant in an uncertain world.

Filing her conversation with Tina away in her mental file cabinet, she took deep breaths and let the tension bubble away. An airplane crossed the sky. *Headed where?* she wondered. *Chicago? New York?* Another plane flew lower, its powerful engines slowing as it approached the Denver airport thirty-some-odd miles away. She tracked the blinking lights, and imagined them carrying passengers to exotic places or bringing them home to joyful reunions.

Reunions. What a shock to see Matt. He said she looked the same. Ugh! He'd caught her cleaning the bathroom. She'd looked just as dull and old as Tina described. He could have called first!

Staring at the star-studded heavens, she noticed a wispy cloud, shiny white against the night sky, like a vapor, visible, but without substance. Did that sum up her life? Had she produced any substance?

The girls. But they didn't need her anymore. At least not much. Her job? She'd traded one harness for another—from helping build Matt's career to building her own. When his promotion required a move to Boston, he'd accepted without consulting her or the girls. She'd refused to go, although it turned out to be a meaningless resistance, since he hadn't wanted her to come, anyway.

Before the divorce, her life had been full and fulfilling. Or, so she had thought. Sunday school teacher, head of the church's community outreach, wedding coordinator, choir member, School Board member, involved mother, hostess—she'd been the ideal corporate executive's wife. Now her duties required the same skills, but as a businesswoman, community activist, and mother—the ideal corporate executive. Two sides of the same coin. Had she slipped back into the old rut? Oh, she loved her job. Loved working with Nick. Loved the challenge and the satisfaction of her success, but at what cost? Was she lonely? Solitary, certainly, and logic said loneliness was right around the corner. Maybe she'd take Tina's advice and lighten up. If nothing else, it would be worth the shock value. After all, Tina had been bugging her for years.

A shooting star streaked across the sky and broke her reverie, then disappeared, burning out in the atmosphere. Victoria grinned and made a wish. If the wish came true, if a handsome knight charged into her life, she'd jump on the horse herself. She'd have to do something about her shoes, and her makeup. When she thought about the sight Matt had seen in her bathroom mirror, she wanted to sink under the water and turn into a goldfish. Yes, she needed a change.

What had he truly thought when he saw her? Not that she cared. She was just curious. Matt was such a master at hiding his feelings—Mr. Diplomacy, an invaluable trait in his career. Beneath his suave smile and perfect manners, he must have been as shocked as she'd been.

Remembering his clenched jaw when she accused him of trying to waltz back into her life made her laugh out loud. Poor Matt. So he thought he'd found religion. Interesting, since she'd tried church and found it to be empty, but that was another subject she did not want to examine. He'd even humbled himself to ask her forgiveness. A sweet sentiment, but he hadn't looked all that penitent. It must be difficult to have a male ego, she thought. It might also be a problem. Matt possessed self-confidence. Once he decided on a direction, he stayed his course. Whatever his reasons, he was back, and for her, that spelled deep trouble.

CHAPTER TWO

BY NINE-THIRTY MONDAY morning, Victoria had already put in half a day's work. Sitting back, she gazed out the window, satisfied with the outcome of a conference call. Nick would be pleased, and that gave her great satisfaction. Thanks to Nicholas Shrock, she had reached the top of her profession. When she and Matt divorced, she hadn't held a job in fourteen years, but Nick had given her a chance.

And she'd proved herself. She'd finished graduate school with an MBA in Business Accounting, then worked her way up to executive vice president and CFO of Nick's industrial real estate development company. With Denver's growing economy, the future seemed limitless.

Mentally shifting gears took a few seconds, then the breathtaking view transported her to another place. Splendor and tranquillity. The Rocky Mountains provided both. Her thirty-sixth floor, luxuriously furnished office attested to her position at INTECH. From her desk, the inspiring scene, which constantly changed with the moods of nature, provided in-house stress management.

On this sunny June morning, the peaks rose majestically above velvety-green cloaked foothills. The peace and beauty of the scene made her take a deep breath and relax.

The buzz of the intercom broke her train of thought. "Call for you on line two. Says his name is Matt Halstead?"

"Thank you, Janice." She picked up the receiver. "Hello Matt. What can I do for you?"

"Good morning." He sounded chipper. "I'd like to talk to you . . . uh . . . about the girls. Are you free for lunch?"

"No, I'm not." Thank goodness. His voice made her stomach flutter, and that irritated her. "I have a business meeting."

"How about tomorrow? Or any day this week? Whenever you say. My schedule's open."

"Mine is full. I have a couple of minutes now. What do you want to talk about?"

"I don't want to interrupt your work. I would like to find out what you have planned for the girls this summer, so I can work around your schedule. Since I'm close now, I hope to see them more frequently. Perhaps they could spend some weekends with me. I don't want to inconvenience you or suggest anything that might conflict with your plans."

Victoria flexed her left shoulder back and forth, then stretched her head to the right to relieve the pinch in her neck. The exercise didn't help. She wanted to yell. Not her only free time. "The girls can see you any time they want, Matt. They have camp in August. Other than that, we've made no plans."

"I don't want to monopolize their time. Without a schedule of some sort, I suspect that could happen. I want to take part in their lives as much as possible, but not at your expense."

"That's very noble, Matt, considering you opted out for five years." *Ouch.* Her inner voice scolded her for her shameful cattiness, but it was true.

"Yes. I made some very bad choices. The Lord is working on that aspect of my character," he said in a soft, humble voice, which shamed her. She hated getting slapped by her conscience. "If I know what to expect and understand what you need, maybe I can keep from tripping on my tongue, and be consistent with your decisions."

Stop being so nice, she wanted to snap. "I don't need anything, Matt." She also didn't like feeling unsettled when she heard his voice. She should feel absolutely nothing.

"I just meant, in regards to your time. I'm sorry, Victoria, I'm not handling this well. The telephone is not my best mode of communication. Can we declare a truce? I don't want to fight with you or cause friction, and I don't want to do anything that will hurt you or the girls."

The silver-framed photograph of the girls, the only decoration on her polished cherry wood desk, drew her attention. Two beautiful dark-haired, dark-eyed teenage girls smiled at the camera with eight thousand dollars worth of perfect white teeth and the healthy vitality of carefree youth. In looks they favored both parents, but Victoria liked to think they took after her. They were happy and well adjusted, despite the break-up of their family. The extra effort and attention she'd given her girls, while she went back to school herself, had been taxing, but worth every minute. Matt hadn't been there then. Did he deserve to be there now?

Yes, her conscience said. *He's their father. He loves them, and they adore him.* The girls would want to spend a lot of time with him. She could make it easy for them, or she could cause problems. Much as she hated having Matt become part of their lives again, she knew she'd be the loser if she objected. "All right Matt. Next week some time. I'll have to check my schedule and call you back."

"Thank you, Victoria."

Her stomach took awhile to unknot. If she got upset every time Matt called, she'd have an ulcer or a permanently kinked neck within a couple of weeks.

When Janice came in, carrying a stack of mail and papers, Victoria gave her a grateful smile, glad to refocus on business. "Thanks for that cup of coffee. I needed the caffeine."

"You're welcome. I didn't want to interrupt your conference call, but I knew you'd want a cup. No matter how early I get here, you're already working."

Victoria's smile turned wry. "Have to keep up with the customers." With the fierce competition, staying up front in the industry took an extra effort. East Coast customers were two hours ahead of her, and European contacts were winding down their day when she started. "Here are some contract changes," she said, handing Janice papers with notes scrawled in the margins and lines scratched out. "Would you redo these and send them to Legal, please. Any important mail or messages?"

"Mr. Shrock wants to see you, and a priority fax came in from London, and these need your signature so they can go out this morning.'"

Picking up a pen, Victoria held out her hand. Quickly scanning the pages, she penned her tight, even signature at the bottom of each letter. "The fax can wait until after I see Mr. Shrock. Do I need to take any files with me?"

"No. Ms. Bates called with the message. She said it was urgent."

"All right." Everything was urgent with Viola and she expected immediate compliance with her commands. Victoria went down a hallway into another reception area.

"Good morning, Viola," she said to Nick's aging secretary. Viola peered over the top of her glasses. Victoria wondered why the woman didn't get bifocals so she could see without pulling her spectacles down her nose. The pose did add an air of intimidation, however, like being called to the principal's office for punishment.

"Mr. Shrock is waiting," Viola said, reproof clear in her tone. "Go right in."

Victoria hesitated a moment in the doorway. The corner office had two walls of window, facing south and west, which extended all the way from floor to ceiling—twice as imposing as her own office. Even from the doorway, she felt like she stood at the edge of a dangerous precipice that dared her to step closer and leap over the edge. Today, Pikes Peak shone clear and snow-capped to the south. The view fit the man, rugged and weathered. The financial storms of recent years had left indelible marks of erosion on his stalwart visage.

Nicholas Shrock had his back to her as he poured two cups of coffee. Victoria frowned. Coffee meant serious business. His doctor had warned Nick to lay off caffeine, so he rarely drank it anymore, unless they were rolling up their sleeves for a tough work session.

"Good morning, Nick. Coffee session?"

Looking over his shoulder, he gave her a weak smile. "I need a shot of adrenaline," he said in a gruff, weathered voice. He looked at her yellow linen suit and blinked. "Maybe I won't need the coffee after all. The sight of you is pure sunshine. I believe I feel more energetic already."

With a chuckle, Victoria said, "This is my power suit. I'm meeting with a business consortium that's funding college research grants. I plan to get a firm commitment on the Black Forest Project."

"You'll dazzle them, as always. They don't have a prayer."

"What's so urgent, Nick?"

At the reminder of his purpose, Nick's expression became closed and somber and his complexion paled, alarming Victoria. Nick wore his emotions for all to see, but exuberant or explosive more aptly described him.

She took the cup he offered and sat across the desk from him. As they sipped coffee, silence stretched between them, becoming increasingly tense. Victoria didn't like the strain she saw on his face.

"Bad news? Am I fired?" she asked, his cue to declare her the best vice president he'd ever had. He didn't rise to the bait. If anything, his countenance became bleaker.

"Ed Carlson died last night."

"Oh Nick, I'm so sorry. You were friends for a long time."

Nick nodded. "Since before I started INTECH, then he came to work for me. He was sweet on my Sarah, you know. That's how I met her. 'Course, soon as I entered the picture, he didn't have a chance."

"You never told me that," Victoria said, smiling sadly. "You still remained friends, though."

"Yes. I'm six years older than Ed, you know." Nick leaned back and closed his eyes. "Makes me feel old . . . and tired."

"I know watching his health deteriorate since his stroke has been hard for you, but he never did have your strength or vitality."

"No, he didn't. I'm going to miss him."

Victoria didn't know what to say, so she sat quietly, willing Nick to read her unspoken sympathy and understanding.

"I've been more fortunate than most men. Ed understood me, then you came along. You see things the way I do. You're more like a daughter than an employee."

Her throat tightened, and her eyes burned. "Thank you, Nick. I feel closer to you than I ever felt to my father."

An awkward silence stretched between them. Finally Nick spoke again.

"I don't know how to tell you, except straight out." He took a fortifying breath. "I'm selling the company."

Victoria jerked up straight in the chair. "You're what?"

"I have to sell the company," he repeated.

"No, Nick. You can't. You're letting grief run away with you. Ed wouldn't want that."

"This has nothing to do with Ed's death. This started long before he died."

Victoria felt like she'd stepped into a nightmare, the recurring dream where she walked down a long, dark corridor and the floor was made of shifting squares—black and white. If she failed to step on the white squares, she'd fall into an endless black abyss.

"Why, Nick? I mean why now? Sure, we've had financial problems, but we've got a handle on them. We've accelerated the debt reduction, so we'll be in the clear within five years."

"The company is doing fine, Victoria. Thanks to you, there is something to sell. But I have financial obligations I can't meet. Before you came to work here, I leveraged my house and all my personal properties against the Black Forest Project. I believed the project would be successful, but it failed. I just got notice that someone bought the notes and won't renew them. Now I have to cash out."

"How much? Maybe INTECH can liquidate enough . . . "

"Twenty-six million dollars, including the savings and loan debt and my personal notes. The company can't possibly foot that bill."

Stunned, Victoria stared at her boss. She knew about the money the company owed Nick. She hadn't known he'd borrowed against his personal estate to get the money. He was right—INTECH didn't have that kind of money. "Go public, like we discussed before. I'm sure I could find investors, maybe even the group I'm meeting with today," she said, thinking out loud. She'd proposed offering public stock before, to recapitalize, but Nick had firmly rejected the idea. He'd been so adamant about retaining control, she'd never suspected he might want to sell out.

When Nick shook his head, a knot tightened in her stomach. "A stock offering would work, Nick. Our prospectus looks very favorable," she argued.

"It's too late." Leaning back in his chair, he shut his eyes for a few seconds. Then, restlessly, he rose from his desk and stood staring out the window. After a minute he started pacing. He was seldom still, especially when he was working out a problem, but this time his movements were different, aimless, lacking his normal focused energy.

"I'm tired, Victoria. I've put forty-five years in the construction business. The past fifteen have been tough. I don't have the heart for the business anymore. I feel like I'm stepping into a mine field every time I enter this office." He forked a hand through his thick silver hair. Deep grooves lined his forehead, and puffiness ringed his eyes, a sure sign of diabetic reaction, but she'd seen his symptoms before, and this wasn't just a simple bout of overindulgence in sweets or too much caffeine. This was different. His sudden aged appearance appalled her.

"I'm sick of fighting everything," he went on. "Taxes, politicians, environmental zealots, impossible regulations, and foreign policy. We're pussyfooting around the Arabs, the Japanese, the Chinese, and a whole mess of Communists that claim they want democracy. And who suffers? Me," he said, pounding a finger against his chest. "The American businessman, that's who. I don't want to play the game anymore."

"Nick, you can't do this. You are INTECH. To sell the company . . . what will you do?" she asked. *What will I do?* Her mind echoed frantically. Who would hire a forty-one year old with only a few years of experience?

Sure, she had her employment with INTECH, but there were those in the industry who believed her meteoric rise had more to do with her relationship to Nick than with her abilities. Depending on the outcome, with financial disaster clouding the horizon, her INTECH experience could even be a detriment. What else? An MBA degree in accounting. Nowadays that was a basic requirement. Before that? Housewife, chairman of the local cancer drive, president of the PTA. Pretty slim recommendations for an executive position. Did she have the energy and skill to start over?

"Do?" His question jerked her back to the present. He stood staring out the window. She'd watched him stand this way many times—straight and full of purpose, legs apart like a general atop a hill, surveying a vast land to be conquered—while he considered a problem. Today his shoulders slumped. "I know some guys who go fishing in Canada every summer. It sounds nice. I think I'll go with them."

Nice? What a lukewarm word coming from Nick. The inevitability began sinking in. "When is this sale going to take place?" she asked.

Nick turned to her with a wan smile. "That's the urgent business. I don't have a buyer."

Stated in such an ambiguous way, it took Victoria a few seconds to absorb his request. He wanted her to find a buyer for his company. She knew him well enough to understand the import of his need. INTECH was his lifeblood. "How much time do we have?"

"Not much. The notes are due September first. With thirty days grace, that's October one."

Two months—three at the most, she thought with dismay. "Can you refinance?"

"No chance. The notes are secured by my company stock." He sat at his desk, facing her squarely, looking defeated. "I may have to file bankruptcy. I can handle that. I knew the possibilities when I borrowed against my assets for the Black Forest Project." He stopped. His eyes grew teary as he fought for composure. He cleared his throat and continued. "Trouble is, I didn't calculate on bankrupting the company too."

Victoria hated hearing Nick's confession and witnessing his fight for control. Mustering a smile, she said, "You've been through worse and come out the winner, and you will again. I guess I'd better get started." *And hope I can pull off a miracle,* she thought but didn't voice. She certainly didn't expect any divine help. She'd learned that the hard way. When she'd cried and begged God to bring Matt back, she'd gotten no answer. At church, instead of compassion, she'd received pitying looks, outright criticism, and whispers behind her back.

All the years she'd taught Sunday school and served on church committees had counted for nothing—with God or with her so-called church friends. The final blow had come when Wilma Stuart, her co-chairman in the ladies' fellowship, had told her she needed to confess her sin and get right with God. Victoria had known Wilma for years. They'd served together on the missions committee and made layettes for the unwed mothers' home. Wilma had known her better than anyone else at church, and she had turned on her as if Matt's defection had been her fault. Of course, Victoria couldn't take offense. Wilma had only been expressing her loving concern, one Christian to another, she'd said, and asked if Victoria wanted to pray with her. In answer, Victoria had turned around and walked out, and she'd never spoken with Wilma or set foot inside that church again. Thank goodness the girls had changed churches when they moved. Otherwise, Victoria would not have attended any of their programs. As it was, those were the only times she'd gone to church since.

And she hadn't missed a thing. She'd done just fine on her own, and she'd do fine again. And her first priority was Nick. He was counting on her to fix this mess, and she wouldn't let him down. As she got up to leave, ever practical, she thought of one more thing.

"Nick, have you consulted a tax lawyer about your situation?"

"No. Barney Giles is a good lawyer, and one of my best friends, but he doesn't handle this kind of thing. I was going to call and get a recommendation."

She hesitated for a second, considering, then made up her mind. "I know an excellent corporate lawyer who just moved back to Denver, and I think you should call him."

"Who is that?"

"Matt Halstead, my ex-husband."

"Are you sure you want me to call him?"

"You need the best, Nick, and Matt is definitely the best."

"You received the report?" the voice on the phone asked.

"Five minutes ago." Cleveland Macy Winslow swiveled away from the view of downtown Dallas and reached for the report on his desk. "I'll study it on the plane."

"What time do you arrive in Denver?"

"Seven tonight. Is everything set?"

"Yes. The city is sponsoring an event at Elitch Gardens amusement park on Sunday for companies involved in an urban renewal project. Ms. Halstead will be there. The pass I secured for you will be in your hotel room. When you arrive at the park, go to the concession area. Lionel Kane, who works with her at INTECH, will meet you there at eleven and introduce you."

"Good." Cleve slipped the papers out of the envelope and picked up a newspaper clipping that was attached to the top of the report. He glanced at the pair in the featured photograph. Nicholas Shrock, sole owner of INTECH. A commanding figure even as he neared retirement. The slender, regal woman next to him was young enough to be his daughter. "You've worked with her, Jeffrey; what's she like?"

"We co-chaired a fund drive. She is single-minded, efficient, manages people well. I hate to admit, I learned a few things watching her operate. She gets results from people without their even knowing what is happening."

Cleve let out a dry chuckle. "Nature of the beast, Jeffrey. Have you ever met a female who wasn't expert at manipulation."

"Yes, well, most women knowingly contrive to get their way. She doesn't seem to be aware she is doing it. Neither is anybody else."

"Is she sleeping with Nicholas Shrock?"

"Good question. Not that can be proved. Everything is in the reports."

"But what do *you* think?"

"I think . . . " There was a pause, as if he were considering the question. "Of course, the report is accurate. Our sources are impeccable. However, I would say they have something more than an employer-employee relationship. She certainly has advanced rapidly in the company. They rarely are seen with other escorts. In public they are careful not to appear too friendly, but I get the impression they share a private amusement."

"That doesn't fit her reputation."

"Not all reputations are earned."

"So the rumors aren't true?"

"There's usually some fact behind rumor. She is not afraid to trim the fat off the goose. INTECH ran a lean staff to start with. With their financial troubles, her carving took on the air of a bloodletting. Truth is, I would not want one of my projects under her scrutiny, not that our projects would not pass muster, you understand."

Cleve couldn't imagine his cool-under-fire, English-bred executive officer ruffled by any corporate hatchet man—or woman, in this case. "She sounds like a formidable female."

"Quite so. If I might be so bold, why has she caught your interest? You have never had me run a security check on a female executive, especially given she is not in our field. Are you thinking to hire her?"

"Do you think I should?"

"That all depends," Jeffrey responded. "How secure is my job?"

"Are you fishing for a raise?"

"If you are feeling magnanimous. Concerning Ms. Halstead, she would make an excellent executive, but her current compensation is generous. I think you'd have to offer more than money to entice her away from Nicholas Shrock."

"I'll keep that in mind. But at this point my interest is strictly personal."

"Interesting," Jeffrey commented. "I have a high regard for her, but she does not strike me as your type."

Cleve glanced at the photograph again. Attractive? Yes. Her stance, and the way she gazed back at the camera made a statement of cool intelligence. Even with the poor quality of the picture, he thought he detected a challenge in her eyes. Altogether, very attractive.

"Tastes change, Jeffrey. Tastes change."

Her watch read 10:01. With the temperature already 93 degrees, the day promised to top one hundred, the weatherman had assured his radio audience. As she waited in line with Jessica to get into Six Flags Elitch Gardens theme park, along with thousands of other fun-seekers, a slow burn pierced the middle of Victoria's scalp. The sunscreen she'd applied to her face wouldn't protect her head. She wished she'd worn a hat. The thin, high-altitude atmosphere intensified the ultraviolet rays. With mankind destroying the ozone layer, she supposed she'd get a brain tumor, or at the very least, skin cancer from this day in the sun.

Perhaps if she could jump around, she'd avoid the laser-like rays. Silly thought. Stuck in a crowd at the gate to the amusement park, she could barely move. She hated carnival rides and crowds, but she felt obligated to be here.

What a farce, she thought. She could be lazing by the hot springs pool in Glenwood Springs while pine-scented breezes gently wafted over her. Instead she stood in a mob, waiting to get inside, so she could stand in more lines. How important was a carnival? She hadn't spotted any other INTECH employees. Besides, she could do her cheerleading and pep-talking at work.

No. She had responsibilities, she argued to herself. With INTECH facing rough waters, she needed to help smooth the way. She alternated between feeling sorry for Nick and feeling sorry for herself. If her project didn't get cut, her career could go stellar. Being at an amusement park wouldn't find a buyer for Nick, but a show of loyalty might help morale. When news of their predicament got out, and it would eventually, confidence at work would sink right through the basement. Besides, she reminded herself, glancing at her daughter beside her, she had a dual purpose. Quality time with Jessica.

Sandwiched in a mass of warm bodies, moving and twitching restlessly like hatching mosquitoes, she had disparaging thoughts about the park's lack of punctuality as she tried to maintain her patience.

"What's the holdup?" Jessica complained next to her.

"I don't know." She raised on tiptoe and tried to see around the giant in front of her. At five feet ten inches tall, she rarely had problems seeing over a crowd, but the man blocking her view topped her by nearly a foot. Her gaze followed his spine upward to his broad shoulders. Realizing she was gawking, she looked down.

A white string clung to the pocket of his dark, form-fitting slacks. She might not have noticed the thread on a shorter, less tidy man. Salon-styled hair, designer shirt, perfectly creased slacks, his clothes were impeccable except for the string—like having a price tag hanging on your clothes, or a label sticking out. He'd be embarrassed if he knew. Now what? She could tap him on the shoulder and explain that she'd noticed a string on his . . . But then she'd have to admit she'd been staring at his, umm, posterior. What a dilemma.

The crowd's focus centered on the front gate. If she reached out, she could remove the thread from the pocket without anyone knowing.

No. She'd ignore it. Mind her own business. Right?

She couldn't. The thread kept drawing her eyes. If she removed the thread, she wouldn't have to look at him anymore. Besides, do unto others, and all that. She'd want someone to remove a thread off her pocket.

A glance around assured her no one was looking. A quick pick and tug.

The string was attached.

Just then the crowd moved, jostled her, and pushed her hand flat against him. Before she could react, a vice-like grip clamped around her wrist, and the man's head whipped around.

Dark eyes, like the inky depths of a deep well, pinned her with an accusing, cold stare. Just as suddenly, the intensity in his gaze dimmed. His eyebrows peaked, and a low, lazy voice drawled, "After my wallet?"

Humiliation ignited flames of heat up her neck. "No!"

She didn't look around, didn't need to. She could feel the accusing stares focused on her. She wished a sudden earthquake would swallow her, but the ground remained firm.

Worst case scenario, I could die. As the crowd began to speculate aloud and one lady affirmed she'd seen her reach for the man's wallet, Victoria revised her thought. *Worst case scenario, I could live.*

A man's voice jeered. Two older ladies tsk-tsked the morals of the younger generation.

Victoria stared helplessly at her captor, silently imploring him to let her go.

"Let go of my mom," an anxious voice demanded. Victoria had forgotten about her daughter. The disbelief on Jessica's face echoed her own feelings. Everything she did lately seemed to mortify her youngest daughter. Now this.

"I didn't . . . I mean, I wasn't . . . it was a thread." Victoria's cheeks sizzled. "I'm sorry."

The man's expression lightened as he become aware of their surroundings and her predicament. His grip relaxed, though he kept hold of her hand. One side of his mouth quirked into a grin. Victoria watched, fascinated at the sexiest grin she'd ever seen.

His grin became a full smile, revealing straight, white teeth. She felt like prime rib—rare—on a platter. She tugged at her hand, but he held tight.

"Apology accepted, Ma'am. Why don't we step over here, away from the crowd?" he said, smoothly leading her through the throng. She followed unresisting to the sidelines. The crowd surged toward the entrance, which had finally opened. Releasing her wrist, he said, "Is that better? You seemed to be having trouble breathing."

"It's the heat," Victoria said, fanning her face with her hand. Her voiced squeaked. "I'm really sorry I embarrassed you."

His devilish grin reappeared. "You'd better keep track of that impulsive hand, before you get in trouble."

Scarlet cheeks turned crimson. She hated her telltale emotions. Her hand itched, and she flexed her fingers, then caught herself, and grinned. Actually, the situation was kind of funny. If she lost her job at INTECH, maybe she could become a clown.

"Looks like the park is open. Will you ladies join me?"

"We can't," Victoria answered quickly. She started backing away. "We, uh . . . we're meeting my other daughter. Thank you for being so understanding." She waved a hand absently.

"My pleasure," he replied. "I'm sorry you . . . "

Before he finished, she grabbed Jessica's arm, and hurried away. Chancing a backward glance, she saw him staring after them, a thoughtful and rather serious expression on his face that made her wonder what he could be thinking. He caught her looking and grinned. Quickly turning forward, she increased her stride, making Jessica hurry to keep up.

"Mother! How could you? I could just die! Everyone was watching."

"I'm sorry, Honey. I was trying to be helpful."

"Couldn't you pretend you're not a mother, just for one day?"

Jessica looked so miserable, Victoria wanted to hug her and make the hurt go away. Knowing she was the cause of her daughter's discomfort held her back. Sometimes she forgot how sensitive a teenage girl could be.

"Come on, Jessica, it *was* kind of funny. Someday we'll look back at this and laugh."

Jessica's pained look held no hint of humor. Victoria raised her hands in submission. "Okay, I promise I'll behave. Today, I'm not a mother. So, let's go have some fun." She linked arms with her daughter and smiled. When Jessica smiled back, albeit weakly, and fell into step, Victoria felt a warm sweep of relief.

"I'M HAVING FUN," Victoria mumbled. Glancing at her watch, she noted that she had six hours to go, *if* she could convince Jessica to leave before dinner. Doubtful. She tossed a paper wrapper into the trash. The double-dipped ice cream cone tasted delicious, but much too sweet and much too much. Especially after a dizzy, death-defying ride on *Chaos*. Victoria hated carnival rides, but she wanted to spend time with Jessica. As the girls got older, they spent more and more time with their friends. Then Matt entered the equation. Rather than a concentrated three weeks in the summer, he'd probably want to be with them on the weekends. With her work schedule, weekends were her only free time too.

Holding a floppy stuffed dog her daughter had won in the arcade, she gratefully sat on an empty bench while Jessica went in search of a restroom. Plopping the toy on the bench, she looked up into the grinning face of the tall man, the one with the string. He sat down beside her.

"Hello again," he said.

"Hello." Trying to appear cool, though she felt suddenly feverish, Victoria gave him one of her polite, strictly-business smiles. When he reached over, she nearly jumped.

"Cute dog," he said, tugging on the floppy ear. "You win it?"

"No. I'm holding it for my daughter."

"I hoped you were a good shot. I need someone to win the Swiss army knife for me."

"You've got to be kidding," she said, really looking at him for the first time since leaving him at the gate. His smile woke butterflies in her already unsteady stomach. "You are kidding." She shook her head. "I'm kind of dense today." She wiped her damp palms on her shorts.

"The amusement park is affecting me too," he said. "The smell of popcorn and cotton candy makes me thirsty. Can I get you something to drink?"

"No, I'm not . . . " Seeing humor crinkle the corners of his eyes, Victoria realized she sounded like a rattled nincompoop.

Get a life, Tina had said. *Go away, Tina,* she mentally ordered, but she sat straighter. "Actually, yes, I am thirsty. I'd like an iced tea, please."

"Don't disappear," he warned.

She admired him as he walked away. So tall. She rarely had to look up to a man.

Watching him return, Victoria experienced an unfamiliar surge of attraction. The combination of deeply tanned complexion, pitch-black hair, and an unreadable expression gave him an air of mystery. Glancing around, she realized others were watching him also. She tried to analyze what there was about him that demanded attention. Perhaps his size, or his classic looks, with his square chin, prominent brow and straight nose. She would paint him in a toga, with a centurion's helmet, standing proud and fearsome as he rode in a chariot through the Roman countryside. Imposing, perhaps dangerous, but not in a crowded amusement park in the middle of the day.

"Here's your tea. I hope you like it with lemon." He reached into his shirt pocket. "Sugar?"

"One sugar, please," she said.

He handed her a sugar, sat down next to her and smiled. "By the way, I'm Cleve Winslow."

"Cleve Winslow? *The* Cleve Winslow?" She stared at him, dumbfounded, as he sat there holding her tea.

"Ah, so you've heard of me. Now you have the advantage."

Of course, she should have recognized him; she'd seen his picture often enough. Every corporate executive in the country knew the name Cleve Winslow. Depending upon your own philosophy, you either revered him or feared him, the Goliath of the corporate world, but she hadn't realized he'd be a giant in person too. In her wildest dreams, she never imagined meeting him or talking to him in an amusement park. Suddenly realizing her silence was rude, but still disoriented, Victoria accepted the cup, willing her hand to be steady. "Thank you."

"You're welcome. Now you're supposed to tell me your name?"

"Oh, I'm sorry." She shifted her cup to her left hand and extended her right to him. "I'm Victoria Halstead."

His eyebrows arched as he reached out and shook her hand. "Victoria Halstead? Your name sounds familiar. Have we met before?"

She couldn't help laughing. Who would expect the great Cleveland Macy Winslow to come out with a tired line like that? She tilted her head to one side and studied him. "Perhaps in Monte Carlo, or Madrid? No, wait, I think Paris."

His burst of laughter joined hers. The deep, rich sound resonated through the air. "I guess I had that coming," he said, "but your name does ring a bell. Are you in business?"

She couldn't believe this bizarre scene. "Is this a set up?" His sharp glance made her wonder all the more.

"What makes you ask that?"

Tina? She would pull something like this, Victoria thought, but she doubted her friend knew Cleve Winslow. "You don't know me, unless . . . do you know Tina Dupres?"

He thought for a moment, then shook his head. "I don't believe so. Should I?"

"No. I just wondered. What *are* you doing here?"

He smiled. "The same thing as you, I imagine."

"I didn't see any children with you."

"Is that a prerequisite?" His eyebrows teepeed. "Isn't this a business event?"

"Yes. That's why I'm here too. So, you were part of the inner-city renewal project?"

"My company donated some equipment. Jeffrey Lassiter, my exec, mentioned this event. I just arrived in town, and I wanted something to do today, so here I am."

"I've worked with Jeffrey on fund drives. Your company is very active in charity work," she said, making a snap judgment, tentatively approving Cleve Winslow. He had earned his ruthless reputation, but she suspected the media exaggerated. Reports painted him to be a playboy, but anyone who supported as many worthy causes as Winslow International couldn't be as notorious as the hype suggested.

Besides, something about him made her feel alive. His brilliant smile made her heart do a little flip. "We try to do our part," he said. He leaned toward her—but not too close. Not close enough to warrant the flutter in her stomach. "Truth is, I feel completely out of place. I don't know a soul here. I thought I wanted to get out somewhere with lots of people and just absorb the surroundings, but I find I'm a little lost."

"I can relate to that. Personally, I detest crowds and amusement parks."

"Really? Why did you come, then?"

"My daughters. And an obligation to the company."

He gave her a measured look, and she gave herself a mental kick. For some reason, she didn't want him to know her position at INTECH. "This fulfills my obligation to bring my girls at least once each summer," she added quickly. Accidentally meeting a handsome man like Cleve Winslow seemed somewhere in the realm of fantasy, and she wanted to keep it there.

"You neatly sidestepped my question. Does your husband work for one of the participating companies, or you?"

She cocked her head sideways and considered him. Was he flirting with her? What an interesting possibility. She smiled. "I'm not married. I work for INTECH, which is an industrial real estate development company."

"And what do you do for INTECH? Let me guess—you're an architect."

"Not even close," she said, laughing. "I'm just an office worker. Nothing very interesting."

"I find that hard to believe, Victoria Halstead." He gazed at her intently until his scrutiny began to make her uncomfortable. Finally, he turned and looked around. "Seems you've been deserted," he said. "How about showing me around the park?"

"I'm sorry. I'm waiting for Jessica. She should be back by now," she said, looking around.

Jessica and a friend were walking toward them, sipping large drinks. When Jessica spotted them, her smile turned into a sour, *I don't like that* expression. Victoria assumed her daughter disliked finding her mother with the man she had embarrassed, humiliating her daughter in the process.

Victoria greeted the girls and made introductions.

"Hello, girls. Are you enjoying the park?" he asked.

"It's okay," Jessica said, glaring at Cleve in a way that bordered on insolence. Victoria wanted to throttle her.

"Mind if I join you for awhile?" he asked.

"Join us?" Jessica responded in a squeaky voice. For a moment, Victoria expected Jessica to make a scene, but her frown suddenly evaporated.

"Mom, Becky and Lisa Pruitt want me to hang out with them and stay over at Lisa's tonight. Then, tomorrow, the high school kids from church are doing a car wash. Can I?"

"What about your father? Didn't you tell him you'd call him tonight?"

"I'll call him from Lisa's, puh-leeeze?" she begged, flashing her most imploring big, brown, calf-eyed look. Victoria rolled her eyes.

"Yes, please let Jessica come with us, Mrs. Halstead," Becky said.

Victoria looked at Becky, then said to Jessica, "I'll have to talk to Mrs. Pruitt first. Go ahead with the girls, and I'll see you at the pavilion at dinnertime. Do you need some money?"

"Dad gave me a twenty yesterday. I'm fine. Will you keep the dog for me?"

"I guess. Jessica . . . " Jessica had already disappeared. Victoria wanted to say something to her about taking money from her father, but what could she say? He shouldered his share of their support. The girls got an allowance out of his child support checks. So now he appeared, unannounced, and started playing Mr. Moneybags. Was he trying to buy their affection? Maybe not consciously, but his actions undermined her authority. She'd have to talk with him.

"Hey, are you still here?" Cleve took her hand and wiggled it.

She glanced at him, startled, and withdrew her hand. "I'm sorry. What did you say?"

"I asked if I said something wrong. Your daughter didn't seem exactly pleased to meet me."

"I'm sorry, I don't know what's wrong with her. She isn't usually rude."

"No matter. She's gone off and left the field open to me. Would you join me now?"

"Well, Mr. Winslow, since we both seem to be on our own, and you're new in town, I suppose my civic duty requires me to act as guide," she said. As she stood, she gave him a cordial, corporate smile.

"Oh, no you don't." At her startled look, he said, "The name is Cleve."

"All right, Cleve." Her voice dropped into the low, modulated cadence she used at work, warm and pleasant, but safely distant. She had an idea that women in general acquiesced to his every whim. Not her. She had developed an immunity to superficial charm. When she glanced up at him, his shrewd smile made her wonder if he could read her thoughts.

"From your reaction, I'd guess you read the tabloids," he said.

"You do enjoy a certain notoriety," she said, smiling up at him.

"You don't seem like the type to believe a bunch of media hype."

"Ouch," she said. "I guess I should apologize again, but I think it's your own fault. You seem to bring out the worst in me, and I don't even know you."

He raised his eyebrows in exaggerated arcs, and she could see laughter tugging at the corners of his eyes and mouth.

"Goodness, a perceptive woman," he said. "I plead innocent to provoking any behavior on your part. As for the rest, I pay my publicist well, and he's a wizard at creating a myth from a few carefully embellished truths."

He looked so proud of his reputation, she laughed out loud. "I have a feeling you are totally outrageous."

"I am. Right now I want to have some fun. Shall we?"

At her hesitation, Cleve gazed down at her intently. "I promise my reputation is totally manufactured." He leaned down and whispered, "But please don't tell."

"So, you're telling me I'm safe with you?" Victoria asked, tilting her head as if waiting for a clever repartee, but serious with her question.

"I'd never promise a beautiful woman she was safe with me," he said, "but I don't play games." His warm smile seemed sincere. "I'd like to spend the afternoon with you."

Tina said she should relax and enjoy herself. Why not? Setting aside her normal reticence, she said, "Yes, I'd like that." She couldn't resist a few hours of harmless flirtation with a handsome man. She probably served as a distraction for him, to stave off boredom, but he made her feel young and pretty and giddy. She couldn't remember when she'd last felt so carefree—not even when she and Matt had been dating. Their relationship had been a sharing of hopes and dreams and noble intentions. With such high ideals, Victoria had always felt slightly gauche and inadequate. Amazingly, her clumsy blundering at the park entrance hadn't driven Cleve off.

He looked around and headed toward a large circular ride that worked on centrifugal force. "Let's try this one out."

When she held back, he said. "Come on, live dangerously. I'll hang onto you, I promise."

He laughed a lot, and she found herself responding in kind. For awhile, she stepped outside her serious-minded, middle-aged career woman role.

They meandered around, ending up at the shooting gallery where they tried their luck. She missed all the targets. Cleve won a teddy bear and presented it to her. They went on a couple of tame rides, and she sat next to him, enjoying every minute.

They stood in another line. She didn't pay attention until they neared the front of the line.

"What ride is this?" she asked, looking up with dread.

"The roller coaster."

The sign said *Twister ll*. Her heart took a dive. The ride consisted of little open cars sitting on toothpick rails that snaked up, over and down, and twisted around. Made out of wood, the structure didn't appear strong enough to support toy passengers, let alone a trainload of humans. "I don't think I want to go on this."

"Come on. I'll protect you."

Swallowing, Victoria glanced from Cleve to the ride and back. Logic fought with fear. After all, people rode the roller coaster everyday—thousands of people. No one got hurt. And how could she not take a chance? The whole day had turned into a fairy tale, all because of Prince Charming. As she stepped forward, she heard Jessica.

"Mom, what are you doing?"

Jessica sat two cars ahead. Victoria smiled weakly and shook her head, trying to warn Jessica to be quiet.

Jessica glared accusingly at Cleve. "Don't get on this ride, Mom, you'll hate it."

"We don't have to go," Cleve said, hesitating.

"Come on, come on, people," the ride operator called out. "You're holding up the line. Either get in or step aside."

Cleve started to pull back, but Victoria slid onto the seat. "It's all right. I've just never ridden a roller coaster before."

"Mom, give me my dog!" Jessica yelled back at her. "I don't want you puking on it. Stay down and hang on."

As Victoria passed the toy forward, she started feeling dizzy. She clutched Cleve's arm with one hand, and the bar with the other. "Don't worry, you wouldn't be able to pry me loose with a crowbar," she muttered. Her throat constricted. The ride must be safe, or the park would shut it down.

The car started moving, and Victoria tensed, fusing her fingers to the bar in front of her.

"Relax," Cleve said, chuckling. "They're still loading the cars. The ride won't start until they're all full."

"Maybe this isn't such a good idea."

"Too late. Don't worry, I'll keep you safe."

"You won't mind if I close my eyes," she said, squeezing them shut.

"Lean on me and forget the ride," he said, his breath warm against her hair. Her eyes flew open in surprise, and he flashed her a teasing grin. "When you feel a rush, just pretend it's from my proximity, not the ride."

She started to scoot away.

"Oh, no you don't. In fact, proper carnival etiquette requires you to cling to me for the duration of this ride."

"Cling to you?"

"Absolutely. A resourceful man invented a roller coaster so he could cuddle with his sweetheart, without facing her father's shotgun. The real thrills are inside the cars."

"Outrageous," she said, shaking her head. She took hold of the bar with both hands, but she didn't move away, couldn't, in fact, as he reached around her and both his hands clamped the bar on either side of her, not actually hugging her, but effectively locking her in. Undoubtedly, flirting and sitting close in public didn't mean a thing to him, but for her, the experience was new and daring. She only hoped Jessica wouldn't look back at them.

The cars began moving, gathering speed. She tried to shut her eyes, but some latent masochistic gene made her keep them open, wide. Up and up, the cars chugged until she peered down at the Rocky Mountains in the distance. Perched at the top, precariously, Victoria feared the cars would fall off the track. She forgot about Cleve and stared ahead, waiting . . . waiting.

Then they fell. Straight down, hurling towards certain death. She barely had time to mutter a prayer—an automatic reaction—then they were going up again. A scream rolled around inside her head, bouncing against the inside of her skull trying to get out as the flimsy little car flew faster and faster. Suddenly, the car made one final plunge, then slowed, coming to a stop a few feet from where they started.

Cleve gently tugged her hands loose and unbuckled her, then helped her climb out of the car. As her legs threatened to buckle, she latched onto his arm. She trembled all over.

"Are you all right?" His deep voice held concern.

"No. Yes. Thank you. I'm okay."

"You don't look okay. Come sit down."

He sounded sympathetic and amused at the same time. She wanted to give him a flippant reply, but the ride had muddled her mind, so she kept quiet and allowed him to lead her toward a bench.

"Mom," Jessica said, catching up to her. "Are you all right? You're positively green. I didn't know anyone could actually turn that color."

"I'm fine, honest." Victoria sat down on a bench. Her stomach stopped rolling, and settled, like a lead pancake, at the bottom of her abdomen. "The ice cream I ate didn't sit too well." At Jessica's skepticism, Victoria said, "Go ahead. Just don't forget to meet me at the pavilion at dinnertime."

Glancing from her mother to Cleve and back, Jessica offered, "I'll stay with you if you want."

"No. Go have a good time. I'll see you later."

"What time?"

"Five o'clock; that's when we're supposed to meet Mandy."

"Okay." Victoria watched as Jessica took off after her friends.

"I get the feeling I've sprouted horns."

Victoria's thoughts were suddenly jerked back to the present. "Why?"

"I don't think your daughter approves of me."

That's because you're not her father, Victoria thought. Poor Jessica seemed to have illusions that her parents would get back together. "Oh, well, you know how teenagers are," Victoria said, passing it off with a casual comment.

"Actually, no, I don't. But I suspect they're really aliens, sent to infiltrate the planet."

"I think maybe you're right." She gazed thoughtfully after her daughter, then pasted a smile on her face, hoping it looked better than she felt, and turned to Cleve.

"Who is Mandy?" he asked.

"My other daughter. She's working, but plans to meet us at the pavilion at five."

"How many daughters do you have?"

"Just two."

"I see. Then you fabricated the one you said you had to meet this morning?"

"Oops. Guilty, as charged," she admitted. "I was so embarrassed, I wanted to disappear. Besides, I don't spend time with strange men."

Cleve laughed, but he didn't sound amused. "I think I've been insulted."

"I'm sorry. I didn't mean that the way it sounded."

He leaned toward her, giving her a stern look. "The first thing you said to me was that you were sorry, and you've been apologizing all day. No more sorry, understand?"

"S . . . "

"No." His short command cut off her words.

Startled, she looked into his eyes, a few inches from her own. Some deep emotion seemed to be smoldering in the depths of his gaze, and, for a second, the cliché about eyes mirroring the soul flashed into her mind. She blinked. That quickly, the coals had sparked into a different light, making Victoria's pulse race and her hands sweat.

He didn't move. Neither did he release her from his gaze. "Say it again and I won't be responsible for my actions," he warned in a deep, husky voice. His grin challenged her to push his button and see what happened. Her mouth went dry. Her stomach felt like the inside of a beehive. Prudence and common sense told her to gather her wits and walk away. Normally, she would do just that, but this was not a normal day. The temptation to play along—just to see what would happen—buzzed around in her head. She hadn't flirted with a man since she and Matt had been dating in college. The idea scared her; at the same time a wild exhilaration pumped through her. Suppressing the grin tickling the corners of her mouth, she shoved caution to the back of her mind and took up his dare.

Widening her eyes innocently, she tilted her chin up and said, "Sor . . . "

He moved closer. She panicked, and stepped away.

"Chicken," he taunted.

She blushed and felt foolish. For a moment, she thought he intended to kiss her. Whether he had or not, she would never know, but she could not play hugs and kisses with a man she'd just met. However, she'd certainly given him that impression. "I don't know what got into me."

He laughed and rolled his eyes. His light response made her see the entire scene for the silly bantering it had been. Nothing serious. No sexual innuendoes intended. His teasing was a game—one she'd seen played out at countless social events. She'd never wanted to play. Never felt comfortable or confident enough to play. *Go out and have some fun,* Tina had said. Victoria wondered if she could remember how?

Feeling awkward, she giggled. "I'm innocent," she protested.

"Sure. You're about as innocent as a thief with her hand in someone's pocket."

"You're not going to let me forget that, are you?" She tried to look disgruntled, but spoiled it by grinning.

"You have a dimple," he said. "And a turned-up nose. Like a pixie."

A pixie? "Ugh. You sure know how to turn a gal's head." She wrinkled her offending feature, but she wasn't upset. In fact, she felt lightheaded and certifiably silly. A twinge of conscience made her glance around. Seeing no one she knew, meeting no curious stares, she let out a sigh of relief. They were just two unremarkable bodies in a busy hive of humanity. Make that one, she amended to herself. There was nothing unremarkable about Cleve Winslow. And he didn't know she was the financial officer of a nearly bankrupt corporation. For the moment, it didn't matter. No yesterday and no tomorrow. Just live for today and have fun.

Cleve casually put his hand on her shoulder. "Lady, you're something else. And thanks to you, I'm having a wonderful time."

CHAPTER FOUR

VICTORIA WAS STILL exhilarated from Cleve's attentions when she arrived home. He had stayed with her through dinner, enduring Jessica's antagonistic looks and Mandy's barrage of questions. Watching the girls ply Cleve for information had been a revealing role reversal for Victoria. Did she prod and pick as relentlessly when she met Mandy's boyfriends? She vowed to be more diplomatic in the future.

After dinner, the pavilion had become a dance floor. Jessica had gone with the Pruitts, and Mandy had a date with Tony. Victoria had planned to leave early, but Cleve asked her to dance, and somehow the evening just slipped away. When the band quit just before ten, he had walked her to her car and asked for her phone number.

The light on her answering machine was blinking. She hit the play button.

"Hello, this is Matt. It's almost ten. I tried earlier but didn't leave a message. I'll call again tomorrow night."

Matt. She needed to talk to him, but not now. She had better things to think about. Every word, every gesture, and every smile Cleve had directed her way made her feel beautiful and desirable—feelings that had no point of reference in her experience. Steadiness and purpose had marked her relationship with Matt. This was different. Cleve was handsome, in a princely sort of way, and the day had been out of a fairy tale. She wasn't ready to close the book. She remembered the feel of his hand on her back as they danced in the pavilion, under the stars. She could see his face, a study in masculine beauty, and his eyes, dark and mysterious like the depths of a woodland pool—an artist's fantasy. Even without his physical presence, the vision made her dizzy.

Victoria wondered how her carefully regimented life could be so disrupted in one single day. Indulging in fantasy went against her character. Flirtation was a foreign language, yet she'd jumped in, awkwardly communicating. Awkward was the word. She laughed, the spell broken.

Could Cleve Winslow have been as affected by her as she was by him? Not a chance.

She had just climbed into bed when the phone rang again. *Not Matt,* she hoped as she picked it up. "Hello."

"Did I wake you?"

The sound of Cleve's deep, smooth voice kicked her heart rate into overdrive. Pushing the pillows against the headboard, Victoria leaned back, extending her legs and stretching.

"No. Just getting ready for bed. I enjoyed myself today."

"Me too. Your voice reminds me of warm honey," he said. She clutched the phone tighter, thinking his voice should be a registered lethal weapon. "Meet me for breakfast tomorrow."

"Oh, I can't. I have an early meeting."

"Dinner then?"

"Another meeting. I'm sorry," she said, truly disappointed. "Monday's are always bad."

He laughed as if in agreement. "All right, are you free Tuesday for breakfast? I have to leave town Wednesday morning, and I won't be back for a couple of weeks."

"Tuesday works," she said, deciding she would cancel anything, if necessary.

"Great. I'll meet you in the atrium at your office building at seven."

After hanging up, she turned out the light and laid down, but her thoughts kept her awake. What strange twists her life seemed to be taking. She could hardly make sense of the sudden turmoil. Matt back in their lives . . . Nick trying to bail out . . . now enter Cleve Winslow. She felt like she'd been dumped into the middle of a novel, but what kind? Romance, mystery, or fantasy? She wanted simple order and security. Given a choice between adventure and tranquillity, she'd opt for the latter every time. She'd thought she had that with Matt, but her peace had shattered when he left. Cleve Winslow certainly didn't offer tranquillity, but maybe Tina was right. Maybe she needed a little adventure.

Charts, diagrams, and spreadsheets covered Nicholas Shrock's desktop. Victoria leaned across, facing Nick.

"Flow tests show ideal LFG or landfill gas recovery conditions," Victoria concluded. Sitting on the edge of her chair, she took a deep breath, replenishing the supply of air she'd exhausted during her presentation. Pausing just long enough to gather her thoughts, she continued.

"The Black Forest Research Center can't miss. We get paid to accept waste, from which we produce the fuel to generate the electricity for the center. Plus, we provide the research material at the same time."

Nick leaned back in his chair and clasped his hands behind his neck. "I had my doubts when you dredged up this project, but I'm impressed. Your Methergy is the ace that could make this a winner. However," he added, popping her bubble of self-satisfaction, "it's still a big risk. We've never attempted anything like this before. How about feasibility studies?"

"We're doing tests now with the help of a team from the University of Northern Colorado. Preliminary studies indicate a possible recovery rate as high as eighty-seven percent. . . . "

"Nick?" Victoria said, stopping on a question. She'd been watching her boss, thinking he looked more tired than usual. "Are you feeling all right?"

His smile lacked his usual sparkle. "I'm fine, just a little stiff. Comes with old age. So, what is this Methergy program of yours going to cost?" he asked.

"Government loans and university grants will build the center and additional recovery systems. Our total capital outlay won't be over three million dollars. About half that will be start-up costs."

"Do we have the available funds?"

"Well . . . almost. We know where they're coming from. We're getting a sizable payment from London on the Saudi Arabian complex."

The distracted look that crossed Nick's face made her stop. "You know, Nick, we could table this until we actually have the EPA approval."

"I thought we planned to get the plant construction finished before November."

"We could extend the deadline and pay off some of your note. I know it's only part of your debt, but maybe you could get an extension."

He shook his head sadly. "I appreciate the thought, but I'm afraid it's too little, too late. There are two balloon payments due. The smallest is three million. Even if I got an extension, we'd be facing the same thing again later. No. Thanks for the offer, but I think we'd better go ahead with construction at the Black Forest site."

"You're sure?"

"Yes," he said. "Now, how about permits?"

She reached into her briefcase and pulled out a file. "County permits, commissioners' approval, interstate-trucking permits, state approval. As for prospects, Lionel has lined up enough pending contracts to make the project an immediate producer. This could become the company's biggest asset. Long-range projections show this will generate enough revenue to pay off the debt."

Pausing, Victoria sorted through her papers then grinned triumphantly as she held up a handful of letters. "Letters of support from high places. Everyone wants credit for saving the environment. With proper technology and cost containment, I foresee a day when every industrial plant and every town will have a non-polluting methane power plant."

"Looks like you've covered every contingency," Nick said. "Is there a down side?"

"Negligible," she said, grinning smugly. "Worst case, we'll get paid to bury everyone's garbage, and we won't make a fortune producing cheap energy. The landfill is already there. This is a win-win situation, and we haven't even touched the possibilities of recycling."

He raised his hands expansively. "How can I resist? So, what's next?"

"The roadbed to accommodate the trucks, then we excavate to enlarge the site. Mountain Excavators is ready to move as soon as the county engineer approves the site."

"Get Bart Jensen on the project right away," he said decisively.

Her eyes twinkled with satisfaction. Nick had caught her enthusiasm, as she'd hoped. The Black Forest Research Center Project had once been his dream, but his timing had been bad. Since he'd announced his own financial crisis, he hadn't seemed interested in any aspect of the company, but she had counted on his visionary excitement resparking his dream. "He's already working on it, Nick, just waiting for your go-ahead for the next step."

"Good. Now, how did your meeting with the mall people go this morning?"

She smiled. Nick was snared. He couldn't change his innate love of doing business. He might be discouraged and depressed, but the thrill of a new challenge, a new building, was in his bloodstream, essential to his living and breathing. "They are interested but not ready to commit. They will, though. Housing is getting critical. Turning that old shopping mall into a residential community with an indoor park makes sense." Victoria started sorting and stacking the Methergy papers.

"I don't know how you keep coming up with these ideas," Nick said. "You are a wonder."

"I learned from the best," she said, returning the compliment. "But I can't take credit for this one. The girls and I were at the mall. Jessica wanted to leave, Mandy didn't. Jessica made a comment that Mandy ought to live at the mall—that she could move into Foley's and sleep in the linen department. Anyway, the next time I passed the empty mall, I thought what a shame that the new, super-malls are killing the older ones. Then the idea hit me. Transform the mall into a residential, commercial project. Upscale condos and assisted living facilities, eye doctor, dentist, clinic, cleaners, restaurants and shops: a perfect community for retired people."

"With your enthusiasm, I'm sure you'll sell the idea."

"I hope so. They're looking at engineering reports this week, then I'll meet with them again next week."

"There are dying malls all over the country. You may find yourself very busy."

Nick smiled, but the fact hit her that he wouldn't be around to run the projects. Maybe she wouldn't be, either. New owners usually brought in their own management. She might be standing in the unemployment line.

Victoria got the last table for lunch in the popular sports theme restaurant. She was looking over the menu when Tina breezed in like a miniature whirlwind. Watching her friend, Victoria couldn't help but smile. Petite, pert, and pretty, Tina naturally attracted attention, as she wound her way between tables.

"Hi kid, been here long?" Tina asked as she pulled out a chair and sat down.

Turquoise eyes greeted Victoria with their ever-present sparkle of amusement. The brilliant colors of Tina's various tinted contact lenses were always startling. Sometimes she color coordinated her hair to match, but not today. Despite the ten years difference in their ages, Tina was her closest friend. Outwardly vivacious and carefree, she laughed off her good deeds and played the flighty female, but Victoria knew Tina had a firm hold on reality and a marshmallow heart. Victoria smiled. "Not long. I'm ready to order, though. I'm starved."

"Good. Me too."

Tina waved her hand and flashed a big smile at the approaching waiter. They gave their orders, both opting for salads.

"Okay, how was yesterday?" Tina asked as soon as the waiter left.

"Hot and tiring. You know I hate amusement parks," Victoria said noncommittally, hoping Tina would drop that subject.

"Yeah, I know you're a wimp. So, you survived the dreaded day. Excellent. You're making progress."

"Very funny. I'll have you know I even rode the roller coaster."

"No! I don't believe it."

"It's true," Victoria said with a small nod of her head.

"You must be sick. Who talked you into that?"

"No one. I wanted to try it," Victoria answered evasively.

"No way. You'd never go near a roller coaster if you were sane." Tina shot her a shrewd look. "You met a man." Victoria's blush gave her away. Tina grinned triumphantly. "He must be something, or else he dragged you on."

"Don't be silly. He suggested going on the ride, and I agreed. It wasn't that big a deal."

"Uh-huh. I know you better than that. So . . . his name?"

"Cleve."

"Cleve. Hmm. A strong name, sounds decisive, no-nonsense." She nodded. "What's he like."

"Nice."

"Nice?" Tina snorted. "Nice wouldn't get you on a roller coaster. He must be dynamo."

"You could describe him that way." He'd been intruding on her thoughts all morning. "Actually, dynamic is lukewarm."

Tina gave a little whistle. "Your eyes are off in Lala-land. I don't believe this."

Victoria blushed. "Hush, you're attracting attention."

"Okay, okay," Tina said in a quieter, conspiratorial voice.

Just then the waiter brought their lunches. Victoria hoped the food would sidetrack Tina, and they could move on to another subject.

"How's the salon? Have you started redecorating?" She took a bite of spinach salad.

"No . . . next week. They had to special order the wallpaper. So how did you meet Mr. Wonderful?" Tina asked, refusing to be distracted. Before Victoria could finish her bite and answer, Tina went on, waving her fork as she talked. Victoria half expected the piece of chicken on the end to go flying across the room.

"Let's see. You fell at his feet in a swoon, and he had to pick you up. One look at your rapturous beauty, and he fell instantly in love. Right?"

"Close."

Tina always caught the humor in every situation. Her chuckling had Victoria grinning as she recounted the run-in with the thread. By the time she finished, Tina's laughter was drawing curious looks. Then she nearly choked on a bite of lettuce. Victoria watched, dismayed, unsure whether to jump up and pound Tina on the back or crawl under the table and hide. Tina quit choking, narrowing Victoria's responses.

"You're embarrassing me," Victoria accused. "Some sympathizer you are. It was not funny."

"Are you kidding?" Tina dabbed at her eyes. "You ought to write that up and send it to *Reader's Digest*. Don't they have a column for most embarrassing moments?"

"The whole scene would have been funnier if it had happened to you, instead of me," Victoria commented dryly.

"Then he'd have fallen madly in love with me, not you. What does Cleve do for a living."

Victoria hesitated too long on that question.

"What is this guy, a Mafia hit-man or something?"

"No, he's an executive with a large corporation," she answered evasively.

"What corporation? What are you trying to hide here?"

"Just a corporation . . . okay, okay. Winslow International."

Tina whistled low. "Cleve as in Cleveland Winslow?"

"Yes."

"Aren't you getting in a little over your head? Even I've heard of 'The Cleveland Winslow.' He eats little girls for breakfast."

Victoria laughed. "That's all hype. He's really very nice."

"Sure, and pigs fly. I think you ought to run while you still have a chance."

"I don't run, Tina. Besides, I'm a big girl."

Tina reached over and placed her hand on Victoria's arm. "I know. I just don't want to see you get hurt, again. Okay?"

Victoria's irritation disappeared. Tina had seen her crash and burn before and had helped her pick up the pieces and start over. "Don't worry. I'm not going to get hurt."

Victoria glanced up and saw the object of their discussion enter the restaurant with a group of very large men in suits and a couple of women in business attire. Victoria recognized several players and coaches from the Denver Broncos football team, also a couple of reporters. She had worked with some of these people at various charity affairs.

Cleve looked right at home with this group. His comparable size and stature made her think he must have been a player at one time, perhaps even a pro. As the group approached, he looked straight at her. She had been about to mention his presence to Tina, but his reaction stopped her. After an instant of recognition, a shuttered expression covered his face, and he turned away. His rejection surprised her..

"By-the-by," Tina said, drawing Victoria's attention, "I heard Matt is back in town."

With a mental shrug, Victoria switched topics. "You're slipping. That's old news." She watched the group disappear into a meeting room at the back of the restaurant.

"Give me a break. He's only been back a week."

"Who told you?" Victoria asked.

"Privileged information. You know I never reveal my sources."

"You should hang out a shingle. Tina Dupres: Hair Stylist, Counselor, and Gossip Columnist. Too bad you don't get paid for all your hats."

"Yes, well, my work has its own rewards. So, have you seen him?"

"He stopped by the day he got to town, to see the girls."

"My source says he looks gorgeous. I can't quite picture that. I mean, Matt's good looking in an academic sort of way, but gorgeous?"

"Matt looks good. Being single seems to agree with him." The admission did not agree with her. "He looks like he's been working out, and he's dressing with more style. I could never get him to do that."

"Maybe he's a late bloomer."

"Well, whatever, he seems to be happy and successful."

"So are you, don't forget. You look terrific, and you've climbed to the top of the heap all by yourself. Matt had your help."

"Which he no longer needs. He did ask me to go out for dinner, though."

"Really? And you said?"

"Absolutely not."

"Hmm." Tina's gaze held speculation. "I always thought your split was a shame. Maybe he finally got some smarts. You two had a great thing going, before he got PMS and flipped out."

"Men don't get PMS, and I'd call running off with another woman more than a little crazy."

"Yeah. Monumental in the mistake department, and despicable, but his betrayal made no sense. Matt is Mr. Solid Citizen. And you have to admit, it takes guts to come back and try to make amends."

"He must think I'm really gullible. I haven't forgotten why he left."

"Why you think he left," Tina corrected. "He never married her. In fact, that fizzled pretty fast. I've always wondered what really happened. Have you ever asked him?"

Victoria avoided the question. "The point is, Matt isn't coming back to me. He missed the girls, and Denver. And he's starting a new career."

Thankfully, Tina had let her off the hook—for now. "I heard about his partnership. Pretty impressive. You know the old saying about still waters run deep. There's more to Matt than appears on the surface."

"You always had a crush on Matt. You should have been the one to marry him."

"I would have, but you'd already tied the knot before I met him, remember? I'm kidding. Of course, he's going to have to prove himself. That should be interesting."

"Not to me, it won't."

"Lighten up. He is the girls' father. At least you can be friends. Well, I gotta run. Here's my share," Tina said, tossing a twenty-dollar bill on the table. "Don't forget, my Fourth of July barbecue is next Saturday. Why don't you bring Matt?"

"No way! Besides, he's taking the girls somewhere for the weekend."

"Okay, bring Cleve Winslow."

"He'll be out of town too."

"Well, for crying out loud, bring the pizza delivery boy then."

Victoria laughed. "I'm perfectly happy without a date."

"You're hopeless."

"Great meeting," Victoria commented to Leah Talbot, First Step's Executive Director. The foundation was Victoria's brainchild. Originally started to help single teenage moms get on-the-job-training and provide on-site daycare for their children, the idea had blossomed into a program that helped people take that first step out of poverty into full-time employment through apprenticeships at INTECH and a few other corporations that had come on board. Construction, maintenance, cooking, day-care, equipment repair—the list of opportunities kept growing. "I'm excited about your interior decorating program. Getting Artistic Interiors to donate training is a real coup. A six-week class at their studio runs about two grand. I can't wait to see some of their projects."

"Classes start next week. We're giving them an office floor and a residential floor in the old furniture warehouse that INTECH's converting. When the models are ready, we'll hold a black-tie open house."

"Brilliant. We'll launch sales at the same time. Maybe I'll get some ideas for my house. The girls would love to change everything."

"How are the girls? Enjoying their summer?"

"Yes. They're so busy, I hardly see them anymore. Tonight they're with their father. He just moved back to town."

"Oh. Well, that's good. I mean, that takes a little of the burden off your shoulders. The responsibility of raising teenage girls has to be hard."

"I never thought of the girls as a burden," Victoria said. She regretted the curtness of her tone as soon as the words were out.

"Of course not. I didn't mean . . . It's just, sometimes you look so tired."

Victoria let out a big sigh. "Like tonight. Ignore me, Leah. I'm just exhausted. I think I'll go home and go to bed early."

Lately, the volunteer work had become a burden, Victoria thought as she drove home, and she wondered why that was so. Helping others had always been important and satisfying to her. As a young child, she'd been fortunate to recover from vaccine-associated polio with very little residual effects. Her stamina had taken years to regain, and she never had become physically strong.

Her mother had encouraged her in things like academics and art. The fact that she would never excel in sports was of no account, her parents had said, but they had been strong people and her brothers were star athletes. Her father had doted on her brothers' accomplishments. Her lack of physical prowess had made her all the more determined to succeed. The sting of being a weakling in a robust farm community had spurred her to champion anyone with any kind of handicap, which her mother had encouraged. *"For unto whomsoever much is given, of him shall be much required,"* her mother had often quoted. She had lived by that Bible verse, giving tirelessly to others. Volunteering with her mother had given mother and daughter a special bond that Victoria missed.

Her mother had died ten years ago. Victoria kept the verse taped above her mirror and had carried on her mother's legacy, volunteering her time at church—until Matt left. When she moved, the verse came down, but the need to give remained strong. Victoria became embarrassed when people praised her good deeds. Her motives were not purely selfless. The giving affirmed the fact that she had much—a backward reasoning, perhaps, but assurance, nonetheless. Even if she couldn't prove her worth to anyone else, she was able to give—and give—and give.

Once in awhile, however, like tonight when exhaustion hit her, spasms would grip her shoulder muscles, or cause cramps in her legs, and feelings of cynicism and futility would creep into her thoughts. She flexed her shoulder and moved her head side to side and wondered what good it did to help people who expected handouts or else didn't care. Yes, she had much to be thankful for, but the requirement to give back seemed more and more like a thankless and useless burden. How much was enough? And besides, just once she would like to be on the receiving end.

Chapter Five

CLEVE SAT AT the bottom of the escalator in the atrium, for all appearances, engrossed in a newspaper as he watched Victoria enter the building. She wasted no time crossing to the escalator, eyes forward and head held high, giving the impression of strong purpose and single-mindedness. She walked with a saucy hitch in her gait. Her hair flowed with life. Sleek, shiny, the blunt-cut ends reached just under her jaw-line, alternately brushing one side of her neck, then the other. Watching her gave him surprising pleasure.

Briefly, he considered greeting her at the bottom of the escalator with a kiss. He'd thought about kissing her ever since she backed away from his challenge at the amusement park. This time he wouldn't give her time to think about it. Wondering how she'd react made him grin. Shock? Or, more likely, she'd slug him after he'd ignored her yesterday. For once, he had wanted to thrash the paparazzi. He shook his head and wondered at his reaction to this lady, who so strongly stirred his imagination. Reminding himself of his mission, he planted it firmly at the forefront of his thoughts.

Her psychological profile revealed an overachiever—goal oriented, focused on career advancement, fueled by success and steered by cool logic. This one-dimensional, black and white image, created by her brief, phenomenal career and limited public life had helped him formulate a plan to gain her trust.

However, now that he'd spent time with her, he recognized a missing, vital element. The file photograph had failed to capture her essence, so that he almost hadn't recognized her. The cool logic and careful reserve that characterized her reputation were a facade. He'd caught her with her guard down, and he'd felt the warmth and seen the color, which made the picture come alive.

He'd reread her profile and analyzed his observations. She was more vitality than beauty, more character than sophistication. Even with her success and business savvy, he'd almost call her naïve, a compelling combination that would work in his favor. The challenge excited his hunter instincts. With this new knowledge, he scuttled his intentions to lure her with promises of power and money. She wouldn't be influenced by greed. His revised plan called for Victoria Halstead to fall madly in love with him. Logic made it expedient. Merely contemplating the idea made his blood simmer.

As she got off the escalator, he folded the newspaper and stood up. "Good morning, Victoria," he said, stepping forward. "You're right on time."

She raised her eyebrows. "Good morning, Mr. Winslow. I did not expect you to be here."

"I could say the same. About yesterday . . . "

"Yesterday?"

Her raised eyebrows told him the lady was definitely ticked. Her formality made him smile. If she wanted to pretend she hadn't seen him at the restaurant, he'd play along, however, they had definitely made eye contact. "We'll walk to the restaurant, if that's all right with you?"

"Certainly," she replied.

She fell into step beside him, stretching her stride to keep up, yet still looking professional and even graceful in the process. She had on a standard corporate uniform: khaki straight skirt, tailored white blouse, navy blue blazer, and low-heeled navy leather pumps. If clothes were messengers, today she meant strictly business. Efficient, sensible. He preferred the pink outfit she'd worn at the restaurant the day before. She'd looked much more approachable.

Traffic noise made conversation useless, which relieved Victoria, since she couldn't think of a thing to say. They stopped in front of a nondescript, cement-block building. Large blue lettering above the door said *Manny's Cafe*. A hand-painted sign taped to the door announced the Blue-Plate Special $4.99.

Inside, the sounds of friendly chatter and the clinking of dishes accompanied the rush-hour bustle. Taking a deep sniff, Victoria sighed. "Fried onions and potatoes. Smells heavenly."

Cleve grinned. "I knew we were going to get along. Come on." He took her elbow and guided her to the back where a waitress beckoned them to an empty booth. Shiny, green tape covered rips in the Naugahyde seats. The finish had been scrubbed off the Formica tabletop. Victoria slid onto one side and turned her coffee cup right side up.

"Have you been here before?" Cleve asked.

"No."

He motioned toward her cup. "You seem comfortable with the routine."

"What? Oh, you mean the coffee cup?" She smiled.

"The upside-down mug is usually a truck stop set-up. So you can get your own coffee."

"My parents had a drugstore with a small cafe," she explained. "I've waited a few tables and slung a little hash."

"Where is your hometown?" he asked.

"A small town out on the western slope, near Paonia. I doubt if you've heard of it."

"Apple and peach country. I used to hunt off McClure Pass and the Grand Mesa."

That surprised her. Grand Mesa attracted locals more than tourists. "Do you still have family there?" he asked.

"A brother." She didn't expound. Didn't want to. That part of her life had nothing to do with her present. Besides, this man hadn't earned a deeper look.

"Somehow, I can't picture you growing up in a small town. I'd have guessed city bred."

Appearances. How shallow. "Well, you know what they say. Clothes makes the man."

The waitress interrupted to fill their coffee cups and take their orders. Cleve ordered two blue plate specials.

"Wait." Victoria put out her hand toward the waitress. "I can't possibly eat that much food."

"That's all right," Cleve said, and the waitress hurried away. "Humor me; you have to try it."

Seemed she had no choice. Another strike against Cleveland Winslow. She did not like domineering men. After this breakfast, she'd not see him again. No doubt he felt the same. So, why had he shown up? A point in his favor, she supposed. At least he didn't break dates, or rather appointments. This breakfast did not constitute a date She believed he had an agenda, but what?

The fast service relieved some of Victoria's feelings of awkwardness. Her eyes widened at the sight of the huge plates of food the waitress set before them. Arranging the napkin in her lap, she picked up her fork and held it poised above the plate, wondering where to start. Cleve took a mouthful of potatoes and sausage smothered in gravy, chewed and swallowed, then closed his eyes and hummed his appreciation. Then he opened his eyes and grinned.

"It's just scrambled eggs and sausage and potatoes."

"Cholesterol au gratin, swimming in flour and water paste."

"No, no. The sausage gravy is something special, honest."

He was watching, waiting for her to take a bite. Scraping most of the gravy off the potatoes, she took a modest forkful. As soon as the food hit her tongue, her taste buds woke up and begged for more. "Very good," she said after she swallowed. "Not what I expected." She dipped the next bite in the gravy.

Apparently satisfied, he attacked his food with enthusiasm.

She ate about half the food on her plate, took a swallow of coffee, then looked at her watch. "I need to get back to the office. Thank you for breakfast."

He reached across the table and took hold of her hand. "Whoa, you've hardly eaten. Finish your breakfast, and I'll walk you back."

"I can't eat another bite. I'll drink my coffee while you finish." And she lapsed into silence.

He took his time on purpose, she thought and wondered what game he was playing. She avoided watching him, her head turned slightly away, but in her periphery she could see his gaze upon her . She tried to appear relaxed and absorbed in the surroundings, but his scrutiny jangled on her nerves. She caught herself turning her fork over and over, and stopped. She squirmed in her seat, shifted position, crossed and uncrossed her legs, and couldn't seem to stop. The clatter of dishes rang out each time the kitchen door swung open as waiters and waitresses hurried in and out. Someone dropped a dish, and it shattered noisily, making her tense. His voice, when he suddenly spoke, startled her.

"Good. Better, even, than I remembered," he said as he finished and wiped his mouth on a napkin. "I used to come in here when I worked in Denver. That's been fifteen, sixteen years ago. Their breakfasts kept me going all day."

"I didn't know you lived here before."

"I went to college in Boulder for two years and worked a warehouse job near the railroad station at night. I fell in love with Denver then. I've always wanted to move back here."

"Why didn't you?"

He shrugged. "You live where the money is. For me, that meant Dallas. Now that I can work out of anywhere, I decided to try Denver. Meeting you has cemented that decision."

"That's ridiculous," she said, irritated that he'd expect her to be moved by such nonsense.

"I'm very attracted to you," he said. She couldn't help a small snort of disbelief. Ignoring it, he leaned towards her across the table. "When I return, I want to spend time with you."

"Mr. Winslow," she said, drawing his name out as if she spoke to a slow-witted child. "You'll forgive me for not understanding. Yesterday you pretended not to recognize me. Today you want to build a relationship?"

"The name is Cleve." He reached across the table and took one of her hands. She pulled it back.

"Yesterday was a fluke," he said. "Bad timing."

Her eyebrows shot up. "Bad timing?" she repeated.

"Did you see the woman following us?"

"No, should I have?"

"Not particularly. Paparazzi. She'll sell anything to anyone for a buck—true or otherwise. If I had indicated interest in you, you would become her latest target."

"You were protecting me?"

He shrugged. "I didn't think you'd appreciate having your name hooked to mine. Especially the way she'd report it."

"Really?" She had to credit him for ingenuity. "How?"

"I have a . . . a certain reputation in the tabloids. Every woman I meet becomes linked to me in some romantic way, usually sordid and greatly exaggerated."

Imagining herself on a tabloid cover made Victoria laugh out loud. "As a matter of fact, no one would believe it," she said. "I have a certain reputation of my own."

He looked at her with interest. "What might that be?"

"I'm considered an ice maiden around here."

"I don't believe that. People around here must be affected by the altitude."

"Oh, it's quite true," she said proudly.

"Not a chance. I know you."

She shot him a quick glance. Her amusement faded. "You don't know me at all," she said.

"Yes I do. You forget, I rode the roller coaster with you. That makes me an expert. By the way, I figured out why you look familiar. I read about you in a Denver business magazine last month. You don't work for INTECH; you run the whole, cotton-pickin' company."

"You're exaggerating. The article didn't say that."

"Perhaps not in those exact words. Your approach to business impressed me. I bet you could give my board some fresh ideas. Maybe I'll talk you into giving my people a seminar."

She felt her cheeks color. Real or not, his flattery got to her. The idea of doing seminars intrigued her. "Timing accounted for a lot of my success," she explained. "I was in the right place at an opportune time. A growing market, low interest rates; Colorado naturally attracted new businesses. The area is still growing, especially here in Denver. Every direction you turn, there's opportunity. INTECH, for example: I can see the company doubling or tripling in the next two years." She splayed her hands down on the table and leaned toward him. "We have a project that could bring a whole new field of development to Colorado."

"Is this project a secret?"

She laughed. "No, but you don't want to get me started. I could talk about it for hours."

"Okay, so tell me about it."

She tried to gauge his sincerity. He gazed directly back at her. "If you're really interested, I'll take you to see it."

His smile dazzled her. "Great. I have to be in Dallas for the next ten days. I'm moving my headquarters to the Denver office, and I've bought a house, so I have to arrange the moves. I do want to spend time with you. I like your entrepreneurial spirit and your vision. I think we have a lot in common. May I see your project when I get back?"

Another line? She didn't think so. "I'll show you, but . . . "

"Good. It's been a long time since I've enjoyed myself as much as I did with you on Sunday." Cleve grinned wolfishly. "Usually, when someone tries to get into my pocket, I end up on the short end."

"Now wait a minute. I explained that."

"Yes, you did. And your impulsiveness made my day. My wallet survived, intact, and I came out way ahead. Now admit that you enjoyed yourself too."

"All right. I enjoyed Sunday."

"Very good. Now, repeat after me. 'Yes, Cleve, I'll see you when you get back.'"

She grinned. "Yes, Cleve. I'll see you when you get back. But right now, I need to get back to my office."

Standing, he tossed a twenty-dollar bill on the table.

He escorted her to the bank building, up the main elevator to the corporate level. At the corporate elevators, he looked around the empty corridor, then stepped close to her, making her back up against a wall beside a large potted plant that effectively shielded them.

His kiss caught her off guard. It was quick, but thorough, tasting of sausage gravy and making hash of her senses. When she put her hands against his chest to push him away, he immediately stepped back, then grinned down at her confused expression. He looked so smug, she half expected him to crow. This man was accustomed to getting what he wanted. Why he seemed to have set his sights on her, she couldn't fathom. He could have enjoyed the amusement park with almost any woman, and one younger and prettier at that. One, perhaps, who would welcome kisses in public elevator corridors. Moving away from him, she walked to the bank of elevators. He followed, and stopped her when she reached out to push the button. She pivoted around to face him.

"Why did you do that?" she asked, keeping her voice low to cover a multitude of emotions.

"Couldn't resist. And I want to be sure you remember we have a date. I'll see you a week from Friday. We'll do something."

"I didn't commit to a date. I'll have to check my calendar. I might be busy."

"That's almost two weeks' notice. You can clear your calendar if you want to."

Victoria raised her eyebrows, thinking to object to his high-handed challenge, but honesty stopped her response. Misgivings or not, she did want to see him again, which defied both logic and common sense. On the negative side, the man displayed over-confidence and aggressive tendencies, necessary traits for a man in his position, but not great attributes for a personal relationship. Keeping things in perspective, however, Cleve wanted a diversion, and so did she. He was charming and outrageous—pleasant company and fun to be with. He made her feel young and vibrant. He made her nerves skitter around inside her like popcorn in a hot, buttered skillet. She particularly liked popcorn.

"I'll see what I can do," she said. She punched the *UP* button to call the elevator.

He started to leave, then turned back. Over the top of her glasses, she caught his grin. "Don't pick any pockets while I'm gone," he said.

Egotistical brute, she thought, tamping down the quiver that tried to turn up the corners of her mouth. She had no one to blame but herself, letting him get away with his teasing. Letting him kiss her. The elevator doors opened. As she stepped back into the elevator, she gave him a reproving look like she would give a probationary employee who had just blown his job. "Thank you for breakfast. Oh, and have a nice trip, but don't hurry back."

He frowned as the doors closed. Victoria felt like she'd been granted a reprieve. She needed to set some ground rules before she considered entering any kind of relationship with him. She was no ingenue, looking for glamour and notoriety. In fact, she was not looking for a relationship, period. She would make that clear when he returned—if he returned, which she doubted. More than likely, she'd never see him again. But if she did, she'd be on her guard.

As she rode the elevator to her floor, she mulled over everything she knew or had heard about Cleveland Macy Winslow. Notorious for his cold, methodical business dealings, he had maneuvered hostile takeovers, axed companies or divisions that had posted second quarterly losses, and handed walking papers to numerous high-salaried corporate executives. The man kept to himself, a loner by his own design. Not a man to initiate a relationship. Not a man ruled by passions. So what did he want from her? Those questions piqued her curiosity.

On the way to her office, she muttered good morning to several people without even registering who they were—an unusual lapse, for her.

Was he telling the truth? Could Cleveland Macy Winslow be attracted to Victoria Halstead? She'd need all her wits to withstand his charm, but she already knew she wouldn't back down from the challenge. Besides, she needed a buffer to protect her from Matt's determined pursuit. She'd been appalled to discover she was still susceptible to the only man she'd ever loved. Matt threatened her equilibrium. Cleve made her feel strong, a challenge to test her mettle. And what better defense against vulnerability than the attentions of a dynamic, attractive man. Two weeks—less, actually. Anticipation set a smile on her face.

First Step has been busy, Victoria thought proudly as she thumbed through the impressive report on the corporation's charity foundation. The mayor's office was compiling data on corporate involvement with charities. For a private foundation, INTECH's innovative program ranked among the best.

Once a pastor had said she had a servant's heart. When she had turned to church for solace after her miscarriage, people had been so supportive, she'd wanted to repay their kindness. The warmth and satisfaction she'd gained in the process had spurred her to increasingly more service. She loved watching a project come to fruition. Loved the joy a little act of kindness would bring to someone's face. At work, she insisted on anonymity, which made the results all the more rewarding, like a secret she hugged to herself.

Starting the program had allowed her to continue her charity work on a larger scale. The INTECH employees partnered the project as mentors, trainers, or tutors, or they could work on fund-raisers. They reaped the personal gratification of giving and earned credits toward time off as well as commendations in their employment records.

This report documented the number of hours employees had contributed. Their volunteer hours more than doubled the previous year's stats, she noted with satisfaction.

There were reports from the company kitchen, the in-house day care training program, the construction apprenticeships, and the new interior design training. During the program, participants honed skills in reading, speaking, budgeting, and appearance. They composed resumes and took part in mock interviews, preparing them for the real thing. The program's success rated so high, companies with entry-level positions sought First Step graduates. Many companies had joined their efforts, expanding the areas of training and adding money to the program.

Nick had been so pleased with the program, he'd created The Sarah Shrock Foundation, in honor of his deceased wife. They'd hired a full-time director, Leah Talbot. Under her guidance the program had become a model for the private sector.

Janice entered Victoria's office with a sheaf of papers. "These need your signature. The top one is the cover letter for the First Step report."

"Good. Thanks, Janice."

"If you don't have anything more, I'll drop these off at the mail room on my way out."

"Send the report by courier. The mayor wants it by tomorrow." Victoria scanned the letters, signed them, and handed them back to her secretary.

"That's all for today. You go on and have a nice evening." Victoria closed the Methergy folder she'd been working on earlier and sat back in her chair, smiling with the satisfaction of completing the preliminaries of a big project, especially a project of her own design. She could hardly wait for the construction to begin.

She'd spent eight months investigating and organizing the methane fuel utilization project. Methane regeneration plants were already operating with varying degrees of success in several cities, but her development plans included extensive research on a methane propulsion system that could revolutionize transportation. With preliminary details completed, the project could begin, if . . .

Since Nick revealed his financial crisis, doubts had crept in to cloud her excitement, and she wondered if this were an exercise in futility. Any success ultimately depended on a new owner. Assuming Nick sold the company, would the new owner complete the research center?

Countries worldwide were stepping into cooperative programs in every arena, but there were so many risk factors. Eastern Europe's volatile state, the fickle international market, trade deficits, human rights barriers, emerging third world countries with antiquated technologies.

Even so, Victoria believed Methergy would be the cohesive ingredient in attracting a buyer for Nick's stock. She would certainly do her best to convince them.

Rubbing her temples, Victoria thought about going home. Both of her daughters had plans for the evening. Between friends, fun, and father, the girls hardly ever stayed home. Over the Fourth of July weekend, they were going out of town with Matt, leaving her with three free evenings. Victoria hated holidays without the girls, but Matt had a right to their time too.

Tina's annual barbecue bash was Saturday. She put on spectacular parties and always invited plenty of singles. Victoria had promised she'd go, though she didn't feel much enthusiasm at the prospect. She rubbed the back of her neck. She'd been sitting at the computer too long. Maybe she'd stop by the health club on her way home and work the kinks out of her body.

The phone rang as she put away the day's work. After ignoring the first two rings, she remembered Janice had gone home.

"Victoria Halstead speaking."

"Victoria, this is Matt. Are you busy?"

"I'm just leaving."

"Do you have plans tonight?"

Victoria's mind went on alert, immediately looking for an excuse. The health club, and . . . she couldn't come up with anything more pressing than washing her hair.

"If you're free," he hurriedly interjected, "I'd appreciate your help. I need some advice. Will you have dinner with me?"

He needed her? She doubted that. "What's going on, Matt? Is it about the girls?"

"Partly, yes. Will you come? We could grab a bite somewhere around here close."

She had to eat anyway. She'd find out what he wanted, have her say, then leave. That couldn't be construed as a date. "Okay, Matt. I want to talk to you, anyway. Where shall I meet you?"

"I'll pick you up out in front of the building in, say, twenty minutes? That way you can leave your car in the parking garage where it's cool."

"All right." After she hung up, Victoria felt shaky. *How silly,* she chided herself. They shared responsibility for raising their daughters and they needed to discuss problems that concerned their welfare. So what help did he need? Was he going to back out on taking the girls somewhere for the weekend? Didn't divorced fathers do that all the time? She'd never had to worry about that when he lived on the East Coast. She could feel her blood heating up.

Give it a break, her logical self insisted. *You're getting paranoid.* Matt wouldn't let the girls down unless a real emergency came up. At least with his daughters, he was as dependable as an old shoe.

Maybe he had found another woman, and he'd forget this nonsense about getting back together. That thought should have perked her up but did the opposite. She considered standing him up, even as she freshened her makeup in the ladies' room. She combed her hair, applied fresh lipstick, spritzed on some perfume, then hurried downstairs to the front entrance.

CHAPTER Six

MATT PARKED HIS Mercedes at the curb. Victoria slid into the cool, air-conditioned car. "Hi. Thanks for picking me up," she said. "My car's been closed up all day, so it'd be an oven. Boy, it's hot. We must be breaking records again."

He gave her a stiff smile. Her palms grew damp.

"Hello, Victoria. The radio just said the temperature is 101 degrees, and thank you for coming with me."

If her insides weren't threatening a panic attack, she'd have laughed at his greeting: polite, correct, and making sure he responded to her comments. She hated his cool. No matter what, he never broke a sweat. Nothing ever cracked his composure.

Glancing at him, she noticed his hand trembling when he reached for the turn signal. She looked down at her own hands, clasped in her lap. On second thought, if tremors were an accurate barometer, his nervousness equaled hers. As he pulled out into traffic, she smiled and relaxed back into the plush leather seat. "You're welcome. I almost didn't, you know."

"I know, I could hear the rejection in your pause on the phone."

"Truth is, I'm nervous, Matt."

His head snapped around, and he almost ran a stop light. He slammed on the brake, then turned to look at her. "Why?"

"I don't know. I suppose because we haven't been alone together or really talked for five years." She took a deep breath, then plunged ahead. "I'm worried about what you want to say to me that can't be said over the phone. I feel like I'm on trial and I don't know the charges, but whatever they are, I'll be found guilty. I don't know what you think of me. For that matter, I don't know what I think of you."

"Kind of like facing the dentist?" he asked.

"Something like that."

Matt seemed to relax, then the car in back of him honked, and he started driving again. He drove several blocks before he spoke. "How about if I promise not to get out the drill?"

She laughed. "It's no big deal. I just thought you should know."

"I didn't know anything made you nervous, except heights, of course."

"Are you kidding? I get nervous all the time."

"You hide it well. To be honest, I'm nervous too."

She almost blurted out that she knew, but she held her tongue.

He glanced over at her. "After your first miscarriage, when you got involved in church, you told me God gave you grace to get through each day. Do you remember that?"

She nodded, but didn't respond—didn't want to get into a discussion on religion.

"I didn't understand. I looked for my answer in my work. I kept too busy to grieve, but my denial sure didn't help us. Now I know what you had found. Now I realize God's strength covers my inadequacies, and He never fails me."

She gave him a forbidding look, like she would level at Mandy or Jessica when she wanted them to drop the subject. Her warning worked. Matt's smile acknowledged her hit.

"I'm sorry. I get carried away. It's still so amazing to me. I discover something new every day. I hoped our faith would give us a common bond, something we would share. Please, don't take offense. They say the worst zealot is a new convert. I'll curb my enthusiasm, and let's just relax tonight, okay?"

"Sure." She couldn't, but she wasn't going to admit her agitation. "By the way, where are we going?"

"Al Fresco's. You used to like eating there. I hope you still do."

"Terrific. It's one of my favorite places," she said, pleased he'd remembered.

They were early, so the maitre d' seated them right away. The waiter brought a loaf of bread to the table, and Victoria broke off a hunk. Instead of dipping the bread in the dish of olive oil and herbs, she broke it in half, then in half again, and again until she had a pile of shredded bread in front of her. When she looked up, Matt was watching her so seriously, she felt a moment of dread.

"Victoria, I want to apologize."

Her fingers stopped. "Oh?"

"I didn't mean to interfere the other day when I gave Jessica twenty dollars. She told me you were displeased."

"Displeased? She said that?"

His half-smile seemed a tad strained. "My interpretation."

Her fingers crumbled the small piece of bread she still held. She dropped it on the plate. "You're right. The girls get an allowance out of the child support you give me."

"I realize I should have asked you first. I gave in to an impulse without thinking. I don't want to undermine your authority. I can't promise not to spoil them on their birthdays, or when they are with me, but I promise I won't hand them money again without asking you first."

Victoria chewed on her lower lip. She'd worked up a perfectly justifiable case against Matt's interference. Now she couldn't give voice to her irritation without sounding like a shrew. That irritated her all the more. An ex-husband, especially given the fact that he had left her, wasn't supposed to be cooperative and understanding. "I accept your apology," she said.

"There is a condition," he added. "If the girls need anything beyond their normal expenses, will you let me give you the money?"

"I don't need your money, Matt."

"I know you don't. You never have."

He sounded almost sad, which startled Victoria. He didn't accuse or sound bitter, yet his statement stung.

"Victoria, please let me. I need to help."

She shrugged. "Okay. I'm not so proud I can't accept help. Besides, I may be out of a job after Nick sells the business."

"If that happens, you'll find something else. You'd be an asset to any company."

"Thank you," she said. His assurance erased the irritation and the sting. His statement may have been merely polite, but his endorsement encouraged her. "I wish Nick would hold off for awhile, but he seems desperate."

"I'll make certain he gets the best market price for his stock. That's why he hired me, which, by the way, I appreciate. He said you recommended me. I can't tell you how much that means to me. I promise I'll do a good job for him."

"I know you will. I wouldn't have mentioned you if I didn't believe you were the best lawyer available." Odd, but Matt seemed embarrassed by her praise. She only spoke the truth. After all, she'd helped him get there, though he seemed to have changed—blossomed, like Tina said— in the past few years. Although he seemed genuinely humble, there was a buoyancy, an assurance about him that inspired confidence.

"Speaking of Nick," he said. "We need to set up an audit."

"It should be soon, for Nick's peace of mind. Maybe after the holiday weekend. I could have Janice call your office to set up a time."

"Yes, that'd be great."

"Who does your audits?"

"I'll be handling it myself. I want to give INTECH my personal attention."

Panic welled up inside her. "That's not necessary. We did one eight months ago, when Ed Carlson had his stroke. Everything's in order."

"I'm sure you're right, but I want to look for any legal points that might help."

"Oh. I hadn't thought of that." She hated the idea of Matt examining her work, even though she knew the company books were in perfect order. She might not have made every entry—they had a full staff of bookkeepers—however, the ultimate responsibility lay at her door. What if she didn't pass . . . ? *Don't be paranoid,* she silently argued with herself.

To ease her tension, she asked about Matt's new job. He launched into a monologue about his partners. The old man, Lansing Stone, was a forgetful old man who should have retired years ago. His son-in-law, Lincoln Halverson, was one of the most respected tax lawyers in the country, but also one of the worst practical jokers. His son, Lansing Halverson, not yet a full partner, had great potential if he'd forget the ladies and apply himself to law. Matt's descriptions of the office antics had Victoria laughing and accusing him of making it all up.

Victoria couldn't remember Matt being this enthusiastic when he worked for Global Data Technologies. Reserved, unruffled, and supportive of company policy, Matt made the ideal corporate executive. He never had complained, but he'd never raved about his job, either. He had chosen a firm path and never wavered. She'd believed Matt's job fit his personality. Apparently she'd been wrong. For a second, she wondered what else she'd been wrong about, but she pushed that thought away. She didn't want to know.

As they ate Caesar salads, she asked where he was taking the girls.

"Linc is letting me use his house in Breckenridge for the weekend."

Victoria's eyes lit up, then she remembered she wasn't invited and a lump tightened her throat. "That's wonderful. They love Breckenridge. Be sure you watch the fireworks at the lake."

"We will." Matt looked at her intensely for a second, then changed the subject. "I'm very impressed with your success, you know. But not surprised. Tell me about your job."

She wondered when he was going to explain the reason for their dinner, but she wouldn't prod. She described the mall conversion project they were proposing and the methane project, generalizing and trying not to put too much emphasis on her own role in the business. She took pride in her achievements, but she didn't want to sound like she was bragging.

The waiter brought their entrees. Matt had thick, creamy chicken lasagna, and Victoria had seafood linguini. As they ate, Victoria remembered how they used to order different entrees, then trade bites. For a second, she considered forking a bite off his plate, but she resisted. She didn't want to give Matt the wrong impression or encourage familiarity. The easy conversation between them amazed her. She'd heard of marriages where couples had become great friends after divorce, but they just couldn't live with each other. Did that describe them? Could they be friends?

She studied him over the rim or her coffee cup. His face was so comfortably familiar, yet he looked different in subtle ways. Deepened lines at his eyes and mouth made her think he smiled more often, but a sadness crept into his gaze when he looked at her.

"You've changed," she said.

"How so?"

"I don't know. Your face is more expressive; I can almost read your thoughts."

"We did live together for seventeen years. I'd be surprised if you couldn't."

"Is that so? Can you read my thoughts?"

He considered for a moment. "Not often. You hide your feelings pretty well."

"That's what I would have said about you, but I suddenly realized you aren't hiding anymore, that's all. I'm just making an observation. Silly, I suppose."

"No, definitely not silly. One thing I've learned is that my need for privacy has to do with trust. I was afraid to trust anyone with my feelings—afraid I'd be misunderstood or rejected. Once I relinquished control and gave my trust to Jesus, I lost that fear. Feelings don't go away when you hide them, they fester. I made that mistake with you—us. I'm trying to be more open and put my trust, including my emotions, in God's hands."

Moving restlessly in her chair, Victoria picked up a chunk of bread and dabbed it in oil. His admission could be construed as an accusation. She'd been equally private during their marriage. *Self-preservation,* she thought bitterly. Lately her own emotions seemed to burst forth regularly, making her edgy. She wished Matt wouldn't drag God into every conversation. Once upon a time, she trusted God, but He had let her down too. Matt was watching her with a look of gentle understanding, and she realized he'd caught her staring. Unreasonable anger shook her. How dare he presume to know how she felt. Tamping down her emotions, she pushed her plate away. "So, why do you need my advice?"

"I found a condominium near here, and I want your opinion, if you would?"

She was appalled. "I can't help you buy a place."

"I'm not asking you to. I want a woman's point of view. I'm hoping Mandy and Jessica will spend some time with me, and I want a place they'll like. Also, you're much better about kitchen layouts and closet space and all the practical things woman look for, for resale value."

His explanation sounded logical, but she felt threatened by his request. Not that she still cared for Matt, at least not romantically, so she didn't fear his rejection. She'd grown a thick skin over her wounds. She just didn't want to get involved in his personal life. "Why don't you ask your partner's wife, or a professional decorator? Why don't you ask Mandy and Jessica?"

"I could, of course. I'm sorry. I shouldn't be bothering you. I value your opinion, and you always seem to see below the surface. Linc's wife doesn't know me, and I don't want a professional decorator near the place. I want to pick out furniture and do my own arranging. Even if it doesn't look as good, the results will reflect my own tastes. Do you understand?"

"Sure, I felt the same way about my house."

"And the girls—I want them to approve, but they'll either like the place or not. They can decorate their rooms. I doubt they'll have an opinion beyond that."

She understood and felt flattered that he asked her. Besides, she was curious what type place appealed to him. "All right, Matt. I'll look at the condo with you."

"Thank you, Victoria. It won't take long. We're only a few blocks from the complex."

He took her farther into Lodo, south of the railroad station in lower downtown. In a bygone era when the railroads had thrived, the warehouse district had bustled with commerce. For many years the buildings had stood empty and crumbling, until a few visionaries moved in and began restoring. As old buildings were turned into restaurants, professional office and residential condominiums and specialty shops, the area became a trendy community nestled in the heart of the city. Matt drove down a side street and parked beside a large brick building.

"Are you sure we're safe here?" Victoria asked, looking around the deserted street nervously before she got out of the car. Though she'd read about the renovations and development in the area, INTECH specialized in industrial development, and she had not ventured farther than the historic shopping area of Larimer Square, several blocks away. Once upon a time, Lodo had been home to winos and derelicts—a place to be avoided, especially after dark.

"Perfectly safe," Matt said, offering his hand to help her out of the car. She accepted, but withdrew her hand as he led her to the entrance of the building. He punched a code into a keypad next to the door, which released the lock with a click. Then they entered a brightly lit hallway.

Two metal staircases led up to opposite sides of the building. The brick walls appeared to be ancient. Freshly painted white pipes ran exposed along the tall ceiling. A single large impressionist painting in the hallway broke the austerity.

A handsome young couple dressed for an evening out came down a stairway. They were discussing a two-hundred-dollar-a-plate dinner for the opening night of a Broadway play at the Bonfils Theater. Victoria usually attended the popular annual benefit for cancer research. The couple smiled and said "good evening" as they passed and walked out into the night. Since there hadn't been another car outside, Victoria expected a limousine to pull up, but the couple strolled off nonchalantly down the sidewalk. She realized they were within blocks of the theater complex and many of the gourmet restaurants and night spots.

They took the elevator to the top floor. "Here," he said, unlocking a large double door.

When Matt flipped on the lights, Victoria felt dwarfed as she silently appraised the cavernous room. Across a large, polished wood floor, a row of tall windows faced a breathtaking view of the mountains. Another row of windows with a southern exposure led to a large roof area shared by a similar unit across the open roof and one on the east. The cedar decked roof had umbrellas, tables, lounge chairs and potted trees and planters filled with bright summer flowers.

"The high ceiling and windows give it a larger appearance. Actual measurements are thirty by fifty, plus the loft and a private sunroom."

"Hmm," she responded, disconcerted that he'd sensed her awe. In her mind's eye, she pictured a grouping with leather couch and chairs facing the mountains and a dining-room table in the corner nearest to the roof top garden with a long marble-topped bar between the two, forming a subtle room divider without obstructing the openness.

"Come see the rest," Matt said, breaking in on her imagination. He walked to the left, around a walled partition that supported a second floor loft.

The partition formed one side of a bedroom area, obviously the master bedroom. The lack of furniture kept the room from seeming too intimate. Instead of succumbing to nerves, Victoria took her time checking closets and storage. A doorway led to a bathroom and large closet. A

mirrored wall camouflaged an entertainment center. The reflected image of Matt, watching her, set her feet in motion.

In back of the bedroom, a stairway wound up to a loft. Victoria started to climb up, but Matt called her to see the other side of the partitions.

Around the south side, a state-of-the-art kitchen faced the rooftop garden patio. The ceiling over the work area, which supported part of the loft, lit up when Matt flipped a switch. The gourmet kitchen, the lovely roof garden, the breathtaking mountain view—the condominium fit an urbanite's dream. *Was it Matt's dream?* she wondered. He claimed he wanted a home to share with their daughters. While the loft was appealing, in an upbeat, trendy manner, Matt had always gone for traditional. Had he changed so much? She really didn't want to know. She stood in the kitchen, her hand idly wiping back and forth across the cool tiled counter, as she wondered what had possessed her to come here. Matt was watching her, his head cocked at an angle, an expectant look on his face. When she looked up, he smiled, tensely.

"Well?"

She hesitated a second. "It's nice." Matt held onto his smile, but Victoria couldn't miss the disappointment in his eyes. She hadn't meant to sound unenthusiastic. "Lodo is a prime location right now, and it's close to your office. You could do some great entertaining here." If anything, her assurances seemed to deepen his disappointment. Well, what did he want from her? She'd listed all the positives she could think of. The condo fit the needs of an urban, professionally successful single adult, but she kept that thought to herself. "Show me the upstairs," she said.

"All right." He led the way up the stairway. The landing above the kitchen, large enough for a small sitting room or office, looked out over the roof garden. Partitions on both sides housed doorways to two bedrooms that shared a bathroom. A three feet tall privacy wall surrounded the perimeter of the loft.

"Matt," she said, spinning around to face him. "This is charming. The girls will love staying here."

"Do you think so?" he asked. He didn't sound convinced.

"Absolutely," she declared.

He seemed to relax at her assurance. "One last thing to see," he said. "Come on." He went back to the landing and climbed a set of steps that rose to a skylight which opened like a door. He stepped through and extended his hand to her.

The hatchway led to a private rooftop gazebo large enough for a set of wicker furniture and a profusion of potted plants. Pivoting around, Victoria caught her breath and felt a weakening ache spread through her legs as the reality of their position threatened her equilibrium. She grabbed Matt's arm and moved close to him.

"You okay?" he asked, putting his arm around her waist to steady her.

"Yes," she whispered. As she gazed at the splendor of a sunset in full bloom, her heart swelled, and her eyes clouded. To the north and east, the city shone like burnished copper as the setting sun glinted off tall glass buildings. As they watched, the western sky transformed from pink to coral. Purple silhouettes of jagged peaks stood against the wash of colors, and brilliant gold lined the wispy clouds.

Matt's voice, low and reverent, broke their awed silence. He spoke to the heavens, repeating a Psalm she had heard before, although she only remembered the first line.

"The heavens declare the glory of God; the skies proclaim the work of his hands. Day after day they pour forth speech; night after night they display knowledge. There is no speech or language where their voice is not heard. Their voice goes out into all the earth, their words to the ends of the world.

"In the heavens he has pitched a tent for the sun, which is like a bridegroom coming forth from his pavilion, like a champion rejoicing to run his course. It rises at one end of the heavens and makes its circuit to the other; nothing is hidden from its heat."

Mesmerized by the magnificence before her and the poetic beauty of the words, Victoria's spirit reached out to embrace the wonder of the scene.

"When I saw this," Matt said, turning to encompass the full circle of view, "I forgot about the rest of the loft. I keep coming back to stand here. I'm driving my Realtor nuts, but I can't get enough. Every time, the Lord creates a new masterpiece, reminding me of the depth of His love. Up here, I can almost picture Jesus coming back in the clouds. I wish I could share this with the world. You could, with your talent; you could capture this."

She could hardly speak over the tight ache in her throat. When she did, her voice came out in a hoarse whisper. "I could never do this justice. The view is magnificent!"

"Yes, it is."

She felt the warmth of his gaze on her, though she didn't dare look at him. A slight movement told her when he looked away, looking out at the scene with her. Neither spoke again. Neither had to. The touch of his arm and hand against her side warmed her. In his stillness, she sensed his own stirred emotions and felt close to his spirit in a way she hadn't experienced since the day Jessica was born.

As the sunset deepened to crimson, Victoria visualized an artist's rendition of Christ, painted in the classic manner of Michelangelo—Christ triumphant, arrayed in glory and splendor, surrounded by a host of angels, garbed as for war. To even attempt such a masterpiece would take genius, devotion, and divine inspiration. The scope of such a creation caused her to tremble. Knowing she fell far short of even one of those qualifications, for a crazy instant, she wanted Matt's comfort. She needed to be hugged and cherished. Afraid to speak out loud and reveal her need, she whispered, "This is a wonderful home, Matt. I know you'll be very happy here." She turned and left him standing on the roof.

After a few minutes, he followed her down. She was waiting for him by the front door. They descended the stairs in silence and didn't speak until they were in his car. She thought Matt seemed preoccupied, and she felt lonelier than usual.

Before he started the car, Matt turned toward her. "With the girls gone, what are you going to do this weekend? Do you have plans?"

"Not really. Tina's having a party, and I have things to do around the house."

"I was thinking . . . now, don't say anything until you hear me out. Linc's house in Breckenridge has a separate room and bath in the attic. You could come with us; even take your own car up if you want. You could spend time with us, or go off on your own to paint or whatever you want."

His invitation threw her. Why would Matt ask her to go with them to the mountains? Did he feel sorry for her? Heaven forbid. That he wanted her opinion on the warehouse condominium seemed strange enough.

"I don't think so, Matt, but thanks for the offer. I'd feel awkward and so would you. You and the girls go. Enjoy yourselves. Don't worry about me. I'll be fine."

"All right, but, if you change your mind, I'd like you to come. So, what do you think about the condo's investment potential? I'm so bowled over by the gazebo, I can't assess the value objectively, so I need an unbiased opinion."

Always the diplomat, she thought, relieved at the change of subject. "I'm no expert," she said. "And I have no doubt you've run comparisons and projections on the real estate market. I think the building is nice and the unit is great. The kitchen is a dream. The views, the privacy, the security, everything seems ideal. From what I could see, there's plenty of storage. The gazebo enhances the value, I'm sure. If you don't take the condo," she said lightly, "maybe I will."

"I hoped you'd feel that way. I made an offer, but I haven't received an answer yet."

"What about your car?" she asked as an afterthought.

"There's an underground garage with plenty of parking. The building is covered by an excellent security system. When the girls visit, they can come directly upstairs from the garage. Actually, they'll be a lot safer here than driving home to your house at night."

Victoria bristled defensively. "The girls are perfectly safe when they come home. They always lock their doors, and they have a cell phone in the car."

"What if they have a flat tire?"

"They call the automobile club from the car. They call me. They can call the police if they need to. Honestly, Matt. You used to accuse me of coddling them. You are the one sounding overprotective."

"Okay. I'm sorry, Victoria. You're a long way out on isolated roads, but I have to admit you have been fine."

"Yes, we have," she said.

They had arrived at Victoria's car. As he pulled to a stop, Matt thanked her for her help, and she thanked him for dinner. They parted politely.

❧

Before he returned the key, Matt went back to stand in the gazebo. Although he felt the continual presence of the Lord in his life, the rooftop oasis called to him like a mountaintop where he could meet with God in the midst of the city. Tonight he had much to think and pray about. The evening hadn't ended well. Matt had hoped for . . . expected a miracle. God hadn't intervened, and Matt was ashamed to realize he'd been trying to dictate to the Lord again. Perhaps he fell a little short in the realm of patience. He wanted Victoria back now. "Oh, Jesus, will I ever get this Christian business right? I gave You my relationship with Victoria, but I keep grabbing it back. I feel like I have to do something, or it'll never happen. Some faith, huh?"

My child, do you not understand? If you have faith as small as a mustard seed, you can say to this mountain, "Move from here to there" and it will move. Everything is possible for him who believes.

Matt felt exposed and naked before the Lord, who knew the depth of his belief and the breadth of his weakness. He wanted to weep. "Lord, you know I believe. Help me overcome my doubt."

As he stood there, the night enveloped him in a soft veil. The mountains were silhouettes against the twilight sky. Stars were beginning to appear, though faint because of the city lights. House lights and streetlights lit up the city for as far along the Front Range as he could see. Each light represented humanity. People in cars, on streets, in houses. But here, on the rooftop, he was alone with God.

He could still feel Victoria's presence, though she was no longer there and might never stand there again. The sense of spiritual connection between them had given him hope. For a moment, she'd drawn close to him, but then she'd left.

He had meant what he said about being with the Lord on the rooftop. Had she felt God's presence too? At her house, when he had told her he'd asked the Lord's forgiveness, she'd scoffed at him. For awhile tonight, when he'd recited the Psalm, he had felt a harmony between them, but then she ran away. From him or from God? Or both?

According to the girls, she no longer attended church. She dropped them off, then returned to pick them up, keeping the car running as if she couldn't get away from the buildings quickly enough. Since Mandy had gotten her license, Victoria had stopped taking them. Knowing how much church had meant to her, he had assumed she had gotten too busy with her career to attend. Now he knew how poorly she'd been treated when he left. The trust she had placed in the church had been destroyed. Did she blame God for the failings of Christians?

Gazing up at the stars, Matt silently repeated, *This is the confidence we have in approaching God: that if we ask anything according to his will, he hears us. And if we know that he hears us—whatever we ask—we know that we have what we asked of him.*

His heart constricted as if a vice clamped tighter and tighter around it, until he could no longer stand. Dropping to his knees he begged, "Jesus, please, restore my family. I know I'm asking a lot, and I don't deserve it, but You told us to ask according to Your Father's will. You created us and established marriage. You came to earth to restore us to you. Please help me restore my relationship with Victoria. I love her, and I want to be the husband You called me to be, but I can't do that unless she forgives me. I'm hanging onto Your promise. I don't know what Your plan is, but I know You are working in my life and in Victoria's. Please take care of her and protect her. Please soften her heart toward me."

Remembering scripture verses and praying helped. Even so, Matt struggled to hang on to hope. How could anything break through Victoria's resistance? He might not be responsible for the church's lack of compassion, but his betrayal created the circumstance. Destroying her faith was one more sin the Lord had blotted off his account. Matt's regret threatened to crush him. The consequences that remained were worse than the loss of his family. He had caused Victoria to turn from God.

Oh Lord, how many sins have I committed that I don't even know about? If Tori never returns to me, don't let me keep her from knowing you.

Would she ever forgive him? And if she didn't find her way back to God, could he ever forgive himself?

Victoria worked through the lunch hour, eating a sandwich at her desk. She had pushed aside a paper plate with crumbs and an apple core when her door swung open.

"Ah, Victoria, you're working too hard again," a masculine voice scolded.

Lionel Kane, vice-president of sales, was leaning against the door-jamb, striking a deliberate pose of nonchalance. A lock of blond, streaked hair fell casually over his forehead, but Victoria knew it was jelled in place.

"Lionel," she acknowledged curtly. Janice had gone to lunch, so he'd barged in unannounced and uninvited. His intrusions had become a bad habit. Lionel's smooth line and self-confidence gave him an air of competence with people. It also gave him an overlarge ego. He expected everyone to fall under his spell, and most often he got his way. Even her best friend, queen-of-the-singles Tina, succumbed to Lionel's charm. Victoria was not impressed. Too bad he hadn't targeted Tina for his attention. "What can I do for you?" she asked.

"Ah, love, you need to be rescued, and I'm here to save you."

She gritted her teeth and frowned. "As you can see, Lionel, I am busy."

He stepped into the room, shut the door, then sauntered over and perched on the edge of her desk. "Tina let slip that you're going to her party alone." He quirked an eyebrow and continued. "Naturally, I told her I'd be happy to pick you up."

Victoria pictured her hands wrapped around Tina's neck, squeezing. "I'm sorry," she said, smiling sweetly. "My plans have changed. I'm going to the mountains with my daughters. We're leaving tonight and won't be back until Monday, late."

"Oh. I thought, I mean, Tina said they were going to be with your ex-husband."

"Yes they . . . we are." The declaration was out before Victoria could clamp her mouth shut. She had a sinking felling she'd just sprung a trap and caught herself inside. Tina was going to razz her but good. She'd been trying to fix Victoria up with Lionel, a ridiculous notion. They were totally mismatched. But Tina would flip at this turn of events. Victoria vowed she'd have a long heart-to-heart talk with her best friend as soon as she got back from the weekend to which she'd just committed herself.

With an air of superiority, Lionel advised her not to jump into the frying pan, and he offered his shoulder and any other services she might need, then he sauntered back out. As he disappeared through the door, Victoria sunk down in her chair. What had she done? She didn't want to go to the mountains with Matt. She could go off on her own. No, that wouldn't work. Lionel would tell Tina, and she would ask the girls if we had a good time.

She was stuck. Oddly, her spirits lifted. She did want to go to the mountains with her family. She'd keep her distance from Matt. He'd promised she could be on her own and join them only if she felt like it. Lionel had forced her decision, but the more she thought about it, the better it sounded. She'd drive her own car and take her art supplies. Perhaps she could capture a sunset like the one she'd seen from Matt's roof. Breckenridge was an artist's paradise. Before she could change her mind again, she called Tina.

"This is your own fault, you know," Victoria told her friend. "If you didn't feel compelled to play matchmaker, I'd still be coming to your party."

"I didn't want you to be alone. I know you. If you came by yourself, you'd play wallflower and ruin my fun."

"Wait a minute. What does my socializing have to do with your fun? You're always the life of the party."

"So everyone thinks, but it's hard work, you know. I have to set the tempo. That's the secret of my success."

"Well, your sacrifice certainly pays off," Victoria said in a dry tone. "I've heard people lie, cheat, and steal for invitations to your bashes."

A trilling laugh came through Victoria's phone, making her smile. Tina bubbled like an effervescent spring, joyfully rising to the surface and spreading cheer like the ripples in a pond. Victoria couldn't stay mad at her.

"You don't have to leave town to avoid Lionel. I'll find him another date, though I can't see why you dislike him so much."

"He's a lecher. Every time he comes close, he has to touch me. And he acts like he's doing me a favor."

"Well, he's charming and successful. I won't have any trouble getting him a date."

"I've no doubt he'll get his own, unless you're offering yourself."

"No way. I think he's handsome, but so does he. I might make my living making people beautiful and, it's true, vanity is involved, but my dates have to think more about me than about the curl over their forehead."

Victoria laughed. "So you don't waste time feeling sorry for me, I'm going to the mountains with the girls."

"I thought the girls . . . wait a minute! The girls are going with Matt for the weekend. He didn't back out, did he?"

The fat was in the fire now. "No, and don't jump to conclusions. I will be by myself; I'm just sort of tagging along. I'm going to do some sketching."

"Do tell?" Tina's laughter vibrated along Victoria's nerves, making her wonder what had possessed her to make such a rash decision. "Wow! When I tell you to take chances, you plunge off the high dive. This ought to be really interesting. Don't forget your hair appointment next week. I can't wait to hear the juicy details."

Chapter Seven

MANDY AND JESSICA were thrilled, even after Victoria explained to them, firmly, that going to the mountains with them did not mean their parents might get back together. Moreover, this was his weekend to spend with them, and she would not intrude on their time together.

When Matt arrived to pick them up, Victoria was lugging her bags downstairs.

"Mom's going with us!" Jessica shouted, whirling around excitedly. Amanda beamed, and Victoria began to doubt the wisdom of her choice. If Matt looked smug, she'd take her bags back upstairs.

A thoughtful frown creased his brow. "Did the girls pressure you into going, Victoria?"

"No. They never said a word. I just couldn't resist the idea of a weekend in the mountains."

The lines in his forehead disappeared, and he smiled. "I'm glad. Let me take your bags," he said, reaching for her suitcase. "Girls." He motioned them to get their own bags.

"I'm taking my car. And it's open."

"Ride with us, Mom. There's room," Mandy said. Jessica echoed her.

"No, thanks. I want my car to drive around and find places to draw."

"I'll give you directions to Linc's house, just in case we get separated," Matt said. He took a pen and small notepad out of his pocket and explained as he wrote out instructions. "I don't think you'll have any trouble. Have you had dinner?"

"I'm not hungry," she said, wanting to set firm boundaries before they left.

"You might be, by the time we get there. We're going to Wellington's. You're welcome to join us." He didn't try to talk her into it, which she appreciated, but Wellington's . . . her favorite mountain restaurant. How could she resist?

"I pay my own way."

"Absolutely."

She grinned. "We'll see. The mountain air does give me an appetite."

All during the drive up, she waged war between impulse and logic. Spending a weekend with her ex-husband rated high on the crazy scale. Of course, she wasn't *with* Matt, she argued back. And the girls would be there. On the descent from the Eisenhower Tunnel, as she passed Lake Dillon, she considered driving on to Vail and getting a hotel room. However, when she reached the exit to Breckenridge, she turned off. She and Matt were mature adults. Just because they were divorced, they didn't have to be enemies. They needed to get along, for the girls' sakes.

The house, three blocks east of downtown, sat high enough to have an unobstructed view of the mountains. Transfixed, Victoria stared out of the attic room's dormer window. In the fading sunset, the majestic purple peaks rose against a sky washed in pink. Rays of light shone on the underside of a few lazy clouds, giving them a golden glow. The scene reminded her of the view from Matt's gazebo, and she understood his special affinity to something supernatural in the place. On that rooftop, she'd almost felt like an intruder.

Matt's claim that he'd discovered Jesus irritated her. In some odd way, she felt cheated. She had been a Christian for years. She believed Christ was part of God and He had come to earth as a man to teach about God's love and forgiveness. God the Father, Son, and Holy Spirit. She clearly remembered the moment in church when she had turned to Jesus for comfort and felt a peace that had to be supernatural. In those early years, after she'd lost her first baby, the prayers and reading of Scripture and the music at church had assured her that her own precious baby had gone home to Jesus. Did she still believe that? Yes. How could she not? Just looking at the beauty of nature pointed to a divine artist, but she had never experienced a personal closeness with God like Matt seemed to have found. Sixteen years she'd given to God, putting her energy and time into helping at the church. During that time, Matt only attended on special holidays. He had run off with another woman. She never betrayed their wedding vows. Yet, when Matt left her, God deserted her too. She cried out to Jesus for help, but He didn't answer.

All her life, she had been forced to be strong and self-sufficient. Sometimes she wanted to step back and let someone else make the decisions and carry the burdens, but life just hadn't worked out that way. Thinking about her responsibilities philosophically, taking charge, being in control provided the only assurance of success. If you relied on others, even God, you were setting yourself up for disappointment.

But tonight's sky, so breathtakingly beautiful, seemed to be painted just for her. She refused to waste a moment worrying about theology. As Matt said, the sunset was like a special present, designed just for her. Of course, there must be others gazing at the same view, but that didn't take away from the peace that filled her. Somewhere out there, she had a baby boy, and surely her child dwelled in the realm of beautiful sunsets with God. If nothing else, she could take comfort in that. Reluctantly, she grabbed a light jacket and went to join the others downstairs.

They linked arms and walked four abreast to the restaurant. Jessica and Mandy had tried to push their parents together, but Victoria maneuvered around until the girls were sandwiched between their parents. The scent of pine mingled with a potluck of delicious smells. Sounds of gaiety spilled out of doorways. A cool breeze teased Victoria's hair against her neck, sending pleasant shivers down her back.

They feasted on wienerschnitzel and stroganoff in the lovely Victorian setting. Lace covered tables were decorated with candles and vases of wildflowers. The gentle strains of classical music played softly in the background. By the time they polished off Black Forest cake, they all complained about being too stuffed to move. Afterwards, they strolled along Main Street, peering in shop windows and enjoying the balmy summer evening.

Back at the house, the girls suggested a game of cards. Victoria excused herself, claiming the mountain air made her sleepy. In her attic room, she opened the windows, pulled back the curtains, and laid in bed staring out at the crisp sky. The stars sparkled brighter in the mountains, something to do with the thin atmosphere. Muted sounds floated on the air; faint voices, rustling branches, an occasional burst of far-off laughter, and the haunting song of a night bird. She hadn't expected to sleep well in a strange bed, in the same house as Matt, but the next thing she knew a chorus of birds heralded the arrival of the sun.

After a quick shower, she dressed and went downstairs. The house was quiet. She walked to town, bought a fresh croissant and a latte from the only business open that early, and sat outside on an empty bench.

A man walked by with a newspaper tucked under his arm. He smiled and said hello. A lady came by accompanied by two dogs, trotting unleashed at her sides. One—an adorable black puppy, zigzagged erratically as he checked out every flower and post and discarded scrap of paper in his path. His paws were still disproportionately large for his body, making his movements clumsy and comical. The other, a huge black furry mongrel, came over to investigate Victoria's breakfast. The puppy followed, its tail wagging so hard it could hardly navigate. Victoria popped the last bite in her mouth, then held up her empty hands. The big dog nearly climbed into her lap, but the lady called "Bear" and it obediently ran over and sat at her heels.

"Sorry if they bothered you," the woman said. Victoria said they hadn't, and the woman walked off down the street, her dogs following.

Sitting back, inhaling deeply, Victoria absorbed the early morning serenity. Hushed sounds of humanity reached her, but no one else appeared. Columns of dark green pine trees climbed the mountainsides, their pointed tops lit by early sunlight. In the soft light of dawn, they looked like soldiers, marching through velvety paths of summer-green ski slopes. Near her bench, blue columbines bobbed gracefully on long stems as bees climbed inside their cupped petals, then backed out, and flew on to gather nectar from other flowers. Pansies, daisies, cornflowers, snapdragons, delicate irises and sturdy, red Indian paintbrushes crowded together in a profusion of sweet scents and vivid colors that begged to be captured on paper. Victoria finished her drink and went back to the house for her art supplies.

Matt was in the kitchen, at the rear of the house when he heard the front door open and Victoria's footsteps on the stairs. A few minutes later, she came down, her satchel of art supplies under her arm. Her hand was on the front door knob when he went down the hallway to greet her.

"Good morning."

She turned to face him. "Good morning," she said. Her gaze swept from his hair to his chest, then up to meet his eyes. Her hand curled into a fist at her side and she blushed, making him aware of his inappropriate appearance. He'd gotten out of bed and slipped on a pair of jeans. He was barefoot, bare-chested, and embarrassed. "I should have put on a shirt. Sorry."

At his apology, she relaxed her fist and smiled, and his heart did a somersault. The morning air had curled wisps of her sleek, dark hair. The crisp mountain air, or the brisk walk up the hill from town, had kissed her cheeks. When he crossed his arms over his bare chest, he thought the color deepened.

"You don't have to dress up on my account."

"I was going to have a cup of coffee out on the patio. Would you like a cup?"

"No, thanks. I had a cup downtown. I'm going sketching. The early light gives everything a lovely pastel glow and great shadows."

"The girls and I are going to go four-wheeling and then maybe do some fishing. You remember that glacier lake we found above Frisco? The views up there would make great sketches, if you want to come with us."

A spark of remembrance, an instant of interest in her gaze had him hoping, but she shook her head. He hoped what he saw was regret. "That would be lovely, but I already have my subject picked out. Besides, I don't want to cut in on your time with the girls."

He'd expected her to turn him down, so he shouldn't feel so disappointed. She was determined not to be part of a family foursome. Now what? Victoria's many fine qualities included tenacity. Right now, that virtue could be his worst enemy. He knew if he pushed, she'd only resist harder.

"I'd . . . we'd love to have you join us. Anytime. Without exception, Victoria. That is a standing invitation." When resistance narrowed her eyes, he held up a hand, and quickly added. "I know . . . I promised, and I meant it . . . you are free to do whatever you want. This is your weekend to relax. I just want you to know you are welcome."

"I do. Thank you, Matt . . . for not crowding me."

"Yeah, sure. Well, have fun. We'll probably see you later." Victoria opened the door. "Oh," he interjected. "We want you to watch the fireworks with us this evening, if you'd like."

As he stood in the hall waiting for her reply, she hesitated.

"I'll consider it," she answered. Non-committal, but her pause gave him courage.

"The girls want to spend part of the holiday with you," he added, hoping he didn't sound like he was manipulating her. It would be silly for her to sit by herself, away from the girls.

"See you later," she said. Before she got out the door, Mandy called from the top of the stairs. "Wait, Mom! Aren't you going to spend the day with us? We're going four-wheeling to the top of the Continental Divide. Jessica and I will make a picnic lunch."

Matt cringed at the hope in Mandy's voice. Victoria shot him a look that pleaded for reinforcement. What could he say?

"I'm sorry, Mandy," she said. "I've already made plans. You all have fun and I'll see you later." With a little wave, Victoria went out and shut the door.

Mandy moaned in protest.

"It's all right, Honey," Matt assured his daughter. He watched through the window as Victoria walked down the street. The little swing in her walk, as she descended the hill, gave her a jaunty stride, as if she hadn't a care in the world. He knew better. His Tori didn't have it in her to be mean. Her refusal had cost her.

⚜

Fireworks rained down like celestial jewels against a black velvet sky. Victoria leaned back on her elbows on the blanket they had spread on the ground. Matt reclined on the other side with Jessica and Mandy lounging between them.

Sharp pine and the loamy fragrance of damp leaves and mosses scented the warm, silken breeze. Water lapped gently against the shoreline of Lake Dillon.

The ease of sharing the evening with her daughters and Matt surprised Victoria. He'd kept his word, leaving her to her own plans all day. She'd filled a sketchbook with drawings of the mining town's restored Main Street with its brightly colored, Victorian-styled buildings. The ruggedness of construction and materials stamped the town uniquely western. Notes on color and lighting were scribbled all over the sketches for future reference. One day soon, she'd set up her easel and paint at home.

She smiled as she thought of the pastel pictures she'd quickly drawn of the glorious wildflower garden in front of a charming old shop.

"Your teeth are gleaming," Matt said in a quiet voice, but loud enough to break into her thoughts. "What are you smiling about?"

"Did you see the pictures I did today of the cat and the birds?"

"No. I'd love to see them."

"Well, this cat reminded me of Bill—the skinny, straggly cartoon cat in the funny papers. Totally inept, poor thing." Matt chuckled as she described the cat slinking low through the flowers as if it were invisible and the birds with a flurry of flapping wings dive-bombing the poor feline.

"I had a wonderful day, Matt. Thank you for inviting me."

"My pleasure. I hope you don't take offense—I know you have every reason to avoid my company—but it feels right to have you here."

Victoria made no comment, but she thought about how she felt. Companionable, and safe. Not safe, really—unfeigned perhaps fit better. Like a moment out of time, a short vacation from the pressures of performing, she didn't have to be anything or anyone but herself. As much as she loved her life and job and role as primary supporter of their daughters, sometimes she needed to set her cares aside for a few hours and relax. And she'd indulged herself all day.

Bending closer to Matt and speaking in low tones so Jessica and Mandy wouldn't hear her admission, she said, "I'm glad I'm here." Matt reached over and squeezed her hand in a casual, friendly gesture.

Several booms reverberated almost simultaneously. Fiery petals opened one by one, filling the sky with an array of colorful blooms and reflecting on the still lake like star dust dancing upon the water. Emotions welled-up in Victoria as she sat, enthralled by the beauty. She felt the contact of a warm body and reached down to smooth Mandy's long sleek hair. She was surprised, but not disturbed, to find herself rubbing arms with Matt, their daughters having moved to snuggle against their laps. Like years past, two young girls would each claim a parent's lap and cuddle against them until the fireworks ebbed and they would fall asleep. Only now the girls were nearly grown and too large for a lap.

"Lean on me," Matt said against her ear. When she hesitated, he said, "I won't bite, but Mandy's too heavy for you to support."

Victoria leaned against his shoulder, gingerly, at first, then gradually relaxing. The scent of his spicy after-shave blended with the smoky scent of aspen wood from the open pit fire he had built earlier that evening to barbecue the trout he and the girls caught. They'd convinced her to join them for dinner. She loved fresh trout, so she'd given in easily. She also loved the masculine scent of the man sitting next to her, and for a moment she forgot the recent past and remembered a time more distant, when love had surrounded them like a warm blanket.

As they watched the fireworks display, Victoria admonished herself to remember this man had turned his back and walked away from her. For today, he was being kind and generous, but her future did not include Matt. She fervently hoped Jessica and Mandy wouldn't misread this weekend. The girls' too obvious attempts to reunite them were doomed to fail and disappoint them. At least they'd have this holiday to add to their memories.

Mandy snuggled closer; Victoria leaned down and kissed her forehead.

When they got back to the house, the girls said goodnight and went upstairs, leaving Victoria and Matt alone. Before she had a chance to excuse herself, he stopped her.

"The night's too beautiful to waste sleeping. Please, come share a nightcap with me," he said. "I have some iced tea left from dinner."

She looked hesitant but said, "Just a small glass."

After handing her a glass, Matt opened the double doors leading to the porch. "Let's go outside, where we can see the stars."

At their approach, some small creature skittered away, rustling leaves beneath its little feet. Faint people sounds drifted up from town. The dark silhouette of the mountains dwarfed them.

"It's so peaceful here," Victoria said. "I envy your partner having a home here."

"Breckenridge has always been one of our favorite spots, hasn't it? Maybe I'll see about buying a place here." He looked for a reaction, but her eyes were closed, and she made no comment.

"Someone back East told me he couldn't understand why everyone rhapsodized over a pile of rocks," Matt said. "That's what he called the Rockies. Can you imagine? When I stand here, I can almost see God sitting on His throne on top of Peak Eight. People who aren't used to mountains find them intimidating, but to me they're inspiring and comforting."

"I feel small down here," she said. "Insignificant. Kind of puts things in perspective."

"I used to think meeting God face to face would be an earth-shaking experience that would take place on top of Mt. Elbert or Mt. Massive. Funny thing is, I met Him in a snowstorm in downtown Boston. The only thing shaking was my bones, from the cold."

"Here's to the mountains," she said, cutting him off. She raised her glass in a toast. "May they stand tall forever."

"And to their majesty and strength, their testament to God's power," Matt added. As Victoria took a sip of her iced tea, he watched her and felt the frustration of being so close to sharing God's grace with her, only to have her cut him off. *Oh Lord, when will the time be right?* "The girls and I are going to church tomorrow," he said. "Would you like to join us?"

"I don't think that would be wise, Matt. The girls would interpret that wrong. They're getting their hopes up too high already. Besides, God and I aren't on speaking terms."

"*You* aren't on speaking terms, Victoria. Jesus is always listening and waiting to talk to us."

"That has not been my experience, Matt."

He didn't know what to say. She wasn't asking his opinion or his experience. Matt had always assumed Victoria was a believer, but now he wasn't so sure. She knew who Jesus was, but it seemed to end there. Matt knew he couldn't prove the reality and intimacy of a relationship with Jesus. Faith and acceptance required a personal decision. Hadn't he ignored God for years? Once upon a time, he had considered Victoria to be a strong Christian because of her dedication to church and to helping others. She was certainly a fine, loving, selfless woman, which made him all the more desperate for her to know Christ as he did. Although Matt knew Christ held no one to be more valuable than another, Victoria deserved God's love far more than he ever had. Somehow, because of his betrayal, she felt God had let her down. How could he show her the Lord had always been right beside her? No one could have convinced him of the truth. And if he tried to tell her, she would think he was judging her. *Tell me what to say, Lord.* But no words came.

Disheartened, he leaned against the railing next to her. At first he could feel her tension. The silence stretched out. Other than an occasional whiz or pop of fireworks, the evening was relatively quiet. Gradually, he felt her relax. As a bright shooting star crossed the sky, she sighed, a sound of contentment. Even so, Matt sensed a sadness in her silence. He missed the empathy that had freely flowed between them, once upon a time. He hoped his comment about their loving Breckenridge had struck a chord. He fully intended to look for a Victorian home in the quaint town they could enjoy as a family.

He shifted his weight back so he could see her from the corner of his eyes. He didn't want to stare directly, but he craved any opportunity to gaze at her. Her confidence and character had transformed the pretty girl into a beautiful woman.

"Do you remember the night we met?"

"Oh yes. Very clearly." She laughed. "I was so nervous, and you frowned like you were looking at a bug under a microscope. Then you introduced yourself, and you were so polite."

"I thought you had to be the wrong girl. I expected studious and, well, different. I wasn't expecting you to look like a cheerleader. When I got up close, though, your eyes were so serious, I knew you were the right person. Then you smiled. I saw your dimples and fell in love."

"Dimple. I have only one."

"Which made it all the more special."

"So you say."

"Yes, I do." He took her glass and set it aside with his. Placing his hands on her shoulders, he turned her to face him, holding her at arm's length. She didn't resist. "I don't know why you decided to come this weekend, but I'm glad you did," he said. His voice threatened to break. "Having you here has made this weekend very special for me. I hope . . . " His voice trailed off and he cleared his throat. "I'm sorry. I feel rather nostalgic tonight. Victoria, you are beautiful. You always have been, but never more than tonight."

She started to turn away, but he held her still. "Don't go, please. I won't push you."

"I know. But I don't understand." Her eyes glistened in the moonlight.

"Just accept my thanks," he said. He moved closer, until his breath fanned a wisp of her hair. Their bodies didn't touch. He saw awareness in her gaze. When he leaned forward, her eyes closed. He kissed her eyelids and tasted salty dampness. "I'm sorry. Please, Tori, don't cry." With his thumb, he smoothed her cheek tenderly, then he settled his mouth lightly against hers. She was warmth and sweetness. Her tentative response made him shudder with unbearable longing. Her lips parted in a quick intake of air just as he released her. He stepped back and felt a stab of loneliness.

Reaching as if to steady herself against the porch railing, she took a deep breath. Her hand shook as she smoothed her hair back from her face. She looked at him with confusion and shook her head. "I don't want this, Matt. Goodnight." She turned and rushed into the house.

"Goodnight, Tori," he called softly after her. She was running away. She was so careful not to expose her feelings. Somehow, he had to break through her emotional barrier. He wanted to chase after her and break through her shield, but not tonight. This weekend was for reestablishing friendship. *Patience,* he told himself. *Patience.*

She ran up the stairs to the attic room, where she shut and latched the door. Tori. She hadn't been called that for years. Even before he'd left, Matt had stopped calling her by the endearment only he had ever used.

She couldn't seem to stop trembling. The strength of his effect on her surprised her. In fact, she'd expected to prove that she wouldn't feel anything. She sternly admonished herself to keep things in perspective.

Matt was an affectionate man, and staying friendly—for the girls' sake— was important. And that's all the kiss had been. A friendly gesture. The fact that their marriage had failed didn't change the fact that Matt was a nice guy. An attractive, nice guy.

She no longer harbored the seething anger towards Matt that had sustained her through her final year of graduate school and the first exhausting months of proving herself. Some of that anger had been focused on God, who had deserted her at the time she needed Him most.

Fatalistically, she had shouldered that struggle as one more battle in her war on life. How she longed for the war to be over, but for her, it seemed, that would not happen until she gave up. And that she would never do. She'd learned as a child she had to fight to be recognized. Not physically, but with her mind and will and determination. She had to work harder than anyone else, think smarter, and last longer. With Matt's return, and all his talk about trusting Jesus, she felt like she was entering another battle, striving to hold her own. Doubts about her own decisions and motivations shook her thoughts. Getting the divorce had seemed like a clear, simple matter, with no alternatives. Now she wondered if things could have been different.

Maybe she hadn't fought hard enough for her marriage. Maybe she hadn't loved enough or given Matt enough attention. They had married out of honor and duty, not love—at least on Matt's part, no matter what he claimed. Desire. Dreams and ideals. Youthful passions had sealed their fate. She had often wondered, if she hadn't gotten pregnant, would they have married?

Matt had asked if she remembered the first time they met. She remembered every single moment they'd spent together. Even at their first meeting, when he'd walked into her dorm, Matt had become more than the tutor her economics professor had recommended. The bounce to his step, his dark hair thick and blunt-cut as if he trimmed it himself. She remembered his beautiful hazel eyes and long, thick lashes behind his black, horn-rimmed glasses. His frown—she'd been holding her breath, waiting for him to take a look at her and refuse to help her.

Except for her brothers, she'd had no experience with men. In the small farming community, physical stamina was a valuable asset. Naturally athletic, her brothers had been local celebrities. Their family life, even their drugstore and soda fountain had revolved around school sports. Victoria had been proud of her brothers, but their abilities had emphasized her ineptitude. People compared her. She didn't blame them. She had compared herself and came up lacking.

Her brothers were strong and handsome with big smiles and well-developed builds. She had been tall and gangly—a string bean, her father had called her. Exercising hadn't helped. Giving that up, she had poured her efforts into school and excelled in academics.

So, when she couldn't keep up with her college economics, Victoria had expected rejection or pity from the economic department's star graduate student. Then he'd introduced himself in a soft-spoken, deep baritone, and he'd been so polite and kind. No pity. No condescension.

Matt had accepted her as a fellow seeker of knowledge, a kindred spirit, never mentioning her lop-sided smile or her weakness. His patience, his dedication to purpose, his gentle humor melted her self-consciousness.

When he asked her out for coffee, she thought she'd arrived in paradise. They sat in the student union and drank burned coffee and talked about dreams. He talked, and she listened, enraptured. With four years left for a law degree specializing in economics and tax law, his life's plan was a carefully plotted journey. He'd drawn a straight line between then and the future, no detours allowed. He knew every route marker, every obstruction, every short cut between points A and B, and he'd calculated the cost down to every tank of gas.

Victoria had fantasized about being his navigator, but she had recognized the futility of her imagination. Romance played no part in his itinerary. His interest in her was strictly platonic—until homecoming weekend, when he rescued her from the forced attentions of her inebriated blind date. After that, Matt had become her protector, but more—he began treating her like a woman.

Tutoring sessions became special occasions. Chances to talk and touch and gaze into each other's eyes. Matt always held himself in check, though, until finals were over and he no longer tutored her. Then, they celebrated.

The weather had been unseasonably warm for January in Colorado. They'd taken a picnic to Boulder Canyon, and spread sleeping bags, for warmth, on a ledge under a rock outcropping. Matt made a fire and opened a bottle of wine. A wind kicked up; they huddled in their warm hideaway, drinking wine and sharing dreams. As the light had faded, Victoria's love had blossomed. When she began to shiver, Matt opened the sleeping bag and covered them for warmth. The closeness brought awareness. Awareness sparked hunger, then passion. Although she had been raised to believe premarital sex was wrong, she had set aside her ideals for love. As the fire burned down, their passion blazed to life, and dreams were forgotten for the pleasure of the moment.

If only they'd waited—taken time for courtship, she'd often thought, Matt might have truly fallen in love with her, but they had stopped the clock by their own actions.

The second semester had started. Their schedules kept them apart—Matt with classes, plus a part-time job at a private law library, Victoria with classes and houses to clean. Fatigue had plagued her. She'd lost weight and her stomach was queasy more often than not. Her energy level dropped, her grades fell, so she finally went to the doctor. She would never forget Matt's reaction. She'd avoided seeing him for two weeks, until he'd finally cornered her, demanding to know what was wrong. She'd evaded his question, refusing to look at him. As long as she lived, she would never forget his question and his reaction to her answer.

"You're pregnant, aren't you?" he'd asked.

She'd jerked her head around and stared at him in horror. "How did you know?"

"Oh no," he had groaned, and buried his face in his hands.

They had married. And struggled. After an accident caused her to miscarry, she'd gone to work to support Matt through law school and turned to God and the church for solace. Then Amanda had been born, so after graduation, Matt had taken a corporate job, with benefits.

To his credit, Matt had tried—they'd both done their best to make their marriage work. They had adjusted to parenthood, building a family life for their daughters. Life went along without a wrinkle until Matt had left. Whatever had caused Matt to stray, a job opportunity or the woman he'd almost married soon after their divorce, Victoria realized in hindsight that she had stagnated in their marriage. Perhaps Matt had felt the same way, only recognized his weariness sooner.

So here she was, twenty-four years later, picking apart the past as if doing so would have some relevance in her life. No longer young and naïve, she knew better than to repeat past mistakes. Furthermore, she had no intention of lying awake any longer, rehashing her marriage and divorce. She was an intelligent woman who learned from her mistakes.

She turned over and punched the pillow into shape. She learned from her mistakes and did not repeat them. And that meant Matt. He belonged in her past, and there he would remain, no matter how he affected her heart. She would not give in to nostalgia. She'd get over her emotional lapse in a day or two.

CHAPTER EIGHT

Needing distance from Matt, Victoria left Breckenridge early. She intended to go home and work on reports, but the beauty of the day beckoned. On impulse, she turned north and looped through Rocky Mountain National Park then stopped to eat and browse in Estes Park.

The girls were already home, watching television in the den, when she arrived. Taking a glass of iced tea and a book, she retreated to the living room. When the phone rang, she ignored it.

"Mom. Phone's for you."

"Okay, I got it." She picked up the portable. "Hello."

"Victoria? Finally. I've been trying to reach you all weekend."

Her heart did a little flip. Cleve Winslow. She hadn't really believed he'd call.

"Victoria? This is Cleve Winslow."

"Oh . . . yes. Hi. I just got home. I haven't checked my messages yet."

"I didn't leave any. I wanted to talk to you, not a machine. I've missed you."

Victoria gave a skeptical laugh. "You've seen me only three times. I doubt that made enough of an impression to miss me."

"Wrong. So, how was your holiday?"

"Wonderful. I went to the mountains with my daughters. How about you?"

"Good. I combined a little business with a little fishing in Corpus Christi. Looks like I'll have everything wrapped up here and be in Denver Friday. Did you clear your calendar?"

"Friday? I have meetings. What time?"

"Late afternoon. I haven't booked a flight, yet. You'll know when you see me."

Arrogant man. "Friday's are usually slow. I suppose I can do some juggling," she replied.

"Victoria, I've been working like a fiend to get everything wrapped up here. I think about Denver, and I get impatient to get back. I need to see you."

He sounded serious. She remembered his kiss, before he left, and the promise it held. Romance and adventure without complications and unwanted emotions. Then she remembered the drum roll his kiss had set up in her stomach, and her hand, holding the receiver, started to tremble. Good thing he couldn't see her reaction. She had never been particularly adventurous. Was she ready for that kind of ride? A casual relationship with no expectations had to be better than waiting to see what Matt would do next, and maybe he would get the hint and stop his unwanted pursuit.

"All right. I'll see you Friday."

After Cleve hung up, she stared out at the darkness for a long time. Why did Cleve Winslow make her feel like an inexperienced teenager? What did he want from her? And what about Matt? His attentions seemed excessive for an ex-husband. Hormones, she could control. She couldn't seem to analyze her feelings for Matt, and that made her more nervous than thoughts of Cleve Winslow.

Tuesday morning, Victoria met with Nick and Bart Jensen for a progress report on the Black Forest Project. Victoria had never worked with Bart before, but he had excellent credentials.

"Everything's going fine," he reported. He sat slouched in a chair, one foot perched atop the opposite knee. His boots were scuffed and scored.

A battered cowboy hat, stained dark around the sweatband and curled on the sides, teetered on his bent knee as he jiggled his foot.

"Will the site be ready on schedule?" Victoria asked.

"Yes, ma'am."

The man's brevity made Victoria want to shake him. She wanted to know every detail of the project's progress or problems. But Bart was a man of few words. The way he had settled into the chair reminded her of a rock that would require dynamite to move.

Nick glanced at her and winked. "Humor me, Bart. I haven't been following this one. What have you done so far?"

Bart dropped his foot off his knee and switched legs, raising the other boot and resettling his hat. "We dug out the old dry pond next to the dump. I worried a mite when water started gushing in. Turned out we'd crushed an old pipe. Looked like it'd been leaking for years."

"Our maps don't show a water source on the property," Nick said. "We drilled a new well for the industrial buildings."

"Yes sir, traced it myself. There's an underground artesian spring half a mile southwest of the dump. Clump of cottonwoods gave away the location, else I would've missed it. Probably fed the pond at one time. The pipe runs catty-corner across your property towards the northeast."

"Where does it go from there?"

"Empties into a pond not far north of the fence line. Did you know they're running buffalo?"

"That must be new," Nick said. "They had a few head of cattle when we were surveying, but nothing significant. Is that a problem?"

"Shouldn't be. We rerouted the pipe around the dumpsite. Even figured room for expansion, so the water pipe shouldn't make no difference."

Nick frowned over Bart's revelation, and Victoria wondered if the proximity of the water source could cause problems. Bart didn't seem to think so, but then he came from a generation that didn't have to worry about government regulations or environmentalists. "Will the site be able to accept waste loads?" Victoria asked.

"It'll be ready on time," Bart proclaimed, "We still got eleven weeks before the deadline."

"Of course," Victoria answered. "I'm not doubting your abilities, Mr. Jensen. I'm concerned that the land is actually compatible to the project as the reports indicated. I don't want to be suddenly faced by opposition. I don't understand how we missed the water line and spring."

"Call me Bart, ma'am. I don't stand on formality. Don't worry about that spring. We took care of it. We've got some digging to do, then we'll lay the groundwork and pipes in the excavated area. The old landfill is ready to go. I don't expect any problems. We'll be ready when that first truck rolls through the gate."

"Thank you, Bart. I appreciate your patience. I'm afraid I'm pretty ignorant of all the details."

Bart grinned. "I've seen your reports and the plans and blueprints you had drawn up. You might not understand the details on the drawings, but I know you studied them yourself. You ain't ignorant, Miz Halstead. I'd say you're right smart. No one can know everything."

Victoria smiled at his praise. "Thank you, Bart. You've answered all my questions."

"Keep us posted." Nick stood as Bart unfolded his lanky body and rose.

"Ma'am," Bart nodded towards her and put his hat on before he left the office.

Victoria stood and started to leave, but she hesitated a second, wondering if she should speak up. Oh well, she never had been able to keep her mouth shut. She sat back down and looked Nick in the eyes. "You know, this project could be the salvation of INTECH. You wouldn't have to sell."

"Victoria, you've done an excellent job. I'd have to be blind not to see the potential here. The gambler in me would love to meet the challenge, but I just don't have the energy to pull it off. Let someone new do it who has the resources and passion to create a new industry. That's what you're talking about, isn't it?"

"Yes. I'm sorry, Nick. I don't mean to push you, but I'm going to miss you. It won't be the same around here without you at the helm."

She saw the sorrow in his eyes and the resignation in the sagging lines across his forehead and around his mouth. The tough, nothing-is-impossible giant of industry had lost his vision. He had challenged and pushed her to do more than she'd ever dreamed possible. A knot of emotion thickened her throat. She pitied herself as much as Nick. They had forged a team in the past few years.

Victoria alternately fretted about her clothes, the audit, and the fact that she was fretting about either subject as she rode the elevator to her floor. She should have worn the tailored, navy blue suit. Instead, she'd chosen her new mauve suit to bolster her confidence. Now she worried that the outfit's sophistication would give the wrong message.

There should be a law against audits, Victoria grumbled inwardly, especially this one. As INTECH's executive vice-president, she shouldered responsibility for the financial health of the corporation. She'd rather face the IRS, the FBI, or the treasury department than to have Matt examine her company books.

Her stomach growled, more out of anxiety than hunger. The toast she'd eaten for breakfast had stuck in her throat. Nervous twitches in her shoulder warned of impending spasms. If she could just relax! She'd thought she'd gotten over trying to live up to Matt Halstead when they'd divorced, but she'd miscalculated. Old feelings of inadequacy churned through her system again. Crazier still, Matt had no idea—never had known about her insecurities. Hiding her fears behind constant activities and projects, she'd spent her entire married life proving her value, but it hadn't been enough to hold him. Today, as he scrutinized her career, would he find her lacking in this too?

No! She had fine-tuned INTECH's accounting. The department was beyond reproach. The current crisis had nothing to do with the company operations. Without boasting, she could claim her policies and strategies had set the company on a solid footing. She had not known that the company's long-standing note payable to Nick jeopardized his personal estate.

Still fretting, she decided to move the audit to the conference room, so the memory of today wouldn't be tied to her office. She and Janice carried all the files to the larger room and arranged them in order. Then she checked to be sure she had everything. The conference table and executive chairs made a pleasant work area, and she hoped the mountain view would take some of the strain out of the proceedings. Victoria arranged her notepad and pens so she would face Matt and the auditor across the table with her back to the windows.

Janice carried in coffee cups. As she started a fresh pot of coffee, she said, "I don't see why they have to go through these records again. We did all this when you took over."

"The audit is merely a formality. Mr. Shrock hired new legal counsel, and they like to do their own analysis. By the way, I'd appreciate you warding off any interruptions today."

"I'll take care of everything," Janice said. "I'll be at my desk if you need anything," she added, "like antacids, or a straight-jacket." They exchanged a brief smile, and Janice stepped to the half-opened door, then backed back into the room.

Two men blocked the doorway. Janice stared at Matt, a bemused expression on her face. Seeing her reaction, Victoria decided she should have revealed Matt's identity.

"Victoria," Matt said, smiling warmly. "This is Stan Brady, my auditor."

"How do you do, Stan. This is my secretary, Janice. Stan Brady and Matt Halstead."

Matt reached out to shake hands, and Janice quickly shifted her papers and shook his hand. The look on her face teetered somewhere between awe and adoration, tickling Victoria's sense of humor. Just then, she could have hugged Janice. Her reaction made Victoria forget her own nervousness.

Turning her attention to the auditor, Victoria noticed him—tall, thin to gaunt, hungry—eyeing the stack of journals as if they were slabs of prime rib. In her mind, Victoria nicknamed him Ebenezer, as in Scrooge.

Janice murmured something about being at her desk if they needed anything and hurried out of the room.

"We're ready to start," Victoria said and held out a hand toward the table. "Please, have a seat." She indicated two chairs facing the windows.

"All the records for the past twelve months are there," she said. "Also, the report of the audit eight months ago, when I took over this office."

"Thank you, Mrs. Halstead," Stan Brady said. He set his briefcase on the table and opened it to reveal a laptop computer. He arranged a pen, pencil, and notepad in precise order next to the computer. "I won't need the last audit. I rely on my own calculations."

"As you wish." She looked at Matt, who stood watching her, a warm smile on his face. A sudden mental picture of herself tripping and falling at his feet made her move away.

"Nice dress. The color is great on you," Matt told her.

She'd been right. She should have worn the other suit. Pouring the coffee, she purposely set Matt's cup at the table next to Stan Brady. Matt picked up his coffee, walked around the table, and sat in the chair next to where she'd put her notebook. Irritated at having her plans thwarted, Victoria scooted her chair a few inches away from him before she sat down. Stan ignored them, burying himself in the journals.

Matt's attention had shifted to the papers in front of him, and the process began. He wanted details of operations and finances. He seemed conversant with every aspect of the company, which didn't surprise her; however, his questions centered on areas that had been nonproductive. Explaining tabled projects and costly overruns made

Victoria feel irritable and inadequate. She shouldn't be required to justify losses that preceded her advancement to financial officer. Matt understood the former economic climate that had precipitated INTECH's problems. His intense scrutiny, as she answered his questions, made her squirm.

She tried to read his thoughts, his body language, but he gave nothing away. She wondered if she'd imagined his emotional expressions the previous weekend.

His deep, calm voice usually had a soothing effect, but today it jangled her nerves. As he probed, she wanted to demand he look at the progress *she'd* made. She explained how she'd orchestrated contracts to build industrial plants in Kuwait and Saudi Arabia. When she tried to give him positive projections, he mumbled agreement and jumped to something else.

He was so immersed in INTECH's files, he hardly glanced at her. Frustration knotted her mind. She told herself to relax. Emotions in the business world were counterproductive. He needed complete information to help Nick, but she wanted Matt to recognize her success. She had steered the company back on course. She answered his questions carefully, keeping her feelings under tight control. The overhead lighting made her want to take off her jacket, but both men still wore their suit coats and appeared perfectly comfortable.

At noon, Victoria rose. "Gentlemen," she said with wilted dignity, "We need a break."

They readily agreed. She checked her watch, then made an unhurried exit. Closing the door, she marched straight to the ladies' room.

Janice had sandwiches waiting for them when they returned. Victoria invited the men to help themselves, then picked up half a chicken sandwich. The bread seemed like sawdust, and the filling tasted tinny. She set her food down after two bites and drank a cup of coffee.

Stan Brady downed two sandwiches, then returned to his computer. Matt removed his jacket, rolled up the sleeves of his impeccable white dress shirt and pulled his tie loose, leaving it hanging at an angle, then he took a seat close to the window. Victoria thought he looked more like the man she used to know, and she started to relax. When he picked up a thick green folder and sifted through the contents in silent concentration, Victoria watched with foreboding. She recognized the Black Forest Project folder.

Quizzing her on project revisions, plans, costs, and legal implications, he'd nod and jot notes as she answered. He wanted every detail, from the date of purchase to the present.

At four o'clock, Stan closed his laptop with a snap and looked up. "I have everything I need for now," he announced. "I'll have more questions after I examine this data."

"Excellent," Matt said. "I'm finished for now. Everything is in impeccable order. As far as attracting a buyer, I would say we're in a good position. As far as finding any loopholes to help Nick immediately . . . " He shook his head. "I'll have to study these findings closer, but everything seems tight. That's not a surprise, though, with you in charge."

She blinked as his comment soaked in. Suddenly, the past seven hours seemed like a stroll in the park. Smiling, she magnanimously offered any other help she could give them.

Matt thanked her and gave her a beautiful smile before he followed Stan Brady out the door and shut it softly. Victoria stood at the desk and stared at the closed door. She was so tired, she couldn't seem to think.

Janice opened the door and peered cautiously into the room. "Are you all right?"

After looking at her secretary blankly for a few seconds, she placed a hand on the small of her back and rubbed at an ache. "I'm fine," Victoria said. "Let's quit for the day. I'm bushed."

"Me too. The whole company knows about the audit, and some of the speculation got crazy. I tried to stop conjecture, but I don't know if I succeeded. I think everyone in the whole building found a reason to stop by my desk today. I feel like I've been through a war. I can't imagine what you've been through," she said.

Victoria smiled. "The thick of battle," she replied. "File these journals, then go on home."

"Thanks," Janice said.

⁂

When she heard Tony's car in the driveway, Victoria put the steaks on the grill. She heard the door slam, then the car drove off.

"Amanda? Isn't Tony staying for dinner?"

"No, Mom."

"Oh. I put a steak on for him. How was your golf lesson?"

"Rotten." Mandy came out onto the patio. Her expression could have scared the sunshine away.

"What's wrong, Honey? Did you and Tony have a fight?"

"Yeah. I hate him."

"Goodness. What did he do?"

"He made me look like a klutz. He embarrassed me in front of . . . of other people."

"Oh dear. I'm sure he didn't mean to. Don't be too hard on him. Sometimes it's best not to take lessons from a friend. I suppose I could help you, but I'm not very good. Your father is a great golfer. He could teach you."

"No. I mean, I'd get embarrassed with Dad too. Maybe I should give up, or take real lessons, from the golf pro."

"That could get expensive. Your father wouldn't embarrass you. You could go to a different course to practice."

"Hmm. I'll think about it."

"You do that. Meanwhile, the steaks are almost done. Please call Jessica for dinner."

"Sure." Mandy went inside and yelled down the stairs for her sister. Then she went into the kitchen and poured a drink, humming as if she hadn't a care in the world.

CHAPTER NINE

CLEVE WAS DUE back that day, but Victoria didn't know what time. He hadn't called since the night she got back from the mountains. All day she anticipated his return. Every time she left her office, she expected messages, but he didn't call. She began to feel foolish when she asked Janice for the fourth time if she'd missed any phone calls.

She told herself she didn't care whether she saw him or not, but the expectation of his return put her on edge. By the time she got home, her nerves had knotted up. When Matt showed up to collect Jessica for the weekend, her patience was stretched to the limit. He wanted to talk about sending the girls to camp, but Victoria cut him off, saying they'd discuss camp arrangements later. She practically pushed them out the door. After they left, she felt terrible.

What was wrong with her? She'd snapped at Jessica for no real reason, because a man she barely knew had said he'd call, and he hadn't. So she'd been stood up. So what? She decided to quit waiting for the phone to ring and take a cold drink out on the deck.

After changing into comfortable clothes, she cut up fresh strawberries and blended them with frozen lemonade. Then she relaxed on the deck off her bedroom, putting her feet up on a stool and sipping her drink.

A breeze blew down off the mountains, cooling the air. The late afternoon sun behind her cast tall, jagged shadows across the golf course below. Victoria watched electric carts buzz along, carrying golfers to their next shot. A squirrel scolded her from the big spruce tree next to the house. A shiny red Jimmy wound up the road below her, turned up her road, then disappeared behind the trees. She didn't recognize the car, but there were three houses past hers before the road dead-ended.

She'd dismissed the car from her mind when the doorbell rang. She wasn't expecting anyone—except Cleve, and he didn't know where she lived. She looked down at her paint-splattered white shorts and yellow halter-top. Not exactly dressed for company, and barefoot to boot.

The doorbell pealed again. "I'm coming," she shouted as she hurried down the stairs to the main floor entrance. She opened the door and looked through the security screen door.

"Oh, Cleve," she said, disconcerted. He stood at the door looking like every woman's fantasy, staring at her with a bemused expression.

"I didn't expect you," she explained, and tried to smile. Taking a key from a brass hook near the door, she unlocked the deadbolt. When he stepped into the foyer, she had to crane her neck to see his face. She couldn't believe he was really there.

"I told you I'd come."

"I thought you'd call. How did you know where I live?"

He shrugged. "I asked," he said and gave her a smile she recognized as uniquely Cleve. Smug, and at the same time, secretive, like he had a private stock of knowledge that no one else knew. Enigmatic. His mystique enhanced his attractiveness. Made her want to dig beneath the surface and see what made him tick.

What did he see in her? No mystery surrounded her, no enigma. Nothing below the surface, but more of the same, and right now, the surface looked a mess. She *knew* what he saw. Matt had told her often enough. Sprite. Elf. Pixie. Her turned-up nose and the reddish highlights in her hair, which matched her freckles, gave that impression. Dressed thus, she knew she looked more like her teenage daughters than like a successful corporate executive.

Poor man, no wonder he looked bemused. He'd no doubt expected cool, composed, serene, like the last moment he'd seen her at her office building—just before he'd kissed her. That memory suddenly made her nervous. As if he could read her thoughts, he reached down and touched her hair, cupping the side of her face with his hand. Her insides went perfectly still as he stared at her, then lowered his head.

She'd been waiting for this moment, and the anticipation had made her edgy. Not because his kiss by the elevators had thrilled her. Startled her, even shocked her, perhaps, but Cleve's kiss created enough impact to help her forget another kiss—on a patio in Breckenridge. She wanted to like this handsome man, to flirt and laugh and erase any lingering bonds to Matt. Blocking out all else, she closed her eyes. His lips touched hers. Light, sweet. He drew away.

Not unpleasant, but no thrill.

"Strawberries," he said. Then he kissed her again.

Better. Her heartbeat accelerated. Much better. His image blurred when she opened her eyes, but she could see him staring down at her, so she smiled. "Hello," she said, sounding out of breath, like she'd climbed a steep hill. "Is that your standard greeting?" she asked.

He ignored her question. "You taste like strawberries."

She grinned, then sobered. "I feel like I've been run over by a loco-motive. I don't want to make a big deal out of this, but, ah . . . do you greet all women that way? I mean, I'm not a prude, but I don't usually fall into the arms of every man who comes to my door."

"I certainly hope not," he responded emphatically. "I'm sorry." He ran a hand through his hair with a jerky motion. "I know this sounds like a tired line, but . . . " He shrugged his shoulders and smiled down at her. "You just looked so irresistible, I guess I lost my head."

"Irresistible? That's got to be a first." *And a stretch of the imagination.* Either he was slipping, throwing out such a trite compliment, or he was very tired. She took a good, hard look, then nodded her head. He'd been packing and moving, then traveled all day. "You look exhausted. Come in, and I'll get you a drink." She turned and walked away toward a corner of the big open room.

In the large, high-ceilinged living room, he didn't appear so tall or intimidating. He crossed to the large window next to the fireplace and looked out at the valley and the golf course below.

"Nice view. Nice place."

"Thanks." He came to the counter separating the kitchen from the living area.

"Strawberries or something else?" she asked. "I have iced tea, pop, fruit punch."

"Your strawberries come by the glass?" He looked so confused, she laughed.

"Strawberry freeze. With fresh berries and lemonade. Want some?"

"Yes, that sounds good. Where are Amanda and Jessica?"

"With their father for the weekend. Makes the house awfully quiet." She stole glances at him as she pureed fresh berries and ice with the yellow liquid. He braced himself against a barstool and gazed off into space. She handed him a glass, and he took a sip.

"Wonderful," he said. "Have you eaten? I passed up the snack on the plane. Airline food never looks very appetizing. Besides, I want to take you out."

"No, I haven't eaten yet. I like to wait until the temperature cools down. If you don't mind, I'd rather not go out. Could I fix us something here?"

"Sounds good. I'd much rather be alone with you."

She ignored that, but her heart did a little flip, anyway. "Are you hungry?" she asked. "I'll fix dinner now if you are. Otherwise, we could take our drinks out on the deck."

"I'd like that. Where's your drink?"

"I left my glass upstairs. Why don't you go out, and I'll join you in a few minutes."

"All right. Don't be long," he added.

She changed quickly. Part of her confidence came from her appearance. As superficial as looks might be, exercising control came easier when she felt properly dressed. Paint-spotted shorts and bare feet did not invoke confidence. Slipping on a sundress, combing her hair and adding a faint dab of lipstick made her feel a great deal better—ready to face the evening and the dynamic man downstairs with at least a thread of assurance.

His reaction proved her right, though his thorough perusal snuffed out any illusions she had about control. At least she could give the impression of control.

"You changed fast," he said. "But you needn't have bothered on my account. You looked fine in your shorts."

"I looked a mess. I hadn't intended for you to see me that way."

"That way was safer," he muttered, his voice flat.

She didn't mistake his warning, intentional or not. "Maybe I should start dinner," she said, heading for the kitchen. "It'll only take a few minutes. I made this up earlier." He followed her and watched.

While she prepared dinner, then later, as they ate chicken fettuccini with salad and crusty sourdough bread, they talked about the frustrations of moving, about his gas and oil exploration and her dreams and goals for INTECH and the Methergy project. After dinner, they sat together on the couch in the living room, looking toward the eastern plains at a distant, rumbling lightning display and sharing their ambitions and aspirations. Both knew from experience the harsh side of business, but they shared visions of achievements and knew how to make them happen.

He seemed spellbound by her stories, laughing with her over her meeting with three Arab potentates. Their initial disdain at dealing with a woman had ended with a signed contract, conceding to all her proposals and conditions to build their industrial complexes. His stories took her into a world she'd only dreamed about, of power and authority in high places. Judging by his enthusiasm, Victoria could see that Cleve's satisfaction came from seeing the success of his efforts, not from wealth and prestige. Factoring in his company's charitable activities, she knew he shared her conviction that true value came from what you gave to society. This new insight into his motivations pleased her.

When he began lightly rubbing the back of her neck, she relaxed and sighed with contentment. Leaning back, she rolled her head to look at him. He gave her a kiss so sweet, her tension uncoiled, leaving her feeling languid and dreamy.

The dream dashed when he stretched out on the couch and started to pull her down. "No. don't do that, please." She pushed away and stood up.

He lifted his head and looked at her, then forced himself to sit up. "Guess it's time for me to leave."

He smiled. No anger. No resistance. He acknowledged her control, and she liked him all the more for it.

"It's been a long two weeks, and I'm exhausted," he said. "Could we do something tomorrow? Take a drive in the mountains, perhaps?"

"I promised to help landscape a shelter in the afternoon, and there's a fund-raiser in the evening. Why don't you come with me?"

"All right. What time shall I pick you up?"

"Be here at eleven and dress casual. Jeans or shorts would be a good idea. You'll have time to go change before dinner." She walked him to the door and gave him a chaste kiss. He accepted her restraint and left, like a good boy.

Yes, she felt much more confident about the future of this friendship. And she hadn't thought about Matt once. Well, maybe once, she admitted. She tried not to compare the two men, but Matt served as her only yardstick. Naturally, she would see similarities or differences. Cleve was a very physical man. So was Matt, but in a different way. Matt invited you to participate. Cleve overpowered. He had behaved tonight, but she wondered how long he'd be satisfied with kisses and cuddles. Her own reactions shocked her. For an instant, she had wanted to lose control, but to do so went against everything she believed.

She didn't love Cleveland Winslow. She hardly knew him. What she did know of him should convince her that a relationship made no sense. The man lived in a world she knew nothing about.

Victoria took Cleve with her the next day to borrow Nick's truck and pick up a load of decorative bark for a new family shelter. Several civic groups had teamed up to restore and refurbish a large, old house. Volunteers were painting the outside and hanging wallpaper on the inside, adding the finishing touches. Cleve pitched in without a grumble, climbing into the truck bed to shovel the bark out into a wheelbarrow. Victoria could handle the lightweight load, so she pushed the wheelbarrow and started a pile on the ground. As she returned, she heard a whistle and looked up.

Tina Dupres stood with her back to Victoria, facing the pickup, admiring Cleve. Moisture glistened on corded muscles that rippled as he wielded the shovel. Victoria experienced an odd stab of possessiveness. Chagrined, she reminded herself that Tina was her best friend.

"Tina," she called out. "Aren't you wallpapering inside or something?"

Tina swiveled around and grinned. Her eyes lit up as she noticed the wheelbarrow, then she turned toward the truck to see Cleve stop and watch them. "Is this gorgeous hunk with you?" she asked.

Victoria blushed, and Cleve grinned. He jumped down from the truck and came over to stand next to Victoria. "If you're referring to my humble self, then the answer is yes. Cleve Winslow," he said, holding out a grimy hand, then stopping and wiping it on his jeans before reaching again to shake her hand.

"This is Tina Dupres," Victoria introduced. Tina looked her usual punk-beautiful self. Today, the streak in the front of her spiky hair matched her bright lavender-tinted contact lenses. The twinkle in her eyes belied the garishness of her appearance.

"Victoria lied," Tina said, grinning outrageously. "You're not nice, and you're not lukewarm—no, that's not what she said, either. She said dynamo was a lukewarm description for you, but that's off the mark too. Do you hurl thunderbolts?"

"Every chance I get," he replied with a grin.

Cleve seemed perfectly comfortable with Tina's audacious behavior, whereas, Victoria wanted to brain Tina, or crawl in a hole, or both. Tina didn't mean anything by her flirting. "I sure could use something cold to drink. Come on, Tina. I know you need to get back to work inside."

Tina started to follow Victoria, then turned back and winked. "Subtle, isn't she?"

Cleve had filled another wheelbarrow when she came back out with two iced teas. They each had a few sips, then she set them on the porch to finish later.

Victoria was pushing the last wheelbarrow load when Tina came around the corner, a volunteer in tow. "Hey, I found reinforcements."

Victoria looked up and stumbled, nearly landing in the wheelbarrow. The volunteer rushed over. "Here, let me do that."

"Thank you, Matt." She shot Tina a lethal glare. "I didn't know you were involved with this project."

Either he didn't see the nonverbal interplay between the two women, or he purposely ignored it. "Tina recruited me, and I'm happy to help. I haven't had time to get involved in local projects yet, but the firm gave toward the restoration." He dumped the bark, then walked over to Cleve. "Hi, I'm Matt Halstead."

"Cleve Winslow," Cleve said, shaking Matt's hand. He sent Victoria an inquiring look. Tina cheerfully jumped in.

"Matt is Victoria's ex-husband. He just took a partnership with Halverson's law firm.

"Congratulations," Cleve said politely. Matt responded, equally politely. Victoria wanted to scream. Tina had set her up, and Matt blithely played along. Or had he instigated this cute coincidence?

"If you're going to help, grab a shovel." She took Cleve's arm and drew him away, but not as far away as she wanted. If she hadn't promised to do the flowerbed, she would have left. Instead, with the help of three sets of hands, she decided she and Cleve could leave earlier than planned.

They worked side by side turning the soil around trees and planting flats of petunias, marigolds and a variety of bushes. Wasting no time on polite and friendly chitchat, Cleve and Matt quickly prepared the soil, while Victoria set the plants in the ground. Once the flowers were in and watered, they spread the mulch around them, and then Victoria plopped down on the porch steps in exhaustion. Cleve sat beside her. Matt leaned on a shovel and watched them, a calculated expression on his face, and she wondered what he was thinking. Cleve had to be a revelation to him, unless the girls or Tina had clued him in. Which she doubted, since Cleve had just gotten back in town.

Swiping at the grime on her forehead, Victoria smeared dirt across her skin. Cleve laughed and finger-painted stripes on her face. "There," he said. "You're ready to go on the war path."

She saw the mischief in his eyes. "I'll show you war path, not-so-white-man." She dipped her fingers into her glass of iced tea and drew a line of mud on his face.

"Painted lady plays with fire," Cleve said, his ferocious growl spoiled by his grin. Before she could react, he poured tea on his hands and rubbed them down her arms. Jumping to her feet, she took off running around the house. He chased after her, rounding the side of the house in time to get hit with a stinging stream of water. He looked so surprised, she doubled over laughing, wildly aiming the hose, and liberally dousing him with the cold spray.

Grabbing her hand, he turned the spray back on her. They were laughing and struggling when the hose suddenly went limp. Wet and bedraggled, they turned to face Matt.

He shrugged his shoulders and grinned. "Figured I'd better do something, before you washed the new paint off the walls."

☙

"You made the auction, with your generous bid on the buffalo hunt sculpture," Victoria said as they sat in her living room after the charity auction. "After that, the bids all increased. I know the foundation appreciates your help. A lot of kids will benefit from the money they made tonight."

Cleve had kicked off his shoes and stretched his legs out, crossing his feet on the coffee table. The curtains billowed back from the open sliding glass doors as a summer storm front moved into the foothills.

The atmosphere seemed charged, and the breeze whipped up keening sounds as it soughed through the dark trees outside. Distant flashes of lightning and rolls of thunder heralded the advancing storm. The weather suited the man next to her. His presence, wherever he went, seemed to generate powerful currents. As he rubbed the sensitive skin at her hairline, tingles ran up and down her spine.

"You bought two ski packages and that sweater," he said. "They're nice enough buys, but you said you didn't want any of them. You're the soft touch." He gazed at her, his eyes alight with warmth. "Sure doesn't fit your ice maiden image."

"You keep rubbing my neck like that, this ice maiden will melt into a puddle."

"I'd like to see that."

"I don't think so," she said lightly. Now that she recognized and could return his witty, half-innuendo banter, she enjoyed flirting. "Your company is well-known for philanthropy, which convinces me your dastardly reputation is a sham."

His fingers stilled, tightened to a grip. "Don't," he said, his jaw set in rigid lines. "I bought good will tonight, period. I take advantage of anything that opens doors or makes things go my way. Don't mistake me for one of the good guys."

Victoria blinked and shook her head. "I'm confused. One minute you're pulling me close and the next, you're shoving me away. Why are you determined to be a heavy?"

"Come here," he said, tugging her towards him. She turned to face him, her eyes searching for an answer. He didn't smile, in fact he seemed almost angry. She started to place her hands on his shoulders; he grabbed her wrists and held them out.

"I want you to accept me as I am, not as someone you create in your imagination. Your ex-husband? He's a good-guy. I know his type. Polite, pleasant, politically correct. Boring. If you want nice, go back to him. I don't know what happened, and I don't want to know, but I do know this. He wants you back. You used me today for a shield."

"No, Cleve. Matt's showing up surprised me. Tina set me up, and you can be sure I'll tell her I didn't like it. I enjoyed being with you today."

"I know. And I don't mind being your shield, if you really want protection. Just don't use me to make another man jealous. And don't lie to yourself, if that's what you want. I can't be like him. I don't want you thinking I'm some closet Mr. Clean who secretly harbors a kind heart. I don't. I take what I want, and if someone gets in my way, they'd better move or get run over."

"That fits your reputation."

"Do you believe it?"

She thought for a moment before she answered. "To an extent, but I know there's a lot more to you than that."

"You're right, but not what you think. Are you strong enough to accept me, or will you run the first time I do something you don't like?"

She stared into his eyes, trying to understand his challenge. The dark intensity, as he stared back, made her nervous. She had to lighten his mood. "Not unless you do something illegal, immoral, or fattening."

He scooted closer, trapping her against the end of the couch. "None of the above, but I like to push the limits. I think you do too. Beneath that controlled image of yours, you want excitement and adventure. You try to hold back your impetuous streak, but sometimes you can't resist. And I speak from experience. I got soaked when you got a hold of that hose."

She leaned back against the arm of the couch. "And that's about as adventurous as I get. I'm an accountant. That impetuous act didn't cost anything. And that's the key. Wanting isn't reason enough. I have to count the cost. I want a lot of things that I'm not going to get."

"So you pretend you don't want them? You give up? Funny, I don't see you as a quitter."

"Not quit—choose. There's a difference. Just because I want something doesn't make it right. That something might be bad for me or might hurt someone else."

"I'd never hurt you," he said, taking her hand. The teasing gleam faded from his eyes. "I could be very good for you, Victoria. No games." His eyes became darker, more intense, and far more compelling than they were when he tried to charm her. "I'm almost forty years old, and I'm tired of being alone. I want what everyone wants—a home, a family. I don't mean I want to start having kids. I'm too old for that, but I like Amanda and Jessica. Victoria, I can't begin to put a name to this attraction between us. I've never felt a desire so strong before. I've never been down this road, and I want to see where it goes—with you. Only one rule. Trust. I have to know that you won't ever use me or lie to me."

She stared at him, mesmerized. He stared back, waiting for her to say something.

"I don't know what you want me to say. I'm not even sure what the question is. I don't lie or use people. And if this isn't a game, why do I feel like I just got off a seesaw? Right now, I'm pretty confused, but you've given me a lot to think about, and I promise you, I won't be able to think about much else. The last five years, I haven't had time to be lonely or anything else, but you're right. Whatever the outcome, we're on this road together."

Cleve stood and pulled her to her feet. "You are a rare treasure. A woman who applies logic to emotions and who's not afraid to keep walking. And that's just two of the things I love about you. And I think I'll say goodnight before you decide to throw me out."

JANICE BACKED INTO Victoria's office, pushing the door open as she struggled with a large basket of flowers.

"Oh, how beautiful," Victoria exclaimed at the profusion of snapdragons, dainty blue iris, daisies and roses. "Put them over there, on the table."

Beaming at her boss, Janice set them down and handed Victoria the attached card. "I know today isn't your birthday. Is there a special occasion or just an ardent admirer?"

"No idea," Victoria said, opening the envelope. She suspected—hoped—the flowers came from Cleve.

These remind me of you and the garden you drew in Breckenridge. Sorry I doused your fun. Forgive me? Love, Matt.

"Janice, take them . . . no, never mind."

"An unwelcome suitor?"

"My ex-husband." Victoria sighed. *Love, Matt.* Oh-h-h, why did he have to add that? She didn't really want a reminder of Matt filling her office, but she couldn't resist the beautiful blooms. Janice grinned at her, and Victoria realized she had a traitor in her midst. Matt had won an ally in her secretary.

After lunch, Mandy and Jessica popped into Victoria's office looking for a handout. Mandy had the day off, and the girls were going with their church youth group to a Christian rock concert at Red Rocks Amphitheater that night. Since both girls were saving their money for camp, Victoria dug into her wallet. She might not want to go to church herself, but she was happy the girls belonged to the youth group. They never lacked for activities, and they were always well chaperoned. While she thought their emphasis on Jesus was a tad overdone, the church taught the young people to make moral choices and take responsibility for their actions, which reinforced the values she personally tried to teach her daughters.

When Matt called, the flowers he'd sent had worked their charm. At least her anger had cooled.

"I honestly didn't know Tina asked for my help so she could interfere with your plans," he said. "I'm sorry. I wouldn't have come if I'd known. I hope I didn't make you uncomfortable."

"Tina means well. She's tried to arrange my life before. I do wish she'd give up, though. Setting us up wasn't fair to either of us."

"I'm glad you aren't angry. You know I care about you, and I'd never purposely put you in that kind of a situation. Victoria, I'm trusting in the Lord to work out everything in our lives for His best and our best, whatever that may be. Our future is in His hands, and He doesn't need Tina's help, or mine. I told Tina that, and she promised not to meddle again."

Victoria ignored Matt's reference to God, refusing to get into a discussion with him about religion. Besides, Tina's promise not to meddle was so ludicrous she couldn't help smiling. "Not if she can restrain herself, anyway. You know Tina. Her impulses take wing, and she just gets carried away."

"Let me take you out to dinner tonight, to make up for harassing you."

"I'm sorry, Matt. I already have plans. Besides, your flowers are enough. And they are lovely. Thank you."

"You're welcome. Another night, perhaps."

"Perhaps."

◈

Her plans were dinner with Cleve. He picked her up at work.

"I hope you're hungry," he said as he pulled away from the curb. "I skipped lunch. My office furniture arrived this morning, and I wanted to make sure everything got set up the way I instructed."

"You're decorating your own office?"

"Yes. The amount of time I spend there, I want the furnishings arranged to suit me. I've never met a decorator yet who could resist putting her own artistic touch on her decorating. Let them do the rest of the building, but not my office."

"Makes sense. I like my office, but I only contributed the art work."

"I have very exacting tastes. I'll be glad when the move is finished, though. I'd forgotten what a nuisance it is."

"Where are we going?"

"To my house. I hope you like Chinese. I stopped and got some before I picked you up. We can reheat the food in the microwave."

"Your house? I didn't know you'd moved in."

"I haven't. The moving van is there. It's a day early, and I want to make certain everything is all right before the movers leave."

"Oh. We could have done lunch tomorrow, instead."

"Tomorrow I'll be supervising a landscape company and meeting with an interior decorator. I'm letting them do paint and wallpaper." He turned off Interstate 70 in the foothills west of Denver and drove up a winding road to a brand new house perched on a hillside overlooking Denver. Three men were unloading a grand piano from a moving van.

"Do you play the piano?" Victoria asked.

"Not I. Sometimes I hire a pianist for a party, or perhaps one of my guests will play. The piano gets used enough to stay in tune. Do you play?"

"Only two-finger chopsticks."

"Would you mind taking our dinner into the kitchen while I speak to the movers? Kitchen's to the left," he said, handing her the large sack he'd brought from the car.

While Cleve talked to one of the men, Victoria followed the movers as they rolled the piano across the dark gray marbled entry way into a spacious living room overlooking the city. Polished oak banisters curved up along marbled stairways on both sides of the entry leading to two separate upstairs wings.

The enormous windows in the living room were bare of coverings, and the stark white walls seemed sterile without any pictures to break the expanse. The men put the piano in a corner by the windows. Boxes were stacked everywhere and pieces of furniture covered in white cloth were set haphazardly around the room. When the men brushed past her to go out for more furniture, she moved down a short hall to a room with a large crystal chandelier hanging from the center of the ceiling. Through that room, she found a kitchen that could have been in any gourmet restaurant. A shiny stainless steel range with double ovens took up nearly one whole side of the room. A chopping block island held a small sink and disposal, while the main sink and commercial size dishwasher took up another wall. Victoria couldn't find a cloth or paper towels to clean a space on the counter, so she used a Kleenex and was surprised to find very little dust.

"A crew came in and cleaned," Cleve said, coming up behind her. "There should be utensils in the sack with the food. My housekeeper arrives tomorrow. Hungry?"

"Starved. I had only an apple for lunch."

They rewarmed the cartons of food and took them out to a deck off the back of the kitchen where the movers had set up a glass-topped wrought iron table and chairs. Victoria set out the paper plates and plastic silverware, while Cleve put ice in plastic cups and added water.

"Sorry, it's the only thing to drink. Next time I'll have something fitting for the occasion."

"Water is fine."

He raised his glass to her.

"To my first guest on my first night in my new home. May this be the beginning of many evenings here together."

Victoria looked thoughtful, then raised her glass. "I'll drink to the *first* half of your toast." She took a sip. "I don't know about the rest."

"I hope there will be many," Cleve replied, as he sat in a chair next to her. "I entertain a lot, mostly business and charity. I might even enjoy them if you're here with me."

Victoria left his comment unanswered and busied herself spooning out the contents of the containers on their plates. "Szechwan beef, um, and sweet and sour shrimp. I love this stuff. Here's some hot mustard."

As they began eating, Cleve said, "Tell me about the development industry. That's one aspect of business I haven't been involved in."

"Nick started out building custom homes, one at a time, but that market dwindled when housing tracts became popular. He could have made a killing doing that, but he said he didn't want to compromise his quality, so he had to find something else. He's a remarkable man," Victoria said, warming to her subject. She admired her boss so much, she could expound his virtues for hours. She picked up a piece of shrimp with her fingers, swirled it in the sauce, then popped it in her mouth and licked her fingers before she continued.

"He switched to commercial offices, small, upscale retail, warehouses, and industrial complexes," she said. "He has a theory that everyone wants to do the big, glamorous architectural feats, like skyscrapers and courthouses and cathedrals. Someone has to do the little projects, the buildings that house the medium-sized businesses that keep the others going. He concentrated on filling those contracts, the ones too small for the big guys and too big for the average contractor. We keep our prices reasonable and fit every job to the client."

"Interesting," Cleve commented. "INTECH has certainly found its niche. From what I understand, you guided the company into some of those areas yourself."

"I can't claim all the credit. Some opportunities opened up about the same time Ed Carlson, the previous CFO got sick, and I had to step in. The timing gave me a lucky break."

"You saw a possibility and made the most of the opportunities. Isn't that what you told me Saturday night? You make a choice, and then you make things happen?"

"Yes, that's what I said, and I believe our choices determine our future," she asserted. They'd been talking about the physical side of a relationship. About making a choice to participate or abstain.

"I agree," he said. "That's why I could never be happy working for someone else. I have to be in control, making the decisions. We're a lot alike, you and I."

His acknowledgment ranked as high praise. He talked to her as an equal, with respect for her knowledge and achievements. That this phenomenally successful man considered her a peer amazed her. After going through an audit with Matt, feeling full of doubts and deficiencies, Cleve's affirmation boosted her spirits.

"Victoria, I haven't told anyone else this," he said, conspiratorially leaning forward towards her and lowering his voice. "I have a feeling you'll appreciate my secret. It reminds me of the project you were telling me about, where you're going to convert methane gas to electricity."

Her interest aroused, she leaned forward, propping her elbow on the table and resting her chin on the heel of her hand.

"I'm looking at alternative vehicle fuel sources," he said. "Especially residential applications. When I get unpacked and set up, I'll show you the small shop I'm putting in the basement. Environmentally conscientious projects are smart business right now. Every business that effects the environment needs to address those issues."

"You are so right," Victoria said. "I can't wait to show you what we're doing at the Black Forest. The process is amazing."

"When can I get a tour?"

"I can probably arrange to take you out tomorrow . . . oh, I forgot. You have appointments."

"I can work around them. I'd much rather see your project. Now, I'd better check on the progress here. In fact, come help me, and I'll get you out of here faster."

"I'll do what I can." She cleared up the remains of their dinner, threw away the trash, and put the rest in the huge refrigerator. She found Cleve in the living room checking a packing list against the numbers on the furniture.

"Here," he said. "Compare and mark off numbers and do a once-over for damage—just obvious scrapes and dents. I could leave this for my housekeeper. She'll go over everything again with a magnifying glass, I'm sure. But I like to check things for myself."

After an hour, they finally accounted for every item. With the covers removed, all the exquisite oriental furniture stunned Victoria. The pieces were of a heavy wood, not black-lacquered in the typical fashion, but glowing with a rich, golden wood finish. She was rubbing her hand over a satin-smooth chair arm when Cleve joined her.

"Beautiful, isn't it? Philippine mahogany, hand-made in China before World War ll. Unlike some oriental furniture, this period utilized simple lines and warm, sensuous wood."

"I've never seen anything so smooth and elegant." Her hand continued to trace the graceful curves.

"You'll have to see the effect when the rugs have been laid and the paintings are hung, but I guess we're finished for now."

When he returned her to her car, they arranged to meet at her office the next morning for the Black Forest tour. Then he kissed her goodnight, a kiss firm enough to relay admiration and need, but short enough to make no demands in return.

He followed her from downtown, all the way out Sixth Avenue, then down C-470 south another ten miles to her exit. Then he proceeded on east, headed back to his hotel, but he'd gone thirty miles out of his way to get there. A warm glow started somewhere near her heart and began to spread. Far from feeling pressured by his attention, she felt cherished and respected.

Before they headed out to the Black Forest site, Victoria showed Cleve the diagrams and test results on the Methergy Project. With papers spread all over her desk, they stood bent over, going through paper after paper as she explained the process. His intelligent questions showed an immediate grasp of the project and revealed a more than cursory interest. An idea began to germinate in her mind. Cleve's company might want to invest in this particular project. Although his company concentrated on energy development, more precisely oil, he had talked about environmental consciousness and research. She watched him study one paper after another and waited expectantly for his comments. Finally, he looked up. "You've begun work on this project?"

"Yes. The test system is in. You've seen the preliminary results. They've drawn responses from half a dozen top universities. The project has been cleared through all the necessary channels, and expansion areas are being excavated right now."

"What about buildings?"

"We hope to complete the shell of the main headquarters before winter sets in. That will entail the basic construction, nothing fancy at first. We'll expand as the project prospers."

Setting the papers down, he stood straight and stretched. "How soon can we leave?" he asked.

"Right now," she said, stacking the papers and tapping them against the desk to align them. She slipped them into a file folder and set it aside. "Let's go."

An hour later, Cleve parked the Jeep next to a monster earth-mover.

"I never get used to the size of these things," Victoria said, practically shouting to be heard. "Makes you see things from an ant's perspective. Come on, I'll introduce you to Bart Jenson."

"Bart Jenson's working on this project?"

"Yes, do you know him?"

"Only by reputation."

Giant yellow machines lumbered along like prehistoric mastodons, destroying everything in their paths as they carved a wide crater out of the flat land. The noise level made conversation impossible. Victoria spotted the site boss and headed toward him, skirting the excavation area and holding a hand over her nose and mouth to filter out the dust. Cleve kept pace with her, but she noticed him looking around, taking in every detail as they walked.

A research park had been Nick's dream. Methergy was Victoria's baby. She had followed every step since its inception. Now she watched Cleve nervously, wanting his approval, needing him to give her words of confirmation. A slight frown marred his forehead, and his eyes squinted against the dust, giving her no clue to his thoughts.

Bart spotted them and pointed toward a construction trailer. He joined them there, and Victoria introduced the two men.

"This is quite a setup," Cleve commented. "When Ms. Halstead told me about the project, I didn't expect to find the construction so far advanced."

A broad grin split Bart's face. "This is all still preliminary, but we built the test system to be the initial plant. No sense doubling the work and materials."

"Then you're already producing electricity?"

"In negligible amounts. Just enough to run our tests. Come on, I'll show you around."

They walked to a point some distance from the excavation work until the noise level became bearable.

"That's better," Bart said. As he explained the development process, he pointed out the various systems to Cleve. The site development currently stands at forty percent."

"That sounds like a long way from production," Cleve said.

"Actually, we could go into full methanogenic production now."

"Which is?"

"That's the period when the greatest quantity of high quality methane gas can be produced."

"Then what is the holdup?"

"Development. Construction is a lot easier at an inactive site. We are expanding the site from thirty-five to eighty acres. First we excavate, then lay the pipes below frost line to eliminate freezing that can kill the methane-forming bacteria. We have to factor in soil conditions and adequate water. An old pipeline ran through the middle of the site. And there's constant seepage from an artesian spring on the property. We rerouted the pipeline, and we've designed an irrigation system to accommodate the landfill."

"Who else does the water affect? I assume the pipeline supplies water elsewhere."

"The spring feeds a small livestock pond on the next acreage. A creek runs out of that, but doesn't go anywhere. That seems to be the end of the road."

"You've put a lot of time and money into a worthless landfill. Will the return justify the cost?"

Bart turned to Victoria. "Ms. Halstead can answer than question. I just wield the hammer."

Victoria smiled. "Some hammer," she said, then turned to answer Cleve. "If we only produce and sell electricity, then no, the project wouldn't be worth the cost. However, the ultimate goal is research and practical application of the gas we convert. The plant will produce both the experimental medium and the energy to operate the laboratories.

That's the beginning. From that point, the possibilities are limitless." Victoria paused long enough to take a breath. She was warming up to her favorite subject.

"We have the land, proximity to the city, the airport, energy industries, medical industries, space technology industries, the list goes on and on. We're far enough away from the centers of government to attract cooperative foreign research efforts." She pointed her index finger at Cleve. "Who knows," she said, taking a plunge into her newest idea. "You might be interested in some of the applications from this research."

He looked around, considering. Nodding slowly, he said, "That's possible. Garbage to electricity isn't exactly in my line of development, however."

"But this is only one part of the project. See those towers?" she asked, pointing to a complex configuration of pipes and two towers next to the water reservoir.

Cleve looked where she pointed. "That's something different?"

"Yes," Bart answered, "Besides the electrical generation, we are building a small Binax gas processing system. The towers house a plant which separates carbon dioxide from methane gas to produce vehicle fuel."

Cleve's eyebrows peaked. "Indeed. Is the result like natural gas as a vehicle fuel?"

"Yes. The vehicle conversion is the same, and the fuel is interchangeable."

"How will you market the gas?"

Victoria spoke up. "Again, we're talking research. We are building our own refueling station—very small. We'll convert the research project vehicles and track fuel consumption, cost, performance, maintenance, engine response—whatever might pertain to the fuel usage."

She expected his approval. Instead, his eyebrow drew together in a thoughtful frown.

"Bart, thanks for the tour," Cleve said, shaking the engineer's hand. "I've absorbed all I can handle for one day. I'd like to come back and watch the operation, if that's all right with you?"

"Sure, any time. I'll keep Ms. Halstead informed of our schedule."

"Victoria?" Cleve took a hold of her elbow. "We'd better get out of Mr. Jenson's way. I'm sure we've disrupted his day enough."

"My pleasure. Ma'am." Bart tipped his grubby old hat in her direction.

On the way to the car, Victoria's insides were a bundle of knots, waiting for Cleve to make some comment. Her excitement about the project didn't mean anyone else would match her enthusiasm.

Even with all the positive evidence surrounding the project, Victoria harbored a lot of insecurity, as she always did. She hid her doubts well. Everyone thought Victoria Halstead was supremely confident, a perception she nurtured to enhance her image. And Cleve's opinion meant a great deal. He was at the cutting edge of the energy industry, and he'd confided his interest in alternative vehicle fuel sources. She knew he was chewing over some thought; she could almost hear the wheels of his mind cranking over, but he kept his impressions to himself. As he opened her door, she couldn't stand the suspense any longer. Screwing up her courage, she said, "Well? What do you think?"

He looked at her abstractedly, then he grinned. "I'm speechless," he said. He got in the car and started up, backed out and drove down the dirt road leading off the property.

"I'm still trying to take in the scope of your development," he said, glancing over at her. "The papers you showed me don't begin to cover the reality."

Victoria let out a pent-up breath and smiled. "For a minute I wasn't sure what you thought."

He flashed her a quick sideline glance. "You had doubts about your project? If anything, you should feel very smug. I'm honored you gave me a personal tour."

"Maybe I'm buttering up a prospective investor. Your own idea lends itself to our vehicle fuel applications."

Cleve smiled. "Good point. I can see how you've earned your reputation. When the time comes, and you're ready to develop research complexes, I might get in line."

As they drove back to town, Cleve suggested an early dinner. At the mention of food, her stomach let out a grumble. She laughed and accepted his offer. He pulled into a restaurant southeast of town.

Over dinner, Cleve urged Victoria to talk about the Methergy project and her plans for the Black Forest Research Center. His interest spurred her to reveal more than she'd told anyone other than Nick, who shared her dream. As she enthused about her ideas, he seemed to get caught up in her vision. When she started talking about international cooperative research, he reached across the table and took hold of her hands.

"When you shoot for the stars, you're headed for another galaxy, aren't you?"

Flustered, she stopped. "I got carried away, didn't I?"

"No. I admire big thinking. No one ever reached the Eiffel Tower by heading for Paris, Texas."

She grinned. "I have a tendency to forget such mundane things as 'the Seven Wonders of the World' when I get to talking about my project."

"That's why you'll succeed. That's another one of the things I love about you."

She laughed.

"You think I'm kidding?"

"I know you're teasing me, and I'll have to admit I'm vain enough to enjoy it."

"As you get to know me, you'll discover that I don't tease."

"That's not true. What about the water fight?"

"You started that. I was defending myself."

"Sure," she said, grinning at him.

"When you smile, you have one dimple that seems to be winking at me."

Her smile immediately disappeared into self-consciousness. She hadn't thought about her off-kilter face in a long time.

"Hey, don't stop. Did I say something wrong?"

"No. I had some nerve damage as a child." She shrugged. "The weakness used to bother me a lot. Now I forget most of the time."

He frowned. "You have a beautiful face. What you see as a flaw, I see as a beauty mark."

She looked earnestly into his face. "That's very kind of you, Cleve. I'm not ashamed of my looks, but I certainly never tried out for any beauty contests. Anyway, it doesn't matter."

"Anything that upsets you matters, and I'm not kind, remember?" He let out a resigned sigh. "We need to get better acquainted. Come spend the day with me tomorrow."

"I can't," she said, regret coloring her voice. "Besides, I thought you were picking out wallpaper tomorrow."

"That can wait. In fact, I want you to see the rest of the house and furniture first. Then you can help me."

"Oh no, I've known friendships to disintegrate over choosing wallpaper. I'd be interested to see what you'd pick, though."

"Okay, how about dinner at my house. Everything is unpacked, and there's something I want to show you."

At her look of disbelief, he held up his hands. "I really do, honest."

"I'd like to, Cleve, but I need to spend the evening with my daughters. I promised to take them shopping for camp."

"The next day, then. Whenever you say, just don't make me wait too long."

"All right, how about Thursday?"

"Thursday it is."

Later, as she drove home, she thought about Cleve and his declaration. He'd been teasing, of course. Three times he'd said he loved something about her. She liked hearing his praise, even if he didn't mean it. She still couldn't believe she—middle-aged, unexciting Victoria Halstead—had two handsome men vying for her attention. Both wanted her advice on their homes. Both claimed to want a relationship with her. She couldn't trust Matt. Could she trust Cleve? He talked about love. He probably said he loved things about lots of women and meant every word. A dynamic man like Cleve enjoyed women. So, he praised her project, told her she was brilliant and beautiful. Who was she to argue?

The more she got to know him, the more fascinated she became. He was a hard, ruthless businessman. She could understand that. You didn't get to the top of an industry without grabbing opportunities—and stepping on a few toes in the process. She recognized in him, however, a deeply hidden sensitivity. He allowed her to see glimpses of his vulnerability—a rare privilege, she believed. Cleve would never let his guard down unless he trusted completely and absolutely. And that was the crux, the need that drew her. Trust held primary importance for him, as it did for her. She wanted a man she could trust totally. Once she'd trusted Matt that way. The deep cut, when he'd betrayed her trust, still hadn't healed.

TWO BEAMS OF light bobbed and jerked around the steel behemoths like fireflies flitting about on a summer night. Jokes and curses bounced off the hulks of metal. The sounds magnified like clanging gongs through the still night air, though unheard by any but a few scavenging coyotes and a marauding owl.

The men were in no hurry, no one would come to the remote spot until shortly after dawn. By then, they would be long gone.

"I'll hold, you pour," one said, his accent slurred by the whiskey they'd been drinking.

"You always get the easy jobs," the other voice complained. "What makes you the boss?"

"I got the connections," the taller figure said. "Shut up, and let's get this done. My mouth is watering for some of those Cajun chicken wings and a bottle of tequila."

"Stuff's too hot for me. Gimme a meatball sandwich with lots of sauce and melted cheese and a cold brew."

"You ain't getting nothin', man, if we don't get this done and get outta here. Come on, pour that stuff in here." He laughed maliciously. "This is so-o-o sweet. Boy are they in for a surprise when they crank up these babies."

Victoria's mind was focused on engineering reports when Nick came to her office.

"Good morning, Nick! I'm glad you're here. I want you to look at these reports." Taking a good look at him, she noticed his deep frown. "What's wrong?"

"We have a problem at the Black Forest." His jaw clenched. His fists balled. "Every last piece of machinery, every earth-mover, dump truck, grader, and anything else that moves seized up this morning."

"Seized up? As in won't work?" Mega-dollar signs and delays pressed down on Victoria's head. Cost overruns topped the pile. "How could that be? They were running fine when I visited the site yesterday."

"You went out to the site?"

"Yes, I took a friend on a tour. I couldn't resist showing off."

"You have plenty of reason to be proud. Only now you're going to be upset. Looks like someone sabotaged the equipment."

"Sabotaged!" Disbelief struck her, making her head pound in earnest. "Why?"

Nick shook his head. "I don't know. Vandalism, maybe. They found an empty whiskey bottle by one of the trucks. That could have been left by one of the men, but Bart strictly enforces no alcohol on the job."

"But Nick, are you sure sabotage caused the equipment failures?"

"Not yet. We'll know after the mechanics look over the equipment, but that many breakdowns at once rules out coincidence."

"You're right, but it doesn't make sense." Her disbelief turned to anger. All that work and planning. All her dreams. It wasn't fair.

"Vandalism rarely does. Some sickos get a kick out of destruction."

"I don't think so, Nick. That's a long way out in the middle of nowhere for someone to just happen along and decide to destroy something."

"You think someone went out there on purpose to do this?"

"Logically? Yes. Vandals might smash things and make a mess, but to disable every piece of equipment? Too specific. Maybe someone has a grudge against one of our subs."

"Maybe."

Feeling violated, as if the vandals had attacked her, Victoria reminded herself that the only victims were machines. "What are we going to do?"

"First we'll wait to find out what's wrong. Soon as Bart calls, I'll let you know."

Matt stood outside Victoria's closed office door. Her secretary was gone. He tapped on the door, hoping she hadn't already gone to lunch. Hearing her voice, he went in. She glanced up, said something into the phone, and hung up. As she rubbed her neck, he saw the weariness in her eyes and the slump of her shoulders . "Hope I'm not interrupting anything." He shut the door. "Your secretary is gone, so I took the liberty of barging in. Bad day?"

"That's putting it mildly. I hope you're not bearing more bad news."

"No. I stopped to take you to lunch. From the look of things, you need a break. How about it?"

She shook her head. "Thanks. Today I'm tempted, but I'm snowed. Vandals hit the Black Forest site last night. I'm dealing with insurance." She flinched and flexed her shoulder.

"Here, let me do that," he said, moving around the desk to stand in back of her. Brushing her hand away, he began gently massaging her neck. "You've got a knot here. How bad is the pain?"

"It just started."

"Good. Maybe I can work the tension out. Tell me about the vandalism. What happened to your equipment?" He rubbed in circles, working down and out her shoulder blades.

"They poured sugar in the gas tanks. Sugar! Every piece of equipment shut down—the earth-movers, graders, trucks, everything. Ouch!" She grabbed his hand. "That pinches!"

"I found the spot, then. Relax." He gentled his touch as she rotated her head side to side. She let her head hang down and her arms go slack. Using his thumbs, he slowly worked the sore area. Just feeling the tight knot and touching her skin brought back memories of other muscle spasms, other neck rubs. Sometimes he'd have to stop rubbing to control his guilt and anger so he wouldn't get too rough.

She had cleaned houses while he'd attended law school. Not just cleaned. As in everything she did, Victoria had to excel. Moving furniture, lifting, scrubbing until the strain to her healthy nerves would overload, compensating for the lack of impulses on her right side, and sending her muscles into paralyzing spasms. Sometimes he'd been able to massage the spasms out. If she'd strained too hard or had added emotional stress, only strong medication would help. "Let your stress go, Tori. You'll recover from this setback. There's nothing you could have done to prevent this."

Closing his eyes, he concentrated on his fingers and sent a silent plea. *Let me help her, Lord. She tries so hard to be tough, but she's so vulnerable.* He kept his voice low and soft, like a lullaby. "You don't have to carry all these burdens, honey. Relax. Let Jesus carry them for you."

When her shoulders stiffened under his fingers, he knew his words were to blame. "Shhh, it's okay," he whispered, just loud enough for her to hear. He kept massaging. *She is as resistant to me as this knot in her neck. What am I doing wrong, Lord? I believe You want us to get back together, but I'm just not making any progress. What should I do?*

As Matt imagined his fingers sending loving messages to the overloaded nerves centers causing Victoria's muscle spasms, an answer came to his mind as clearly as if God spoke to him. *You had to choose. So does Victoria.*

Matt knew it was true. He resisted for forty-two years. He'd had to lose his family, his honor, and his pride in order to gain everything. He wanted to spare Victoria that pain, but she had fought so long and so hard to prove her worth, she wouldn't willingly give up control of her life. And he gave her no example. He had failed God and Victoria before. Was he fooling himself? Was winning Victoria back wishful thinking on his part and not the Lord's will at all? *Please, give me another chance.*

For whom? a voice inside asked. *Victoria or yourself?*

The question pierced Matt's heart, and he felt ashamed. He wanted his family back for selfish reasons, however, God designed marriages to last for a lifetime, so restoring their marriage obeyed God's will. Yet according to Jesus' answer on divorce, his unfaithfulness gave Victoria just cause to divorce him.

Yes, he desired the love and acceptance, the peace and joy of his family back. And he wanted the chance to be the husband and father God called him to be. But more than that, he wanted Victoria to experience the total, unconditional love he'd found in Jesus. She'd been trying to win that kind of love all her life, pushing to reach a level of success that she could never achieve in order to win her father's love. She didn't realize she already had that love and more. She only needed to grasp the boundless, faithful, unchanging love that overflowed. Matt prayed they could share that love together. As his prayers took wing, he began to feel a little give, a little softening beneath his fingers. Gradually, Victoria's shoulders relaxed. Speaking softly, making his voice as soothing as possible so she wouldn't knot up again, still massaging, he whispered, "Tori, I love you."

When she didn't respond, he sighed. Perhaps she didn't hear. He stopped massaging, leaving his hands resting on her shoulders.

"That feels better. Thank you."

"You're welcome. You know, sugar isn't something most people carry around with them. Especially in quantities big enough to stop a fleet of road equipment. I could believe vandalism if they'd found dirt in the gas tanks."

She craned her head around towards him. "I agree. Broken windows, overturned dumpsters, thoughtless pranks—that would fit vandalism. But they left everything else alone. No messes. This act took planning. Why would someone go to all that trouble? And why us?"

"You're going to hurt your neck again doing that."

She swiveled her chair around. "This couldn't happen at a worse time. I've got people trying to find equipment, but the push is on to complete all the road construction projects before winter. Everything available within a thousand miles is tied up. With our tight schedule, every delay affects subcontractors, equipment, delivery dates, materials. Each step multiplies into cost overruns. You know the situation. We simply can't afford delays."

"I know. I wish I could help."

"Me too." She gave him a weak smile. "Enough whining. What did you want to talk about?"

"Nothing urgent. Amanda was talking about college, asking about options. I want to talk with you so we're on the same page before I say anything. We need to agree on what and where and how we're going to handle her financing."

"She has a full scholarship to Fort Collins. You know that."

"She's talking about going to Fort Lewis."

"That's in Durango!"

"I was afraid she hadn't said anything to you. Her talk may be nothing, but we need to discuss our response, in case she's serious. I can see this isn't the best timing. We both need to think about what to do before we react, *if* she should approach us. This might be a passing whim. I think one of her friends is going there."

"Yes, we do need to discuss it. Thank you, Matt. I appreciate you coming to me before you give her advice. We could so easily work at cross-purposes. I, for one, don't need any more aggravation in my life. I'm sure you feel the same."

"How about that lunch? You should get out of here for awhile."

"Thanks, but Janice is bringing me back a sandwich. Give me a couple of days to think about the college business. Okay?"

"All right. Would you mind if the girls stay with me again this weekend? The church youth group is going river rafting, and I promised I'd ask you if they could go. I'll go with them. You can come, too, if you want."

She shuddered. "No thanks. Rafting with a bunch of teenagers isn't my idea of rest and relaxation. You're welcome to take them."

"Thanks. I'll call you tomorrow—to see how things are going."

Piles of rock, bark, and mulch bordered Cleve's driveway. When Victoria pulled in and parked, Cleve was talking to two men who were building a moss rock wall. He motioned her to go inside. The scene from the entryway stopped her. The transformation from packing crates to completed décor filled her with awe. Her eyes were immediately drawn to a large Oriental carpet in the center of the living room. With the ageless sheen of old silk and wool, and a rainbow of colors softly muted by time and countless slippered feet, the lovely rug depicted a palace garden in full bloom. The rest of the room was fit for an emperor. Graceful oriental furniture, the grand piano in the corner, intricate tapestries and paintings on the walls, and a fabulous panoramic view of Denver blended to create an opulence of wealth and grandeur, but the carpet drew her attention away from the rest.

"Take off your shoes and step on the rug," Cleve's amused voice said behind her.

"I'm afraid to. It might take flight."

"I always feel that way, but it won't, I promise. Go on," he encouraged.

She threw him an impish grin, then kicked off her shoes, padded across the entry, down a step into the living room, and stepped gingerly onto the rug. The contrast from the cold marble floor to the luxuriant rug gave her the feeling of wading into a pool of soft, warm water.

A moment later, Cleve joined her. He handed her a fluted crystal goblet. "Sparkling cider," he explained.

"Thanks." She accepted the glass. Looking down, she caught sight of his stocking feet. No toes sticking through threadbare socks. She'd always had to supervise Matt's wardrobe, or he would have worn his clothes, especially socks and sweaters, until they disintegrated.

Watching her expectantly, Cleve asked, "What do you think?"

She looked up, startled, almost blurting out, "no holes," but she caught herself. "The room is wonderful. Did you pick out all this furniture and furnishings yourself?"

"Absolutely. I bought the rug first, at an auction. Then I needed the right furniture to complement the rug. Collecting all the furnishings has taken years."

"I'm just surprised. I can't quite put the picture together."

"Don't you like the results?"

"Yes. I mean, I can't picture you picking these styles. I expected heavy wood and leather furniture and outdoorsy pictures, maybe a moose head or a trophy fish above the mantle, not a silk tapestry of a garden."

His mouth twitched into a grin. "That tapestry is five hundred years old. I love beautiful treasures. Collecting rare art is my passion." He watched her intently as he moved closer to her.

She laughed nervously and stepped back, feeling like a poor copy of a Picasso in an art museum.

"Don't back away," he said, reaching his hand up to cup her neck. "You fit here, you know."

"Hardly. I'm more the rummage sale, conglomeration-of-odd-pieces-and-styles type."

"You're looking in a warped mirror. That's not how I see you at all."

"Oh, really? How do you see me?"

"You remind me of this carpet."

"You've got to be kidding," she said, choking back a laugh. "The carpet is a treasure. You come out with the most imaginative lines."

His jaw tightened. "I don't hand out lines, especially not to you. I thought I made that clear."

His curt tone wiped away her humor and her smile. "Nothing is clear," she said. "I don't understand any of this." Men negotiated with her, made sales pitches to her, but they didn't call her beautiful or compare her to rare carpets. He'd hinted at caring about her, and she'd thought of little else since.

"I know." A sympathetic smile erased the harshness in his features. His hand caressed the side of her face. "I want you to take me seriously. You are lovely—no, don't give me that skeptical look."

She hadn't probed her own feelings toward Cleve—hadn't dared— but she wanted him to mean what he said. *Convince me,* she silently demanded. "You date gorgeous young models and famous socialites. There's no way I compare."

"They are the ones who don't compare. This rug, for instance, has beauty and warmth. There's magic woven by hand, one stitch at a time, into the fabric, which has endured and will last as long as the carpet. Like you. You are resilient and creative. When I'm around you, I feel like I could conquer anything. Magic, you see."

"I haven't believed in magic since I was four years old."

"Come here." He set their glasses aside and drew her to him. "Let me make a believer out of you." He kissed her longingly, thoroughly. Her toes curled into the thick pile beneath her feet, a silky foundation both firm and insubstantial. He stepped back, and she felt the coolness of air against her face and opened her eyes to gaze into dark eyes as dazed as her own.

"Magic," he whispered. "When I saw the rug laid out, I imagined you here with me."

"No," she said, her voice unsteady. He moved too fast. The romantic picture his words painted intrigued her, but the image was illusion.

"Yes. When I'm with you I feel like I've come home," he said, his voice gone husky.

"Stop," she said, panic building inside her. Something—the carpet, Cleve's kiss, his touch, his declaration—beckoned her to enter an exciting, daring, and very seductive make-believe world. The only time in her life she'd felt such overwhelming emotions, she had lost control and made disastrous decisions. She couldn't trust herself when emotions ruled her heart. "This is crazy," she said. "We've only known each other a few weeks."

"I've never been confused by my feelings, Victoria. I've wanted you since I read that article. I may be rushing you, but there's no doubt on my part." He stopped and took a deep breath. "I need to make a confession. Come sit down."

He led her to the couch. "And please, hear me out before you react, all right?"

Looking for some hint in his expression to reassure her, she slowly nodded. He studied her, as if gauging the best way to make a presentation. She thought she caught a glimpse of the calculating businessman, and it made her nervous.

"I appreciate your skepticism. I don't trust emotions, either. First and foremost, I'm a businessman. I handle my private life the same way I run my corporation. When I want something, I learn everything about it. Then, if reports confirm the potential value, I formulate an offer or a plan to obtain my objective." He paused to get a response. So far, she agreed, so she gave him a little nod.

"When I'm contemplating acquiring a company, I collect data—everything available. Standard procedure." He paused long enough for Victoria to suspect she wouldn't like his disclosure. "I have a thick dossier on you," he said.

He stopped. She stared at him, stunned. Confused. Furious. What could she say? Nothing. She fought to control any emotion that might give him an edge, though to what end, she had no clue.

"You are extremely intelligent, self-possessed, and shrewd. You have an intuitive business sense mixed with consistently faultless logic. When

I decided to come to Denver, I planned to meet you. Fate stepped in first, almost as if we were predestined to meet."

"I don't believe in destiny. I choose my way. What happens is a result of those choices, not destiny. As for investigating me without my permission—I find that offensive and degrading."

"I'm sorry, I didn't mean to upset you. It's a simple precaution. There's a lot at stake. I could have kept my investigation to myself, you know, but I want honesty between us." Cleve let a slow smile transform his face, turning the wattage up high. She knew he used his charm to maximum power, and she refused to be impressed.

"There are lots of women in corporate management with better qualifications than I. Why all the trouble? Are you looking for a token female in your organization?"

"I'm not looking for an employee. I'm looking for a partner. When I read that article, I knew I'd found the right one. You strike a chord with me."

"You're looking for a partner? Surely you know the risks involved in a partnership."

"Not a business partner." He speared his fingers through his hair. "I'm really botching this. See how you affect me?" He stopped and looked at her as if waiting for her acknowledgment. She gave none. "I've been trying to figure out how to approach you on this, but it isn't like negotiating with another company, and I've never done this before. I guess straight out is the best way. I want to marry you."

"What?" She jumped to her feet, reacting to a need to move. "Why?"

Cleve stood and walked to the windows, the distance reassuring her. After looking out for a moment, he pivoted to face her. "Many reasons. I told you some of them the other day. I've spent half my life building a business. You know the old saying—it's lonely at the top. Well, the cliché is true. I want certain qualities in a wife. Compatibility. You and I are compatible in every way. I want a partner who shares my visions and understands my life. You are motivated, determined to succeed, and not afraid to do what's necessary to accomplish your goals. I want someone—you—to share and celebrate the victories. And there will be many. Together, we'll be unbeatable." He stopped and put his hands in his pockets.

"Let's see if I understand. You read about me, then checked me out, and decided you want to marry me. Sounds like a business deal to me."

"Yes—I think that's best. Emotions only cloud the issues. In this case, the decision came first. I'll have to admit, since I met you, emotions have confirmed my choice, but your profile alone convinced me you are the right woman. The report clearly showed you have the most important quality. You are completely trustworthy and loyal. I want that trust. That is more important than desire or any other transitory emotions."

"I'm glad to know I passed all your tests." She couldn't keep the sarcasm out of her voice. "If I find myself out of a job, I'll put you on my résumé as a reference. While we're being so honest, I'll level with you," she said. "You scare me. I'm afraid of you and what you make me feel. Right now I'm angry. Maybe I'm a little flattered. I'm certainly confused. I don't like having my emotions all stirred up. Calm and simple, that's my style. And you've laid this all out like such a simple plan. Such a deal I have for you, today and today only. Sign up now and you'll live happily ever after. Aren't you going to whip out a contract and a brand new pen so I put my signature on the dotted line, all legal-like? Is there a notary in the house?" She looked him square in the eyes, her chin jutting out defiantly. Inside she quivered like a frightened kitten staring down a big, bad wolf. She expected him to pounce, or throw her out after she threw his offer back in his face. He did neither. In fact, his eyes seemed filled with understanding.

"Marriage is a contract, Victoria, and I never enter into an agreement without understanding the fine print and agreeing with the conditions. However, what started out to be a simple, straightforward offer has gotten complicated. I didn't count on wanting you so much, and that makes me nervous. I learned a long time ago to meet fear head on. It's the only way to win, and I want to win."

She shook her head. "I want to win, too, but my idea of winning is nothing like yours. I don't have to check out my friends. I believe in people, and I'm rarely disappointed." That wasn't entirely true, an inner voice mocked, reminding her about Matt. She ignored the thought. "I thrive on small things, like my daughters' accomplishments or a successful project. I'm not looking for fame or fortune and certainly not marriage. A little romance, maybe. That's what I expected. Not this."

"I know. I want everything aboveboard between us. Honesty and trust. I can give you romance. I can give you anything you want. My offer's on the table. You can think about what I've said, ask questions, make me a counter-offer, anything you want. I'm just opening negotiations."

Now they were on familiar ground. She looked at him thoughtfully. "No pressure?"

"I can't promise that; after all, I'm human. But I'll always back off if you say stop."

Victoria had to admit, he'd been more than open and honest, and she appreciated that. A relationship based on logic could work. A partnership with a man as successful and dynamic as Cleve Winslow, even short term, tempted her. Besides, her emotions were in enough turmoil over Matt. Maybe she needed this to bring those emotions into balance.

"I'll agree to be friends. Then we'll see." They had no real future. His ideal woman wouldn't come with a ready-made family. With time, he'd realize that. Meanwhile, he'd promised two things she'd been missing for a long time. Romance and trust.

"Well, friends gives us a start," he said.

Wrapping his arms around her, he hugged her, not moving, not kissing, just holding her as if she were precious. "You won't be sorry," he whispered just before he placed a light kiss on her ear. Although she resented being investigated, his thoroughness and openness were things she could approve. She smiled and hugged him back, feeling comfortable in his arms until her stomach growled and broke the spell.

"Umm. I guess you are real, thank goodness. Magical creatures don't get hungry."

She laughed and felt a great relief. Reality restored her control. "You did invite me for dinner, if I remember correctly. And you promised to show me something."

"Right. Come on, I'll show you my idea first." He led her downstairs to a walkout basement. Stacks of boxes were everywhere.

"Don't mind the mess. I'll sort out everything eventually." He walked through to a workroom with a clean workbench and a wall of tools neatly hanging on hooks. Opening a drawer under the bench, he withdrew an object that he handed to Victoria.

She studied the gadget, and turned to him expectantly. "A high-tech faucet?"

"Pretty close. Let me show you."

She followed him to the garage where a pipe ran along the back wall and disappeared down into the basement. Midway along the pipe there was a T-joint with valves and gauges on either side of the joint. He closed one of the valves and uncapped the joint, then screwed the gadget onto the open pipe. "This is pressurized, so I use the valves to release and regulate the flow."

"Is that a gas line."

"Yes."

"And that faucet? It's an adapter?" She looked around the garage and her eyes widened. "That's like one of the spigots on a quick-fill fueling station like we're putting in at the Methergy site. Can you use that to fuel a car?"

"That's the idea. This is only the prototype. It isn't perfected for mass marketing yet, but this little widget could turn every residence into a fuel station for natural gas."

"What would a hook-up cost?"

Cleve smiled. "The installation and cost of natural gas will beat the average car's fuel bills. Interested?"

"Interested? Who wouldn't be?" she said enthusiastically. "This is just the kind of product I envision our center producing," she said. "Why are you working here and not at Winslow International?"

A boyish grin lit his face, and he shrugged. "Why should my engineers get all the fun while I sit behind a desk and read their reports or sit in conference rooms and watch lengthy presentations? Making gadgets like this is the reason I became an engineer in the first place."

"What are you going to do with it now?"

"I kind of thought we could fool around with the project, make it work."

"We as in . . . ?"

"You and I. My natural gas tap would be a perfect offshoot of your Methergy fuel project, except your fuel would have to be sold to the utility company."

"You didn't start this invention yesterday. You didn't even know about me or Methergy until recently."

"Haven't you ever felt that some things, like the two of us meeting, are just meant to happen? I started this because the idea germinated and wouldn't leave me alone until I did something about it. Isn't your Methergy the same thing?"

She nodded her head. "I guess so. And you want me to be a part of your project?"

"I want you to be part of everything in my life."

An invisible hand squeezed her lungs. "This is moving too fast, Cleve. I can't."

He raised both hands as if backing off. "Okay—no more sales talk. Let's go eat."

While they ate the delicious pasta dinner left by his housekeeper, Victoria told him about the vandalism at the Black Forest site and the precautions they were taking. He sympathized and offered to help. Just having him listen, sharing her frustrations and worries, eased the burden.

He asked her to stay. He made the suggestion after dinner, but he didn't push when she declined. They made a date to play golf, and he let her go after a sweet goodnight kiss.

Chapter Twelve

"CHERRY CREEK MALL," Mandy said.

"No. Park Meadows," Jessica insisted.

"Southwest Plaza is on our way, so we'll go there." Victoria said in a tone that brooked no argument. "What do you want for dinner?"

"Fajitas," Jessica said.

"You got to pick last time we went out," Mandy said. "I want a stromboli."

"We'll try the new Italian place near the mall," Victoria decided. Jessica slunk down in the seat, crossed her arms, and pouted. Jessica's disapproval didn't spoil her appetite. She finished off a large plate of lasagna. Mandy barely touched her stromboli. The girls had spent several days with their father. When Victoria asked them what they'd been doing, she heard a full hour of "dad did this" and "dad did that," until she wanted to take them to their father's loft and let him take them shopping. Not one to admit defeat, however, especially to Matt, Victoria took them to the mall.

After tromping from one end of the mall to the other, discarding umpteen perfectly good pairs of jeans, shorts, and tee shirts, Victoria decided ten hours of work beat even one hour of shopping. By the time the stores closed, they managed to outfit Jessica with enough clothes to get through two weeks at camp, and a new, simply fabulous pair of shorts and golf shirt made Mandy happy. Victoria hadn't realized Mandy cared that much about golf, and she offered to play a round with her on the weekend, which Mandy politely declined.

The next day Victoria received an urgent summons to Nick's office. When she got there, Viola told her to go right in, then turned back to her typing. Victoria thought she seemed miffed.

Nick looked up and grinned as she entered the office. "Come in, come in."

His smile reassured her. She'd feared another disaster. "Good news?"

"Great news." He picked up a thick sheaf of papers. "This," he said, waving the document, "is a bona fide offer to buy INTECH."

Victoria plopped down in the chair in front of his desk, feeling like she'd been hit in the face with ice water. "An offer," she repeated. He looked so pleased. She felt like crying. Nick really was selling the company.

The implications began sinking in, filling her with despair. What about her projects? The mall endeavor would probably stand, but what would happen to Methergy, her dream-child—the culmination of all she'd achieved? Would a new owner recognize the project's value and potential?

Her job. She'd worked so hard, spent so many sleepless nights solving corporate problems. She had corrected the course of the company's finances, but new owners usually meant new management. Corporate hierarchy was as shaky as a political staff position in an election year. What if she lost her job? Unemployment wouldn't cover her two thousand a month mortgage payment plus expenses. She could sell her car and take the old Jeep back from Amanda.

She thought of her reserved parking place. A silly thing to think about at a time like this, but the reserved sign held her name and title, representing her position of authority. The thought of job hunting alarmed her. Top management jobs were a scarce commodity, and her qualifications ruled out less. Maybe Cleve would hire her, but that would only complicate things.

Through her torrent of anxieties, she realized Nick was waiting for her to share his relief and happiness. She struggled to gather her thoughts. "Well, Nick, that is news. I never expected an offer to come in so fast. How? Who?"

Nick laughed. "Your reaction matches mine. I'm glad I'll be able to pay off my debts; at the same time I wanted a miracle to happen, so I wouldn't need to sell."

"Is the offer a good one?"

"Adequate. When half your life's spent building a business, in your mind it takes on a great value. No offer would be enough based on my idea of what the business is worth. Matt gave me a ball-park figure, running several different formulas, and he came up with a range of twenty to twenty six million, tops, for an asset buyout."

"So, what is the offer?"

"Twenty three million, and they want to close soon, which suits me. I'm running out of time."

"They are buying the company assets?"

"Yes."

"We still owe eighteen million on the Black Forest land. That only leaves five of the eight million the company owes you. How will you pay off your notes?"

"I'll have to sell the house. I had the Cherry Hills house and the beach house in Malibu appraised. I should net just enough over the three million on those to build a small place and have some capital left."

"Oh, Nick. You love the Cherry Hills house."

"It's just a building, Victoria. I don't need all that space. I never use half of the rooms. Maintenance costs a bundle. The house holds memories of Sarah. I built it for her, and she loved the house and the gardens, but my memories live here. . . . " He thumped his hand over his heart. "Not in a building."

"What will you do?"

"I own a few acres in Sedalia that I've always wanted to develop. I'll build a small house, a couple of outbuildings. It'll give me something to do."

"You're going to become a gentleman farmer?" Victoria asked teasingly.

He grinned at her terminology. *"Rancher,"* he corrected. "I always wanted to be a rancher. So maybe I'll build a mini-ranch and raise miniature animals."

She laughed. "Sounds like a nice plan to me. Who made the offer?"

"A corporation called Matsuko, from Japan. They make computer components, but they've diversified into mining investments in Canada and real estate in the States. They want to invest in research and your project caught their attention. Thanks to you, they are interested."

"Really? Good. I hoped that wouldn't die in the process."

"No, in fact they want you in charge, working with their people, of course, and they have money to develop the whole complex."

"That sounds too good to be true."

"We'll find out. I made an appointment with Matt to look over the offer and negotiate the sale. You'll come with me?"

"If you need me to," she agreed reluctantly. The audit had been a trial. The thought of working with Matt didn't thrill her.

"I need you to," Nick affirmed emphatically.

Where do you want these?" Cleve asked, hoisting Victoria's golf clubs out of his car.

"In my car." She opened the garage and unlocked the trunk. "Maybe I'll stop at the driving range sometime next week. Maybe I'll even take a lesson from the pro. I need to do something before I try to play with you again."

"You did all right."

"Not!" she said with a short laugh. "I was lousy, even by my standards. You may not believe me, but I usually hit ten strokes below today's score. Even at that, I'd seriously hold you back. You should be on the pro circuit."

Cleve shook his head as he stowed her clubs in her car trunk. "I've played in a few pro-am tournaments. My scores come out fairly low, but my blood pressure goes through the ceiling."

"You're a classic Type-A personality," Victoria stated. "You'd probably get high blood pressure waiting for me to reach the green." She started into the house as she talked, and Cleve followed her up the stairs to the main floor.

"You hit a nice 180-yard drive. That's acceptable in anyone's game. You just need practice for consistency. We'll play again next week."

Victoria laughed and looked back at him over her shoulder. "You are a glutton for punishment. How about some iced tea? I don't know about you, but I'm dying of thirst."

"Sounds good."

In the kitchen, she fixed two glasses, handed one to Cleve, then removed her hat, shook her head, and combed through the flattened strands of her hair with her fingers.

Cleve leaned against the counter and tilted his head back as he drank. Fascinated, Victoria watched his Adam's apple move as he swallowed. Crazy, but everything about this man captured her attention. As they'd golfed, she'd caught herself watching him, as he swung a club, as he powered the ball three hundred yards down the fairway with enough slice to wing a right-handed dog-leg at the far end. He was a born athlete, like her brothers, only he didn't treat her like a klutz who couldn't do anything physical. Of course, neither had Matt. They had bungled and learned together—the two pencil pushers, her brothers had teased. Cleve would impress them. His height, musculature, and natural grace of movement, gave him the attributes of a first-class competitor. Victoria raised her glass and took a long drink.

She was leaning against the island work counter, an arm's length across from him. Cleve put both hands around her neck and drew her close. She felt her pulse throbbing under the slight pressure of his thumbs.

"Watching you every time you hit the ball put me off my game," he said.

"Oh? You scored pretty low. You want me to believe you were having a bad day?"

"I'm sure I hit at least twenty strokes over my average. Speaking of strokes." He began caressing the back of her neck.

"Huh-uh," she replied, shaking her head and giving him a flirtatious grin, even as she started to move away. He held her still.

"Cleve. It's dinner time, and I promised to feed you."

"My appetite goes beyond mere earthly fare," he said, his voice low and gruff. He leaned down and kissed her.

He'd promised her romance, and he'd spent the whole day making her feel beautiful and capable, an unbeatable combination. She loved every minute of his attention and Cleve for giving her such bliss. Wrapping her arms around his neck, she returned his kiss and promptly forgot about anything else until he suddenly released her, drawing back far enough to look down at her. She recognized supreme satisfaction in his lazy grin.

"We have company," he said in a husky voice.

Whipping her head around, Victoria saw Jessica, Matt, and Amanda framed in the doorway. The stunned expressions on their faces stopped her cold. Jessica looked sick, Amanda's mouth formed an incredulous "O" that oddly matched her wide-eyed stare, and Matt looked like he'd been karate-chopped. As she pushed away from Cleve, he held onto her waist, so she had to shrug off his hands. She frowned up at him and realized he was enjoying the situation. He didn't even straighten up, and his grin could only be called arrogant.

"Hi," she said, her voice squeaking. "What are you doing here?"

"We live here, remember?" Amanda said.

"Of course I remember," Victoria responded. "I just mean I didn't expect you until tonight."

"Obviously," Matt said.

His scowl angered her. How dare he judge her, she thought, certain he put an unfair interpretation on the situation. It was only a kiss—not even that passionate. Her daughters picked a lousy time to walk in. This would make their animosity toward Cleve worse.

Victoria felt Cleve's arm circle her back and his hand settled on her waist. As she turned toward him, she caught a glimmer of glee in his eyes, and her gratitude for his moral support died. She poked him with her elbow. "Cleve, you remember Matt," she said. Cleve and Matt murmured some polite acknowledgments, and Victoria swallowed a strong urge to kick the entire group out of her house.

"The girls and I have been water-skiing at Chatfield Reservoir," Matt explained. "They wanted to shower and change here, rather than ride back to town in wet suits. We should have called. I never thought we might inconvenience you."

Inconvenience her? He seemed to be forever popping up and apologizing for inconveniencing her. She blamed the embarrassing situation on him for barging into her house unannounced and uninvited. Victoria noticed their attire. The girls had on wet bathing suits with beach towels draped around them. Matt had on trunks and a wet tee shirt. His dark tan almost matched his brown hair, which was mussed from the wind and water. He looked too young to have two teenage daughters. Life wasn't fair. She suddenly felt every day of her forty-one years. She glanced at Cleve, wondering if he knew she was older than he. But, of course he knew. He'd investigated her. "It isn't inconvenient," she said. "We just finished a round of golf and were getting something to drink. Would you like some iced tea?"

"Yes, I'd like a glass, thank you." As Matt stepped into the room, Cleve moved his hand up to rub the back of Victoria's neck. Matt's frown intensified. "Girls, go get changed."

"Mom," Jessica said before they went to their rooms, "we want you to go to dinner with us."

"Sorry, Honey, Cleve and I have plans."

"Hurry up, girls. I'm starving," Matt said as the girls protested.

After she got Matt's iced tea, Victoria excused herself and hurried to the bathroom to regain her composure. Her image in the mirror made her groan. She looked like she'd been doing more than kissing, with her reddened mouth and her hair and clothes a mess from playing golf in the heat, but she knew defending herself would only make the impression worse. Running a comb through her hair and holding a cold, wet washcloth to her face helped.

When she returned to the kitchen, Cleve and Matt were discussing the merits of different golf courses. While they sounded cordial, their folded arms and rigid stances made the animosity between them clear. When the girls reappeared, Matt turned to Victoria.

"I'll have the girls home early. I have to be in court first thing in the morning. I'll see you in the afternoon."

Victoria blinked at him, then remembered the appointment with Nick about the offer. "Right. Have a nice dinner." *My, aren't we polite,* she thought, wishing they'd hurry up and leave. Her frustration made her antsy.

"We'll be home by ten o'clock, Mother," Amanda said, glancing at Cleve.

"Good. I want to hear all about your weekend." Victoria didn't miss the warning in her daughter's message or the disapproving looks both girls gave her as they left. As soon as the door closed behind them, she turned to Cleve.

"What was all that about?" she demanded, her hands fisted on her hips.

With a complaisant smile, he raised his eyebrows. "What was all what about?"

"You know what I'm talking about, Mr. Winslow. I'm talking about that proud dance you did for my family. My daughters saw us in an embrace that probably looked . . . compromising. Rather than being a gentleman, you had to flaunt it."

He grinned. "Compromising? Now there's an old-fashioned notion. You think pretending we weren't kissing would make them forget what they saw?"

"No, of course not. But you didn't have to rub their noses in it."

"Your daughters better get used to seeing us together. And your ex-husband needs to understand he is no longer in the picture."

"If you're trying to make some sort of statement to Matt, don't bother," she said, her anger at both men stretched out of proportion by her own jumbled emotions. "He might be upset about the girls seeing me like that, but he certainly can't judge my actions." Victoria couldn't keep the frustrated tears out of her eyes or the bitterness out of her voice.

"His reaction had nothing to do with your daughters. The man's jealous."

"That's ridiculous. Matt left me for an assistant in his office . . . a young, blond assistant."

"He's obviously changed his mind. Your ex-husband wants you, and I have no intention of letting him have his way."

"You have . . . " Victoria sputtered and shook her head as if to clear her confused thoughts. She felt like she'd just been dunked in a water trap. "This has gotten out of hand. Look Cleve, I apologize if I've given you the wrong impression, but this has got to stop. I've been acting like I have no responsibilities and no one to answer to, but that's not true. My daughters are too impressionable. I can't tell them not to give in to temptation, then turn around and indulge myself. I've tried acting sophisticated, but I can't even fake it." She tried to be matter of fact about this. What a ninny she must sound like, explaining to a man like Cleve why she couldn't be caught kissing him. She looked down and realized she was wringing her hands together. She made herself stop.

"I'm sorry," she said. "I think you'd better leave before I make this any worse."

He stared at her in disbelief, then his eyes narrowed. "Every time I come over here, you try to throw me out. I'm not buying the distressed act, Victoria, and I'm not going anywhere until we get this straightened out. Are you still in love with Matt Halstead?"

"No," she answered quickly, surprised by his question. "We're friendly, because of the girls. I guess we'll always have that tie, at least till the girls are grown."

"What are you doing tomorrow afternoon?"

"Tomorrow?"

"With him," he said, nodding his head toward the door.

"That's business. Nick, my boss, is selling the company, and Matt is handling the sale."

The mention of a sale caught his attention. "He's got a contract?"

"Yes. Matsuko Corporation of Japan. Have you heard of them?"

"Electronics, aren't they? Computer parts or something? Why would they want a real estate development company?"

"They're diversifying. We have a meeting with them tomorrow afternoon."

"Isn't that a conflict of some kind—your ex-husband representing your boss?"

"No, of course not. Matt's the best in his field."

"You didn't recommend him, I suppose?"

"As a matter of fact, I did. I'm not so petty that I can't separate my personal life and my job."

Matt Halstead always seemed to be in the center of Victoria's life, and Cleve didn't like it. Halstead wanted more than his daughters' welfare. Victoria's reaction concerned him too. She might not be involved with her ex-husband, but she was a little too emphatic denying any feelings for him and a little too quick jumping to his defense. Cleve figured he'd better back off if he wanted to keep an upper hand. "I guess I overdid the caveman bit, huh?" he asked, flashing her a boyish grin.

"A bit," she agreed.

He reached out and captured her hand and entwined his fingers with hers. "I'm the one who needs to apologize." He shrugged his shoulders. "I'm a jerk. I don't handle competition well, I'm afraid. I don't like to lose."

Her eyes grew wide. The idea apparently had not occurred to her. "You think you're competing with Matt?"

"With Matt. With your daughters. Victoria—" He placed both of her hands on his chest and covered them with his hands. "—I know your loyalty is to your daughters and you have a responsibility to be a role model. I'm not asking you to betray that. That's part of the trust and loyalty I find so important. I'm not looking for sophistication. I want to be part of a real relationship. I'm asking you to make room for me."

"Why?" she asked.

He shrugged, a gesture he hoped looked nonchalant. "I told you before, I'm tired of being alone." She just kept watching him expectantly. This discussion had gotten far too serious, but his future depended upon planting her firmly on his side. Weighing her reactions, he figured he could count on her strong maternal instincts. Backed into a corner, she'd fight like a wild cat for her children. Perhaps for Matt Halstead too.

"Honey, this is new to me, and I'm having trouble understanding my emotions myself. You've become important to me, but I don't know much about relationships. That's one of the things I admire about you—your relationship with your daughters. My mother was so busy keeping the peace, she was too tired to care about anything." Just voicing it took him back to a cold, seedy hotel room, his father on one side with a swollen eye, caked blood under his nose, smelling like sweat and his mother cowering on the other side, whimpering with fear. The memory brought a fresh wave of bitterness. His father had lost another fight and wanted to hit somebody who couldn't hit back. Bulldog Winslow, his father had called himself, middleweight boxer—never a contender. "My father was so involved in fighting his own war, we were just one more punching bag." Cleve had been twelve when he managed to return a punch that knocked his father out cold and gave them the chance to escape. They'd never gone back. His mother had not thanked him.

Cleve looked into the soft brown eyes that were gazing back at him intently, and knew he'd revealed more than he'd intended. He knew it when she pulled her hands free and cupped his face. He saw the knowledge in her eyes before she closed them and raised up on her tiptoes. He felt the promise in her kiss. Her tenderness, empathy, and understanding made him uncomfortable, even as he reveled in the strange sensation. He wrapped his arms around her and hugged her. Resting his face in the crook of her neck, he held her tight. He'd won this round. He had her sympathy. He had a feeling he'd won more and lost more than he'd bargained for.

✿

"I don't like him," Jessica told her dad and sister in the car.

"That's obvious," Mandy said.

"Your mother has a right to see whomever she wishes, and you girls need to be polite and make an attempt to get along with her friends. She works hard to give you girls a nice home and provide all the things you need," Matt admonished his daughters. His anger contradicted his words. *Lord, can't she see this guy is no good? That he'll only hurt her?* Matt despised violence, so why did he feel like hitting something?

"But Dad," Jessica objected, "You give Mom money for us, and we earn our own money."

"Compared to the time and energy and love she gives you, my contributions amount to nothing. Neither do yours. Your mother deserves a life, without your hostility or interference. If you can't like him, at least keep your opinions to yourselves." *And that goes for me too. Okay, Lord. Help me keep my mouth shut.*

"I haven't been hostile," Mandy objected. "He's not a bad guy. Jessica's upset because she wants you and Mom to get back together. I want that, too, but I'm not childish about getting my way, like *some* people."

"You think you're so smart. You don't know nothing."

"Anything," Matt corrected.

"Yeah, well he's lying to her," Jessica declared.

Matt gave Jessica a sharp glance. "What makes you say that?"

"I heard him. At Elitch's, I got in line for a drink, and he was talking to another man; he called him Kane. I've seen him at Mom's work. They didn't see me. The guy said he'd introduce Mr. Winslow to Mom, and Mr. Winslow said he didn't need him to, cause he'd already met her. The other guy seemed ticked off that he didn't get to do it, and Mr. Winslow sort of told him to get lost."

"Your mother is a beautiful woman. I can understand how he would want someone to introduce him."

"Yeah, but he pretended he met mom by accident, when he planned to meet her all along. Otherwise, why would he be at Elitch's? Guys like him don't hang out at amusement parks," Jessica reasoned.

"Mom works with a guy named Lionel Kane," Mandy said. "She can't stand him. She told Tina he was a conceited creep. Tina laughed and called him cute. I guess he's always pestering Mom. She'd never go out with him."

"Oh yeah. I bet he's the reason Mom went with us to Breckenridge. Tina said we could thank her, cause she tried to get Mom to go to her barbecue with a guy from work, and Mom told him she couldn't 'cause she was going with us."

"I wondered why she changed her mind so suddenly," Matt said. "I'll talk to your mother about Mr. Winslow. Meanwhile, behave and straighten up your attitude. All you're doing is making her unhappy."

"Yeah, Jessica," Mandy agreed.

"You, too, young lady. Keep her informed about what you're doing and where you're going. She worries about you."

"But Dad. She treats me like a child. I'm an adult, now. She doesn't have to worry."

"You're an adult when you start acting like one, and that means being considerate of your mother's feelings. Telling her what you're doing won't hurt you. Understand?"

"Yeah," Mandy said.

"Jessica?"

"Yeah, Dad. I hear you."

"Well?"

"I'll try. But I don't like it."

Victoria was cleaning the kitchen when Mandy and Jessica came home. Their exuberance seemed exaggerated, Victoria thought. Both girls vied to tell about their weekend—the water-skiing, their father's neat speedboat, choosing furniture for their bedrooms at Matt's condominium. Mandy had picked out a rustic Aspen wood poster-bed and dresser set with southwestern accessories. Jessica had gotten ultramodern, black lacquered furniture and neon-bright yellow, red, and green comforter, pillows, and a matching chair.

Matt took them to church. They loved having a parent there, like they were a real family. That gave Victoria guilt pangs, but going with them would be hypocritical. There were enough hypocrites at church without her adding to their numbers.

They bragged about their dinner, letting her know she'd missed something special. Matt had grilled salmon and potato wedges, and the girls had made a fancy fruit salad, using half a pineapple for the bowl. They ate dinner on the roof garden, Mandy explained, with a white cloth on the table, real napkins, good dishes and fancy glasses.

And Matt took them to a rock concert at Fiddler's Green to hear Eric Clapton, Jessica added. He was *sooo* cool—not Eric—Dad. All the women stared at him. Eric Clapton was cool, too, of course; that went without saying.

Mandy and Jessica ran out of steam, and an uncomfortable silence gripped the kitchen.

"Sounds like you had a wonderful weekend," Victoria said.

"The best," Jessica said. She gave her mother a challenging look as if she felt she had to defend her father.

Victoria caught the meaningful look that passed between Jessica and Amanda. Where Jessica's eyes held accusation, Amanda's held sympathy and understanding, which startled Victoria. She knew her youngest daughter was daddy's girl—always had been, so Jessica's hostility toward Cleve made sense. Mandy adored her father, but Victoria sensed maturity and acceptance in Mandy's gaze.

"Dad's super," Mandy piped in. "I think he's trying to make up for the years he missed. It really isn't necessary, of course, but I think he feels bad."

Instead of defusing Jessica's animosity, Mandy's comments fueled her sister's temper. "You said you were going out for dinner, Mom," Jessica said. "That's why you couldn't go with us."

"I said we had plans. They were to eat here. I had already prepared the meat."

"You stayed here so he could hit on you some more," Jessica accused.

"Jessica!" Victoria and Amanda exclaimed at the same time. Victoria paled at her daughter's verbal attack. Mandy grabbed her sister's arm and dragged her toward the stairs. "Get downstairs before you really blow it," Mandy ordered in a low growl loud enough for Victoria to overhear.

"I don't care," Jessica said, her voice quivering with anger and frustration. "I hate him! He's going to ruin everything." Jessica ran down to her room and slammed the door.

Victoria flinched at the sharp bang of the door. Mandy walked over and gave her a hug.

"Don't let her temper bother you, Mom. She's being dramatic again."

"I know." Victoria hugged Mandy tight. "Thanks, Honey." When she drew back, she saw tears in her daughter's eyes. She smoothed one away with her knuckle, then wiped her own eyes and smiled.

Mandy smiled back, then kissed her. "Goodnight, Mom. I'm really tired." She picked up her purse and the gym bag that held all the paraphernalia she'd taken to her dad's for the weekend and followed her sister down the stairs.

VICTORIA FIDGETED WITH her hands as she and Nick sat in the waiting room of the law firm. The offices were located in a renovated Capital Hill mansion. The second floor reception area had probably been a sitting room. The offices had no doubt been bedrooms. Classical music played softly in the background. Everything, from the reverent hush to the gold leaf in the wallpaper announced wealth and elegance. Victoria caught herself gnawing on a fingernail. She dropped her hand into her lap and forced herself to be still before she ruined the nail coat she'd so carefully applied the night before.

Matt had certainly moved uptown, she thought. What he'd told her about his partners didn't jibe with the setting of their firm. Facing her ex-husband on his turf, amid such elegant surroundings, after the scene he'd witnessed in her kitchen, had her heart pounding with mortification. She smoothed her skirt with one hand. The soft silk of her shirtwaist dress normally soothed her, and its rich teal color usually gave her confidence. Since Matt had seen her at her worst and most embarrassing self several times, she wanted him to see her today as the successful executive she'd become.

"You look wonderful, Victoria," Nick whispered to her. "Your ex-husband might be a great lawyer, but he's a fool."

"Thank you." She took a deep breath. Just then the secretary called them.

When they entered the office, Matt rose and shook hands with Nick, then turned to Victoria, clasping her hand and smiling. She smiled politely, outwardly composed, inwardly stilling her accelerated heartbeat. Her hand was damp. How could he be so relaxed? He greeted her with more enthusiasm than she'd anticipated. He really had a nice smile. She discreetly withdrew her hand from his and moved toward a chair by his desk.

"Let's sit here," he said, stepping to a grouping of Windsor chairs across the room and holding the back of one for her. When she was seated, he went to his desk to get a clipboard with a yellow legal pad, giving her a chance to study him. He perfectly suited the elegant atmosphere. His light gray double-breasted suit set off his hazel eyes and the silver highlights in his thick brown hair. He looked handsome and distinguished with an aura of confidence that would inspire trust. Matt was known for his integrity. *True at least in business,* she silently allowed. As far as she knew, she thought with a twinge of bitterness, his only breach of trust in his entire life had been his betrayal of their marriage vows.

Nick handed Matt the large, thick envelope that contained Matsuko's offer. Matt took the papers out and glanced through them, then set the offer down.

"This is a preliminary meeting," he said, addressing Nick. "Before we get into details, let's recap your goals and see if this is even feasible."

For half an hour, they talked generalities of Nick's situation, the company picture, and the basic offer. Nick said he could accept the terms of the offer. Matt listened intently, asked pertinent questions, and took notes, but Victoria noticed his glance kept straying to her.

"I'd like to study the offer," Matt said. "Then we can discuss it before you decide whether to counter or accept, and what to revise."

"Fair enough," Nick said. "Victoria will be handling much of this for me. If she feels you two can work together, I'll basically turn the deal over to the two of you."

"I'm certain you're aware of our situation, Mr. Shrock," Matt said, smiling at Victoria to include her. "I have the utmost respect for Mrs. Halstead. If she has no objection to working with me, I'm sure we can negotiate a contract for you that will meet your needs and give you the best possible deal."

Victoria nodded. What else could she do?

Nick stood and offered his hand. Matt rose and accepted the handshake. "Good," Nick said. "Now, drop the Mister and call me Nick. The

Matsuko representative wants a meeting as soon as possible. Can you hurry things along?"

"I'll study this tonight and have a basic analysis ready tomorrow afternoon. If you'd like, I'll contact Matsuko and set up a meeting."

"Fine. Just let us know when," Nick said. He walked to the door. Victoria followed him.

"Victoria, could I talk to you for a minute?" Matt asked before she stepped through the door.

She threw Nick an inquiring look, and he said, "I'll wait for you out here. No hurry."

Matt shut the door and turned to Victoria. She folded her arms across her chest. "When you look like that," he said, smiling, "I feel like I just tracked mud all over your clean carpet."

She nearly smiled back, but refrained. "What do you want, Matt?"

He walked over to his desk, looked down, as if reading something, and drummed his fingers on the desktop. After a few seconds, he looked up, directly into her eyes. "I promised the girls I'd talk to you. Besides, I think you need to know about Cleve Winslow. He set up you're accidental meeting."

She felt her face turn red. Heavens, did everyone know about her humiliation? "I don't think so," she said. "Wait a minute . . . set up? What do you know about how I met Cleve?"

"Jessica told me . . . "

"Jessica exaggerates."

"She overheard two men, Cleve Winslow and a man named Kane talking about you at a food stand," Matt continued.

"What? She never told me that."

"She didn't know how you'd react. She said the man named Kane was supposed to introduce Winslow to you, but he said he'd already met you. Then Kane said he'd fulfilled a favor he owed, and Winslow told him to get lost."

Mind buzzing with thoughts, Victoria tried to make logic of Matt's revelation. "I'm sure there's an explanation. He told me he'd planned to meet me."

"It's not like no one knows who you are. He could easily have gotten a legitimate introduction. Victoria, I know I have no right to interfere in your life, but I don't trust Cleve Winslow," he said somewhat hesitantly. "I care about you, and I don't want you to get hurt."

"You're a fine one to talk to me about trust." She lifted her chin a fraction of an inch.

His hand smacked the desktop. For a few seconds, he hung his head, then he looked up at her. "Victoria. I love you. I can't stand by and let that man take advantage of you. Especially when it's my fault you're vulnerable to start with."

"Don't flatter yourself, Matt," she said, controlling her temper with some difficulty. *How dare he be so pompous.* "As far as taking advantage of me, you are the only man who's ever done that. Seventeen years worth. I am not a child, and I am no longer vulnerable. You cured me of that weakness. Cleve is a very nice person, and we have a great deal in common. He respects me, and strange as it may seem to you, he finds me attractive."

"Finds you attractive? You're probably the most beautiful woman he's ever met." At her stunned reaction, Matt groaned. He moved toward her, but she stepped away.

"Oh Tori. What have I done? Did you think you weren't attractive? Did you think I left because of you?" He shook his head. "It wasn't *your* shortcomings that drove me away. Don't you see? *My* failures are what caused me to leave."

Eyes wide, Victoria tried to take in Matt's words. Lately, she seemed to go from confusion to confusion. "This isn't the time to talk about this, Matt. Nick is waiting for me."

"I know. I'm sorry, I just had to warn you." He reached out and took her hand. "Victoria, please think about what I said. He's made a career out of manipulating people. Don't fall for his line. You're too good for him."

"I think you're mistaken, Matt," she said tightly. "But thank you for your concern. I've got to go now." She removed her hand from his and went to the door. Matt opened it and followed her into the reception room where Nick waited.

As they rode back to the office in the limousine, she could sense Nick studing her. She smiled stiffly and apologized for keeping him waiting.

"That's all right, I didn't mind. Victoria, is this going to work? If you're not comfortable working with your ex-husband, I'll get another lawyer."

She wanted to shout *No, it won't work,* but she couldn't do that. Nick needed the best, and, after all, he'd gone to Matt at her suggestion. "It's all right, Nick," she said with a wry grin. "Matt has an overblown sense of responsibility sometimes, but that will work in your favor. There won't be any problems."

"Good." Nick settled back against the seat. "He's honest and forthright, and any fool can see he's crazy about you. You know, a man can get real mixed up when he gets to be a certain age—about Matt's age. He wakes up one morning and half his life is over, and he doesn't seem to have anything to show for it. He's had dreams, and he hasn't lived up to his own expectations. He sees the years flying by and he gets real scared. Something inside just snaps, and he's liable to do something real foolish."

"Did that ever happen to you?"

"Matter of fact, I bought a big Harley motorcycle and hit the road. Alone."

"But you came back."

Nick laughed mirthlessly. "Sarah gave me two weeks, then she came after me. She'd bought leather chaps and a leather jacket with fringe. Told me she was my old lady and she refused to be left behind." Nick chuckled. "Can you picture my sweet Sarah trying to be a tough motorcycle mamma?"

"No. So, did you quit and go home?"

"Mercy no. Sarah climbed on the back, and we spent six months touring the country. Had a ball. Thank goodness, Ed held down the fort while we were off playing, or there might not have been a business to come back to."

"Well, at least you weren't leaving because of Sarah," Victoria said bitterly.

"For a smart woman, you certainly are dense. You missed the whole point. Chances are, Matt didn't leave because of you. He was running from himself. He must have been going through some terrible delusions when he left. Obviously, he finally figured that out and regrets his mistake. He's one of the good guys, Victoria. I like him."

She smiled at her boss. Much as she'd like to take her ex-husband out and hang him, she couldn't fault Nick's assessment. "That's the real kicker," she said. "I do too."

"Fact is, I think you care for him more than you're willing to admit, even to yourself. It's a shame to see two fine people letting their pride keep them apart. Loneliness is a terrible thing, Victoria, believe me. Give the man another chance."

"Nick?"

"Yeah?"

"Do you know Cleve Winslow?"

"So it's true," he said, his thick brows furrowed.

"What do you mean?"

"I heard you were seeing him. Met him at the amusement park, did you?"

"Does the whole world know how we met? Yes. We've seen each other a few times. I value your opinion, Nick. What you think about him?"

Nick was thoughtful for a minute. "Best way I know to judge a man is by what he does, not what he says. Take a look at his life—how he does business, how he treats his family. Listen to his actions. Cleve Winslow has a reputation for ruthlessness."

"Would you trust him?"

"I don't know him, except what I've read. Let me tell you a story." Nick settled back against the leather seat and crossed his arms. "You heard about the scorpion that begged the horse to carry him across a river?"

"No," Victoria said. "What happened?"

"Well, the horse refused, said he wasn't a fool, he didn't want to get bit. The scorpion said, 'Why would I bite you? You'd die, and then I'd drown.' The horse thought about what the scorpion said and figured it made sense, so he agreed to give the scorpion a ride. Halfway across, the scorpion bit the horse. As he was going under, the horse asked, 'Why did you do that? Now we'll both die.' The scorpion shrugged and replied, 'It's my nature.' You can't fault someone for being what they are," Nick said. "But you don't have to get bit."

"That's pretty cynical," Victoria said.

"Perhaps, but it's realistic. You're an optimist. You look for the good in every situation, and I'm not saying there isn't good to be found. Just keep your eyes open."

"Sounds easy enough, but the truth is, I'm losing control. Jessica is angry all the time, and Mandy's off in her own world. The rest of us don't exist as far as she's concerned. Matt warns me about Cleve. Cleve warns me about Matt. The Black Forest Project is limping along, and I don't know which end is up."

"When things start piling up and I can't see my way clear, it helps me to get off by myself and do some praying. Amazing how answers suddenly appear."

"You're starting to sound like Matt."

Nick grinned. "He's a smart man. I believe in you, Victoria. You're a sensible woman, and you've got spunk. These problems are a cakewalk after what you've already overcome. When the choices come, you'll make the right decisions."

"I hope so. I'm beginning to wonder."

"I remember when you applied for a job," he said. "You were scared, strung-out, emotionally battered, but you had gumption. You sneaked past Viola and demanded to talk to me. I asked you why I should hire you, remember?"

She recalled every word they'd exchanged. Nick had sat behind his desk frowning like a judge. To top it off, the windows in his office had made her want to turn around and run, but she'd stood her ground. She'd urgently needed a job. That first position didn't pay much, but the hours fit her class schedule. Besides, she'd been rejected at seven interviews. Nobody had wanted to hire a thirty-six year old housewife who hadn't worked in fourteen years. "I said I would have your files and archives organized in one month or you didn't have to pay me."

"Yes, and when I asked for references, you told me you'd served on every charity board in the city, including my favorite charity for cancer research. That clinched my decision, you know."

"I know. I remember Sarah, always sweet, always smiling. I adored your wife. Even while she went through chemotherapy, she volunteered regularly. I suppose I was crass to use that connection, but desperate straits call for desperate measures," she said. "Still, you gave me the chance and believed in me. I didn't dare fail."

"You're a survivor, Victoria. I saw your determination then, and I see it now. And you give. I've been repaid a thousand-fold for hiring you that day." Nick hesitated for a moment. "This is none of my business; you've never said anything about God to me, though I know you see to it that your daughters go to church. My Sarah had strong faith in Jesus Christ. She didn't talk about religion a lot, but her prayers got us through some tough times. Took a good, long time, but eventually, they even got through my hard head. It's something you might consider."

She could see Nick's eyes glazing over and felt tears gathering in her own eyes. Nick had never mentioned religion to her before. Sarah had been the kind of gentle, sincere Christian who truly reflected unconditional love; so Nick's faith shouldn't surprise her, but it did. As a strong, self-sufficient man, Nick did not like relying on others. Convincing him to trust in Jesus must have taken some strong and convincing arguments. Reaching over, she patted his hand. "I'll consider it. Thanks, Nick." She turned to look out the window as if the corner of Broadway and Colfax were the most fascinating street corner in the world.

Matt's accusation about Cleve setting her up nibbled and pecked at the edges of her mind. She couldn't believe he had deceived her. He made a big issue about trust. Besides, what was his motive?

She pushed the questions aside, concentrating on the sale to Matsuko and the tasks to be completed for the Methergy Project. But the thoughts kept intruding, causing the beginnings of doubt to enter her mind. The story came from Jessica, and she wanted Cleve out of their lives. Would she lie? Would she make up a story that could easily be refuted? Cleve was out of town for a few days, but she'd ask for an explanation as soon as he got back.

She missed him. He was becoming important to her life, a situation she could not allow. She couldn't stand to go through the hurt she'd experienced after Matt left—was still experiencing, if the truth be known. In all honesty, just seeing Matt made her grieve and yearn for the happiness they'd once had. Crying over past history was pointless. There was no going back.

⁂

Nick received the formal contract in a meeting at Matt's office. After the Matsuko representative gave a verbal overview of the contract and received some preliminary reports from Victoria, he left. Victoria and Nick stayed while Matt silently scanned the contract for a few minutes, then he leaned back, folding his hands behind his neck.

"It's a thorough document, full of a lot of legal jargon. It'll take awhile to wade through it. I don't want to overlook anything that might not be to your advantage, especially since we're dealing with a foreign company. I'll try to get a higher price, but they are obviously aware of our need for haste, so I doubt they'll budge. We have to be certain INTECH can satisfy its liabilities. Part of that liability is the debt to you."

"I'm working on that. I don't want Nick to take a loss if I can help it," Victoria said.

"What about the savings and loan debt?" Matt asked.

"I've tried to negotiate with the new finance company, but I don't get any response," Victoria said. "Now that we have a buyer and can pay off in cash, maybe I'll get some action."

"It would be reasonable to expect them to knock off as much as, say, two million, maybe three if we're lucky," Matt speculated. "I've never dealt with them, but I'll be happy to try. Do you want me to contact them for you?"

"That's a good idea," Nick said. "Victoria's going to be busy next week." Then Nick stood up, abruptly ending the session. "You two do whatever it takes," he admonished. "I'd like to wrap this up as soon as possible."

"Let me get you a copy of the contract to go over." Matt walked them to the stairs, stopping at the secretary's desk to get copies made. "I'll do what I can to hurry things along, Nick, but don't expect to retire in two weeks. Two months might be more realistic. Even that's optimistic."

"Victoria said you're the best, and I trust her judgment." Nick shook Matt's hand. "That's why I'm going fishing next week. Between you and Victoria, I have complete confidence. When I get back, I'll sign the offer, and we can set a date for the closing."

On the way back to the office, Victoria asked, "When did this trip come up? When you mentioned fishing before, it was a maybe, and way in the future. You don't even like fishing."

"Well now, I don't know that for a fact." His eyes twinkled as he chuckled. "I can't say as I ever gave it a fair shot. These buddies of mine are going fly fishing in Canada, and they guarantee I'm going to like it. I figured I owe it to them to at least go along and find out."

"When do you leave?"

"Tomorrow."

"Tomorrow! But that doesn't give us time to go over anything before you leave."

"Don't worry. You handle everything so well, you won't even know I'm gone."

Victoria wanted to finish up all the red tape on the Methergy Project before Nick got back, but the EPA, the government, and every supplier in the country seemed to have taken the summer off. She developed a genuine hate for electronic receptionists that gave a long list of instructions as to what number to press to reach what department, then patched her through to a message center after she pushed the appropriate number. When she did contact a real person, he responded as if his mind had gone on vacation.

To compound her frustrations, all of the vandalized engines at the Methergy project had to be rebuilt. Even as a priority job, it would be weeks before they'd be operational. They had found some equipment to rent, but not enough to meet their deadline.

Summer had taken time off too. Violent thunderstorms, hail and power outages halted work at the Black Forest job site for two days. Friday afternoon, an hour before quitting time, the skies cleared and the sun shone through.

On the way home from work Victoria bought a paperback bestseller with the intention of escaping into a romance for the entire weekend. The girls were having dinner with their father, so she would have the house to herself, and she could curl up on the deck and read until dark. When she pulled into her driveway, Matt's car was parked beside the garage.

The domestic scene in the kitchen stopped her short. Jessica shredded lettuce into a large wooden bowl as Mandy put a casserole dish in the oven, and Matt sat at the counter talking to the girls as they worked. Victoria noticed that the table was set for four.

"What's going on here?" she demanded.

Mandy looked up and smiled. "Hi, Mom. Jessica and I are fixing Dad's birthday dinner. He offered to take us out, but he's tired of restaurant food, aren't you, Dad?"

Victoria was stunned. Matt's birthday. How could she have forgotten? Last year and the two years before that she'd cooked his favorite food and eaten it alone while the girls had been in Boston to celebrate with him. "I'm sorry," she said. "I forgot."

Matt had gotten up. "I didn't expect you to remember," he said. "Evidently the girls didn't clear this with you. I'm sorry. If this interrupts your plans, we can go out."

"No, Dad," Jessica cried. "We fixed this just for you. It's all right, isn't it Mom?"

Both daughters looked at her beseechingly. What could she say? "It's fine, really. I had a hectic week; I guess that's why I forgot."

She wanted to excuse herself and hide in her room until Matt left, but that would be silly; besides the girls would be crushed. From the looks of the table, set with her best china, crystal goblets, and a bouquet of snapdragons and wildflowers, the girls had gone to a lot of trouble. "I'll just go change," she said, and she hurried out of the room.

Victoria put on a soft pastel sundress instead of the shorts and tee-shirt she'd intended to wear. She brushed her hair and touched up her makeup quickly. She didn't want them thinking she'd gone to any trouble to look nice for Matt's birthday. On the other hand, birthdays were special, and she could at least look decent for the occasion.

CHAPTER FOURTEEN

THE GIRLS INSISTED their parents take their iced tea out on the deck until dinner was ready. Victoria sat on a wicker chair; Matt stood looking down at the golf course. An awkward silence stretched between them until Matt turned around to face her.

"I'm sorry . . . " they said in unison, then smiled uneasily at each other.

Matt sat in the chair next to Victoria. "Well, if we're both sorry, then everything should be all right. Let's enjoy the evening. It's beautiful out here."

"I love it. I spend a lot of time out here when I'm home."

"Which isn't much, if your job success is any indication."

"Not as much as I'd like, especially in the summer. According to the weather reports, we should have a nice weekend. I could have done with some of this sunshine this week."

"Rain mess up your plans?" Matt asked.

"The Black Forest Project is behind schedule. We found some equipment, but the storms cost us three days. We're racing the clock. We're trying to excavate and get the roads done so construction on the buildings can begin. We want to at least have the exterior of the complex finished before winter."

"Forecasters are predicting more wet weather."

"So I've heard," Victoria said. "We might be able to handle the rain, but I don't dare have crews operating in thunderstorms, so I'm paying them to sit out there under shelters. At least that way they can work in between rain showers. On top of that, we had no power yesterday and today, so we're setting up emergency generators."

Listening to her discuss her work, Matt thought what an amazing, dynamic executive she'd become. He deeply regretted he hadn't been around to help her achieve her success. His only contribution had been inadvertently causing her to refocus her life after he'd walked away.

After she quit speaking, he stared at her until she turned away from his scrutiny. When she reached up and started rubbing her neck, the motion broke into his bemused thoughts. "You've got a stiff neck," Matt said. "Here, let me." She mumbled a refusal, but his fingers had already begun kneading her tense muscles.

"Ummm. That feels wonderful."

"What have you been doing to get like this?" He pressed the tightly corded muscles in her neck, massaging gently, but firmly up, then down into her shoulders.

"Too many hours at the computer. I usually don't spend entire days on it, but this week I had no choice." She yelped and jerked as he hit an ultra-sensitive nerve.

"Sorry. I'm a little rusty." He lightened his touch, but kept massaging. "You should know better than to let yourself get this tight," he chided. "I don't imagine you've been miraculously healed in the past five years, have you? Last I heard, nerves don't regenerate."

She tensed beneath his fingers, and he splayed his hands to broaden the area of massage.

"I keep it under control most of the time," she said. "Occasionally I get kinked up. It's an occupational hazard."

"It shouldn't be. If you take a break every half hour, loosen up your muscles, you shouldn't ever get spasms."

"If you're going to preach at me, you can quit," she said. Her voice sounded pinched, like her muscles. "You forfeited the right to lecture me when you walked out of my life."

His hands paused, then continued. "You're right, and I'm sorry. I'm just concerned about you. I couldn't stand to see you paralyzed with pain like you used to get."

Her shoulders rose and fell as she took a deep breath. "Believe me, I don't want to repeat that experience, either. I'm careful, and it's paid off; I haven't had an attack like that in years."

She started to get up, but he held her back with a firm hold on her shoulders.

"Victoria." He moved around in front of her and hunkered down to face her, taking both her hands in his. She looked startled, then her eyes narrowed in suspicion, and she started to pull away.

"Please," he said, "listen to me for a minute. I've been waiting for the right time, hoping we could become friends again first, and I think we've done that. Victoria, I did some terrible things, and you paid the price for my mistakes. Even before I left, I was never the husband I should have been. I am very, very sorry. Losing you is the worst thing that ever happened to me. Can you forgive me for the past? For betraying you? For leaving you? For hurting you?"

"If it will make you feel any better, then yes, I forgive you."

He let out the breath he held and buried his face in their hands. *Thank you, Lord.* His eyes burned. He didn't care. He looked up into her eyes. Any emotion she felt, she hid deep inside. "Thank you. I know I don't deserve your forgiveness, but, with the Lord's help, I'm trying to be the man God wants me to be. Victoria, will you give me a chance? We've both changed. Will you go out with me and let us get to know each other all over again? There's a new play I think you'd enjoy. We could go out to dinner first."

She looked down at their hands. Hers were shaking—barely, but enough so he noticed. "I'm sorry, Matt. I don't think that's a good idea." She stood up, pulling her hands out of his grasp. "Dinner should be ready," she said. "I think I'll go see what's causing the holdup."

Watching as she walked, stiff-backed, into the kitchen, he fought back a wave of hopelessness. He should have known when he saw her dismay at the cozy family scene that she wasn't going to forget the past. And he didn't expect her to. He hoped they could get over that hurdle and go on to rebuild a relationship. She'd been flustered by his apology, but he had no idea whether it helped or hurt his cause. It didn't matter. Gaining her forgiveness was all important, second only to the Lord's forgiveness. But the Lord also had set his sins aside and remembered them no more. If only he could find the key to unlock her feelings. If only Victoria would blow up at him and get it out, so the hurt could heal. He thanked God that she didn't hate him, but her ambivalence frustrated him. "Lord, I'm stumped. What do I do now?"

The answer came swiftly as a scripture Matt had read this morning leaped into his mind. *Trust in the LORD with all your heart and lean not on your own understanding; in all your ways acknowledge him, and he will make your paths straight.*

"Thank you, Lord. Please, trip me if I step off the path."

Matt's cheerfulness and nonchalance during dinner made her wonder if their serious conversation had really taken place. Maybe she had imagined the importance he'd placed on her forgiveness. He directed his attention to the girls, effusively praising them for the best lasagna and the most delicious Caesar salad he'd ever eaten. He exclaimed over the design created in whipped cream on the top of the rich chocolate Texas sheet cake they'd made for his birthday, then proved his compliments by eating two pieces.

Victoria had felt wary when she sat down to eat, but relaxed as Matt all but ignored her presence. She would have begun to doubt his declaration and might have thought their conversation had been a figment of her imagination, but several times she caught him staring at her before he quickly looked away. She saw an emotion in his gaze that she couldn't identify. In fact, he'd never displayed much emotion of any kind before. So much about him was intimately familiar, yet a subtle difference about him baffled her.

She decided the best way to handle Matt's request was to pretend it had never been made. Her intentions were easier to make than to keep, however. All evening she thought about his earlier expression. Even after she went to bed, the vision of his intense gaze preyed on her mind as she kept trying to put a name to the emotion she'd seen in his eyes.

She knew she had made a serious mistake accompanying Matt and the girls to Breckenridge. He was reacting to seeing the four of them together as a unit. She understood because she'd felt moments of raw yearning as she remembered the four of them cuddling on a blanket under the stars while brilliant displays of fireworks exploded overhead.

Yearning—that was it. He was envisioning what might have been, but it was too late. She'd spent five years purging Matt from her heart, and she refused to open herself up to that kind of vulnerability again. She had worked hard to rise above the deep sensitivities and insecurities that could undermine her determination and success. Only she knew how precariously she balanced. Matt was one of the few people who could knock her off her perch with a word or a look. He was more dangerous than ever with his new sensitivity and humility. He seemed sincere, but she couldn't take that chance. If he betrayed her again, she doubted she'd have the strength to survive. If she avoided him, perhaps he'd give up. Matt was an intelligent, sensible man. All he needed was time to put their present circumstances into perspective and realize his emotions were not love.

Energized by the bright, cloudless day, Victoria arrived at work earlier than usual. The construction crew wouldn't start work for another hour and a half, but she had high hopes that they could make up for some of the time lost to the weather. As she reached her office, her private phone rang. She hurried across the room and picked up the receiver.

"Hello."

"Ms. Halstead? Bart Jensen here. I'm at the site. We've had another incident. The night watchman's hurt. Construction trailer burned down. I've called an ambulance. Called the fire department and the sheriff, too, but there's not much they can do."

"Ambulance?" Shocked and sickened, Victoria stared out the window, seeing nothing. "What happened?"

"I'm not sure. Otis thinks he started the fire—says he might have left water heating on the stove when he chased after the dogs. He heard gunshot, then the dogs took off over the hill. Otis grabbed a gun and followed them in the jeep. I'm thinking more vandalism. He found the dogs, dead. When he got out of the Jeep, someone hit him over the head and stole the Jeep. He managed to make it back. I found him passed out near the trailer. He's got a nasty gash on his head."

Victoria heard sirens in the background.

"Ambulance is here."

"Get Otis taken care of. I'm coming straight out."

Victoria wrote Janice a note, grabbed her purse, and was headed out the door when the phone rang. She almost ignored it, then thought it might be Bart again, so she answered it.

"Victoria? I missed you at home, so I thought you might be at work this early."

"Matt? I can't talk. There's been an accident—no, not an accident, a break-in at the Black Forest Project. They beat the night watchman and burned the trailer. I've got to get out there."

"I'm going with you."

"I don't have time to wait, Matt. I've got to go."

"I'll be at the front entrance in five minutes. It'll take you that long to get your car out of the parking lot."

"You're right. Besides, I just remembered, I'm low on gas. Okay, Matt, five minutes."

When they reached the site, firemen were sifting through the rubble and a sheriff's team was checking the area where they found the dogs. Workmen stood around in groups, talking in low voices. The scene looked like the aftermath of a battle.

"*Why* would anyone do this?" Victoria asked in stunned disbelief.

"Someone wants to delay this project," Bart said, coming up to them. He and Matt introduced themselves, then Bart turned and ordered the men to get to work. They dispersed, and soon engines roared to life.

"That's a pretty sound. At least they left the equipment alone," Bart said. About that time, one vehicle died, then another, and another. "Well, so much for that."

He ran over and motioned for everyone to kill their engines. He asked a few men to stay for cleanup, sent one of the crew supervisors to the hospital to check on Otis, and told the rest to take the day off, with the exception of the mechanics, whom he put to work checking vehicles.

Using Matt's cell phone, Victoria called the hospital. The receptionist said Otis Drake was in surgery and they had no information as to his condition. Next, Victoria called Janice. Her secretary had gotten her note, reported the incident to the insurance company, sent Leah Talbot to the hospital, and was already assembling copies of the company backup files that would have been destroyed in the fire. Thanking her, Victoria hung up. As she stood looking around, the full scope of the destruction crushed down on her. With everyone busily putting things back to rights, the work would commence without too much delay, but Victoria felt like she'd been personally trampled. Leaning on the car, she rested her forehead against the warm metal. An arm encircled her shoulder, and she turned into Matt's embrace, giving in to his comfort.

"Hey, everything will be all right," he said softly. He held her close and rubbed her hair with soothing strokes while she grieved with silent tears, letting him absorb her shudders. Leaning on his strength felt good, and she was tempted to let him take charge. She knew he would accept the burden. Moreover, he exercised restraint for her sake. That alone gave her the strength to pull herself together. With a sniff, she lifted her head.

"Oh, Matt, I ruined your shirt." She touched the wet mascara smudge on his shoulder. He took a handkerchief out of his pocket and handed it to her. She wiped her eyes, then dabbed at the stain on his shirt. "The smudge won't come off."

"Don't worry about my shirt. Are you all right?"

"Yes," she said, looking into his concerned eyes and smiling. "Thanks for coming with me. I doubt Bart would appreciate me ruining his shirt."

Matt smiled back. "My shoulder is always at your disposal. Looks like Bart's finished with the crew."

"Good," she said, standing straight. "Let's find out what's going on."

Bart and Victoria had a powwow and decided to get the construction back underway by the next morning if possible. He'd already ordered another construction trailer to be delivered that same afternoon. Luckily, Bart kept his daily log and test results on a laptop computer, which he kept with him. While they were conferring, Matt questioned the fire inspector.

Victoria wandered around the proximity of the trailer, kicking around the dirt with the toe of her expensive, soot-covered walking shoes that she'd put on in the car on the way.

Formulating their plan of action should have restored some feeling of stability, but the senseless, deliberate violence of the attack left her dazed as her mind searched for any possible reason or motive. There was none. What could they—could she have done to prevent this heinous evil from occurring?

"The Sheriff agrees this is more than random vandalism," Bart said when he and Matt joined Victoria. "It appears the dogs were deliberately lured to a poisoned deer, where someone waited in the trees for Otis, bashed him over the head, then made off with his Jeep."

"Have they found the Jeep?" Matt asked.

"Not yet. They expect it's abandoned nearby. There's the hope of getting fingerprints, but these guys are pros. They got a good cast of tire tracks coming and going from the scene where they found the dogs. That might help."

"I spoke with the inspector. They found traces of gasoline around the area of the trailer, so they're pretty certain arson caused the fire," Matt said.

"Yeah? That's about what I expected," Bart said. "Poor Otis thought he started the fire. He's worried about losing his job."

"Isn't he one of our construction apprentices with the First Step Program?" Victoria asked.

"Yes, ma'am. He works the crews during the day and stands the watch at night. He's a good guy, hard working and honest. I let him sleep in the trailer for a few hours in the morning, then again in the late afternoon. He used the hot plate to fix his meals; had a whole stash of cans of spaghetti, chili, and stew. Sends most of his money to his wife and kids. Told me he's not a deadbeat."

Even with the hot sun beating down, Victoria felt a shiver race up her spine.

The mechanics reported finding dirt in the gas tanks, which meant flushing out the fuel lines and the tanks, but at least the engines sustained no permanent damage. All in all, the vandalism caused only minimal delay to the project. Victoria considered the quick recovery small consolation compared to the serious injury to Otis Drake. Hot, dusty, and tired, Matt and Victoria headed back to Denver.

"It doesn't make sense. Why would anyone want to botch up the Methergy Project?"

"Last night's attack seems to narrow it to an attack against INTECH," Matt reasoned. "Burning the trailer wouldn't affect a sub-contractor."

"I agree. But why? No one stands to gain by delaying the project, and that's all these attacks are—delays."

"What about a personal vendetta against Nick? Could someone be trying to get even with him for some reason?"

"Stopping the project wouldn't hurt Nick. He's about to lose his business. Sure, he's selling, but he won't make anything on the deal, in fact he's going to have to sell his house to break even."

"There's got to be an angle we aren't seeing," Matt insisted. "Someone stands to gain if the project stops."

"That seems logical, but I just don't see who," she said, shaking her head. "They must be desperate to beat up a night-watchman and kill the dogs." She reached for the car phone and started dialing. "I hope Otis will be all right," she said as she put the receiver to her ear.

The hospital couldn't give her any information, other than Otis came out of surgery and went into recovery. When she voiced her frustration, Matt turned and drove to the hospital.

Leah Talbot was waiting outside recovery. She explained that Otis had a skull fracture and the blow to his head had caused swelling and pressure. The doctors had taken measures to relieve the pressure, but all they would tell her was that the operation had been successful. Whether Otis would recover remained to be seen. The doctors gave high likelihood to some permanent impairment—mental, motor, or both. Only time would tell them what and how much. He would be transferred to intensive care soon.

"What about a family?" Victoria asked.

"His wife and two children are in Oklahoma. I spoke with his wife earlier. She's upset, but has no way to get to Denver. They just got off welfare. It looks like they'll have to go back on."

"Arrange for them to get here, if they want to come. Send the bills to corporate, and get them into a temporary shelter, see if you can get them in the program. Otis might recover better if he knows his family is all right."

When they got back in the car, Matt turned to Victoria.

"Would you mind if I say a prayer for Otis now?"

His question surprised her. Mealtimes at home, or with the girls at bedtime had been the extent of their prayer life. Other than that, she couldn't remember the two of them ever praying together, in a car or anywhere else. Right now, it seemed appropriate. "That would be nice," she said, and she bowed her head. When Matt took her hands, she almost drew back, but his touch comforted her.

"Lord, You know what happened to Otis, and I know he's in Your hands. He's had a rough time in life, and he was just getting on his feet. His wife and kids need their father and husband to take care of them. It's Your will that a man care for his family, Lord, but he can't do that right now. I—we just want to ask you to heal him and restore him to his family. And, Father, please protect Victoria and all the workers on this project. Someone wants to stop it, and we've already seen that they'll do anything to get their way. These people are evil, Lord. Stop them now and bring them to justice. Amen."

Matt squeezed Victoria's hand. She squeezed his back. She didn't look up, but just sat there with her head bowed and her eyes closed. The prayer moved her so deeply, her insides were choked up and her eyes burned. Matt talked to God as if he knew Him well—as if prayers were conversations with a friend. And he had such confidence. Victoria felt certain Otis would be all right. God might not hear her prayer, but she had no doubt He heard Matt's.

What did it take to feel that sure about God? Victoria wondered. After a fall down a flight of stairs caused the miscarriage of their first child, turning to God brought her a measure of peace.

She'd been five months pregnant, and her son had not survived the fall. What had begun as an unwanted pregnancy had become the most important event in her life, and losing her child had sunk Victoria into a deep abyss of despair, intensified by an imbalance in her hormones. Upset himself, and inept when it came to dealing with his hysterical wife, Matt had turned to school and work for his comfort. For a time, he had tried to help her, but she'd been inconsolable, and he'd given up. Going through the motions of living, she had resumed cleaning houses.

Victoria remembered the day Rachel Harmon found her scrubbing the floor and crying. She had fixed Victoria a cup of tea and shared her own story of grief and God's loving comfort. Rachel had miscarried three times and could not have children. She told Victoria that her sweet babies were with Jesus and so was Victoria's son.

Picturing him with the angels gave Victoria the comfort she needed. She began going to Rachel's church, where the uplifting music, the litanies of praise, and the Scripture readings soothed her grief. Rachel encouraged her, and the church members welcomed her. Jesus offered a haven of compassion Victoria readily accepted.

Through a class on spiritual gifts, Victoria learned she had the gift of serving, which made perfect sense, and the church gave her an outlet to use her talents and abilities to help others. Feeling needed and loved, and grateful to have discovered such divine purpose and acceptance, she had dived in with enthusiasm and all of her abundant energy.

Victoria had found fulfillment at church. Matt supported her activities, even though his job kept him too busy to go with her. Then God blessed them with Mandy and Jessica. They'd had a nice home, lots of friends, and the respect of everyone around them, at least until Matt left her. As soon as word of their divorce got around, everything changed. The church people who had become like family didn't need her anymore. Everyone gave advice and even sympathy, but no acceptance. Finally, when she didn't follow the deacon's scriptural advice, she'd been shut out—not literally, but they might as well have pushed her out and closed the door in her face. All her hard work and all the hours she'd given counted for nothing. Instead of thanks for all the things she'd so selflessly donated to the church, she'd been treated like a sinner. So much for a loving God. All the confidence she'd felt as a Christian had turned sour.

So what had Matt discovered that she'd never been able to find? She always tried to live a good life and follow the Golden Rule, but she had never attained the assurance and intimacy that Matt had. And how could Matt have gotten it, after what he'd done? He said God had forgiven him.

She'd forgiven him, too, but that didn't negate the fact that he'd broken his vows. God is love. She knew that. But she'd also been taught that God hated sin. God forgave sin. Okay. If someone did something wrong and didn't know better, she could understand how they could be forgiven, but Matt had known better. So, did it boil down to forgiveness? Was God only for people who did terrible things, then repented? It seemed so. She just didn't understand.

"Tori, Honey, don't cry." Matt spoke gently as his thumbs brushed the tears from under her eyes. Looking up, she saw such compassion in his eyes, she almost started crying all over again.

"Sorry. I seem to be a leaky faucet today. I'm not usually this emotional, but I didn't get much sleep last night." She sat up and buckled her seat belt.

On the way back to her office, Victoria finally remembered that morning. "Matt? What did you want this morning when you called?" she asked.

"I just wondered if you sent all the documents to Matsuko?"

"No. I intended to do that this morning, but I got sidetracked, and I forgot all about it."

"Understandable. It isn't all that urgent, except Nick seemed anxious to get the deal wrapped up."

"I'll send the documents first thing tomorrow morning."

"I'd like to see everything you send them. In fact, make photocopies, and I'll pick them up tomorrow."

"All right." She sat angled toward him. The events of the day suddenly came rushing back at her, making her weary clear through her bones. Matt looked as tired as she felt, and as dusty and disheveled, but so very competent and strong. She'd leaned on him all day, and he'd given her the support she needed. What would she have done without him?

"Matt, I really appreciate you going with me today. I would have managed alone, but I want you to know, it meant a lot to have your moral support."

"I'm glad. I couldn't do much to help, but I couldn't let you go out there alone."

⚜

Victoria sent a copy of INTECH's assets and current projects to Matsuko Corporation the next morning. That done, she focused on business, shelving thoughts of the impending sale. Matt showed up at her office just before noon to collect the copies he'd requested.

Getting up, she handed him a thick folder. "I could have sent these over. Sorry. I'm not thinking clearly."

Matt took the folder, then leaned over and kissed her cheek. The gesture surprised her, but before she could pull back, he stepped back.

"No problem. I needed to see another client in the building. Besides," he said, smiling, "I hoped to talk you into lunch."

"Is there something you want to discuss?"

"Yes. I have a few questions about INTECH and ideas about the purchase offer."

"I'm sorry, Matt, I really shouldn't. With Nick gone on vacation, I'm swamped." She awarded him a smile of regret as she stepped back behind her desk, putting a safe barrier between them.

"You need a break. Too many hours behind that desk will give you more neck cramps. We have a lot to discuss on Nick's behalf, and I know he's anxious to have this completed."

With a shrug, Victoria capitulated. The intimacy of the previous day had made her uncomfortable. She didn't want him to misinterpret her gratitude, and she didn't want spending time with him to become a habit. The sooner they had lunch, the sooner he would leave. She followed him out of the office, telling Janice to go to lunch herself.

Matt called ahead on his cell phone, so a table was ready for them at the restaurant. They ordered the lunch specials. While they waited for the food, Matt asked about Otis and the fire investigation. She brought him up to date. Otis's condition remained the same. Then he asked if she'd read the Matsuko contract.

"I skimmed the document once through over the weekend," she said. "I've been awfully busy, especially with Nick gone. He doesn't realize his importance around there."

"I'm not criticizing. I'm the one who was supposed to study the document. I value your insight. On first glance, what did you think?"

"Well, I expected the asset buy-out, but a stock buy-out would be faster, less complicated and better for Nick. However, just because Nick wants to hurry things along, doesn't mean speed is their priority."

"The emphasis on haste concerns me. With the deadline on the notes coming up soon, our ability to negotiate decreases. They know we're desperate. If we had more time, I'm sure we could get a better offer. Has Nick considered a public stock offering?"

"I've tried to talk him into going public several times, but he adamantly opposed the idea. Didn't want anyone else having a say in his business. I doubt there's time to put it together now. Besides, he seems to have lost heart. He just wants out."

"Do you think that's a knee-jerk reaction? Is he likely to regret selling later?"

Victoria leaned forward earnestly. "I'm positive he's going to regret selling INTECH. The business is his life. He's tired right now, and I worry about his health—he's diabetic and has heart problems—but all he needs is a long vacation. I know he would come back reenergized."

"I formed pretty much the same opinion after our meetings. But his wishes must be respected. I'll negotiate the best deal possible, and I'll have to work toward its culmination. Meanwhile, perhaps I'll get a chance to discuss some options with him. Maybe a week of fishing will revive his energy."

Victoria relaxed back into her chair and smiled. "I'm glad Nick retained you to handle this sale. I know you will protect his interests, whether he likes it or not. I don't know about this trip reviving him, though. I can't imagine Nick sitting still waiting for a fish to bite a hook. He's probably going bonkers right this very minute."

"Speaking of fish," Matt said as their entrees were set before them. "This is the way to go fishing. Fresh trout, deboned and delicious, without getting my hands smelly."

"My sentiments exactly."

While they ate, they talked of this and that, their conversation drifting from one topic to another. Once again, the relaxed atmosphere between them surprised Victoria. Her concerns about his expectations after the previous day seemed foolish now. She'd worried that he'd use this time to further his cause or misinterpret her presence.

She'd forgotten her misgivings by the time he dropped her off at her office. She got out of his car, then turned around and leaned on the open passenger window. "Thank you for a wonderful lunch, Matt. Would you keep me apprised of your discoveries as you study the contract?"

"I certainly will. Oh, and Victoria?"

"Yes?"

"I love you."

Straightening quickly, Victoria mumbled, "Good-bye, I have to run," then she turned and hurried into the building as if the hound of heaven nipped at her heels.

WHEN VICTORIA GOT back to her office, a voice-mail message from Cleve awaited her. She returned his call.

"I just read about the fire," he said. "Why didn't you call me? I'd have gone out with you."

"Everything happened so fast, I didn't have time to think."

"Is everything all right?" he asked.

The sound of his voice and the concern she heard in his tone lifted her spirits. "We're back at work, if that's being all right. The night watchman's condition is critical, and he might not fully recover."

"The paper said he'd been assaulted. Could he tell you what happened?"

"No. He muttered a few incoherent words. He seemed to think he caused the fire."

"Maybe he did. Could the whole thing, his injury and the fire, have been an accident?"

"I wish. The police think it was arson. Looks like someone's trying to sabotage the project."

"You should have called me," he growled at her over the phone. "Reading about it in the paper made me sick. I can imagine how you feel."

Victoria swiveled her chair away from the desk and looked out the window. "Sick describes my state pretty well," she said. "I try not to dwell on it."

"I want to see you. Will you be home tonight?"

"Yes."

"Good. I have an early dinner meeting. I should be done by six-thirty. I'll come by."

Victoria spent the afternoon struggling with a business projection. After reading the same paragraph three times, she still didn't know what she'd read. She understood the technical language of the report. She simply couldn't concentrate. Leaning back in her chair, she rubbed her neck. The fire, the project delays, the emotional trauma caused by the violence all weighed heavily upon her, compounding her distress. Nothing in her life made sense. Since the moment Matt reentered her life, her goals, her bright outlook, and her promising prospects crumbled under one disaster after another.

Logically, she knew no correlation existed, but she'd felt his intrusion at every turn. And he had to keep mentioning God and Jesus, a ploy, she decided, to convince her that she should take him back. Well, she refused to be manipulated, which was why she'd felt edgy and distracted since they'd gone to lunch. She blamed part of her agitation on lack of sleep. Matt had invaded her thoughts far into the night. At lunch he'd been businesslike—until he ruined it when he dropped her off. How dare he claim to love her now. Why wouldn't he leave her alone? His persistence made no sense. Perhaps he regretted his mistake, but it was too late.

She no longer cared for Matt. She was not going to love him, and they were not going to be a happy little family again. Case closed. Besides, Cleve had entered the picture. She enjoyed his company. He challenged her intellect. Being around him stimulated her creativity like an injection of vitamin B12. She didn't know if she believed his declarations, but she certainly could not trust Matt.

Analyzing the numbers in front of her, she worked and reworked the same calculation, but the figures weren't coming out as she'd expected. Either she was wrong, or the profitability did not measure up. She saw an opportunity slipping away, but INTECH couldn't pursue a project with a low profit margin. She was fighting to swallow two headache tablets when the door opened and Nick came into her office.

"Nick!" She got to her feet and gave her boss a hug. "Boy, am I glad to see you. When did you get back? Tell me about your trip? How was the fishing?"

"Hold on," he said. He plopped down in a chair and grinned up at her. "This old, tired brain can handle only one question at a time."

Victoria leaned against her desk. "Well, how are you? How do you feel?"

"That's two more. Let's see. I'm fine. I feel okay. I got back a couple of hours ago, came straight from the airport. Great trip. Saw some of the prettiest country I've ever seen. Fishing is . . . " He shrugged " . . . fishing."

"You sure you feel okay? You look tired. Fishing must be hard work."

"Humph," he grunted. "Fishing is boring. I look tired 'cause I haven't done anything for over a week."

"Is that so? I guess you aren't ready to become a full time angler?"

"Not on a bet."

"Then maybe you'll call off this sale and get back to work?" she said, expressing her wishful thinking.

"Nope to the first, but I'm not retiring until the deal closes. How is it coming, by the way?"

"The deal is progressing. I met with Matt at lunchtime to discuss it. The sale will take awhile, Nick."

"Not too long, I hope. So, fill me in. What's happened since I left?"

Her elation faltered. "Would you like a cup of coffee?"

"Uh oh," he said. "Maybe I don't want to know." He refuted his words by leaning back in the chair and crossing his legs.

Victoria handed him a cup and waited for him to take a sip.

"The Black Forest site got hit again." She told him about the attack on Otis and the fire. Otis's vital signs were holding, but he'd slipped into a coma in the ambulance and still hadn't regained consciousness.

Nick rubbed his unshaven chin and shook his head. "You see why I want out of this rat race? I don't care if that whole project blows up in smoke. It isn't worth risking lives."

"But Nick, the Black Forest has been your dream." The weariness that had crept into Nick's voice and posture appalled her. He sounded like he needed a nap. He looked like he needed a long vacation.

"I don't have many priorities these days. A message came while I was gone from the company that bought up all my mortgages. Seems they got worried when I left town so sudden, as if I'd renege on a loan," he said with disgust. "They told me as long as I keep making interest payments on time, they won't foreclose on my house, but they reminded me the balloon payments are coming due, and they expect them on time. Strange how they seem to know so much about me. They're like a bunch of vultures sitting on a telephone pole waiting for me to default."

"Oh, Nick," Victoria said sympathetically. "I need to get you paid back. I've been trying to figure out how to do that before this sale goes through."

"The company can't afford to pay me and keep operating."

"I could cancel the Methergy project."

"No, no. Matsuko wants that. Increase security out there and go ahead. We've never given in to threats before; no sense starting now. I'll take a run out tomorrow and talk to Bart. By the way, I'll be out of town again for a couple of days. I'm taking off Thursday."

"More fishing, Nick?"

"No, I've had my fill of that sport. I'm going gold panning. Who knows, maybe I'll strike it rich, and we won't have to worry about any of this nonsense. Before I go, I want to sign acceptance on Matsuko's offer."

"This weekend is the mayor's dinner. You can't miss that."

"Yes, I can. You know I hate those things. You're going. You can be my stand-in." He grinned at her glare. She didn't like the social obligations any more than he did, and he knew it.

Victoria sat on the deck in front of an easel that held a partially filled canvas. She dabbed deep purple on the mountainside as she created a painting of the Breckenridge sunset that she'd sketched over the Fourth of July. Her style was like a mixed metaphor. Lines and perspective had to be perfect, but splashes of magenta and gold overflowed the lines, spilling emotions all over the canvas.

Mandy and Jessica were both home, but not for long. They were arguing about what movie to see.

When the doorbell rang, Victoria was in the middle of a sweeping brush stroke. "Mandy, get the door, please. It's probably Cleve," she called.

She saw Mandy and Jessica exchange disgruntled looks, then Mandy went to the door.

"Hi, Mr. Winslow," she greeted politely. "Mom's out on the deck."

"Hello, Amanda," he replied, smiling charmingly. "Call me Cleve, please. Here, I brought these for you and your sister." He handed her a sack from one of the exclusive department stores in Cherry Creek Shopping Center.

Peeking inside, Mandy let out an exclamation of delight. "Thank you, Mr. . . . Cleve, I mean. Wow, nobody's ever given me Godiva chocolates before. Jess, look."

Grinning, Cleve followed her into the house and, spotting Victoria, went out onto the deck. "I think I found the charm for at least one of your daughters."

Glancing around, Victoria saw Mandy tempting Jessica with the box of candy. Jessica looked mutinous. "She's got a real quandary," Victoria said. "Accepting the candy, which she is dying to do, I assure you, might seem like she's approving you. She'll come around. She's a daddy's girl, that's all."

Victoria looked up at the handsome man towering over her. "So, where's mine?" she asked.

"Huh-uh," he said, shaking his head. "If I give you chocolates, you'll be too busy indulging to kiss me. I'm no fool." He leaned down, bracing his hands on the chair arms, and kissed her. "Much better than Godiva."

He wiped at a smudge on her nose with his finger. "Paint," he pronounced. When she rubbed her nose with the back of her hand, he said, "Now you've got paint on your hand."

She set down the brush, picked up a cleaning cloth and dipped it in turpentine, then cleaned her hand. In the background she heard Jessica making sarcastic comments. She hoped Cleve didn't hear her.

He studied the canvas. "I didn't know you were an artist. You're very good."

She felt herself blush. "The picture will be better when it's finished," she said.

"Mom drew several pictures while we were in Breckenridge," Jessica said from the doorway.

Victoria closed her eyes and wished her daughter would pop out to Never-Never Land. When she opened her eyes, Jessica stood there with a big-eyed innocent expression, a promise of devilish mischief. "Dad especially likes the one with the cat stalking the birds."

"Come on, Jessica, we'll be late for the show if we don't leave now," Mandy said.

Yes, go on, Jessica, Victoria silently enjoined. Bless Mandy. She should become a diplomat.

"I wanted Mom to do a fireworks picture. It'd be really neat with us sitting on a blanket, Mom, Dad, Mandy, and me—like we did on the Fourth of July—with a big firefall in the sky over us."

"Jessica! Come on," Mandy demanded, grabbing her sister's arm.

Shaking off Mandy's hand, Jessica said, "I'm not going."

"Jessica," Victoria said in a quiet, threatening tone. "Either go with your sister or go downstairs, now."

With a smirk and a toss of her shoulders, she said, "Okay," and walked out.

Mandy grabbed her purse and followed. "We'll be home about eleven, Mom," she called over her shoulder.

After the door slammed shut behind the girls, Cleve gave Victoria another kiss.

She grinned up at him. "Good evening to you too," she said. "Hmm. I can't decide which is better? Your kiss or a piece of chocolate. It's a close call."

"Let me help you decide," he said, pulling her to her feet and kissing her again.

"Kisses win," she said. "Besides, they aren't fattening."

He suddenly hugged her close and held her tight. "I keep thinking about that attack at your project. What if you'd been there?"

Leaning back in his arms, she noticed the furrows in his brow, the intensity that made his dark eyes almost black. "I wouldn't have been there, Cleve. The attack happened in the middle of the night."

"The time doesn't matter. It's your project. Some lunatic wants to stop the project, and you're the center of it. I shudder every time I remember the picture of the burned-out trailer I saw in the paper this afternoon. I want you to stay away from there."

"I'm perfectly safe, Cleve. When I go to the site, there's a full crew of big, tough construction workers."

"Have you stopped to think your arsonist might be an employee? Who would have better access and knowledge?"

"No. I can't believe that."

"Maybe someone who's been fired. Shut down the stupid project until they find who did it."

"I can't do that, Cleve. You wouldn't stop."

"That's different," he muttered. "I care about you, Victoria. I don't want anything to happen to you."

Reaching up to touch his face, she said, "Nothing is going to happen to me."

Taking a deep breath, he held her tight, as if his holding her could somehow insure her safety. Then he said, "I realize I'm falling into your daughter's trap, but tell me about the Fourth of July. Did your ex-husband go to the mountains with you?"

"Why does it matter?"

"Let's just say I'm curious."

"I accompanied Matt and the girls to the mountains. I stayed in my own room, and I went off on my own most of the time."

"Except for watching the fireworks at Lake Dillon."

"We shared a blanket, with two teenagers in between us—all perfectly innocent," she insisted. "Mandy was leaning against me and Jessica was leaning on Matt."

"That paints a cozy little family scene."

"It wasn't important."

"Apparently your daughter disagrees."

"Jessica is a big girl. She understands, whether she wants to or not."

"I doubt that. You spend the weekend with your ex-husband, who is pursuing you like a dog after a T-bone steak, and you don't think an evening as a family is important?" he asked, his voice challenging. "You're not fooling your daughters. You're fooling yourself."

"You're trying to make something out of nothing, for crying out loud."

"Are you telling me the entire weekend was strictly platonic?"

Her eyes slid away from his gaze. Matt's kiss meant nothing. A mere symbol of friendship, short and undemanding. And so gentle and sweet it had almost made her cry. And he'd called her Tori.

"Yes. Strictly platonic," she insisted.

"I want you to stay away from him."

"You don't have the right to dictate who I see."

The muscles in his jaw clenched tight, and his piercing glare almost frightened her. She watched as he fought and controlled his anger. It happened so quickly, the change amazed her. Cleve Winslow had remarkable self-control. He would be a formidable opponent.

"You're right. I'm sorry. I seem to lose my head where you're concerned. Do you see the power you have over me?" His smile aimed at making amends. His mood had lightened, but she could see by the way he gazed at her, as if nothing else existed, that the depth of his emotions still remained, close to the surface.

"I told you before that I want to marry you. Now I'm asking. Victoria. Will you marry me?"

His smile relaxed the harsh planes of his face, making him seem like a different man, more human somehow. She reached up and put her hand on the side of his face, lightly abrasive with the growth of beard that began anew as soon as he shaved. A man with a five o'clock shadow at noon, Cleve never did anything by half measures. If he loved her, his love would be all consuming. *If.* Did she dare entertain such a possibility? What could she give in return? How would she hold his affection?

She looked for answers in his eyes. "What makes you think you want to get married? And why me?"

"Always the accountant, huh? All right, let's see if I can analyze this." He took her hand and led her to a wicker love seat, sat down and pulled her down next to him, putting his arm around her and tucking her close to his side.

"Imagine your life in five years. Your daughters will be out on their own by then. What do you see? What will you be doing?"

"I'll be working overtime to pay college bills, no doubt."

"What else? What about your dreams?" he probed.

"I haven't had time for dreams. I've struggled to get this far. Until recently," she confessed, "I thought I'd arrived. I remember the morning Nick told me he was going to sell the company. I'd been sitting at my desk congratulating myself." She let out a short laugh at the irony. "Every-thing I wanted seemed within my reach."

"You say that as if it's no longer true. How has the situation changed?"

"My dreams have turned into a nightmare. Nothing is certain all of a sudden. My job is up in the air, and that could affect everything I have. My emotions are all jumbled up, and, to add color to my nightmare, the girls are both acting strange. I suppose they're just growing up and exerting their independence. Maybe they are reacting to my turmoil." Victoria contemplated her situation. Cleve gave her shoulder a little squeeze of encouragement, letting her know he wanted to understand, but he kept quiet, allowing her the space she needed. Maybe sorting out the recent events would help her understand herself.

"I struggled so hard to get here, and I've had enough victories to believe perhaps I'd won the battle. I guess I developed a false sense of security. When things started happening, I got bombarded from all direc-tions. INTECH is up for sale. Matt shows up and puts on the pressure. You—you haven't exactly been subtle. Jessica is belligerent, blaming me for the trouble between her father and me. Mandy just goes her own way, oblivious to what anyone else is doing. Add the problems with the Methergy Plant—I'm back in the thick of battle, but I don't know which way to aim my guns."

She felt his light kiss on her temple. He hugged her and rested his head against hers. "One against the world, fighting to secure a place. I've felt that way most of my life," he said. "The battles are different, of course, but underneath it all is that feeling of being alone. No one to share the burdens, and no one to celebrate the victories. I've always felt that way, but I never gave it much thought," he said. He shifted position so her head rested on his shoulder. She closed her eyes.

"I never met a woman before who made me see what it could be like to have someone share my life. There's this gnawing ache, like I wake up in the middle of the night and there's no one to hold, or I have something to say, but no one is listening."

On the canvas of her mind, she saw a lonely man, prominent and powerful, yet solitary in the crowd, set apart by his own dynamism. Who could measure up? How could she? "Hasn't there ever been someone you loved?" she asked.

"Once, when I was just starting out. She wanted to help me build an empire. My business was growing and prospects looked great, but then something happened, and she left. I blamed her, but I should have known better. I'd been fantasizing about something that didn't exist. I had myself to depend on and no one else. After that I didn't look for more, and I wasn't disappointed."

He pulled her around so they faced each other. "Then I met you and all the rules changed. Casual no longer works. I want to wake up each morning and find you beside me. I want candlelight for two and hugging in front of the fireplace. I want skiing and bicycling with you and the girls, and I want rocking chairs for two on the deck. I'm tired of being alone."

A yearning began building inside her, making her wonder. She struggled to put his words into perspective. The artist in her visualized his idyllic dreamscape vividly. She could see herself painting it, but when she tried to put herself in the scene, the picture wasn't right.

"I don't fit, Cleve. You've built me up in your mind to be something I'm not."

"Why do you have such a low opinion of yourself?" he asked.

"Not low, realistic. I know what I am."

"All right, I'll give you reality. You were an unemployed housewife until five years ago, not even a contender. You got knocked down when your husband left, and don't ever forget *he* walked out on you," he said, pointing a finger at her. "But you got up, put on gloves, and entered the ring swinging. You knocked out a master's degree, got a job—no small feat these days, especially with a huge work force a whole lot younger than you. I expect that was a fight in itself, right?"

Victoria uttered an exclamatory laugh. "If we're comparing job hunting to boxing, I got knocked down, shoved against the ropes, got black eyes and a bloody nose before I bullied Nicholas Shrock into giving me a job."

"That's what I thought. Then you turned the job into a position of power, second only to the owner of the company."

She gave him a sardonic look, her mouth pushing into a lopsided grin. "You're exaggerating."

"I don't think so," he said. "Remember, I've seen your methane conversion plant. The plan is brilliant, and it's coming together against all kinds of odds."

"You're being very complimentary, Cleve, and I thank you, but you're ignoring all the other factors involved. I may have injected some new energy, but the basic plan already existed."

"You're putting yourself down again."

"No, I'm being honest. That credit goes to Nick. And my mall project ideas came from Mandy and Jessica." Suddenly she remembered Jessica's story. She had planned to ask Cleve about that first thing.

"Speaking of Jessica . . . for some reason, she thinks you arranged for Lionel Kane to introduce us at Elitch's. When Matt told me, I laughed. You don't even know Lionel Kane."

The instant surprise and wariness in his eyes confirmed Jessica's story. "Why would you do that, Cleve?"

An embarrassed smile crooked his mouth, and he shrugged. "I told you, when I read that article about you, I was intrigued. Actually, I took one look at your picture and fell in love."

"Oh, come on, Cleve. You don't expect me to believe that."

"I didn't believe it, why should you? I talked to a few people, found out about you, heard your reputation, and decided I didn't need to be snubbed, so I put you out of my mind. But you wouldn't go away. I even dreamed about you. I had to meet you, so what was I supposed to do? Consider my options. What would you have done if I'd made an appointment to see you, introduced myself, and asked you out to dinner?"

That picture made her laugh.

"See? You'd have thrown me out on my ear. I don't do well with rejection, so I insured success. I arranged to get an introduction through Kane."

"Lionel Kane is the last person I'd trust if he introduced me to someone."

His brows peaked. "Fate must have intervened, then. Don't you see? We're meant for each other."

"You don't really believe that. You're too intelligent and sophisticated for that kind of thinking."

"I was cynical—past tense—life taught me that, but you've shown me something different. Victoria, I want you. I have from the beginning, only now I won't settle for less than everything. So, I'm asking again. Will you marry me?"

"Cleve, I don't know what to say." She smiled sadly and shook her head. "I'm so confused. I need time. Please, please understand. I didn't expect this. I'm very flattered that you would ask, but I'm not ready for marriage again, and I may never be ready. After Matt, I just don't want to risk another failure. I'm sorry."

"Come here." Pulling her into an embrace, he kissed her softly, briefly. "I know I rushed this. I hoped . . . but I should have waited. Think about this like a business venture. Without risk, you'd be out of business tomorrow. Calculated risk, if you must be conservative. I know you've taken risks before. Think about my proposal. I will ask again."

Victoria was surprised when Janice announced that Viola was there and wanted to see her. Viola summoned. She rarely left her domain.

"Send her in."

Nick's secretary looked unusually agitated. "Good morning, Viola. How are you today?"

"I am in excellent health, thank you for inquiring. This, however, is not so excellent." She handed Victoria an official-looking envelope addressed to Nicholas Shrock and INTECH.

"What is this?"

"It's a court injunction. A man walked in asking for Mr. Shrock. When I said he wasn't in—which I would have said even if he had been—he wanted to know if I had the authority to sign for Mr. Shrock's mail. Well, I told him my signature was legal tender around here, so he had me sign a form and handed me this envelope."

Removing the contents, Victoria quickly perused the document. Her eyes widened, and she reread the first page again. "Thank you, Viola. I'm going to run this over to our lawyer." Victoria stuffed the papers back into the envelope. "If Nick comes in, call me."

As Viola turned to leave, Victoria picked up the phone. "Janice, get Bart Jenson for me, and also, put a call through to . . . never mind. I'll do that one myself. We have a problem with the Black Forest Project. Any outside calls, especially from media, the answers are *no comment* and *I can't be reached*. See what you can do about canceling or rescheduling my appointments, please."

"What about your appointment with the hairdresser this afternoon?"

"Oh, brother. I forgot all about the mayor's dinner tonight. I guess I can't get out of that affair. My appointment isn't until four-thirty. I'll be ready for a break by then."

Victoria's call came through while Matt was on the phone with a client. As he dialed her number, he leaned back and pictured her. He couldn't help smiling. Then he sobered up. The last urgent call was disastrous.

"Thanks for calling back so quickly, Matt. I need help."

He recognized the raised pitch in her voice and knew she was upset. "What's wrong?"

"More problems with the Black Forest Project."

He sat up straight. "Another attack?"

"Yes, but not like before. This is a legal problem."

"Victoria, has another attorney been handling that project?"

"Barney Giles. He's gold panning with Nick right now. Nick would want you to handle this."

Reaching for a yellow legal pad and a pen, Matt said, "Okay. Tell me what's wrong."

"We received a temporary restraining order to stop construction pending a hearing."

"Hmm. What is the order based on?"

"It cites violations of the Federal Clean Water Act and the Federal Endangered Species Act."

"Who instigated the order?"

"A group called Citizens for Environmental Purity."

"You have EPA approval on the project?"

"Not officially. Tom Condrey at the state EPA has given us a verbal go-ahead. He's excited about the project. He warned us the paperwork could take some time but said we were clear to begin preliminary construction."

Drumming his fingers on the desktop, Matt tried to think of some technicality that could get INTECH around the staying order. He didn't have enough information. "I need to see the injunction. Could you bring it over?"

"I could fax it to you right away."

"You could, but that wouldn't expedite things. If we need to take a countermeasure, I'll need authorization. It's eleven now. I'm free for the next two hours. How's your schedule?"

"This is a priority. I'll make time. Are you giving up your lunch hour for me?"

"I didn't have any plans. I'll order in."

"Don't bother. I'll pick up something on the way. Thanks Matt."

"You're very welcome," he murmured to the dial tone. Victoria didn't need another headache. And this could mean trouble for the Matsuko offer. He picked up the legal pad and headed for their law library. Environmental law wasn't exactly his area of expertise. Good thing he was a quick study.

CHAPTER SIXTEEN

WHEN VICTORIA ARRIVED with the injunction, Matt spent several minutes studying the order.

"Someone has done their homework on this thing," he said, "and their accusations could mean sudden death to your project. If the runoff from your spring empties into Kiowa Creek, as this states, which then empties into the South Platte River, you're fighting the same whooping crane that the Two Forks Dam project fought in 1989."

"And they lost." She sighed deeply and Matt thought she looked ready to crumble. "So what are we supposed to do, give up?" she asked.

"That's only one aspect. Their claim that contaminates from the landfill are seeping into the Ogalala Aquifer is a pretty nebulous statement to disprove. Everything pollutes the aquifer."

"That's the nature of a landfill. INTECH is cleaning the pollutants up."

"And expanding the landfill's operations."

"Whose side are you on, anyway?" she asked accusingly.

"Do you have any doubt?"

For a few seconds she stared at him, then her shoulders slumped in defeat. "I'm sorry, Matt." She pressed her fingertips against her temples and rubbed in little circles.

"That's all right. Let's talk about this later. I'm getting hungry. What's in the sack?"

"Pastrami and Swiss on dark rye."

He grinned. "Kosher dills?"

"Yes," she admitted.

"Hmm, hand that over," he demanded, reaching towards the sack.

She started to give him the bag, then stopped and grinned at him and her dimple came to life. She'd been so serious and distracted by all the problems she'd been facing, Matt was relieved to see her smile. The order hadn't overcome her determination.

"Say please," she instructed.

"P-l-e-a-s-e."

While they ate, Victoria fell back into melancholy, not as far, but enough to disturb him. He switched the subject. When he mentioned Mandy's interest in golf, she finally perked up.

"I offered to teach her myself," he said. "I would have enjoyed spending the time with her. She turned me down."

"She turned me down too. In fact, she sounded bored by the prospect. She had more important things to do, like cheerleading and drama club."

"I got the impression Tony occupied a lot of her time too. What about him? I guess he is a golf enthusiast."

"I don't think that's the attraction. She said he made her feel clumsy on the golf course."

"Maybe she needs to prove him wrong."

"Then why wouldn't she let you or me help her?"

"A bid for independence, no doubt," he said with fatherly resignation. "I guess we have to face the fact that she's becoming an adult."

"Her decision not to go to camp surprised me. She's anticipated that for months."

"Well, her reasoning is sound. She could use that money for college and keep working instead of quitting now."

"I know, her decision just seems odd to me, that's all. Besides, she wouldn't need the money if she'd take the scholarship to UNC. Fort Lewis is an excellent college, but I wonder why she changed her mind?"

He shrugged. "One of her friends, I think. As long as she gets a good education, I guess Fort Lewis is as good a place as any."

"Probably Kim. She's in the church youth group. Nice girl." Victoria set her half-eaten sandwich down and sighed. "I'm not ready for Mandy to leave home. I didn't think her leaving would bother me. She grew up too fast. And Jessica is only a few years behind her."

"Come here." Matt got up and gently pulled her into his embrace. For a moment, she accepted his hug, and he felt privileged to share her feelings of loss. Few people ever saw the tender side that she hid so well. If only he had understood her deep need for affirmation instead of competing with her, they might be sharing this moment as a couple united in love instead of as two single parents who shared the same children. The tears were there, unshed and under tight control, for the things she stood to lose that defined Victoria Halstead—her children and her career. Mandy to college, Jessica to friends and school and outside interests, and Nick, her project, maybe even her job to the financial hatchet. Too many changes, all at once.

"You don't have to be alone in this, Victoria. Let me share your burdens with you," he whispered against her ear. He kissed her temple, where she'd been rubbing it. The intercom on his desk buzzed, and Victoria pushed away from him. He sighed and went around the desk to answer the call.

"I have those records you requested," the voice of his secretary said.

"Good. Bring them in, please." He looked over at Victoria. She had regained her composure and was finger combing her hair in the reflection of the glass covering a photograph of their family taken when the girls were little. Such a beautiful family, he thought. Too bad the picture represented only the past, but kicking himself again accomplished nothing. He intended to change the future.

The secretary brought in the papers. Matt scanned the contents. "This documentation covers the Two Forks Dam project that was killed years ago," he told Victoria. "Environmental groups cited the same violation to stop the dam construction. The project was approved at the state level, but the head of the EPA at the federal level vetoed the project, overturning the authority of the state and local agencies. That set a precedent, but the stakes were a lot higher than reclaiming a land-fill in the middle of nowhere. The dam would have destroyed a prize trout-fishing stream that attracted big money sportsmen."

"I remember that," she said. "Amazing how a few people with money have so much power."

"One pertinent detail regarding the Endangered Species Act: the Two Forks Dam threatened water levels downstream. In this case, they claim our pollution will harm the whooping cranes. We can disprove that. Your project isn't likely to attract attention in Washington, DC. If you get the state approval, you should be home free. That's where we have to concentrate our efforts."

"Does that *we* mean you intend to help?"

"Of course. I have a few connections, you know."

"I certainly do. I helped you get them, remember."

"I've never forgotten that, Victoria. You always went far beyond the call of duty to help my career. I wouldn't be where I am today without your help."

Victoria winced. How petty could she get? She didn't do that to coworkers, so why did she always feel the need to assert her claim as part of Matt's success? Only moments ago, he'd been comforting her, and she'd come close to drowning him in a sea of tears. What was wrong with her? "I'm sorry. I don't know why I said that. You're an excellent lawyer, and you earned your success. I don't blame you for resenting me. You never asked for my help."

"How could I resent you? I might have if you'd ever held your efforts over my head. But you didn't, nor did you ever complain."

"Yet you do," she repeated, amazement dawning on her face. "Why?"

He shrugged. "The past doesn't matter."

"Oh, but it does. I have a feeling the past is very important."

"If I'd been more of a man . . . but that doesn't change what happened or what I did, so just suffice it to say I could never out-give you, and I couldn't live with that. Dumb answer, huh?" She looked so confused, he decided he'd better drop the subject for now. "Don't let it keep you awake, okay? You have enough to think about without me messing up your head."

She looked so perplexed, he wished the subject had never come up. Someday, they'd have to talk about all of the past, but not now. "About the injunction . . . we've got the weekend, let's see what I can do before Monday. Don't get your hopes up. You'll have to stop construction until we can get this overturned. Is there any progress you can make and still abide by this order?"

"I'm afraid not. This is really going to mess up our schedule."

"Victoria, I'm really sorry. I know how much this means to you. I'll do everything I can to clear this up."

"Ladies and gentlemen, I want to thank you all for attending our little party tonight." Appreciative laughter tittered around the room. The *little party* had cost the diners three hundred dollars a plate, and the room was filled to capacity. The mayor explained that those special people accepting awards for their philanthropic efforts would get to designate the evening's proceeds to their favorite charities. Victoria felt a tremor of nerves. Even though it was INTECH being spotlighted and not her personally, she still had to get up in front of all those luminaries and make some appropriate acceptance noises. She hated being put on the spot. Only for Nick. She wished he had come. It should have been him receiving the praise.

An impressive lineup of locally famous dignitaries filed up on stage one at a time to receive certificates suitable for framing and to mouth a few platitudes.

As Victoria waited her turn, she wondered if her hair was in place and if she'd gotten a run in her pantyhose when she bumped her leg against the table. She was sure her lipstick had worn off, but she didn't want to attract attention by trying to reapply it, so she pressed her lips together and hoped that would give them some color. Cleve patted her hand. She made herself sit still. He whispered that she looked beautiful. She took a deep breath.

"I want to thank each and every person in this room," the mayor said. "All of you have shown your willingness to help those less fortunate. Denver is a better place to live because of your efforts. I am proud to be the mayor of such a wonderful city. We have one more award, but I have been asked by a power greater than mine, to step aside. So, ladies and gentlemen, with reluctance, I pass the honor on to our esteemed Governor, Samuel Johnson.

Victoria watched with trepidation as the governor walked on stage. INTECH hadn't been called yet, so, unless the company had been eliminated from the awards, the spotlight would be on her. She wanted to crawl under the table.

"I apologize to your worthy mayor for pulling rank. I pulled rank for the privilege of introducing a woman who has won my utmost respect. She has given freely of her time for nearly two decades. The remarkable fact is, that while the rest of us take pride in our good deeds, she hides her work so diligently, she slips away every time the accolades are passed out. This time we have her. Please come up to the podium, Ms. Victoria Halstead."

Cleve helped her to her feet. "Go on," he encouraged.

Back straight, a smile in place, Victoria walked to center stage. She kept smiling as the governor shook her hand.

"We played a little trick on Ms. Halstead," he told the audience. "We didn't think she'd come otherwise. And I had to promise to share the stage with a co-conspirator. May I introduce Mr. Nicholas Shrock, owner and chief executive officer of INTECH Real Estate Development Company, Victoria's boss."

She watched in a daze as Nick came out and gave her a hug, then stood beside her.

"It's true our company has made a real contribution to society for the past several years, and each employee deserves thanks," Nick said. "Our program is the brain-child of my brilliant chief financial officer, Victoria Halstead, and her dedication has made the program work. Her training program for welfare moms now includes apprenticeships in housekeeping, restaurant skills, construction, maintenance, and on and on. It's a model program for every corporation in the county. First Step works, my friends, and Victoria deserves all the credit."

A thundering applause followed Nick's speech. Victoria's smile started to crack, and she wanted to bonk Nick over the head, then run, but she stood straight and kept her hands folded together to keep them from shaking. Then it was her turn. She stepped up to the mike and accepted a bouquet of long-stemmed roses and a wooden plaque. She stared at the plaque for a moment. Her name, not INTECH, was etched into the shiny brass plate.

"This isn't fair, you know," she said, a slight tremor in her voice. "I had a few words prepared to accept a certificate on behalf of INTECH, and now I can't even remember them."

Everyone laughed, and the governor injected, "I love a woman of few words, don't you?" That tired cliché earned another round of laughter, and Victoria relaxed a little.

She looked out over the audience. The bright lights made it difficult to see faces, but she knew where Matt was sitting, and she couldn't help looking to see his reaction. Locating him, she could just make out his broad grin. Taking a deep breath, she held up the plaque.

"Thank you for this, but I don't deserve it. I made a few suggestions. A lot of people made the ideas work. A wise man once told me that the only way to get a lot done in a little time is to delegate. People need to be needed. You know what? He was right. So, on behalf of Nicholas Shrock, Leah Talbot, our director, all the INTECH employees, and the First Step apprentices, I accept this honor. Without them, I wouldn't be up here tonight. Thank you all."

Victoria stood back while her peers gave her a standing ovation. She started to leave the stage, but Nick stopped her.

"Hold on a minute. Cleve Winslow of Winslow International has a presentation to make."

To more clapping, Cleve came up to the podium. "Aside from the First Step program, Victoria has been involved in many community projects. The new family shelter is just one. The building is finished, but I understand the shelter needs furniture and kitchen appliances. Ms. Halstead, Winslow International would like to donate this check to cover the furnishings." He handed her a check. She looked at it and almost choked.

"Fifty thousand dollars! I should say it will, and more." She waved the check in the air, triggering another round of applause, then gave Cleve an exuberant hug. "Thank you. This will help a lot of families."

The evening ended with dancing to a big band orchestra. Although she shunned the limelight, dancing with Cleve made a nice ending to a perfectly awful day. After two dances, she gave in to exhaustion and had Cleve take her home.

"Don't expect me for dinner tonight, Mom," Mandy said as she breezed through the kitchen Saturday morning.

"Where are you going?"

"I have a golf lesson at nine, then I need a dress for the dance at the country club tonight."

"I thought we were going to the show. We could do lunch and go shopping, instead."

"I'm sorry, Mom, but I'm meeting Kim. Maybe we could do something next week?"

"Sure, have fun. Jessica and I will miss you." Mandy was halfway to the car before Victoria finished speaking. Oh well, that was life with teenagers. There had been little time spent with the girls this summer, and she missed the closeness they had developed in recent years. Soon she would be alone, and that prospect frightened her. She supposed every mother experienced the same letting-go pangs. Hearing Saturday morning cartoons blaring on the television, Victoria called down the stairs, "Jessica, do you have clothes that need washing before camp? I want to get the laundry done before we go to the show."

"I'll get them, Mom," Jessica yelled back.

A few minutes later, Jessica brought an armload, even though Mrs. Green had washed on Thursday. "Can I go swimming at Becky's?" she asked as she dumped the clothes in the laundry room.

"I thought we'd spend the day together. I won't see you for two weeks."

"You can come up to parents' day next weekend."

"I plan to, but that's not the same as spending an afternoon together."

"Come on, Mom. Mandy got out of this afternoon."

Arrow to heart, direct hit. "I didn't realize I was such a burden to you girls."

"It's not like that. Becky will be gone when I get home. I won't see her till school starts."

"Okay, I give up. But I'll pick you up for dinner—that is still a date. Fair?"

"Yeah, okay." Jessica didn't sound thrilled with the edict, but she'd gotten her way, so she gave in without too much grumbling.

Victoria carried the portable phone to the laundry room and called Nick. "Good morning, did I wake you?"

"No, I've been up for hours."

"Did you actually go gold panning, or was that a smoke-screen?"

He chuckled. "I really went. Found enough flakes to whet the appetite, but not enough to buy a cheap breakfast. Working sixty hours a week is easier, and a lot more profitable."

"Not this week, I'm afraid."

"Uh-oh. More bad news?"

"I'm afraid so. We were served an injunction to halt the Black Forest Project."

Victoria heard a whoosh of disappointment from Nick. "Sometimes I wonder if that property is cursed. What is the reason?"

"The order names violations of Endangered Species Act and the Clean Water Act."

"That's ridiculous; we aren't violating any laws. If anything, we're cleaning up the environment. Didn't we get EPA approval on the project?"

"Not yet, but approval should be forthcoming. This may hold the process up, though. I took the injunction to Matt; I hope you don't mind. I didn't expect to see you until Monday."

"You did the right thing. What did he say?"

"He's going to do some checking this weekend, see if he can't get the injunction reversed, but he didn't sound very hopeful. I talked to Bart, and we both felt we should hold off making any decisions. The crew will be there Monday morning, expecting to go to work."

"That's all right. Can we use them somewhere else?"

"I can't think where. Boy, this boils my blood. We have to pay the crew whether they work or not. We can't afford that."

"Calm down, delays are part of the game. You know that."

"Yes, but there is usually some slack built into the contract. We don't have any margin here—not until the EPA approval comes through and we get funding."

"Well, don't bury the body before the last heartbeat. I have faith that Matt will find a way."

"So do I, at least concerning legal matters. I'm sorry I had to call you at home, but you'd have been more upset if I'd waited until Monday. Now, forget about it and enjoy your weekend."

She heard his chuckle. "Listen to your own advice, Missy. There isn't a thing more you can do until Monday morning."

"I'm not even going to think about INTECH, Nick."

But she did, all day. She thought of and discarded numerous plans of action.

At five o'clock, Victoria picked Jessica up, and they went to their favorite pizza restaurant. They ordered Jessica's choice, three meat toppings, no green stuff and extra cheese, but when the pizza came, Jessica ate only one piece.

"Is that all you're going to eat?" "Yeah, I'm not very hungry."

"Did you eat at Becky's?"

"No, just a soda."

"I thought the pizza was good," Victoria said, wondering what was bugging her youngest daughter. Asking her direct questions never worked, but she usually blurted out her thoughts. She seemed unusually close-mouthed and preoccupied tonight.

"It was okay." She picked a piece of pepperoni off the uneaten pizza and popped it in her mouth. "Mom? Will you go with us when Dad takes me to camp?"

"No, Honey. Your father wants to spend time with you."

"Yeah, but he wants to spend time with you too."

"Oh, I don't think so."

"Why are you being so stubborn?" Jessica's voice rose as her emotions spilled to the surface. "Dad wants us to be a family again. You're the one keeping us apart."

"Did he tell you that?"

"No, but I can tell. He asks about you, and he gets upset when you go out with that man."

"That man has a name. Mr. Winslow is very nice, and you need to give him a little respect."

"Are you going to keep seeing him?"

"Probably. I enjoy being with him. You would, too, if you'd give him a chance." Victoria could have bit her lip when she saw the mutinous resolve on her daughter's face. She'd mistakenly thrown down a challenge, and Jessica had picked it up.

"You said you wouldn't date business associates."

"Cleve isn't a business acquaintance. He and I have a lot in common. We like each other for personal reasons."

"You love Daddy. You told me so. You said you'd always love him, but you couldn't live together because he had another life."

"That's true, Honey, but loving someone isn't enough. You have to want a life together."

"Daddy *wants* a life together. You used to want our family back together too. You didn't like it when Daddy left."

"You have to understand. My life and your father's life have gone in different directions. We aren't the same people we were before."

"You told me feelings aren't always right," Jessica said, desperation tingeing her voice. "When Julie got me in trouble at school, and I said I hated her, you said if I decided to like her and acted nice to her and tried to help her, then I would truly like her again. You said love was an action verb, remember?"

How did one argue logic with a teenager, especially when she turned your words against you? Victoria noticed people looking at them. "Shhh. We're attracting an audience."

"I don't care. I bet they agree with me."

"Well, I care. Let's finish this conversation in the car." Victoria paid the bill and got a container for the leftover pizza.

Once they were in the car, Jessica jumped back into her argument. "Everybody says the trouble with teenagers is the breakdown of the family."

"Who is everybody?"

"I don't know, experts, I guess. At Sunday school, they were talking about family values and how we need commitment in our relationships. You're always telling us the same thing."

"Jessica, I know you love your father and me, and you want us to be together again, and I'm sorry that we have disappointed you. Yes, relationships take commitment and hard work, but sometimes things don't work out the way we want. We honestly tried before."

"But Mom, you could try again," Jessica pleaded. "We would be a family again, please."

"I would do almost anything for you and Mandy, but I can't have a relationship just because you want me to. Caring about someone and falling in love are not the same. I care about your dad, but I'm not in love with him, do you understand?"

"It's because of Mr. Winslow, isn't it? I wish you'd never met him. I hate him!"

"You don't mean that. What if I stop seeing Cleve and start dating other men? Are you going to hate them all?"

"It isn't fair," Jessica said, her voice hitching on a sob.

Fair? Was life ever fair? Victoria reached over and squeezed Jessica's hand. "Sweetheart, I know you are unhappy about our situation, but at least your dad is here, and you get to see him all the time. He really loves you, you know."

"I know."

"What happens between me and your father or any other man should not affect your happiness, but that is up to you. You can be miserable or you can make the most of your life, which is a choice only you can make. Maybe being away from both of us for the next two weeks will help you to put your thoughts into perspective. We want you to be happy."

The silent treatment from the passenger side of the car covered any reaction from her recalcitrant teenager, making Victoria want to scream about what wasn't fair. She didn't deserve Jessica's criticism or antagonism. Matt had torn apart their family, not her.

Once home, Jessica wanted to watch a movie. Victoria told her to select one from their videotape library while she made them some popcorn and ice cream sodas. She checked and had a message from Cleve saying he'd try to reach her later.

The evening went downhill from there. Jessica had seen the movie many times, and Victoria hadn't liked it the first time. Once the movie started, Jessica tuned out the rest of life and became enraptured by the poorly written and acted attempt at comedy, while Victoria tried to find something to laugh at and developed a headache instead.

Realizing there was no chance at meaningful dialogue with her daughter, Victoria said goodnight and went upstairs. She swallowed a couple of headache tablets, picked up a book she'd been wanting to read and retreated to her bedroom. The book couldn't hold her attention and she'd decided to go to bed early, when Cleve called wanting her to go to brunch the next day.

"Jessica leaves for camp around noon," Victoria said. "I want to be here to see her off."

"That's fine. They serve until two o'clock, so we can still make it. I'll come by about noon."

"I can't go until at least twelve-thirty."

"All right. So, how was your day?"

"Miserable. I expected to spend the day with the girls, but they deserted me. Ol' Mom takes second place to anything or anybody that comes along."

"Not in my book. I wish I'd taken you with me today."

With a short laugh, she agreed. Sometimes she wished her responsibilities would disappear. "How was your golf game?"

"Not bad. What are you doing this evening?"

"I was watching a movie with Jessica, but the atmosphere got too depressing. She's in one of her snits, so I'm reading, instead."

"I could come over and keep you company."

"You're sweet to offer, but I don't think so. Good night, Cleve. See you tomorrow."

"Good night, Sweetheart."

The sound of an idling engine woke her. The glowing numerals on the bedside clock showed two o'clock. Slipping out of bed, Victoria went to peer out the window. A tree partially blocked her view of a car in the driveway. It didn't sound like Tony's old Chevrolet. The car sat there for several minutes, then Mandy got out and hurried into the house. As the car moved away, Victoria could see the shape of a sports car.

Grabbing a robe, Victoria went downstairs to confront Mandy. She waited in the dark hall outside the bathroom.

"Amanda."

"Oh! Mother, you scared me."

"You scared me too. Do you know what time it is?"

"I guess I'm a little late."

"A *little?* It's two hours past your curfew.

"No big deal, Mom. A bunch of us went to a movie and then out to eat afterwards. We were just talking. I didn't realize the time had gotten so late. No one else had to hurry home."

"You know very well that doesn't hold water with me. I'm not responsible for everyone else."

"I'm not a child anymore, Mother."

"I realize that, but you are still living in this house, and you have an obligation to this family. At the very least, I expect the courtesy of a phone call when you're going to be late."

"I'm sorry. I'll call next time."

"I would appreciate it. I don't want to be an ogre, but I shouldn't have to sit here worrying. Did Tony get a new car?"

"Tony didn't bring me home. We're not seeing each other anymore."

"Oh? Who brought you home?"

"One of the guys, Jase Tanner, gave me a lift home."

"Jase Tanner? Do I know him?"

"You might have seen him. He works at the golf course."

A face materialized in Victoria's mind. A cocky young man Buffy Swinson had described as cute and oh-so-helpful. "Is he the blond fellow who works in the pro shop?"

"Yes. He's an assistant pro." Mandy had a dreamy look in her eye that Victoria didn't like.

"He's too old to be hanging around with your friends."

"He came with Kim's brother. They go to college together."

"Doesn't Eric go to Fort Lewis?"

"Yes. Mom, I'm tired. Are you finished grilling me yet?"

"Mandy, Jase Tanner is not someone you should associate with."

A barrier, invisible but almost tangible, rose up between mother and daughter. The wall seemed so real, Victoria had an urge to claw it down. Mandy's response was cold and final.

"I don't criticize your friends. You have no right to dictate who my friends will be. Goodnight." Mandy turned and walked away, leaving Victoria standing in the dark.

As she climbed the stairs, she thought of her recurring nightmare with the shifting floorboards and bottomless pit. It must have been a premonition, a vision of life with teenage daughters. First Jessica, then Mandy. In one day, the beautiful bond of shared dreams and tears had evaporated into a clash of wills. Victoria felt battle-scarred, and she hadn't even known war had been declared.

CHAPTER SEVENTEEN

TWO OVERSTUFFED SUITCASES sat on the porch. Jessica was dragging a rolled sleeping bag, pillow, and an overnight case through the door. Matt stared at the pile and shook his head. He told Jessica to eliminate half her baggage, and she pouted and insisted she needed everything for bare survival. When he repeated his warning, Jessica started whining. Victoria was rooting for Matt but knew he might as well turn around and talk to the wall.

"Skip it," Jessica said. "Forget the whole thing, I'll stay home. I don't want to go, anyway."

"That's enough, Jessica." That, from Matt, normally quelled any argument, but Jessica's countenance puffed up like a thundercloud about to dump.

Just then, Cleve drove up. Victoria had hoped Jessica and Matt would be gone by now.

"I'm glad I made it before you left," Cleve said, addressing Jessica. He handed her a small box. "I thought perhaps you could use this at camp."

Taking the box, she eyed it as if it contained poison. Her surly expression might have been from the dispute with her father, but Victoria suspected her animosity included Cleve and his present. She started to remind Jessica of her manners when the teenager opened the box. She lowered her eyes to cover her initial reaction, but Victoria saw that first second of interest. Jessica took out a small pocketknife with a Mother-of-pearl handle. Her thumb rubbed the shiny case, and then she stuffed it in her back pocket and squinted up at Cleve.

"Thanks," she grunted. She turned away, grabbed the largest suitcase, and headed for the trunk of Matt's car. Without further objection, Matt stowed the other gear. Victoria suspected he didn't want a scene in front of Cleve—but Jessica had won.

"That was nice of you," Victoria said as they drove off. "I think she liked it."

Cleve chuckled. "Really? How does she react when she hates something?"

"You don't want to know. Suffice it to say, it's not a pretty sight."

"Well, are you ready? We'd better get going if we want to get anything to eat."

"Ready and starving."

Construction at the landfill halted at seven, Monday morning. Matt's contact with the judge had been fruitless. Although sympathetic, the EPA vetoing the Two Forks Dam project in 1989 set the precedent. INTECH had to prove its innocence. The state EPA guru apologized profusely, but the environmentalists' charges tied his hands. A hearing and a complete investigation had to be made, and that could take weeks. He promised to do what he could to speed up the process.

Victoria had calls in to every agency and organization that could possibly help their cause, and she was awaiting replies when Janice buzzed her intercom.

"Victoria, Viola called for you to go to Mr. Shrock's office ASAP. She sounded upset. I asked her if Mr. Shrock was ill, and she said no."

"Thanks, Janice, I'm on my way."

A sense of foreboding made Victoria hurry. One glance at Nick, and she knew something was terribly wrong. His face was ashen, his shoulders slumped as he stared out the window. When she closed the door, he looked up and gave her a faint smile.

"Nick, what's wrong, are you ill? Is your heart acting up?"

"Hmm, that would be the topper, huh? No, I'm fine. Come sit down."

She obeyed, taking the chair across from him, sitting forward in the chair.

"We lost it, Victoria. The sale fell through." His bleak expression held no hope.

"What do you mean, Nick? What happened?"

"Matsuko pulled out, withdrew their offer. They said they were sorry, but they want to build their image here in the States, through research, charity, environmental good-guys, that kind of baloney. They have to avoid anything controversial." Nick's face reddened, and Victoria worried that his blood pressure might explode.

"Because of the injunction?"

"Yup. They politely informed us they can't afford the adverse publicity or the time or money required to fight this thing. And their contract has an escape clause that covers just this type of situation. I can't blame them."

"You've talked to Matt?"

"He's trying to salvage the deal, but it's not going to work. Your ex-husband is a great lawyer, but he's no miracle worker. He said we'd better start looking for another buyer."

Thoughts bombarded her, incoherent and disjointed, darting here and there seeking reason and logic, trying to formulate a plan. An idea hovered, unformed, just out of her mind's reach, but she couldn't seem to grab it. She stood up and started pacing. The thought wouldn't gel. For lack of a better plan, she reached for a temporary fix.

"Can we buy some time, Nick? Get an extension on your notes if we give them some cash? We have seven hundred and fifty thousand dollars sitting in money market. I scuttled the venture with London—the figures didn't work out. I planned to redirect the funds to the Methergy Project, but it could be months before that's rolling again. Besides, you're the top priority."

A minuscule flicker of hope lit Nick's eyes, but the overwhelming scope of their predicament killed the spark before it had time to catch. He shrugged his bent shoulders. "It might work; it's worth a try, anyway.

If we don't find a way out, your Methergy and every other piece of this business will be history."

"We won't let that happen, Nick. We'll find a way out," she vowed. "Maybe Matt could negotiate with the finance companies for you. He's good at that."

"I'll ask him," Nick said. "I asked him to prepare to file chapter eleven bankruptcy before all this hits the fan. Maybe there's some way we can protect INTECH.

"Oh, Nick. I'm sorry. I wish I could do something. I'll have a check for you this afternoon. That's a start. Nick? Are you all right?"

"Yes, I feel fine."

"You don't look fine. When was your last physical?"

Nick smiled. "Now you sound like Viola. One nag is enough."

"Not if you ignore your health, Nicholas Shrock. Well, how long has it been?"

"You know Viola wouldn't let my checkups lapse. It's only been six months."

"I think you should go in for another one."

"I'm all right, honest," he said, holding up his right hand. "I'm not sleeping too well. This money business is hanging over my head. I'll be relieved to get this bankruptcy over and done. Then maybe I can get on with my life."

"I appreciate you seeing me, Ms. Halstead." Margaret Daley, reporter for *The Business Barometer,* stood in front of Victoria's desk and extended her hand.

How ironic, Victoria thought, that a reporter wanted to interview her about her success, when her career teetered on the edge of disaster. Rising to her feet, Victoria took the proffered hand. The young woman, perhaps in her late twenties, looked thin in a lean sort of way, as if eating took too much time. She wore her thick brown hair pulled back in a neat, thick French braid. Her firm handshake and direct gaze reassured Victoria. The reporter took the seat Victoria indicated.

"Why don't you call me Victoria?"

"All right, Victoria. Your progress has been something of a phenomenon. Why is that?"

Victoria smiled. "I'd love to be able to say I came up with a magic formula that solved all our problems, but the truth is pretty dull. We set some goals, did some organizing, some housekeeping, and instituted a team concept. It's amazing what people can accomplish when they have a common purpose."

"Not much without leadership and vision," Margaret said. "As the new member of the management team, what did you do that they hadn't been doing before?"

"Vision is my long suit. I'm a dreamer. Used to get me in trouble," Victoria said with a laugh. "Thank goodness I learned to focus my imagination. Like art, you have an idea, but creating a picture requires perspective and bringing the elements together on a canvas. Same with business. You get a group together, toss out a vision, brainstorm ideas, set goals, and divvy up the tasks, then you meet back to see how things are going. Each team member is accountable to the others."

Margaret laughed. "My stick figures look like squiggles. I have a feeling the concept sounds easier than the reality. Am I right?"

"Well, there are other factors involved. Inspiration and loyalty—dedication to the purpose. The loyalty already existed. Nicholas Shrock is a wonderful boss. I'm the enabler, so to speak, the bolt that holds the cogs together so the machine can operate smoothly. At first we faltered a little. Like in a three-legged race, it takes time to learn to move together. Once the team masters the rhythm, they do fine. When they win a race, or achieve a goal, they get inspired to move on to larger goals. Success makes a great motivator."

"I've heard you called a 'barracuda.' I expected you to be tough and humorless, but you aren't like that at all. How did you come by that name?"

"Trimming fat off a roast requires a sharp knife. If you want the meat really lean, you have to cut close enough to draw blood. INTECH needed a lot of trimming."

Margaret nodded, a look of sympathy dawning in her eyes. "Playing the bad guy must have been difficult for you."

"More difficult than I can tell you. Without the trust and support I got from Mr. Shrock, I wouldn't have lasted a week."

Her line of questioning took a new tack. "I understand Matsuko of Japan is purchasing INTECH. How does that affect you?"

"Unfortunately," Victoria replied. "That offer has been withdrawn."

"Would that have anything to do with an injunction against INTECH to halt operations at a landfill in El Paso County."

Victoria steepled her hands and considered for a moment. "You've done your homework. I guess the cease order will be public knowledge soon enough. Yes, they pulled out because of the injunction. Are you willing to print my side of this issue?"

Margaret smiled and poised her pen. "This is your article, Victoria. Fire away."

"All right." She gave Margaret a brief history, from Nick's original dream to the current project and the injunction.

"Are the charges valid?"

"No. Quite the opposite, in fact. We studied the environmental impact carefully. The spring water never reaches the creek. Nonetheless, we rerouted the spring, piping the water around the landfill. We even recycle our leachate, using an EPA approved collection and treatment system. An extensive gas migration control system surrounding the entire landfill prevents methane gas from polluting the area. Our process reduces the environmental hazards of municipal waste."

"Would you say that your project improves the environment?"

"Definitely. The process takes waste and produces usable fuel. The energy created will supply the research center. I would like to challenge the environmentalists to take an educated look at our project. I'll provide research documents, test results, impact statements, whatever they want to see."

"Well, that is quite a challenge. Victoria, I think we've got an exciting article here. This information is certainly more than I bargained for. I can't wait to follow up on this project." Margaret closed her notebook, clicked off her recorder, and stood.

The two women shook hands. The reporter had listened with rapt attention, jotting notes as fast as her pen would allow. Victoria knew she had an ally and felt a ray of excitement for the first time in a week.

⚜

Victoria got home late. She didn't recognize the red Camaro parked in the driveway. As she trudged up the stairs to her room, she heard giggling.

"Mandy?" A few seconds later, she flipped on her bedroom light.

"Out here, Mom," she called. Mandy's voice sounded squeaky and shaky.

"Are you in the tub?" Victoria moved to the opened glass door and stepped out onto the shadowed deck.

"Hi, Mom. This is Jase Tanner."

"Mrs. Halstead. Nice to meet you."

Victoria was not pleased to meet this young man. Particularly not in her hot tub, off of her bedroom, with no one else at home. The girls were allowed to use the hot tub any time she wasn't sleeping or wanting to be alone. Sometimes she wished the tub was on the other deck, but other times she loved the privacy it afforded her. "How do you do, Jase. Sorry to interrupt you," she said, "but I'm bushed. If you don't mind?"

"That's all right. We're ready to get out, anyway," Mandy said. Grabbing a towel, she stepped out of the tub and wrapped it around her. Then she held one out to Jase.

As he got out, water sluiced off of him in rivulets. The way he stood and moved reminded Victoria of a bodybuilder, showing off his tightly corded muscles. Glancing at Mandy, Victoria thought she detected a blush, even in the dim light. She hoped his obvious posing embarrassed her daughter. Then he picked up his jeans and put them on over the wet suit. At least the jeans covered him, but somehow, his actions seemed suggestive. Victoria shook her head. Dislike for the young man probably clouded her thoughts.

"I'd better get going," he said. "Got to work in the morning. Thanks for the soak, Amanda, Mrs. Halstead. Those jets felt great after a day of golf."

He went downstairs, and Mandy followed, saying she'd see him out. Victoria got out of her clothes and put on a robe, watching the clock, giving them precisely five minutes.

Mandy had just shut the front door when Victoria came downstairs. One look at her daughter, and she wanted to cry. Guilt colored Mandy's face, yet her stance defied criticism. Where was the little girl who ran to Mommy with every hurt or triumph or new discovery? New feelings shone on Mandy's face, but they excluded her.

Victoria held up the empty beer bottle. "I assume this belonged to Jase?"

"He's twenty-one," she said, as if his age made his actions all right. "He worked in the sun all day. I didn't drink any. I didn't think you'd mind," she said, her chin tilted defiantly.

"I do mind. The no-drinking rule applies to all your friends, no matter how old they are. And Jase Tanner is too old for you."

"It's my fault. He said sweet drinks make you thirstier, but the beer quenched his thirst. I told him he could. He only drank one. No big deal."

"Breaking the rules is a big deal. He shouldn't have asked and put you in that position. Mandy, that young man is way beyond your experience. You're flirting with trouble, and I think you know it."

"I am not a little girl, anymore, Mother. You have to accept that."

"I know that, Honey. You are mature in many ways, and intelligent, and I believe you have good values. Sometimes in our desire to be independent, we get into situations beyond our ability to control. I think Jase Tanner is such a situation. He plays a game with his looks and his youth that isn't very nice. There are stories going around about his liaisons with some of the lonely women at the country club. He isn't the right guy for you."

A mutinous look settled on Mandy's face. "That's a bunch of old biddies with nothing better to do than spread false rumors. Are you having an affair with Cleve Winslow?"

Victoria felt like she'd been slapped. "No! Whatever gave you that idea?"

"Oh, you know . . . stories going around at the country club. Well—isn't that what you're doing? Accusing Jase of something based on rumor. You always taught me not to listen to gossip."

Were there really stories going around about her and Cleve? Still, the rumors about Jase Tanner were a different matter. "Honey, I've seen him flirting with some of the women at the golf course."

"And I've seen you necking with Cleve Winslow."

"Amanda! You saw a kiss. Nothing more. Looks can be deceiving. I had hoped you trusted me." She reached up and rubbed her neck. She knew her opinion of Jase was correct. Mandy could be hurt badly by the worldly young man who wanted far more from a girl than innocent kisses. But Mandy's defensiveness would blind her to the truth.

"I do trust you, Mom. You have to trust me too."

With a lump in her throat, Victoria hugged her daughter. After a few seconds, Mandy's rigid stance softened. "I love you, Mandy. You are beautiful and sensitive and trusting. Someone could easily take advantage of your sweet nature. I don't want that to happen, and I'm afraid you're headed for a serious injury with Jase. I've watched him, and I don't believe he holds the same values you do. All I'm asking is that you go cautiously. Stay with a group and avoid getting into a vulnerable situation. Will you do that?"

"Sure, Mom. I love you. Don't worry about me, okay?"

"Now, that I can't promise. I'm a mother, remember? Worrying about our children is part of our job description."

"You're mistaken about Jase, but I'll be careful."

Mandy was petite and dainty and seemed vulnerable, but Victoria knew her daughter had strength of character and stubborn tenacity. She wanted to hold on and protect her daughters, but that wasn't possible. A tear welled up in her eye. She kissed Mandy's forehead and smoothed back her hair. "I'm very proud of you, you know."

With a squeeze, Mandy returned her love. "I know, Mom."

※

"Mrs. Halstead, this is Edith Smith, director of Mountain Glen Wilderness Camp."

Alarms instantly sounded in Victoria's mind. "Is something wrong with Jessica?"

"No, not physically, anyway. We are having a disciplinary problem with Jessica."

"Disciplinary? Are you sure? Jessica loves camp."

"I know that, Mrs. Halstead, which is why I'm concerned. This is Jessica's third year with us, and she has always been a model camper before."

"What has she done, Mrs. Smith?"

"It isn't any single thing, Mrs. Halstead. She seems determined to break every rule we have, and her actions incite the other campers to do likewise."

"Oh dear." Victoria rubbed her neck. "I'm coming to parents' day on Sunday. I can talk to her then."

"I'm afraid that won't be good enough. May I make a suggestion, Mrs. Halstead?"

"Certainly."

"Perhaps there are problems in the home that might be affecting Jessica. She seems distressed about something, but she refuses to discuss what is bothering her. You might consider family counseling."

A nerve pinched at the base of Victoria's skull, and a headache loomed on the horizon. "Thank you for your concern, Mrs. Smith. What do you want me to do about Jessica?"

"You need to come get her tonight."

"Tonight? That's impossible."

"I'm sorry, Mrs. Halstead, but I must insist."

Looking at her schedule, Victoria started rearranging in her mind. It would take some doing, but she supposed she could manage. "I'll see what I can do," she said.

"I'll expect you this evening. Come to my office. Jessica will be waiting in the infirmary."

"Why the infirmary?"

"It is the only place we can control her."

Victoria's intercom lit up as she hung up the phone. "What is it, Janice?"

"Mr. Halstead on the other line. Do you want to talk to him?"

She sighed. "No, but I will." Talk about poor timing. "Hello Matt. What can I do for you?"

"Victoria, I got a call from Jessica. She sounded hysterical and said she wants me to come get her. She wouldn't say why. Do you have any idea what's going on?"

"I'm beginning to. I just talked to the camp director. I'm going to get Jessica tonight."

"I'll drive. What time shall we go?"

"You don't need to go, Matt."

"Victoria, no arguments. I'm going. Shall I pick you up at work?"

"This is exactly the response she wants, Matt. You're playing right into her hands."

"Come on, Victoria. She's only fourteen years old. She needs our support."

She stared out the window, but the mountain scene gave no inspiration today. "Meet me at my house. Can you be there at five-thirty?"

"Yes. I'll see you then."

Pushing the disconnect, Victoria dialed Cleve's office.

"Hello, beautiful. I was just thinking about you."

"Were you? That's the nicest thing I've heard all day. I have to cancel our dinner tonight. I have to go get Jessica from camp."

"Is something wrong with her?"

Nothing strong discipline wouldn't cure, Victoria thought, but she didn't want to tell Cleve about her daughter's poor behavior. "No. Just a teenage problem that cropped up."

"Do you want me to drive you down to get her?"

"Thanks, Cleve, but Matt is going with me."

"Let him go alone. You don't both have to be there, do you?" She could hear the animosity in Cleve's voice.

"I'm the custodial parent. The director called and asked me to come. Matt is her father. If he wants to spend more time with them, then he needs to be involved in this."

"Can't you see what he's doing? Your ex-husband will keep finding excuses to spend time with you unless you put a stop to this."

Victoria rubbed her neck. This time, Jessica made up the excuse. "I can't refuse to let him go with me."

"Well, I don't like it. Can I see you after you get home?"

"It will be late. The drive down takes over two hours." Her head began pounding in earnest. "I've had a rotten day. I feel like I've been run over by a truck."

"Something else happened? More problems with your Methergy Project?"

"No. In fact, it looks like there isn't going to be a project. That Japanese company I told you made an offer for INTECH, well, they backed out. We don't have a buyer. Nick is sick about it, and I'm worried about his health. I feel so helpless. I just don't know what to do."

"I'm sorry, you're really getting dumped on, aren't you? What can I do to help?"

"Nothing, I'm afraid. Just knowing you care helps me, though. Thanks, Cleve."

"There must be something. Look, I'll think about it and see if I can come up with anything. I'll call you later tonight. Meanwhile, don't worry about INTECH. You just take care of getting Jessica, and put everything else out of your mind."

"Thanks for the pep talk," she said. "I feel better just telling you about it."

NORMALLY, VICTORIA LOVED the drive between Denver and Colorado Springs. Both cities were sprawling toward each other, but the fifty miles distance still held miles of open range land, rolling hills, and mountains stretched unbroken along the western horizon. Even in August, lush grass and a profusion of wildflowers bordered the interstate, thanks to all the rain. That reminded her of the Methergy project. The rain wouldn't hold up construction any more. She crossed her arms and turned towards Matt. "I think this is a ploy to force us together."

Matt stared forward down the Interstate. "Is it such a terrible thing that she wants her family reunited, Victoria?"

"How can you say that to me? *Me,*" she said, pointing at herself. "You all act like I caused our family to break up."

"Believe me, I know I was to blame, and I'm sure the girls remember that fact all too clearly. No one is pointing a finger at you." Matt spoke in his lawyer tone, cajoling and reasoning to sway her. He did it well, she thought, his ploy making her fume.

"That doesn't change the girls' feelings. They want their family back, and so do I. Wouldn't it be worth a try?"

"Because we are being blackmailed by a fourteen year old? I refuse to be railroaded into something I believe is wrong."

His grip tightened on the steering wheel, and a reddish flush tinted his face. "Was our marriage so wrong?"

Victoria started to make a sharp retort when she sensed hurt, not anger beneath his question. The revelation hushed her for a moment. "Don't put words in my mouth, Matt." She leaned back and closed her eyes.

He drove for a few miles in silence, then took a freeway exit and pulled into a parking lot. Shutting off the engine, he turned to face her.

She sat up straight, staring forward. The sudden absence of noise sounded like the calm before disaster.

"Victoria, please look at me." His voice, usually so controlled, had a quiver that made her turn toward him. The directness of his gaze made her uncomfortable, but the earnest way his eyes implored her to listen held her attention. He cleared his throat.

"Victoria, will you marry me?"

His proposal came out of left field, almost knocking her flat. She said the first thing that popped into her mind. "I'm not pregnant."

※

Matt clenched his hands. He didn't try to touch her, but he wanted to shake her until she believed he loved her. Of all the answers he'd imagined, he'd never thought she'd dredge that up. Twenty-four years. How could he overcome a doubt so deeply ingrained? Her response held bitterness. She had said she forgave him, but obviously she hadn't resolved her feelings. He couldn't blame her, but her bitterness sure didn't help his case.

"So this time there wouldn't be any questions of motive. Victoria, I love you. I loved you when we got married. Your pregnancy might have pushed the date up, but only until I could support a wife. I could never convince you of that. I didn't know how. Still don't. You worked so hard to make the marriage succeed, you never relaxed long enough to see how much I cared."

"I don't want to hear this, Matt. It has nothing to do with now."

"It has everything to do with now. If you could understand, maybe you'd believe me."

"I believe you were doing your duty. Isn't that right?"

"Duty?" He let out a short laugh. "What was my duty? To leave you and the girls? Hardly. I felt sorry for myself and ran away from duty. To say I was having a mid-life crisis sounds like a shabby excuse, but it's true. I lost my mind for awhile."

"And now you have your mind back, so I should just ignore the lapse?"

"No. But I want you to understand—I didn't leave because of you. I had everything, you and the girls, a beautiful home, a good job. There was no reason for me to be unhappy. I was unhappy with me. I'd lived half my life, and I hadn't accomplished anything that mattered. No one needed me. If I'd disappeared, no one would have missed me—at least not for long."

"That's not true."

"True or not, I felt worthless. The Boston job seemed like my chance to prove myself. I didn't realize I'd never find the answer to my unhappiness in a job or a place."

"Or a woman? What about Melissa?"

"Melissa? I did not leave because of her, but she certainly complicated the situation. I was an old fool, and I made a terrible mistake. I betrayed you, and I know an apology isn't enough, but I'm sorry. I never loved Melissa. . . . "

"Oh, that's great." She shook her head. Her bitterness rose like bile in her throat. "You had an affair with a woman ten years younger than you, and you didn't even love her? What kind of monster are you?"

"Please, Victoria, listen." He closed his eyes as he forked his hands through his hair. *Help me here, Lord. I'm not doing this right.*

"I deserve that. No, I didn't love her. And that's just one more of my sins. She turned to me for help. Her car would break down. Her sink would get plugged. She needed advice on investments. I was flattered. One day she asked for a ride home because her car was in the garage. When we got there, she asked if I'd help her put up a curtain rod. I didn't have a thought in my head about her sexually—honest. She got up on a step stool and accidentally tripped. I tried to catch her, and we both fell over. We ended up in an intimate position and she, well . . . I lost it. I swear, I never touched her again, in fact, I never was alone with her from that moment until she hit me with her announcement."

"She was pregnant," Victoria supplied. "Must have been like reliving your worst nightmare."

"Yes, it was. She asked me to help her get an abortion. I couldn't let her do that. I had accepted the Boston job. You didn't want to come. You and the girls didn't need me, but I believed she and the child needed me."

"Believed? Didn't they?"

"Hardly. One day her old boyfriend showed up claiming he was the baby's father. Melissa admitted she had seduced me to get a father for her child. I was an easy mark. I'm not blaming her. I made a lot of bad choices. I could have walked away."

"What if you had refused to leave your family?"

"She figured I'd take care of her financially. She was right. I would have, one way or another."

Leaning her head back against the headrest, Victoria closed her eyes. No emotion showed on her face. She sat so still, Matt didn't know what to think. He reached for her hand. She moved it away from him. When she opened her eyes, she looked forward, out the windshield. Her shoulders slumped, her eyes had a sheen. She looked controlled, but resigned.

"That's a really sad story, Matt, and maybe I understand a little better, but it doesn't change anything. Duty and responsibility are everything to you. My pregnancy, that woman's pregnancy—next time it'll be something else. Whatever, if a need arises, you'll be honor-bound to respond."

"I won't deny that duty is important to me, but that's not the end of the story. After the divorce, when you wouldn't even talk to me, nothing mattered. I'd lost my family, my self-respect—everything important in my life due to my own disastrous choices. For about two years, I just existed. Did my job, put in a lot of overtime, and felt sorry for myself. My life had no value.

"One Saturday morning in December, there'd been a big snowstorm, so I took a cab to my office. We got involved in a big pile-up. Must have been fifteen vehicles. No one got hurt, but traffic came to a standstill, so I got out and started walking. I hadn't considered the chill factor." He laughed, remembering.

"The storm was what they call a nor'easter. The wind cuts right through your bones with a damp chill that's colder than anything I've ever experienced. As I walked by a church, blowing on my hands, I heard Christmas music coming from inside. A man took my arm and asked me where I was going. I told him and he said, 'Mister, you'll freeze before you get there. Come inside and get warm.' I didn't realize the significance of that until later. He said he had to finish leading the practice for the children's Christmas program, then he'd drop me off at my office.

"I started to say no, but he had the jolliest smile. Looked just like Santa Claus, white hair and beard and all. I asked him if the beard was real, and he just laughed. Anyway, I was so cold, I figured anything beat being outside, so I went in. Someone handed me a cup of hot apple cider. As I waited in the last pew, the heat from the cup warmed my hands, the hot drink warmed my stomach. I watched those children re-enact the nativity."

Matt grinned as the image came to him. "Crooked halos and wings askew, those sweet voices, off key, but so confident and trusting. . . . " Remembered mercy filled him, and he had to stop speaking. He took several deep breaths. Sharing his testimony was harder than he'd expected. As a lawyer, his livelihood depended upon sworn testimony. Today, he realized, was the only case that had ever truly mattered.

Dear God, please don't let me blow this.

"The children sang *Jesus Loves Me*. Suddenly, I realized that my sin hid me from God's light. I was cold and miserable inside out, but Jesus loved me anyway. He sent me an invitation and asked me inside. I accepted Jesus right there in that church, and He forgave me for all the things I've done against Him. Victoria, I want your forgiveness, too, and I want to make up for all the things I've done that hurt you."

Her eyes smarting, Victoria fought off the aching sadness Matt's story wrung out of her. For the first time since he'd left, she felt truly sorry for him. His turmoil, his guilt weren't so different from what she'd experienced when she lost their child. She even understood the comfort he'd found in church. She hoped he would not be disillusioned, as she had been, but he'd set himself up for disappointment if he believed Jesus would bring them back together. Matt had paid a heavy price for his folly. Although his confession and dredging up all those old memories hurt, Victoria felt a measure of release. Thinking he'd fallen in love with another woman, when she knew he didn't love her, had cut deep. She hadn't wanted to face her own failure. Matt reached for her, but she pushed him away.

"You don't need to be noble, Matt, and you can't make up for those years. I'm glad you didn't love her. I felt like such a failure."

"No, never that. You must have hated me," Matt said, incredible sadness in his voice. She stared forward, sitting rigidly, knowing she'd break down if she looked at him.

"Yes, for a time. But I had Amanda and Jessica, and I could never regret that. You gave me my children. How could I hate you? No, I just felt sorry for so many wasted years."

"They don't have to be wasted. We can start over, only with God in our marriage this time."

"God didn't help us before. He didn't help when I prayed for you to come back. Going to church didn't help. Our marriage still fell apart."

"None of that was because of God, Victoria. We never included God in our marriage. You went to church because it fulfilled a need in you. I had an excuse, because I always had work to do, but you and the girls represented me, and I attended on the holidays and felt that covered my duty. We were wrong. We went for ourselves, not because we wanted to be in God's house. And we never invited Him into our house."

"That's not true, Matt. I went to church faithfully. I worked hard to serve God. Maybe not hard enough, though."

"Tori, God doesn't want you to work for Him. He doesn't need anything from us. He *is* everything. But He wants our love. He gave us his Son, Jesus Christ, because He loves us so much. He just wants us to accept Jesus and love Him back."

"I did love Him, Matt. Look, I'm really glad for you, for your success and your newfound faith. I don't really understand the way you feel so close to God. I think that must be for certain people who need to have such a strength to rely on. For me, God's answer seems to be the opposite. God left me to stand on my own two feet and be strong. Maybe that *was* the answer to my prayers back then. I don't know, but I have a new life, and I'm happy in it. We both have to go forward where we are."

"We can move forward together, Tori. Spend time together as a family, like we did on the Fourth of July weekend. We could go out, just the two of us and get to know each other all over again. No promises. No pressure."

"No." She turned to face him. "I feel like the whole world is ganging up on me. Even Mrs. Smith suggested we get family counseling."

"I think she's right. Counseling would help all of us."

"All because Jessica decided to rebel? I'm not buying this, Matt."

"Come on, Victoria, what would we lose by trying? I love you, and I know you loved me once. Real love doesn't die. We just need to rekindle it. We could make it right again. Please, Tori, say yes."

No! no! no! she wanted to scream, and she wished he'd stop calling her by that name. The nickname only he had used conjured bittersweet memories of lost tenderness and intimacy that still made her ache with longing. She backed against the car door as far as she could and wrapped her arms protectively across her chest. Did he think she was crazy? She would never open herself to that pain again. Besides, Cleve had entered the picture, and that thought soothed her fear. She pulled his image to the front of her mind and imagined him on the seat in between them. Cleve was safe. She didn't know why, but it didn't matter.

"Cleve asked me to marry him."

"No! You're not considering marrying him, are you?" His eyes shone with pain. She hadn't meant to blurt it out.

"I'm not considering marrying anyone, Matt. But he makes me feel young and alive like I haven't felt in a long, long time, and it feels good."

"Oh, Lord." Matt covered his face with his hands and slowly rubbed his hands back as if to obliterate something on his skin. He looked at her. "Victoria, you *are* young and alive, but not because of Cleve Winslow. That kind of feeling won't last."

Anger flared, overriding the wrenching emotions his confession and plea had stirred. "You have no idea what I feel or why, so don't give me your sanctimonious baloney!" She turned away from him. Her fury drained away, but the pain inside her burned deeper, gnawing a hole in the pit of her stomach. Tears threatened, for no reason. She was tired. The burdens just kept piling higher, burying her alive. Jessica just added one more shovelful of dirt. Leaning her head back, Victoria closed her eyes and held her silence. Matt started the car and pulled back onto the interstate. They remained silent the rest of the way to the camp.

The confrontation with Mrs. Smith was brief and unpleasant. The director sympathized with her traumatized camper, but rules were rules, and she couldn't allow Jessica to disrupt the camp.

Jessica apologized to the director and to her parents and sat in the back seat sniffling and weeping in noisy silence all the way home. The ride went on forever. At home, Matt instructed Jessica to go to her room while he talked to her mother. She went off with her head hung in abject misery.

"Let me take her home with me," he said after they heard her door shut.

"No, Matt. This is my responsibility."

"Victoria, I can't make up for the hurt I've caused you all, but I can share some of the burden. You have more on your plate right now than you can handle. Please, let me help. I promise I won't indulge her."

"What would you do with her?"

"If you'll let me, I'll put her to work in our archives. They are reor-ganizing our filing system, and I'm sure they could use the help. Maybe work would keep her out of trouble and give her something else to think about."

Why not? she asked herself. The blame could certainly be traced back to him. Let him fix the mess he created.

"For how long?"

"As long as you need. Until school starts, at least."

Tired and defeated, she gave in. "All right. I could use some rest. And I have a mess to face tomorrow with all the appointments and work I can-celed today. I'll tell her."

"Let me."

Matt went to Jessica's room and helped her pack. She filled up a couple of boxes with books and tapes and paraphernalia necessary to a teenage girl. As Matt carted it upstairs, Victoria watched.

"Goodness. You're not moving out for good, you know," she said to Jessica.

"I'm not taking *everything*. Only what I absolutely *have* to have."

"Jessica, you behave for your father. Don't give him any trouble."

"Yeah, sure, Mom. I'm not a child, you know."

"No, I don't know. Most six year olds behave better than you did this week. Good-bye, Jessica."

"'Bye, Mom. Don't worry." Jessica gave Victoria a hug, then got in Matt's car and slammed the door.

"You don't have to slam the door, Jessica," Matt said. He started the car and drove off.

"Sorry. Boy, Mom's really ticked off, isn't she? Like I'm the one screw-ing up her life."

"Don't be crude, Jessica. I won't tolerate gutter language or snide remarks about your mother. She is very upset, and so am I."

The teenager suddenly crumbled into a small girl sitting beside him in the car. Her voice trembled with distress. "I'm sorry, Daddy. What are you going to do?"

Matt glanced sideways at his daughter. Tears spilled down her cheeks. Was this another ploy? She seemed genuinely distraught, but Jessica often resorted to theatrics. What did he know of teenage girls? He didn't understand women, period. Feeling as though he had jumped into very deep water, he issued a quick prayer for divine guidance and wondered how anyone raised children without the Lord's help. He hated to see her so upset, but thought it was too soon to sympathize.

"I'm not going to *do* anything. You will stay with me for the remainder of the summer and work for the firm. No doubt you'll be bored, and you won't have time to visit your friends, but you'll be where I can keep an eye on you."

"Oh, I wouldn't be bored, but you don't have to do that, Dad. I can stay at the loft. I won't get into any trouble."

"I'd like to believe that, but trusting you is a little hard to do right now. I don't understand what got into you. In fact, your whole attitude lately has been out of character. Tell me what's bothering you, Sweetheart? Maybe I can help."

Slumping down in the seat, Jessica crossed her arms. "You can't help. That's the whole problem. I think I screwed up royal."

"That seems likely, but what exactly did you 'screw' up?"

"You and Mom," she admitted. "I wanted to get you together." She sighed loudly. "My plan didn't work like it was supposed to."

"It certainly didn't." *Now what, Dad?* he wondered. As screw-ups went, he was the king. Poor Jessica only tried to help him correct his own mistakes.

"Honey, when I moved away, I hurt you, and I hurt your mother very badly. I betrayed your trust, and I cannot have that trust back until I prove myself trustworthy. Do you see? There isn't anything you can to do help that along. I have to do it myself."

A sad sniff acknowledged his words, and a meek voice answered. "I betrayed Mom's trust, too, didn't I?"

"I'm afraid so. I know your motives were good, but you hurt her." He smiled at his youngest daughter. "We both have to prove that she can trust us."

"All I want is for us to be happy again," Jessica said. "Mom loves you, she told me so. She said that wasn't enough, that you were going different directions. You just need to get your directions going the same way."

"And you thought you could make that happen by getting in trouble?"

"Yeah. It didn't work."

The dejection in her voice caused a lump in his throat. Would there never be an end to the pain he had caused? No one understood consequences better than he did. Matt pulled into a fast food parking lot and shut off the engine. He turned to Jessica.

"Sweetheart, when we go our own direction, we get in trouble. The only way we can get our priorities right is to go the direction the Lord wants us to go."

"I know that, Daddy. I learned about trusting God in Sunday school."

"Do you understand it, Jessica?

"Yes. I accepted Jesus last year at camp. I knew I was doing wrong, but God wouldn't answer my prayers, so I had to do something."

Matt hung his head. He'd been feeling the same way. Desperate. His prayers hadn't been answered either. He didn't want to acknowledge that the answer might be no. Jessica's innocent admission made him realize he was trying to manipulate the outcome too. *Forgive me, Lord.*

"Jessica, sometimes God doesn't seem to be listening, but He always hears us and answers us. We have to keep praying and trusting. The Bible says God works all things for our good if we love Him. See, we must be faithful and patient."

"But what if He doesn't fix it?"

"Much as we'd like him to, God isn't in the business of fixing our mistakes. When we do something wrong, we still suffer the consequences, even though He forgives us. I sinned against your mother and you and Mandy, and against God. I asked Jesus to forgive me, and He did. I never asked . . . Jessica, will you forgive me?"

"I already did, Daddy. I love you."

Swallowing a tear, Matt hugged his daughter close and held her tight. "Thank you, Sweetheart. I love you very much. Honey, you need to accept the fact that your mother and I won't be getting back together. We both love you, though, and that won't ever change."

"I know. Mom said that too." She looked at him hopefully. "You want to marry Mom again, don't you."

"Yes. But that won't make it happen."

"Mom told me love wasn't enough. You have to want something to make it work. You already want to marry Mom. All we have to do is make Mom want to marry you too."

"Jessica," Matt said, warning in his tone. "Your mother is going to keep seeing Mr. Winslow. You have to accept that."

"I'll never accept him," she vowed. "I hate him."

"Jessica. Jesus loves everyone. You don't like Mr. Winslow because he is in the way of what you want. That isn't his fault. If you hate someone, you get sick inside. Hate puts a barrier between you and the Lord. Let Jesus take care of this, okay? Promise me you won't *do* anything. You would only make things worse. Apologize to your mother for your behavior and try not to give her any more reason to worry about you. All right?"

"All right." But she didn't look happy about it.

"I missed you tonight."

Victoria plopped down on her bed and leaned back on the pillows stacked against the headboard, propping the cordless phone receiver against her ear. "Hi. I missed you too. I also missed dinner. We grabbed a hamburger at a drive-through fast food place. I don't even know which one. Shows you how upset I was. I ended up with a stomachache."

"That's too bad. Maybe we can make up for it tomorrow night. Did you bring Jessica home?"

"She's with Matt. Bless him, he offered to have Jessica stay with him until school starts in three weeks. He's going to put her to work in their file room."

"Good. Sounds like she needs to be kept busy. Victoria, I spent all evening thinking about your company's problems. I'm sorry, but I didn't come up with anything helpful. You need someone to come in with a lot of money, someone who isn't afraid of a fight. Getting past that environmental business will take aggressive action."

The ideas that had been bouncing around in her head began to coalesce. Obviously Cleve hadn't seen the solution yet, but her plan made sense, it was logical.

"An inspiration just hit me."

"What's that?"

"I can't tell you over the phone," she said, excitement beginning to stimulate her nerves. "I need to see you. I wish we could talk tonight."

"Now you've got me curious. I could come over."

"No. Can you meet me for breakfast?"

"I have an early appointment. Can we make it six o'clock?"

"Yes, that'll work fine." Victoria named a restaurant that specialized in breakfast, and they said goodnight. It was well after midnight the last time she looked at the clock. She was too keyed up to sleep. Cleve had to see the possibilities—he just had to.

"This restaurant can't match Manny's home cooking, but it's quieter. This place sees a lot of business deals," Victoria said when they were seated. The casual decor fit the crowd of men and women in conservative attire.

"So, tell me what got you so excited last night. I gather you weren't having salacious thoughts about my person."

His comment startled a laugh out of her. "Not exactly." She wondered how best to approach her subject. Mentally crossing her fingers, she plowed ahead.

"I was thinking about your natural gas spigot. It's a fabulous idea, but it needs to be UL tested and market tested—there's so much to do. You need to put the spigot in the hands of a project team, at a research facility like what we're building at the Black Forest Complex."

"I agree, but I thought you stopped the project."

"Oh, we did, temporarily. I believe we can refute the charges. They're ungrounded, but disproving them will take some time and effort."

"Fighting the charges could take months, maybe years."

"You're involved in the oil industry, haven't you ever had to deal with environmentalists and the EPA?"

"Many times. You might say I've become an expert," he said smiling with wry humor. "I'm beginning to feel like one of your prospective customers. You're leading me right down a path. I just haven't figured out where we're going. Care to clue me in?"

Taking a deep breath, she dropped her bombshell. "INTECH has the potential to net millions, but it needs capital and it needs leadership that isn't afraid to dig in and do the job. It needs you, Cleve. *And* it fits right into your operations."

"I don't know anything about commercial real estate development. I'd probably make things worse."

"No you wouldn't." She leaned forward to emphasize her point. "We have a full staff of experts. The corporate leadership needs to have vision and the guts to take chances, and you qualify for both. And I'd help you."

His brow furrowed. "Saving the company would take a great deal of money. You already told me it will take a fortune to bail out the Black Forest debt. I don't know if I could offer enough to make it worthwhile for Nick Shrock to sell."

She could see the wheels turning behind his thoughtful expression. The prospect intrigued him. That was half the battle. Cleve loved a challenge. He couldn't resist.

"Why don't you take a look and see what you think?" she suggested.

He stared at her a moment, mulling it over. Then he leaned forward and smiled. "Why not? If you agree to stay on as executive—we'll make you president—I think we could do it. But don't get excited yet," he warned, holding up his hand. "I'll look at the figures and see what's required to make a buyout work. Can you put together a portfolio for me?"

"I'll fax you copies of all the reports we sent Matsuko. Cleve, you do realize we don't have much time to put this together. Nick is in a bind, and he needs to sell immediately."

He took hold of her hands. "Honey, I know this means a lot to you, and I'll do my best. Don't be disappointed if I can't pull off a miracle, though, okay?"

"You'll do it, I know you will. I'm so excited, Cleve. I just know this is going to work out."

"I'm glad you have such faith in me, but keep a lid on this. Don't get Nick's hopes up until we know we can do it."

"You're right, I'll keep quiet. Oh, Cleve, I can't tell you how much this means to me."

He reached across the table and squeezed her hand. "You don't have to. I'd do anything for you, Love."

CLEVE ASKED VICTORIA to come to his office the next morning. He and his financial team had worked all afternoon and evening and had come up with an offer. He wanted her to see the proposal before he approached Nick. Victoria made excuses to miss an advertising presentation and hurried out to Winslow International.

Two men were in Cleve's office with him, Jeffrey Lassiter, whom she knew, and Charles Dougherty, Winslow International's legal advisor. After introductions, they sat at one end of a massive conference table and Charles gave each of them a binder.

Cleve began the meeting. This morning, she saw the full impact of his keen business demeanor. Watching him, Victoria thought she would be thoroughly intimidated by the man and the surroundings if she didn't know him. INTECH's boardroom was nicely furnished, but much less imposing, and Nick's natural enthusiasm gave their meetings a more relaxed tone.

"After studying your documentation, we agree INTECH has potential, but the risks are high. Our offer reflects that. Charles drew up this offer, so he will explain its contents."

"Thank you, Cleve. Now, Ms. Halstead, as there's some urgency involved here, we factored in expediency as well as financial consideration. For that reason, though not necessarily in our best interests, we are offering to purchase Nicholas Shrock's stock, one hundred percent, instead of buying the assets of the company. I'm certain you can see the value in exercising that option."

Victoria nodded. The transaction would go easier for Nick, and the actual sale could close almost immediately.

"By making that concession, we must look at the extensive debts involved." Charles went page by page through the structure of the offer.

Victoria was amazed they'd put together such an extensive document in so little time. "Do you understand?" he asked when he concluded.

"I believe so. The document is well thought out," she said, thinking that INTECH would be in smart hands with these people.

"Good. Now, given the liabilities involved, we have determined our offer of four-and-a-half million dollars to be a fair price."

Her heart sank like a stone. Tensing to keep her body still, Victoria forced herself to remain calm. The offer, she quickly calculated, would leave Nick destitute. Cleve knew Nick's situation, how could he do this?

She reminded herself that she had suggested the buyout. Cleve's offer involved taking a big risk, and he accepted the challenge for her.

"Thank you, gentlemen," Cleve said. "I think that will be all for now."

The two men shook hands with Victoria and left. Cleve sat down across from her and looked at her until she returned his gaze.

"I knew you wouldn't like the terms," he said.

She smiled sadly. "You've put a lot of time and thought into your offer, and I appreciate it. I know you did this for me, and I can't fault you if it doesn't work."

"All right, let's talk about the offer. What would it take to make it acceptable?"

"A million dollars, perhaps," she said. Fingering her hair back away from her face, she sighed in frustration. "As it is, Nick will have to sell his property to pay off his debt." The hope she'd been clinging to was fraying away. Only threads remained.

"I wish I could give Nick more, but increasing the purchase price isn't feasible. As a businessman, he knew the risks when he took on the Black Forest Project to start with. In essence, he borrowed fifty-two million dollars. The fact that you've cut that debt in half is impressive and reassures me that the debt can be handled over time, but the fact is, Nick lost his fortune to a dream. Look at what I'm buying. The land and project are submerged under an ocean of debt. A new project comes along which might provide enough ballast to raise it to the surface using grants and government funding. That looks great, until Green Peace comes along and says you can't float the ship because it'll pollute the water and poison the whales. Uncle Sam withdraws the ballast, and you sink to the bottom. Now what?"

"But the charges aren't true," she protested. "We aren't polluting anything, in fact we're cleaning up."

"*You* know that, but how do you convince them?"

"We have to fight the injunction," she said, her frustration and anger building.

"Going to court will take a lot of time and probably millions of dollars. I can't fight for the project if I don't own INTECH, and I can't afford to pay more and still have the money to fight the legal battles."

The last thread snapped. Victoria got to her feet and walked over to look out at the golf course. Swallowing the disappointment and frustration that clogged her throat, she fought for control. Many times she'd overcome strong emotions during tough meetings. Emotions were her biggest weakness. She needed to regain her composure before she ruined this negotiation and Cleve's respect. When he came over and put his arm around her shoulder, she knew he meant to comfort her, but his sympathy threatened to defeat her instead. She stepped aside.

"Nick means a great deal to you, doesn't he?"

Wordlessly, she held his gaze. He already knew how she felt about Nick. First she would listen. Then she could figure out how to counter.

"Give me his specifics," Cleve said, turning her ploy back onto her. "Let's figure what he has to work with."

"He's had his property appraised. If he sells his house in Denver and one he owns in Southern California, plus your four-and-a-half million dollars, he's several hundred thousand shy of paying off his debts. He still needs a place to live and an income."

"Does he have a pension or retirement fund?"

"He cashed in his profit sharing plan to invest in the project. What he's built up in the past eight years amounts to peanuts. He owns a small property in Sedalia where he hopes to build a house."

"Social security?"

"Yes, but not enough to pay off the remaining debt and support him." She balled her fists as the frustration bubbled up. "This isn't right! I know business is a risk, but Nick's going to lose everything. I can't let that happen." She walked over to the table and retrieved her purse. "I'm sorry I took up so much of your time, Cleve, and I appreciate your trying to help, but your offer won't work. I'll have to find another way."

"Be reasonable, Victoria. You're emotionally involved in this. Look at this logically. Wouldn't something, no matter how small, be better for Nick than losing everything, including the company and his piece of land?"

That stung, but he had a point. Reasonable or not, she couldn't accept Nick's ruin, nor could she let her emotional involvement lose Nick's last chance. Turning to Cleve, she tilted her head back and looked up at him. "Raise your offer to five million. That's a small concession compared to the overall package. Yes, you'll be taking a risk. You run a high-risk business, and this one will be worth every dime. I personally guarantee it. That's the terms. Take it or leave it."

"You drive a hard bargain, my dear." He chuckled. "But then I knew you would. All right. For you, I'll change it to five million." He leaned down and kissed her. "You do realize, this offer isn't formal yet. My board of directors must approve the purchase." His expression, as he gazed down at her, held sympathy, but little encouragement. Again, her hopes fell.

"Of course, we could get married." He spoke so seriously, she realized he meant every word. She started to say no, but he continued right on. "Hear me out. You would work for me, not INTECH, after the buy-out. You'll be in charge of the merger and the continued operations. We sell the proposal to the board as a package deal with you, my partner, at the helm. They'll approve the terms."

"I can't . . . "

"Sure you can. My proposal is the perfect solution."

"Cleve! That wouldn't be fair to you."

His face gave no indication that her words bothered him or offended him. "I'm not asking for fair," he said. "I'm asking for your partnership and loyalty in marriage."

He watched her patiently as he waited for her response. She felt threatened, which made no sense. He'd asked her before, so his intent was no surprise. He hadn't mentioned love, which was just as well. Loyalty, she could give. In exchange, Cleve would save Nick and INTECH and the Black Forest Project for her. He was giving everything. All he asked was her commitment to him. They were compatible. They respected each other. Without risking her heart, she stood to gain everything. How could she not? As she contemplated her answer, he smiled down at her and reached into his pocket.

"Luckily, I'd already gotten this. Otherwise I might have had to be more conservative." He handed her a small jeweler's box.

Wide-eyed, she stared at the gold box. "Go on, take it," he encouraged.

Accepting the box meant accepting him and the marriage. Making rash decisions went against her character, and she felt the sudden panic and the compelling pull to step off the edge of her world. Her hand trembled as she reached out. He took a hold of her hand. With a sinking heart she recognized the victory in his smile, but she also felt the security of his grip.

"You'd better let me," he said. "You might drop it." Opening the box, he took out a ring with a solitary large emerald set on an intricate rope of yellow and white gold. He slipped the ring on her left hand, then kissed her hand.

"It's beautiful," she said in a hushed voice. "I've never seen anything like it."

"I designed the ring for you. I didn't want to give you something ordinary."

She looked into his eyes and felt her world tilt. "I can't believe this is all happening to me. Thank you, Cleve, for the ring, and for buying INTECH."

He ran the back of his fingers along her cheek, then kissed her lightly. "Consider INTECH an engagement present. I do want my bride to be happy."

She couldn't speak, so she nodded and smiled. She wanted to be happy. Saving Nick would make her happy. And she would make Cleve's happiness her business from now on.

Cleve let Victoria take the offer to Nick. She went straight to his office when she got back to work. Sailing right past his secretary, she rushed into Nick's office.

Nick looked up, startled. "I didn't hear Viola."

"That's because I didn't give her a chance," Victoria said. "This is too important to wait. I have the answer to our problems," Victoria said, waving the offer. She set the document in front of him. "This is a stock-buyout offer for INTECH. It takes over all the company's liabilities." She should have felt triumphant at Nick's stunned look. Instead, she felt the need to apologize.

"Now Nick, the offer isn't big, not as much as I'd hoped, but you will be able to pay off your debts and have enough to build your house. There won't be much left over. Enough, I think, to play gentleman rancher— not on a grand scale, but enough to keep busy."

"How . . . who?" he stammered.

"Winslow International. Cleve is working on natural gas development, and he got excited when I showed him our Methergy Plant."

"Winslow? I never thought . . . " Nick stared at the document Victoria had placed on his desk. " How much?" he asked.

She took a fortifying breath. "Five million." When Nick's face fell, she hastened to explain. "Nick, I wish I could have come to you with a nice, big offer, but that crazy injunction destroyed the asset aspect of the Black Forest property, leaving us nothing but a liability. If we had enough time and money, we could fight it, but I don't see how that's possible, now. At least this will cover your notes and keep you from having to file bankruptcy."

"Victoria, don't blame yourself. You've done everything in your power to save an old man from his own folly. I've been taking my own advice and praying for a solution. It seems the Lord has supplied my needs once again, and, thanks to you, I'll at least come out of this with my hide intact."

A sense of unease swept through Victoria. She had bargained and begged for this deal. Jesus had nothing to do with the deal. Of course, her ability to negotiate was a God-given talent, so why did she feel this bleak emptiness? "I haven't done anything, Nick. I keep thinking there should be something more I could do, but I just can't think what."

"No. You have accomplished amazing things, but there are limitations that even you cannot overcome. My folly caught up with me. I consider myself fortunate to be spared the nightmare of bankruptcy. I've seen good men go through it, and the financial ruin and the shame dragged them down, left them without hope. Some of them managed to start over, but I'm too old for that. And tired."

"I'm afraid this isn't going to give you much to live on, Nick."

"What would I do with a bunch of money? Pay taxes? No, I'll get along just fine; don't you worry about me. Let's get this thing done so I can go gold panning again. My last attempt got cut short so I could go see one of my favorite people get some award or other," he said with a twinkle in his eye.

"Do you want me to have Matt look this over?" she asked, dreading the task. Matt wouldn't like it, she was certain.

"I'll send it over. He'll want to meet with us later, I imagine, but let's let him get used to the offer before he has to look at that ring on your finger."

"Oh." She jerked her hand behind her back, laughed, and extended it so he could see the ring.

He chuckled. "Would have been hard to miss. Thing sparkles like a supernova on a moonless night. You really love him, Victoria?"

"Of course," she lied, hoping her expression wouldn't give her away. Nick would refuse the offer if he thought she was part of the bargain. And she wasn't. Not really. Cleve had asked her before. She'd known he would ask again. He just offered an added incentive.

"I wouldn't want you making any grand gestures to save a stupid old man." At her quick denial, he said, "Don't think I don't realize Winslow's offer comes because of you. What would he want with a bankrupt real estate development company? The man is swimming in oil."

"I told you, he's interested in the Methergy project, and he's developing a home natural gas tap, so they'll have their own use for the research center."

"Well, I'm glad to hear that. Nice to know my dream has value to someone."

When Matt's secretary called to set up a meeting for the next morning, Victoria had an overwhelming urge to say no. Facing Matt and defending Cleve's offer promised to be a nightmare. Revealing her engagement would be worse. His distress, when she'd told him about Cleve's first proposal, had bothered her as much as the girls' antagonism.

But she had to go, for Nick's sake. She had instigated and negotiated the offer, and Matt was going to tear it apart. Victoria wasn't thrilled with the terms either, but no one, including Matt, had found a better alternative. In fact, there was no alternative, except bankruptcy. So,

Matt would be displeased. Her need for Matt's approval had to stop, once and for all. Cleve would never allow any hint of Matt's influence to shadow their lives, and Cleve's happiness had to be her top priority.

Matt noticed the ring as soon as Victoria and Nick entered his office. She saw him glance at her hand, raise his eyebrows, and then set his expression into a polite mask. He never said a word to indicate his displeasure or to even acknowledge the ring's existence, but a wall as tangible as granite suddenly loomed between them. His gaze never met hers. He never came close enough to touch her. He never directed a question to her. Unreasonably, his rebuff stung.

Charles Dougherty came on Cleve's behalf, as Cleve had felt his presence would antagonize Matt, and he'd probably been right. Judging by Matt's frown every time he looked in her direction, her presence wasn't helping much. Charles took several documents from his briefcase. "Earnest money," he said, holding out a check, which Matt took, gave a glance, and set the check on his desk. "And copies of the contract," Charles said, handing one to each of them.

"As you can see," Charles continued, "the cover page pretty much details the offer. A simple stock purchase contract. Ms. Halstead provided the documents to verify the company's assets and liabilities. Mr. Winslow and his accountants have studied a recent audit, and they're satisfied with the results of that report."

At the mention of the audit, Matt's nostrils flared slightly. Victoria doubted anyone else noticed, but she'd seen that indication of his displeasure before. His reaction angered her. So what if he took part in the audit. They investigated the company's finances on Nick's behalf, to be used to procure a buyer. That's exactly what she had done with the audit results.

"This check is drawn on Cleveland Winslow's personal account—a temporary check, at that."

"Mr. Winslow just moved to Colorado and opened that account. The check is covered, I assure you."

"Ten thousand dollars earnest money is inadequate, in my opinion," Matt said. "And if Mr. Winslow's assets are in transition, then we want guaranteed funds."

"The check is a formality to seal the agreement, nothing more," Charles explained. "The amount is immaterial. The bank-issued check is legal tender. You can verify funds."

"We will," Matt said. *"If* we accept the offer."

Victoria recognized the implied insult, and Charles's rigid jaw indicated he took Matt's comment that way too. Was Matt trying to detonate a bomb and blow up the offer?

"These terms call for no down, two million at closing with the balance payable in increments of one third per year for three years at seven percent."

Victoria followed on her copy of the contract as Matt read it out loud. Nick needed the money now. Cleve understood Nick's predicament, so why did the contract call for Nick to carry a note? The clause must be a mistake. As she thought about their meeting, she realized the offer omitted the method of payment. Perhaps Cleve's lawyer had drawn up the contract without checking with him. Of course specifying payoff installments gave the buyer a measure of security. Charles had to look out for his client's interests. Under normal circumstances, she would do the same, and so would Matt.

"Also," Matt continued, "according to this document, Winslow, and not the corporation, is purchasing the stock, yet I find no provision to guarantee the note or the company's debts. Since he's buying stock, and not assets, we need a personal guarantee, with collateral, from Mr. Winslow."

"That is not an option," Charles said. "Mr. Winslow never personally guarantees debt. He doesn't need to. His credit is sterling."

"Nevertheless," Matt replied, "I want a clause to that effect in the contract."

"My client will never sign such terms."

Matt considered each of them in turn. After a minute, he closed the contract.

"I'll contact you when we are ready to meet again, Charles."

Everyone stood, and shook hands with Charles. After he left, Matt turned to Nick, his pose excluding Victoria.

"This contract," Matt said, slapping the document with the back of his hand, "won't save you from bankruptcy. Winslow's a vulture who thinks he's spotted crippled game, and he's circling to feast on the carcass. If you want, we can counter, of course, but you might come out better in bankruptcy—especially if we can get reorganization. This contract might save the company, but it would force you into personal bankruptcy anyway."

Victoria stepped around Matt, putting herself back in the discussion. "The original offer didn't read this way. I'm sure Cleve's counsel used a boilerplate contract document and added the terms without his knowledge. Any negotiator would insert this kind of clause. We just need to ask them to rewrite that clause, or we can take the installments out as part of a counter offer."

His gaze was cold and accusing. "Get real, Victoria. Winslow would never let a legal document go out without checking every detail. I don't like the offer. I want to study the contract with a magnifying glass before we discuss counters. Signing a contract without a personal guarantee is asking to be axed."

Nick pursed his mouth and rubbed his chin with his hand, as if smoothing down a nonexistent beard. "If I had time, I'd accept the three-year payoff with interest, but I can't afford that luxury right now. As Victoria says, we can counter on that point. As to the guarantee . . . it seems to me, if the company goes bad, putting his signature on a guarantee isn't going to save it. They left the personal guarantee out to cover their backsides, so they don't get in a position to lose everything, like me."

Refusing to be rebuffed, Victoria insisted, "Cleve is solid. He isn't going to renege on a contract."

"You don't know that. You're letting personal involvement cloud your perspective. In fact, Mrs. Halstead, you have a clear conflict of interest in this deal, and you should withdraw."

Stung by his insinuations, she struck back. "This offer has nothing to do with my relationship with Cleve. I put this deal together to keep Nick out of bankruptcy. I asked Cleve to make an offer."

"What did you have to sell? Your soul? I hope you got more than that gaudy rock on your hand, because you negotiated a lousy deal," he said, and he turned to Nick, away from her.

"Nick, this could come back on you, at least the debt incurred while you owned the company. If you want to respond to this offer, I strongly recommend we revise this and insert a clause making Cleve Winslow responsible. Furthermore, I think you should insist on a substantial down payment of at least, say, 15 percent and payment in full at closing."

"You know, Matt, I've always done business on a handshake. Clauses and all aside, if he's going to cheat me, he'll do it with or without a contract. I'm betting on his honesty."

Matt shook his head. "What I've seen so far makes me uncomfortable. I have a feeling I'm going to find more things that we're not going to like. I prefer a straightforward deal where everyone understands all the conditions. Let me spend some time interpreting this thing, and I'll give you my recommendations before we do anything."

Heartsick, Victoria listened. More than once she had to bite her tongue to keep from jumping in to defend Cleve and herself. She had expected Matt's animosity, but she hadn't expected his attack. *What did you have to sell? Your soul?* How could he ask her such a question? Did he honestly think she would betray Nick? She wasn't the enemy, and neither was Cleve, but he couldn't see that. Was he jealous? As Nick's lawyer, he had an obligation to point out every clause and term that could negatively effect Nick. She expected no less, but the implication that she would cheat Nick pierced her heart.

"Matt, let me explain something to you," Nick said. "Winslow doesn't need my company—doesn't even want it. You seem to think there's some kind of conspiracy going on here. You should know Victoria better than that. For a man like Winslow to hang a wounded whale around his neck, just to make his bride happy, seems like a mighty fine gesture to me. I got myself into this situation, and I can take the consequences, but a lot of good people will be hurt if INTECH goes under. I hired you to do a job, and so far, you're doing fine. You go ahead with whatever negotiating you feel you have to do, but the bottom line is, unless there's something illegal in that contract, I can live with the terms, and I want to get it done."

Matt turned and stared at Victoria. His scrutiny made her squirm, though she had nothing to hide. She looked directly back. Finally, Matt sighed. "All right, Nick. As your lawyer, it's my duty to tell you every detail in here and how it could possibly effect you now or in the future. When you have a full disclosure, so you can make a knowledgeable decision, we'll do whatever you decide. I know Victoria probably better than you or Cleve Winslow," he said, spitting out Winslow as if he'd gotten a fly in his mouth. "She wouldn't want you to make a decision that could jeopardize your future. Right?" His pointed look seemed like an accusation.

"Absolutely," she said. She wanted to brain Matt. He *did* know her better than to imply some kind of subterfuge or ulterior motive on her part in the offer. If anything, he was the one with the prejudicial attitude. His was the biased viewpoint—colored by the fact that she'd chosen Cleve, instead of him. "I want to insure Nick's future security. Matsuko made a better offer, but the injunction ruined that possibility. Right now we're fortunate to have an option."

As she spoke, an idea suddenly occurred to her. "Don't forget this is a stock buyout. Cleve is assuming the liabilities as well as the assets. Selling his stock won't negate the company's debt liability to Nick. In fact, I've already set up an amortized note schedule."

"Good point. I wonder how Winslow missed that?" Matt mused out loud.

Incensed, Victoria let her indignation sharpen her retort. "Cleve studied *your* audit and my financial reports personally *and* with two of his own experts. He didn't *miss* anything. He felt terrible that he couldn't offer Nick more."

"I'll bet," Matt muttered, barely loud enough for her to hear.

"Well, if you two are done quibbling, Victoria and I need to get back to the office. I'm sure we've taken up enough of your time." Nick shook hands with Matt, then headed for the door.

"Victoria," Matt said, reaching out and taking hold of her arm. "Have you broken your happy news to your daughters?"

"This only happened yesterday. Now that Jessica's living with you, and Mandy's there most of the time, I don't see them much. They haven't been to the house lately."

"Perhaps they don't want to risk walking in on something that might embarrass them."

Her face flamed, and her hand itched to slap him. Too furious to answer, she stormed out of his office.

CHAPTER TWENTY

"LINC, DOES THIS contract strike you as aboveboard?" Matt asked. They were in Lincoln Halverson's office. Matt wanted his partner's opinion. He had a gut-deep suspicion about Winslow's offer to buy INTECH, but he couldn't be certain jealousy and his feelings for Victoria weren't clouding his judgment.

While Linc looked the contract over, Matt recalled the meeting. He'd certainly treated Tori poorly, especially after Winslow's lawyer left. No—poorly put too nice a spin on his behavior. He'd acted like a grouchy old bull that'd been ousted by a younger, stronger bull.

Lord, I really blew it, didn't I?

Jealousy aside, he did know Victoria intimately. She took extreme care not to let emotions rule her decisions. From what he'd seen lately, her emotions overruled her logic, but her loyalty belonged to Nicholas Shrock and INTECH. If she instigated Winslow's offer, she must have been desperate. For Nick's sake? And the engagement to Winslow—did she love the man, or did she agree to marry him as collateral for the sale?

"I'll have to admit, the wording alone makes me uneasy," Linc said. "Winslow's a pro when it comes to creative deals. There's nothing illegal or unethical, but he's certainly covered himself. Actually, you've got to admire the guy, or his legal counsel. It's a great contract, for the buyer."

"But not for the seller. In all good conscience, I can't let my client sign this without strong warning of the possible consequences."

"Which you will do. Didn't you tell me this case could end in bankruptcy?"

"Yes. We had a legitimate buyer, but they pulled their offer when INTECH got hit with an injunction. The legal liability scared the buyer off."

"And Winslow is willing to accept that problem?"

"Apparently," Matt had to acknowledge. "That bothers me as much as anything. The guy never makes a move that doesn't line his pockets."

"Maybe he likes a challenge. Shrock has an excellent reputation in the development industry. At face value, however, Winslow's buying a headache. What about reorganization?"

"It's a questionable alternative. INTECH's legal problems could take years and millions. If reorganization could save the company, and I'm not at all sure it could, Nick would still have to go bankrupt. He owes eight million personally, and he owns one hundred percent of the corporate stock." The more Matt thought about Nick's situation, the less likely a solution seemed. "It's a mess."

"Without studying this thing, I'd say a sale is better than no sale at all. Your client can file bankruptcy now, or gamble on this sale being legit, and if the sale doesn't pan out, he can file later."

"True." Matt shook his head. Everything Linc said, everything Victoria pointed out made sense. "I can't pinpoint the problem, Linc, but this deal doesn't smell good. There's more to this than what shows, I just feel it."

"What? You think they have a hidden agenda in this offer?"

"Yes, I do, but I don't have a clue what that agenda might be. Just a feeling."

"Your feeling wouldn't have something to do with your ex-wife's involvement, would it?"

Matt's expression turned bleak. "I don't know, Linc. It's possible."

"I got a nice note from her after she spent the Fourth of July weekend at our place in Breckenridge with you. Seems like a pretty amicable relationship for a divorced couple."

"We're civil." Matt rubbed his chin, felt the afternoon roughness, a sensation that matched his emotions. He met his partner's intense gaze. "I want my wife back, Linc. She stayed in the attic and kept to herself most of the weekend, but she spent a little time with us, and we almost connected. Have you ever done something really stupid, and every time you try to make amends, your past trips you and you fall flat on your face?"

Linc chuckled. "I plead the fifth." Then he got serious. "You're treading dangerous water, Matt, and not just with your ex-wife. From what I hear, Cleve Winslow can get nasty. If you're too close to this case, I'll be happy to handle the deal."

"Cleve Winslow just got engaged to my ex-wife. He's making this out to be something on the lines of a wedding present for her—you know, save the day and be the hero."

"Whew. Matt, I think you ought to let this go."

"Not yet, Linc. I appreciate the offer, but I'm going to do a little research first."

"All right, but promise me. If you start losing your objectivity, let me handle the case, okay?"

"Okay."

On the way back to his office, and as he sat staring out the window, Matt sorted through the troubled thoughts bouncing around inside his head. He took a cold, hard look at himself, and didn't like what he saw. His own emotions were rubbed raw, and the logic he took such pride in was a tangled mess. He'd twisted facts together with threads of his own design. In fact, he'd been trying to manipulate the outcome. As if forgiveness and acceptance weren't enough, Matt wanted the Lord to fix what he'd broken and give him back the happiness he'd lost. Instead of asking what God wanted, he had decided God's will fit what he wanted.

As a lawyer and an accountant, Matt's whole life dealt with truth and facts. Facing the facts squarely, he made a list, an accounting of his case.

Fact: Divorce opposed God's will.

Fact: God hadn't caused their divorce. He and Victoria had caused the divorce.

Fact: Forgiveness was not a time machine. God didn't undo what had been done or fix what had been broken.

Fact: Love meant giving, not getting. Matt knew the truth. The only love guaranteed was God's love for him, so immense and unconditional that God gave His Son, Jesus Christ, for Matthew Halstead. And all God required in exchange for the gift of His love was for Matt to repent of his sins and return Jesus' love with all his heart and soul and mind and to love others as Christ loved them. First and foremost, that meant Tori. But he'd sought love backwards. He'd been busy trying to win Tori's love, not giving her unconditional love, God's way. Chastising himself, Matt marveled at the fact that the Lord continued to be patient with him.

One more fact remained. While Matt didn't have concrete proof, he knew Cleve Winslow wanted something, and Victoria was a pawn in his game. Perhaps the Lord had allowed him to return to Denver and reenter her life to save her from Winslow's scheme.

Please protect her, Lord Jesus. Open her eyes, and let her see the lies for what they are. Show me the way, Lord. Help me know where to look and what to do.

The Black Forest was an area northeast of Colorado Springs and some fifty miles southeast of Denver. INTECH's property was five miles from the Black Forest. Matt scrutinized the extensive documentation he'd ordered on the property back to the original Sandoval homestead, which had grown into a ranch encompassing thousands of acres. As the population had increased, the ranch had been sold off piece by piece, until the two remaining Sandovals split the ranch in half, one of the halves being the present fifteen hundred acres owned by INTECH.

A topographical of the acreage marked several mine sites on their property and the adjoining ranch land. Matt's interest peaked. When the discoveries of gold and silver brought the gold rush to the Colorado Rocky Mountains, miners panned, dug and tunneled all over the state in search of riches. The crossed pick-axes on the map indicated the Sandovals had caught the fever too.

Could gold be Winslow's angle? Was there ore worth mining on the land? Matt called Nick, figuring he would probably know. Sure enough, he'd checked and found what Sandoval had discovered. Nothing of value. Nick promised to send Matt the survey results.

The equation didn't make sense. Cleve Winslow didn't buy financially decrepit companies without a reason. Certainly not to appease a woman, even an extraordinary woman, like Victoria. Based on his past actions, generosity didn't fit Cleve's game plan, even if the man was in love. Ostentatious gifts, like the ring, seemed more his style.

The Sandoval who had owned INTECH's portion of the ranch had retained the water and mineral rights to the entire three thousand acres. He must have been the mining enthusiast in the family. Matt thought about the possibility of selling the rights back to the neighbor. The adjacent ranch held deeded access to the use of the water already, and since the mineral survey came back negative, those rights probably weren't worth much. Not enough to bail out Nicholas Shrock.

More out of habit than inspiration, Matt instructed his researchers to gather information about the owners of all the adjacent lands. Matt loved detail and judiciously collected minutiae on all his cases. You never knew when an insignificant fact might be the piece that completed the puzzle.

Advance copies of *The Business Barometer*, containing the article about Victoria, were on her desk when she returned to her office. Flipping the top one open to the thoughtfully marked page, she scanned the complimentary account of her life, her career, and the Methergy project. She reread the piece, more slowly, and made a mental note to have Janice send Margaret Daley a bouquet of flowers. The article was the balm she needed to soothe the sting of Matt's attack. Did he really believe she would conspire to cheat Nick? What did he think would motivate her to betray her friend? Didn't he *know* she would never do that? And the jab about the girls . . . his condemnation was so unfair. She'd purposely kept her relationship with Cleve to a low simmer. They'd shared a few kisses, nothing more. Matt's implications made her blood boil. Enough! she told herself, tamping down the hurt. She picked up the magazine again.

The article couldn't help reverse the injunction, but at least she'd defended Methergy in print.

The ring weighed heavy in Victoria's purse. She had carefully wrapped it in a tissue and put it in a zippered compartment. Removing the valuable emerald made her nervous, as if once off her finger the ring might get lost or evaporate into thin air, but she didn't want the girls to see it before she broke her news. She picked up Jessica outside Matt's office at five o'clock, and they met Mandy at the girls' favorite "fancy" restaurant.

The girls had lots of news. The three of them hadn't gotten together since before Jessica left for camp. To Victoria, that seemed like a lifetime ago.

Jessica loved working for her father, though in actuality she rarely saw him during the day. She spent her time in the office morgue with a middle-aged filing clerk and a pre-law student. The newness of earning a check and feeling productive offset the tedium of filing reams of paperwork.

Mandy chattered on about college. She had been accepted at Fort Lewis College in Durango. She and her best friend, Kim, planned to be roommates. Mandy wanted to know when they could go shopping for school clothes. She'd made a list of all the things she needed, enough to last the first semester. Victoria arranged to spend the following Saturday shopping with both girls. Jessica needed clothes, too, and she might as well go broke all in one day.

They ordered, and the waiter placed a bowl of shrimp on ice on their table. Diving in with relish, the girls peeled and dipped the luscious shrimp in seafood sauce as they talked and laughed. Victoria's heart swelled with love and pride for her beautiful daughters. In the pit of her stomach, acid began to burn as she thought how her news would put a damper on their evening. She knew the girls wouldn't share her happiness, so she put off revealing her engagement, deciding to wait until after dinner, maybe during dessert, to tell them.

As they ate their entrees, Victoria toyed with her food. Waiting made anticipating their reactions worse, but she just couldn't bring herself to destroy their good moods. While the girls ate dessert, she screwed up her courage, pulled the wrapped ring out of her purse, and held it clenched in her hand.

"Mandy, Jessica, I have something to tell you."

Instantly they both looked up from their desserts, their forks suspended in mid-bite. Seeing their alert looks, Victoria knew her voice had revealed her tension. "Cleve has asked me to marry him." She took a quick steadying breath. "And I've accepted."

"No!" Jessica wailed.

"Shh," Mandy warned her sister.

"You can't," Jessica whispered loudly, her voice harsh and filled with desperate frustration. "You'll ruin everything. What about me? What about Dad?"

"Honey." Victoria reached out to touch Jessica's arm. When Jessica jerked away, Victoria's heart sank. "Nothing is going to change. You'll still have both of us, and you can still spend time with your father."

"When, Mom?" Mandy asked.

"I don't know; we haven't set a date. Maybe Christmas."

"You're going to ruin Christmas," Jessica cried. "We were going to spend it together, just like the Fourth of July."

"I'm not spending Christmas together with your father. You can spend part of the holidays with him."

"No," she said fiercely. "I won't share Christmas with that man."

"Jessica," Victoria said, a warning in her tone. A glance around reassured her that no one was staring at them. Thankfully, they were early and sat at a secluded, corner table.

"Will he move in with us, Mom?"

"No, dear. We won't live together until after we're married," Victoria assured Mandy.

"I mean, will we live in our house or his?"

"Oh. I don't know; we haven't discussed details. His house, I suppose."

"You're going to make me move schools, too?" Jessica demanded. "Leave all my friends? I won't go. I'll live with Dad," she stated positively.

The ring bit into Victoria's hand. She relaxed her grip, unwrapped the ring, and put it on her finger.

"Wow. Let me see," Mandy said. Victoria held her hand out, and Mandy inspected the jewel. "Fabulous," she declared. "Must have cost a fortune. He's rich, isn't he."

"I suppose he's well off," Victoria answered. Mandy's reaction surprised her. Mandy was gazing at her with something akin to rapture, and she suddenly realized romance played a major role in eldest daughter's thoughts and dreams.

"You love Dad. You told me so," Jessica said, her voice pleading. "You can't marry *him.*"

Victoria didn't know how to explain lost love to her youngest daughter. Then a picture flashed into her mind. "Jessica, remember when you had that big lion that Grandma made you?"

"Yeah, Leo. What's that got to do with Dad?"

"Remember how you dragged that stuffed animal around everywhere we went? You dragged it through the mud, and I had to wash it. Leo's tail came off, and I sewed it back on. That poor lion got so threadbare, I had to cover it up, remember?"

"Yes. You put one of my baby outfits on him."

"I sewed the clothes on to hold the poor shaggy animal together. And you still dragged him everywhere. We took a trip camping, and you caught him on a tree stump, and he ripped open. I sewed up the ragged tear as best I could, and we pretended he had to go to the doctor and get stitches."

"You wouldn't let me take him places anymore. He had to sit in a chair and rest, you said, so he could mend."

"Your father brought you a great big teddy bear to keep you company while Leo recovered. You named it Benjie. You love Benjie. You still keep him on your bed."

"Yeah, so?"

"So, do you still like Leo?"

"Of course," Jessica replied like it was a dumb question. "Just because I love Benjie, doesn't mean I don't love Leo. It's just different. Leo is part of my childhood."

Victoria couldn't help smiling at Jessica's relegation of the lion to her childhood. Obviously, that was the distant past to a fourteen year old. "Honey, that's how I feel about your father. I'll always care about him; he's a part of my past. I have wonderful memories of those years when we were together as a family, but we got torn one time too many. The fabric of our lives ripped beyond repair. Stitches couldn't hold us together anymore, so we put that part of our lives on the shelf."

"Couldn't the rips get fixed now?" she asked, but the sad dawning in her eyes told Victoria her youngest realized the answer.

"I'm sorry, Honey. Life doesn't always work out the way you'd like. Cleve wants to be friends with you if you'll let him." She looked at the girls expectantly, hoping for a positive reaction.

Two pairs of chocolate brown eyes looked back with totally different expressions. Mandy's gaze held such compassion, Victoria was rocked by a new revelation. Mandy was in love. She should have seen the signs before, the way the older girl had been mooning around and taking extra care with her appearance. Victoria connected Mandy's infatuation to the golf lessons and Jase Tanner, and she knew a moment of apprehension. Dealing with the situation would require wisdom and tact.

Jessica's eyes held dark denial. "Your example is wrong, Mom. You and Dad aren't like Leo and Benjie at all. They're stuffed toys, sewn together on a machine. You're people, and God made you so you can mend if you really try."

"Oh Jessica." Victoria felt battered clear to her knees. A child's faith was so dear and so simple. Why did reality have to take that away? Even worse, why did she have to be the one to disenchant her child? "Honey, you are right. We can mend. Sometimes, though, we mend in a different shape. We don't go back exactly the way we were before. When your dad left, I prayed and prayed for God to bring him home. But he didn't come. Instead, I had to become strong enough to get on with life without your father. I'm sorry, but you're going to have to accept the facts."

Jessica listened, but Victoria knew she hadn't convinced her. A struggle loomed ahead on that front, and Mandy wouldn't be there to help. Victoria's resolve tore at her. Should she go through with the marriage when one daughter was so adamantly opposed? But she didn't really have a choice, did she? Jessica would come around. If she didn't, Matt would be happy to have her live with him, but the thought of alienating her daughter tormented Victoria. Was she destined to lose both daughters at once, one to college and independence, and one sacrificed to save Nick's future. Jessica loved Nick like a grandfather. If she knew the whole situation, she'd be more receptive to the marriage. Maybe. And just the fact that she would even consider breaking the engagement for Jessica's sake gave Victoria pause. Testing her feelings about it, she discovered little more than confusion.

Would Cleve go through with the buyout if she broke off the engagement? No. Why should he? Marriages, she told herself, were often based on reasons other than love. Successful marriages. Like Jessica pointed out, people could make things work if they really wanted to. So, what did she want? Companionship, respect, challenge, success? All of those things. Love? She didn't put much faith in that state of mind, but perhaps strong affection would grow out of the others. Could she find them with Cleve? And at what cost? Each question opened more questions and doubts.

Nick invited Victoria and Matt and Viola to his office to witness his signature, accepting Cleve's offer. When they were all together, Nick smiled broadly and thanked them for coming.

"Are you absolutely certain you want to do this?" Victoria asked. "We could still look for investors. The mall project alone would attract money."

"No, Victoria. Matt's tried to talk me out of this, but I've made up my mind. I'm done with the rat race. I want my ranch, humble though it might be. I listed my house and the Malibu property this morning. The Realtor thinks they'll sell for more than we estimated."

The terms weren't much improved. No personal guarantee from Cleve. A larger closing payment, upped to three and a half million, with the remainder in a note at nine percent. Small concessions, but Nick seemed satisfied. In fact, he seemed almost his old, chipper self. Victoria watched him write his large, bold signature across the bottom of the page, signing away his life's work with a flourish. The confident scrawl of his handwriting gave a true picture of the man she knew and loved. With a silent prayer that they were doing the right thing, she added her name to the contract. Matt also signed, reluctantly. When Viola notarized their signatures, Victoria saw tears in her eyes.

For better or worse, the deal was done, bringing Nick's struggle to a conclusion. Victoria had reassessed INTECH's short and long term liabilities and taken money earmarked for the Black Forest Project and the project she'd recently scuttled, coming up with enough, she thought, to keep Nick out of bankruptcy. She'd activated monthly payments on a five-year note to pay off the rest of the money he'd invested in the business. Nick would get all his money. She'd see to that. For a reason she couldn't even name, she hadn't mentioned the amortized payments to Cleve. The day-to-day bookkeeping details wouldn't interest him. Handling the company's finances was entirely her responsibility. Besides, he didn't own the company yet.

☙

Matt was still searching for the illusive pieces to the Winslow/ INTECH puzzle when he received a call from an environmentalist who had been referred to him as INTECH's lawyer.

"How can I help you?" Matt asked into the phone.

"Actually, I believe I can help you, or INTECH, anyway. I represent American Citizens for Responsible Action. Our environmental organization voted to publicly support INTECH's landfill cogeneration plant."

"You're aware that an environmental group got an injunction to stop the project?" Matt responded coolly.

"Yes. I read the article in *The Business Barometer.* Your client has a reputation for following responsible policies and procedures in land development, and methane conversion benefits society if done properly. I believe the local environmental group will withdraw their objection when presented with all the facts."

"I've tried to contact them, but they don't seem to be interested in the truth."

"I have a call in to them now. I'm sure this can be straightened out. I wanted you to know you have our support. We need more conscientious businesses like INTECH, Mr. Halstead."

"On behalf of Nicholas Shrock, I thank you. We appreciate your support. I'm sorry Mrs. Halstead couldn't take your call. I'm sure she will want to thank you personally. By the way, I wonder if you could do me one more favor."

"I'd be delighted to, if I can. Even when situations warrant our interference, environmental groups generate enough bad feelings. I like to reverse that impression whenever possible."

"Someone fed false information to the local environmental group. I'd like to know who. Surely, their own investigation would have revealed the true state of things."

"I'd like to think so, Mr. Halstead."

"Please, call me Matt."

"All right, Matt. And my name is Dale . . . Dale Simms. Unfortunately, every cause has people who jump on the bandwagon for emotional reasons or for publicity. Let's hope that is not the case here. I'll find out and get back to you."

"I look forward to hearing from you, Dale."

❧

"Victoria, there's a call for you on line one," Janice announced excitedly. "It's NBC. I think it's *The Today Show*."

"NBC?"

Her heartbeat jammed into overdrive as she picked up the phone. The network news team had seen the article in *The Business Barometer* about Methergy and the injunction against INTECH, and they had heard from Dale Simms, head of ACRA. Their audience would be interested in a story about two environmental groups battling opposite sides of the same cause. Would she be willing to come to New York and do an interview? Would she ever!

Victoria was shaking and soaring by the time she got off the phone. INTECH needed a big break. Methergy would get its day in the court of public opinion, and the truth should triumph. Hallelujah. Once she explained . . . oh boy, what had she agreed to? Network television. They wanted her to appear before millions of people to push her cause. Impossible, she couldn't do it. She had to do it, for INTECH. "Janice, would you come in here, please?"

The secretary appeared immediately. "What did they want?"

"I'm going to be on network television."

"Wow. When?"

"Day after tomorrow. I fly to New York City tomorrow afternoon. Taping will be early Thursday morning, so I'll return in the afternoon. That way I'll only be gone two days." Reality began to sink in. She began to pace. "What will I wear?" Panic inched closer. "Maybe Nick can go."

"No way," Janice said. "This is so fantastic. You're going to be famous. I'll be the secretary of a celebrity."

"I don't like all this attention," Victoria complained. She realized she had little choice. "I guess it's all right if it helps the Methergy project. Clear my schedule for the next two days, and see if there's anything I need to take care of right away."

Grabbing a pad, Victoria started making a list. She couldn't think of a single outfit in her closet that would be appropriate for the interview. To her list, under Matt and Cleve, she made the notation: Tina—shop for dress.

Victoria dreaded calling Matt, but whatever he thought of her, she knew she couldn't shirk this responsibility. Mandy thought she was old enough to stay by herself, but Victoria didn't agree. Especially not under the circumstances. Picking up the phone, she dialed his number.

"Matt, this is Victoria," she said when he answered.

"Victoria. How are you?" He sounded stilted.

"I'm fine, I guess. I have to go to New York tomorrow." She told him about the television interview and asked if Mandy could stay with him.

"Of course. Do you want me to call her?"

"Yes, if you wouldn't mind. She'll probably object. She's been pushing for her independence lately. I don't want her staying out at the house alone. I don't trust Jase Tanner."

"The young man from the pro shop?"

"Yes. She came in two hours late one night. He brought her home. And he was in the hot tub with her the other night when I got home. He'd been drinking beer. There have been rumors about him making the rounds of the female club members. I don't usually listen to gossip, but this concerns Mandy."

"I'll talk to her." There was a pause. Finally he said, "Don't worry, just enjoy yourself."

"Thanks, Matt, I'll try. I'm scared to death."

"You'll do great."

She felt a little better. She called Cleve.

WHEN CLEVE HEARD about Victoria going to New York, he insisted, as her fiancé and future boss, on going along. Then he upgraded her accommodations from the room booked by the network to a luxury suite. When she'd discovered his plans, Victoria insisted on two bedrooms, saying she needed to get her rest before the show. The prospect of the show made her nervous enough without the added distraction of her relationship with Cleve.

The suite embodied elegance and wealth. Soft background music set a mood of serenity and opulence much like his home. Victoria stepped out of her shoes and wiggled her toes in the plush carpet. Padding over to the window, she drew back the heavy brocade drapes and looked out at the city lights. Hearing a sound behind her, she turned and watched Cleve walk toward her across the living room.

"If I close my eyes part way," he said in a deep, husky voice, "I see an angel surrounded by starlight."

The butterflies in her stomach took flight. "What a vivid imagination you have, sir. Better keep your eyes closed, or you'll discover the maid with a duster in her hand."

"Hardly. By the way, I ordered room service."

"Wonderful. Between the flight and my nerves about tomorrow, I'm exhausted."

"That's what I figured," he said.

They ate a light supper of chicken pasta and salad, topped off with a wedge of New York cheesecake, which more than satisfied her hunger. When she took her last sip of coffee then put down her napkin, Cleve asked, "What time are you supposed to be at the studio?"

"They're sending a car at four-thirty. That's A.M.," she groaned.

He looked at his gold watch. "It's only seven now, Denver time. You have a whirlpool tub. Why don't you go relax and get comfortable, then we'll have a nightcap. That'll help you sleep. I'll arrange a wake-up call, so you won't have to worry about that." He came around the table to help her up out her chair.

"Thank you, Cleve. I believe I will." He twirled her around and gave her a light kiss, then gave her a gentle push toward her room.

Even as she stretched out in the hot, swirling water, her anxiety built. Two thousand miles from home, alone with her very handsome fiancé, she'd landed herself in a precarious situation. A sophisticated man like Cleve wouldn't book a luxury suite with the woman he intended to marry without expecting intimacy. He hadn't asked if he could come. He'd insisted, then taken over the arrangements. So what should she do? Lock the door and not come out until morning? Of course not. He had assured her that he would always stop if she asked him to, and she believed him.

Strangely enough, her convictions caused the real dilemma disturbing her peace, not Cleve's advances. Right now she wasn't sure she knew what they were. She'd been taught that intimacy outside marriage was wrong and, while she wasn't attending church, she still believed in God and living by the Ten Commandments. It boiled down to simple principles of cause and effect. She had ignored those principals with Matt and suffered the consequences, but this was a different scenario. She and Cleve were getting married.

She had told the girls to wait until they got married, and she believed abstinence was important for them. They were young and had no experience with love and adult relationships. At their age, hormones controlled their attractions, and the consequences could be disastrous, as she well knew.

Once she had been that naïve teenager, away from home at a very liberal college where drinking and drugs and sex were part of the party scene. Her roommate had teased her about being a prude and missing out on all the fun. Even so, she hadn't planned to get carried away—it had just happened. They were celebrating the end of the school term.

She and Matt, darkness and isolation, a romantic campfire, cozy sleeping bags to cuddle in, and a bottle of wine. Most of all, she had been madly in love, and she'd had the foolish romantic idea that intimacy would make him love her back. How wrong she had been.

But now she was an adult with no illusions of love. They respected each other, admired each other's acuity, and were attracted to each other. Getting married made sense, giving them the companionship and partnership they both desired. What difference did it make if they consummated their relationship now or if they waited until they signed a piece of paper? None by today's standards, but that didn't sway her. She still held to the moral principles taught in church. Restraint made sense and spared a lot of regret.

Even if God had let her down, she believed marriage and commitment were for life, and she was not going to have another failure. She would have to live with her decision to marry Cleve for the rest of her life. If she had hesitations, she needed to purge them from her system. On the other hand, she reasoned, perhaps if she gave in to intimacy she would gain the subconscious bond that their relationship lacked. Cleve wanted her. She'd seen desire smoldering in his gaze, and it gave her a heady feeling of power. He was very dynamic and very attractive.

And she'd never relax if she kept worrying about their courtship. Better to enjoy the luxury surroundings and see what happened. She dried off and slipped into a pair of silk lounging pajamas and matching robe—a modest ensemble. In the sitting room of the suite, she sank onto the couch, slipped off her slippers, and put her feet up. Cleve sat beside her.

"Tired?"

"Uh-huh." She closed her eyes and rolled her head back, bumping against his arm. He slipped it around her shoulders and drew her close. "I should turn in now," she said.

"Your body clock thinks it's only eight. You probably couldn't sleep if you tried. Here. I poured you a glass of wine. It'll help you relax."

She took a sip, then set it on the table and rested her head against his shoulder.

He tipped her chin up and kissed her softly. It felt good, and not at all threatening. She'd been worrying for nothing. Everything was going to work out fine.

Then, as she relaxed, the atmosphere changed. Cleve's kisses grew intense, and Victoria felt needs that she hadn't felt in years. His masculine strength and the intimacy of their surroundings were seductive. She tingled all over, and it felt good, like love. Her head swam, and she'd hardly touched her wine. When the phone rang, she didn't even hear it until Cleve disentangled himself and got up to answer it.

"It's for you," he said, scowling as he handed her the phone.

"Hello?"

"You sound funny—groggy. What are you doing?"

"Mandy? Hi, Honey. I just had a long bath, and I'm really tired. I was just getting ready to go to bed."

"Oh yeah? With him?"

"No, Mandy. I have my own room."

"Then why did he answer the phone? What is he doing there, anyway? You didn't tell us he was going with you," her young voice accused.

"We have a suite, with two bedrooms. The phone rang in the sitting room." Victoria rubbed her neck. "Mandy, why did you call? Is everything all right?"

"No. I can't believe you went off with him."

"Honey, this is a business trip. I'm going on the show tomorrow for INTECH, and Cleve is buying the company. He's going to be my boss."

"That's pretty convenient," Mandy said, and Victoria couldn't miss the sarcasm. The silence on the line stretched out for a moment. "I called to wish you luck, Mom. I love you."

"Oh, Honey, I love you too. And don't jump to conclusions. Things aren't like they seem."

"Yeah, Mom. Goodbye." Victoria heard the dial tone and hung up. As she set the phone down, Cleve came up behind her and put his arms around her. She stiffened.

He kissed the side of her neck. She stepped away. "That was Mandy," she said.

"I figured that out. She's in Denver, Victoria, not here in this room. Are you going to let her come between us?"

"I guess I am." She turned to face him, apologetically, wanting him to understand. Mandy's call had cleared her mind. She was not alone with Cleve in New York or anywhere else. Everywhere she went and every action she took affected other people in her life, whether they knew about it or not. *And God would know.* When that thought intruded, she wanted to ignore it. Listening to Matt had put that notion in her head. She and God weren't on speaking terms, so what did it matter? It shouldn't, but it did. Once again she had to make a choice. She could indulge in the emotions of the moment, knowing there would be a price to pay, or she could do what she believed was right.

"I'm sorry, Cleve. Please understand. I've told the girls that sex is the most intimate thing two people can share. To me, it's the ultimate act of trust. When Matt left me, he broke that trust, and I made a promise to myself that I would never do that. My daughters trust me. I want them to wait until they get married. I need to practice what I preach."

"They don't have to know. I need you, Love. Let me show you how much," he urged seductively as he pulled her close, lowering his lips to hers.

His kiss was warm and filled with longing. Cleve needed her, and he trusted her. Trust—the assurance of her faithfulness and loyalty—was all she would bring to their marriage. If she gave in, would he be able to trust her? Could she trust herself? No. They did not have the commitment of marriage. For his sake as well as her own and her children's, she had to stick to her convictions. She shook her head. "I'd know, and you'd know."

"For me, Honey," he said.

"No, Cleve. If I don't keep this promise, how could you ever trust me to keep any promise?"

"I trust you." He raised his hands in surrender. "All right, I give up. Let's get married now."

"Now, as in right this minute?" she asked, a laugh easing the tightness in her face, relieving her tension.

He didn't smile. "Why not? Let's fly to Vegas tomorrow instead of Denver."

She shook her head. "I want the girls to be a part of our marriage, and that won't happen if I leave them out of the wedding."

"When, then? Next week? We'll find a Justice of the Peace," he said, pushing for a commitment.

Constriction tightened her throat and her shoulder went taut. She forced herself to relax. Only moments before, she'd almost given in to desire, and suddenly doubts permeated her thoughts again. When she accepted the engagement, the commitment of marriage had seemed far away in the nebulous future. She'd been railroaded into the first. She was not ready to finalize the second.

"I eloped before, and the marriage didn't work. I want a real wedding. It's just too soon. I can't plan a wedding until this business with INTECH is done and Nick is settled."

"As soon as we get a closing date on this sale, I want a wedding date," he growled. "And I want it soon."

Lying in bed, Victoria's mind whirled with so many problems she couldn't relax. Lately, her thinking vacillated in every direction, especially when she was with Cleve. What had happened to her decisiveness and control? For awhile, his presence had empowered her, but his dynamic personality overpowered everything in his path. She certainly didn't feel powerful right now. Somehow, she needed to get a grip on her life. Thank goodness for Mandy's call. Victoria regretted that it had taken her daughter's interruption to bring her to her senses. Even more, she regretted having Mandy catch her in what looked like a secret rendezvous. No doubt she had just blown the trust with her daughter. Restoring that trust would be her top priority when she got home.

Thinking about regret took her back to the beginning of the whole cycle. She and Matt had made a wrong decision, and they had both paid with a lifetime of regrets. She'd often wondered what would have happened if she'd said *no* to Matt. She had to admit, he had not pressed her. They had both lost control, and that was the key. Every time she'd relinquished control in her life, she'd suffered heavy consequences. And here, not an hour ago, she'd almost given up her control to Cleve. Thank goodness she'd regained her perspective.

Victoria tried to block out the discordant background noises and go to sleep. Though the sounds were muffled, they grated on an ear attuned to crickets and country breezes. The wail of sirens and the blare of car horns seemed to ebb and flow through the night. Did they never cease?

In a few hours she would be on national television in front of millions of people. What if she made a fool out of herself? What if the interviewer made her look wrong? The media often championed environmental issues.

Maybe she should pray, she thought. Then she laughed. Matt, with his religious fervor, had planted these thoughts in her head. How she wished solving the problem was as simple as Matt made it seem—not just praying to God, but talking to Jesus as if He were right there—as if He would answer. Maybe prayer really worked for Matt, but she knew it wouldn't work for her. She had learned the hard way to rely on her own strength.

It occurred to Victoria that Cleve and Matt both intensified her insecurities. Compared to Matt, she'd always felt weak and ineffectual. She lacked something, but she'd never figured out what. In her weakness, she had even sought God's love and compassion, a futile exercise. Considering Matt's strength, his sudden need to rely on Jesus and prayer seemed incongruous. Recalling Matt's prayer for a night watchman he didn't even know made her wonder about Otis's condition.

She hoped Otis would recover, and she hoped Jessica and Mandy would accept Cleve. Thinking about the man in the other room gave her the jitters about the future. She hoped she and Cleve would be able to build a marriage out of a business arrangement. In a way, she thought, specifying these hopes issued a kind of prayer—not too committed, though, so she wouldn't be too disappointed when she got no answer.

The wake-up call rang several times before the sound permeated Victoria's sleep. Groping, she managed to turn on the lamp and answer the call. Scooting to a sitting position, she pushed her hair back and opened her eyes, squinting against the light. She was in New York. It was ten minutes to four in the morning. She had forty minutes.

Forcing herself to move, she hurried through her morning ritual. A fingernail caught on her new pantyhose, causing a run. She yanked them off and quickly filed her nail, then grabbed a new pair. She brushed her teeth and combed through her hair at the same time, finding it difficult to move each hand in a different direction at the same time. She applied a minimum of makeup, since they would do touch-ups at the studio.

As her mind began to function, excitement kicked in, and her nerves woke up. In a couple of hours, she would be seen in millions of homes. In her wildest imaginings, she had never dreamed this big. She had pictured standing beside Matt, inspiring him to succeed.

That dream had died, replaced by goals no more far-reaching than the next milestone—master's degree, job, promotion, house, the girls' college, and her projects. Now, as her hard-won career teetered on the brink of doom, suddenly everything seemed to be coming together, but she had misgivings. She'd been struggling and fighting so long, she didn't trust the success that seemed to be within reach. Was this a mountaintop or a false peak? Would this be a crowning moment in her life or a very public humiliation? Thirty minutes flat, she took a calming breath, checked the mirror, then opened the door and entered the sitting room.

Cleve hung up the phone. He straightened and turned. "Perfect, the car is downstairs." He looked her over and whistled low. "You are going to knock them dead."

His praise gave her a shot of confidence. So did her dress. Thank goodness she'd let Tina talk her into it. Tailored femininity. Beautiful, flattering, expensive, and worth every exorbitant penny. She inhaled deeply. "I'm ready. Shall we go?"

The gray world of pre-dawn hung over the city, slowing the pace and hushing the sounds as they drove through the streets. Cars moved purposefully, but without the frantic bustle of daytime. Darkened display windows and empty sidewalks lined the way. Here and there, a dim light revealed a storekeeper stocking shelves or vacuuming floors, preparing for the day. Beside her, Cleve held her hand in companionable silence. She glanced at him, and he smiled.

"I can feel your pulse. You look so calm, but your heart is beating like a jackhammer. Are you all right?"

She opened her mouth to answer and stopped on a squeak. Swallowing, she tried again. "I'm a little nervous. Do you think I can pull this off?"

"Without a doubt. You're going to be dynamite."

Her morale raised a notch, and she was glad he'd insisted on coming.

When the studio found out Cleve accompanied her and that he was buying INTECH—and, furthermore, they were engaged, the interview took on a whole new flavor. They convinced Cleve to join them on stage. Victoria clung to his hand, which made great camera copy. After the introductions, with a few brief comments about Victoria's job and the Mayor's Award, the interviewer zeroed in on the environmental issue, explaining the issue and the unusual event of two environmental groups going head-to-head.

The group from Colorado had declined to be interviewed. Dale Simms participated from a station in Miami, Florida, and he happily prosed on about the benefits of methane conversion to the environment. When Victoria started talking about their conversion project and the future plans for a research center, her enthusiasm took over, and she let go of Cleve's hand. After a few minutes, the attention turned to Cleve, who was asked what had interested him in a real estate development company. He replied that his brilliant and beautiful fiancée had convinced him of its merits, which got a laugh. All in all, it took seven minutes to do the entire interview. Then they were standing, shaking hands, and walking off the set.

"I need a tee shirt saying *I Survived Network Television,*" Victoria said as the studio limo returned them to their hotel. "Did it go all right, do you think?"

He gave her a reassuring hug. "You were wonderful. By now the entire country is wondering why haven't they heard of the brilliant and beautiful Victoria Halstead before?"

"By now, they are asking, 'who is that nobody who has gotten herself engaged to Cleve Winslow?'" she corrected, teasing him back.

"There you go, fishing for another compliment."

❧

Right after Dale Simms appeared on the television interview with Victoria, he called Matt. He reported that he'd gotten nowhere with the emotionally fervent environmentalists in Colorado Springs. Regardless of the facts, the group adamantly opposed all industrial growth outside the perimeters of urban areas. Their agenda didn't surprise Matt, nor did the name of the instigator of their legal action, Sandoval Cattle Company, the owner of the fifteen-hundred-acre ranch adjacent to INTECH's land.

Hanging up the phone, Matt sat back, deep in thought, mulling over the information he'd just received. The Sandoval Ranch was the logical complainant, but why involve an environmental group? Why would they want to stop the project? Water pollution? Doubtful. They could easily test their supply, and if they had a concern, it would seem likely that they would contact INTECH directly. He checked with Nick. There had been no contact with the ranchers. Noise? Traffic? That didn't make sense. Endeavors of a similar nature coexisted all over the west, and the truck traffic would be on the opposite side of INTECH's property. No, they had some reason for anonymity, but what?

The Black Forest Project was a puzzle. Matt examined the pieces. The project wasn't of a sufficient scope to raise a rancher's objection or attract a covetous entrepreneur like Cleve Winslow, so he surmised the site itself was the center of the jigsaw.

The site was deeply in debt, which canceled its appeal as a prime piece of property. Some years ago, it had been near one of the proposed sites for the new Denver Airport and had been attractive for that reason. Several huge ventures had looked at developing in that same area. But the airport had gone north, and the other interested parties had gone elsewhere or fizzled under the strain of economic recession.

According to county tax records, Sandoval Cattle Company belonged to Isabelle Vargas of San Antonio, Texas. A call to the listed phone number reached an answering service that took his name and promised a return call. When he discovered the address was a post office box, a suspicion began to take shape. Someone wanted to remain hidden.

Calling in all his resources, he began his hunt. The corporation was legitimate, registered in Texas to Isabelle Vargas, president. An associate in Texas traced her to a house in San Antonio, where he found renters. The owner, an old lady, lived in a nursing home, they thought. They paid their rent to the post office box. If they had a problem, they left a message with the answering service. Dead-end.

With time to kill until their evening flight, Victoria and Cleve spent the afternoon shopping. They bought a few things for his house—little things like a lovely Chinese tea set and a lacquered tray with a picture of an English thatched roof cottage and garden—that combined their different tastes. The exhilaration that followed the television interview, combined with the intimacy of shopping for their future gave Victoria a euphoria that lasted into the late afternoon. Cleve's support and pride in her during the interview lifted her confidence and set aside any doubts. She floated through the day, basking in his attention.

She arrived home to a deserted house after midnight. Exhausted, she couldn't wait to shower and fall into bed. She dropped her bags at the foot of the bed and checked her voice mail for messages. The last message came in at 11:30 from Tina.

"Call me the second you hear this. This concerns Mandy. Call!"

Her finger trembled as she hit a button programmed to automatically dial Tina's number. Accident? Was Mandy hurt? Since Matt hadn't called, she ruled that out. She was in some kind of trouble. Mandy always ran to Tina when she'd done something wrong, and she didn't want to face her. Boy trouble. Victoria had a sinking premonition that this call involved Jase Tanner.

"Tina, what's wrong with Mandy?" she demanded as soon as Tina answered the phone.

"She's all right, but you need to talk to her. Can you come over?"

"Yes. I'll be there as fast as I can."

"Don't panic, Mom, your little girl is okay, so don't break any speed records."

"All right," Victoria promised. She took a deep breath, then grabbed her purse and hurried out of the house.

Finding Matt sitting in a chair in Tina's living room disconcerted Victoria. He looked especially tired and haggard. Mandy was curled up on Tina's couch, her eyes red and puffy, her face pale, her position almost fetal. The sparkling, confident young woman she'd last seen had disappeared. Mandy kept her head averted, refusing to turn and look at her mother. A knot of dread formed in Victoria's stomach. She turned to find Matt watching her. An angry, forbidding expression ridged his brow. Had Mandy or Tina told him Cleve had gone to New York with her? Had he seen them on TV? But that didn't matter now. Mandy's problem had nothing to do with her trip. First Jessica, now Mandy. What was happening to her children?

Victoria knelt down beside her daughter. "Honey, what's wrong?" Mandy shrank against the end of couch and refused to look at her. "Sweetheart, whatever it is, you can tell me."

Mandy sniffed and shook her head. Victoria looked up at Tina and Matt for enlightenment.

"Mandy, you're going to have to tell her," Matt said, his voice shaken, but gentle.

"Somebody tell me, for heaven's sake. I'm imagining the worst. Were you in an accident? Did someone hurt you? What?" She reached up and cupped Mandy's jaw, gently making her daughter face her. Victoria gasped. A dark, angry bruise marred the side of Mandy's face. "Who did that to you?" she demanded. "Was it Jase Tanner?"

Amanda covered her face and burst into tears.

Rising up to sit on the couch, Victoria took her daughter in her arms and hugged her, rocking her, gentling her with soothing words. Rage and fear gripped her, thinking of that horrible young man touching her beautiful child, but she comforted her child with a mother's touch. When Mandy's sobs subsided, Victoria smoothed the hair back away from her tear-ravaged face and asked what had happened.

"I'm so stupid," Mandy said, her faltering words punctuated by sniffs and sighs. "I thought he loved me. He said we belonged together, and he told me I was beautiful."

"Sweetheart, did he put that bruise on your face? Did he hit you?"

"No, Mom. I ran into a doorjamb." At the disbelieving look on Victoria's face, Mandy let out a shaky laugh, then sniffled. "Honest. I was in such a hurry to get away, I didn't watch where I was going."

Closing her eyes, Victoria steeled herself. She didn't want to ask, but she had to. She opened her eyes and looked straight at Mandy. "Did he force you, Mandy?"

Mandy's eyes widened. She stared at her mother as if weighing her answer, then she slowly shook her head. "No. He wanted me to spend the night with him, but I changed my mind."

Victoria glared at Matt. She had trusted him to take care of Mandy while she went to New York. With his eyes on Mandy, he didn't see her accusation.

"I told Dad I was staying at Kim's. I . . . I lied. I'm sorry, Daddy." Father and daughter stared at each other with such pain, Victoria's heart hurt. Of course Mandy had lied to Matt. He would have stopped her. If she'd been home, Mandy would have lied to her. If she hadn't gone to New York, would she have seen through Mandy's excuses?

She and Mandy had faced the same decision. Thank goodness they'd both come to the same conclusion. Victoria had the benefit of experience and past mistakes. Mandy had no experience—only the advice of her parents. Weighed against peer pressure and young emotions, parental wisdom didn't mean much, especially in light of their own failure. *But Mandy had Jesus,* an inner voice reminded her, *and the teachings of the Bible.* When she faced the temptation, she'd had the strength to resist and flee.

Matt wasn't to blame. Glancing at him, she nearly recoiled with guilt. The grief in his eyes held the pain of broken trust, compounded by seeing a loved one hurt and not being able to take away her pain. If her being in New York with Cleve played any part in Mandy's decision to go to Jase Tanner's, then she was part of that broken trust. Victoria wanted to comfort Matt. She wanted to shake Mandy and hug her at the same time. She wanted to rewind the clock and make different decisions, so Mandy could have been spared this pain. Was that how Matt felt?

"Jase said he loved me, and he needed me to be there for him. He said he wouldn't do anything unless I wanted him to. He . . . he needed me," she said, her eyes imploring her mother to understand.

Scolding for the lie could wait. "And you were in love with him."

"Yes. I thought what we had was beautiful, like our souls were connected. So I went. But nothing happened the way I expected."

"What happened?"

"He promised to fix me dinner. I expected candles and music, silly stuff. He had pizza and beer. I thought, okay, guys aren't very romantic. Mandy looked down at her hands, which were fidgeting with a ring her father had given her for graduation. She glanced at her dad, then looked away.

"He kissed me, and he said he loved me, and I knew everything would be all right. Then suddenly he said he couldn't wait, and he pulled me into his bedroom, and . . . and we sat on the b-b-bed." She took a deep breath. "He turned on the light, and it was like a light came on inside my head, and I knew I shouldn't be there. When I started to get up, he said I couldn't go, and he accused me of leading him on. I said no, I was leaving. He got mad and grabbed my wrist and . . . " She stopped and looked away.

Victoria heard a strangled sound from Matt.

"I was s-scared. I started crying." Mandy drew in a shaky breath. "I thought how you and Daddy were going to be disappointed in me. And I thought, how could I have fallen for such a jerk? And I remembered the Bible says to flee from evil. I didn't know how I was going to do that, so I used Daddy to get me out of there. I told him Daddy was a lawyer, and he'd be in big trouble if he didn't leave me alone. He laughed and said no one could touch him because we were consenting adults. When I said I was only seventeen, he accused me of lying, so I told him to look at my driver's license.

"He was so furious, I thought he would hit me, but he jerked away, so I ran. That's when I bumped into the doorjamb."

Matt stood up and strode into Tina's kitchen, his hands fisted at his sides.

"She didn't tell her dad that much detail," Tina whispered.

"Oh, Mandy." Victoria hugged Mandy and hung on so tight, Mandy had to protest so she could breath. "What are we going to do?" Victoria asked, when they finally calmed down.

"Mandy doesn't want us to do anything," Matt growled from the kitchen doorway.

"Honey, we have to do something. Jase would have hurt you if you hadn't thought so quickly. Next time the girl might not be so lucky."

"No! If I thought you were going to go after him, I wouldn't have told you. I wasn't going to anyway, but Tina made me."

"Thank goodness for Tina." When Victoria turned to Matt, the silent rage that shone in his eyes startled her. The emotions boiling inside of him were ready to blow.

"Matt, what are you going to do?"

He looked at her as if surprised she was there. "Do? Don't worry, I'll handle it."

"Daddy, you promised," Mandy cried.

"You and I will discuss promises later, Amanda. As for Jase Tanner, I said I wouldn't file charges, and I won't."

The grim tension in his face struck Victoria with sudden fear. For the first time she understood the depth of the feelings Matt hid so well. He looked coldly capable of murder. She put a hand on his arm. "Matt, please don't do anything until you calm down."

He jerked his arm away; then he looked at Victoria, and the ice in his eyes seemed to thaw a little. "Trust me," he said.

Their eyes held each other's gaze for a moment, gauging each other's thoughts and intents. Had his restraint ever been pushed so hard? She thought not, but then she believed Matt capable of anything he determined to do. "All right," she answered.

Matt hugged Mandy. "I'm so sorry, sweetheart," he said just loud enough for Victoria to overhear. "I love you so much. I won't let you down again, I promise."

Mandy clung to him. He finally released her and thanked Tina, then said good-bye. When he turned to leave, the tears Victoria saw in his eyes nearly knocked her to her knees.

"What's he going to do, Mom?"

Victoria hugged Mandy and held her close. "Don't worry, Honey. He won't hurt Jase," she said, praying it was true. "I suspect Jase will think twice before he ever tries to coerce another girl. Sweetheart, real love does not demand that you prove yourself." Victoria smoothed back Mandy's long, dark hair.

"It wasn't like that, Mom. I wasn't trying to prove anything. He said he'd been waiting for me all his life. I believed I'd found real love, because he made me feel so special, so ready for love and commitment. When he held me and kissed me, I liked it. Whenever Tony or anyone else kissed me or tried to touch me, I felt icky. I thought we had a future together. I wanted him to love me like you . . . like you and Daddy used to, or like you and Cleve."

Fresh guilt assailed Victoria. "Oh, baby. Kissing and touching are only physical responses. It's the motive behind them that gives them meaning. Tony and most of the boys you've dated are young and unsure of themselves. You like them as friends, so it's natural to be uncomfortable when they want to push your friendship. Jase Tanner is older, more confident, and he appealed to your insecurities and desires by flattering you and making you feel needed. That isn't love. Real love is giving of yourself without thinking about what you're going to get in return. You want to show your love, but it's a two-way street. If he really loved you, he would be willing to wait. Cleve and I are waiting until we get married."

Mandy gave her a searching look. Victoria said a silent thank-you for whatever had awakened her senses and made her stop last night, so she could be honest with her daughter. "I shouldn't have gone," Mandy said.

"I guess I did lead him on. I wanted him to prove his love. I never thought he wouldn't stop if I said to."

"Don't waste your time feeling sorry for Jase. He knew what he was doing. It is true, though, girls don't realize what guys feel, especially young men whose hormones are changing so fast. They don't understand the way girls feel. To them, cuddling and kissing is a beginning, not the end. Don't be in a hurry. When the time is right, you'll meet that wonderful man who is there, in your future, waiting for you."

Seeing Tina watching on the sidelines, Victoria let go of Mandy and gave Tina a hug. "I can't thank you enough, you know."

"No big deal," Tina said with a shrug. "Someone has to man the fort while you're off gallivanting. I hope he was worth it."

Victoria winced at the implication that she'd been off playing and neglecting her family. She'd been in New York on business. It wouldn't do to start in on that topic under the present circumstances, so she held her peace.

"Aunt Tina," Mandy said, joining the hug. "Thank you. I don't know what I'd have done if I couldn't call you."

"You'd have given in and called your father, which is what you should have done. I know you were afraid of what he'd do, but you have to trust him. He loves you, Babe."

"I know," Mandy meekly admitted.

"And you too," Tina said, putting her hands on their heads and pretending to bash Mandy and Victoria's heads together. "Honestly, you're both so dense, sometimes."

"I FOUND HER," the voice on the phone said.

"Isabelle Vargas?" Matt reached for the legal pad and pen that were always handy.

"Yes, much good it did. The old lady is in a lock-up ward at an Alzheimer's facility. She doesn't know her own name half the time."

"What about relatives. Who is responsible for her?"

"Her son is her conservator. Had a tough time getting his name, but I got it. Cleveland Winslow."

Bingo! "Thanks. That's all I need to know. Call me when I can return the favor."

Matt hung up the phone, his mind already racing, looking for the spot to fit this puzzle piece. Winslow controlled the land next to the Black Forest Project, and he wanted INTECH's land. That explained his motives for pursuing Victoria and buying INTECH. He'd gone to a lot of trouble to manipulate that deal. Why hadn't he just made an offer? Dumb question. Winslow didn't purchase companies. He manipulated hostile takeovers. He never intended to buy INTECH. He meant to steal it.

But why? For what purpose? Winslow didn't want more land to run his buffalo. Swiveling around, Matt gazed out the window, staring sightlessly at the tree-lined street while his mind focused on the unfinished jigsaw in his mind. What was so all-fired valuable about that land that would make Winslow go to such extremes? That no-good, lying cheat had charmed Victoria into trusting him. That stung. But worse than Matt's personal pain, Winslow was using Victoria to deceive Nick. Matt couldn't begin to imagine her anguish when she discovered the truth. *Dear God, let her find out before it's too late. I don't know Your plan, Lord, and this is hard for me to do, but I trust You. You are in control of this mess. Please, don't let her be hurt any more.*

Pressing his fingertips against his temples, Matt commanded himself to think. What was on that land that Winslow wanted? Not water. He held the right to use all the water he needed. Not the Methergy Project. Although the alternative energy center might be interesting, it was no gold mine. *Gold mine? Rights?* INTECH's land didn't have any valuable minerals, but what about The Sandoval Cattle Company land?

He spun his chair around and grabbed the phone. "Louise, get Bob Atkinson at the Federal Center for me, please. If you can't reach him, leave a message. Tell him it's urgent. Thanks."

Tapping a staccato rhythm with his pen against the desktop, Matt tried to figure out how to convince Victoria that Winslow had deceived her. She believed he was jealous, which, he admitted to himself, was true. Winslow committed no crime buying INTECH to obtain ranch land. Victoria's reasoning had been clouded ever since Winslow had come on the scene. She thought she loved the man, so she would accept any explanation he offered.

Matt knew with deep gut certainty that Winslow was a cold-blooded crook. At his hands, Victoria faced serious betrayal and heartache. Matt's prime concern, legally and ethically, had to be Nick. However, he had pledged before God to love, honor, and cherish Victoria as long as they both lived. Although he had broken that vow once, Matt knew that promise still bound him and, forsaking all others, he must devote himself to her good, regardless of whether their relationship had any future.

Jesus' selfless life and death for His Bride—the Church—were the perfect example of a husband's love, and Matt prayed he could follow Christ's example and love Victoria and snatch her out of this snare without his own ego and jealousy getting in the way.

Matt's intercom buzzed. "Bob Atkinson is at a conference in Dallas," Louise said. "They expect him back Monday morning. The secretary said she'd have him call you. And Mr. Shrock is on the phone for you."

"Thank you." Monday. Three days away. Too long. Time was running out. Matt picked up the receiver. "Nick. I'm glad you called. Boy, are we in a mess."

"That's an understatement. How soon can we close on this sale? I've got to have that money by next Thursday."

"I thought we had a month yet."

"The finance company called in the notes. After the first of September, they have that option, and they decided to exercise it. I tried to get an extension, but they said no."

"I just discovered something rotten about this deal." He told Nick all the evidence he had uncovered about Cleve's connection to the adjacent land.

"Well, Matt, I'd say he's a smart son-of-a-gun. I don't like being manipulated, but he's got me." Matt heard defeat in Nick's voice. "I have to have the money, so let's get this circus finished."

"There must be an alternative. I just can't see it." Powerless to stop Winslow's scheme, Matt fisted his hand. "I *can't* sit back and let Winslow get away with this. If I help close this sale, I'm helping him cheat you and betray Victoria."

"I don't like it either, but I don't see we have a choice. We've got a hundred people here and a couple hundred more at various sites depending on INTECH to support their families. I don't want to jeopardize the company. You've done a good job for me, but only a miracle can fix this mess now. But you know, Matt? That could happen."

"You're right, and I'm praying for one." But Matt was having a tough time hanging on to hope. Rubbing a crick in his neck, he wondered how Victoria was doing. *Lord, give us a miracle,* he silently prayed. "All right, Nick. It'll take a few days to tie up all the legal ends. I'll make an appointment with Winslow for a closing, and I'll call you back."

"Thanks, Matt. I'm sorry. You tried to warn me, but I don't seem to have many options."

"I understand, Nick, and I'm sorry too." More sorry than you can imagine, he thought. If he hadn't screwed up. If he hadn't indulged in self-pity. If he hadn't grabbed for the top rung of the ladder without checking to see where it led. If only he'd loved Victoria the way the Lord called him to love, instead of putting his own needs first. If only . . . she would never have met Cleve Winslow. Hanging up the phone, he stared at the information he had scrawled on the legal pad. Impotent fury choked him. He raised his fist and slammed it onto the hard wood desk.

Ouch! Self-control, he reminded himself, flexing his hand. Calm down and think. There was always a way. He just had to find it. He picked up the phone and dialed information.

Cleve told Victoria to set a wedding date. The closing on the INTECH deal was set. He would become the official owner of INTECH Wednesday at eleven o'clock.

She felt a moment of sheer panic. "So soon? But . . . but, that's wonderful, Cleve. Nick will be glad." Actually, for Nick's sake, the sooner the better. The deadlines on his notes were coming due.

After she hung up, she spent much of the afternoon making lists. She could sink her teeth into planning a wedding, and perhaps work up a little enthusiasm. Everything would work out, she told herself. Nick, INTECH, and the Black Forest Project would be fine. The pressure she felt would get better after Wednesday. She wanted a nice wedding, but nothing elaborate.

To-do lists swam through her head as she went to Nick's office with her news.

"I haven't set a date yet, Nick, but Cleve and I will get married right after the sale goes through, probably within the month. Will you stand in for my father and give me away?"

He speared his fingers through his thick hair, then started pacing. "Victoria, I want you to put off your wedding plans for awhile," Nick replied to her announcement.

"What? Why, Nick? Is something wrong?"

"I'm afraid so. Evidence indicates Winslow has carried out an elaborate scheme to buy INTECH. He lied to you about himself and why he wants my company."

"What are you talking about?"

"Winslow controls the Sandoval Ranch next to the Black Forest Project. His mother, Isabelle Vargas, is in a nursing home, and he runs her estate. Did you know that?"

A tight fist seemed to grab Victoria's throat. "Matt told you this, didn't he?"

"Yes. He ran a check on all the neighbors. Not only that, but that environmentalist told Matt that The Sandoval Cattle Company instigated the injunction against us."

"That's crazy!" Her mind raced to grasp Nick's news. The accusations made no sense. "Matt picks everything apart, looking for ulterior motives. There's a perfectly reasonable explanation for this." Her frustration spilled over. "I know he wants to stop the sale and ruin my relationship with Cleve, but this is ridiculous."

"Victoria," Nick said in a calm voice, "Matt's in love with you. He wants to protect you."

"From an imaginary bogeyman. Cleve's trying to help, and Matt's determined to discredit him."

"Winslow is using you."

No. She refused to believe Cleve would do that. "Why? Just give me one good reason."

"He wants our land."

"For what reason? Come on, Nick! The Black Forest Development will be an expensive burden around his neck. He doesn't need that, and he sure doesn't deserve your prejudice just because Matt starts making unfounded accusations. If Matt discovered Cleve has ties to that land, okay, I believe that's possible. But think about it. We scrutinized their land at the same time we checked out the whole area, looking for marketable value. We found nothing. Nada! Grazing land at best, and marginal, at that. The land is too dry. The soil's too poor. So what if it doubles Cleve's holdings? Double worthless still equals worthless."

"There must be some reason. It's too much of a coincidence."

"Show me one. Give me some proof."

"I don't have any. Matt . . . "

"Matt isn't the one who's about to save INTECH from bankruptcy, Nick. Cleve made the offer because I begged him to. He's buying your stock because he cares about me. How much more proof do you need?"

"I only want to keep you from getting hurt. I don't trust him."

"Nick, please?" Couldn't he see they had no options? Why was he fighting her on this? Because of Matt. She could only blame herself for getting her ex-husband involved, just as she'd gotten Cleve involved. She had taken the steps necessary to save Nick. Whatever else happened— even if Cleve had an angle—the sale had to go through. .

Nick stopped pacing and opened his arms to her. "All right, I'll give you away," he said. "He'd better not hurt you, though, or I promise he'll wish he was dead."

"Oh, Nick," she said, giving him a hug. She could have wept with relief. She and Nick had never argued before. It hurt worse than fighting with her own father. "Nothing bad will happen, you'll see. Thank you for caring, though."

"I still wish you'd reconsider. Postpone the wedding for a year. Think carefully before you take such a big step. If you'd run a comparison between Matt and Cleve, I think you'd be surprised by your conclusions."

"Matt and I tried, but we couldn't make our marriage work. I don't have any reason to believe things would be any different if we tried again."

With a sigh, he gave in. "Let me know when and what kind of monkey suit I have to wear."

꧁

When Victoria told the girls about the wedding, Jessica stated emphatically that she would not come. Mandy, though not thrilled, agreed to join in the nuptials.

With all his accusations, Victoria expected to hear from Matt, but he didn't call. His lack of concern almost disappointed her. So much for his protestations of undying love. For the next couple of days, no one even mentioned the wedding, which made her apprehension more apparent. With no need to defend the plans, her doubts pushed to the surface.

She had to face the truth. She didn't love Cleve. She had never traveled in his circles nor desired to do so. They employed totally different and possibly incompatible business methods. Their partnership, she feared, would be more figurative than real. In a difference of opinion, he would have the final say. And the differences would come. Where she believed in personal, hands-on involvement, he wheeled and dealed from on high, making decisions based on expedience. To him, people were a commodity, expendable unless they turned a profit. His methods matched the philosophies of many large corporations. Defying that bottom-line logic, she only ordered layoffs when absolutely essential to protect the company and the remaining jobs.

And there were even greater personal considerations. Given the girls' ages and their animosity, Cleve would never be an active stepfather figure to Jessica and Mandy. That meant her relationship with her daughters would become strained. That fact, more than any other, broke her heart, but what could she do? Would Cleve call off the sale if she called off the engagement? Everything hinged on the answer to that question—a question she dare not ask.

"Bob, thanks for returning my call. You back in Denver?" Matt asked his caller.

"No, I'm still in Dallas. I get back tomorrow night. What's up Matt, your message said it was urgent?"

"Yes. I only hope you can shed some light for me." Matt stood by his desk in his loft condominium watching Jessica play with a neighbor's grandchildren out on the rooftop patio. He pulled a pen and note pad out of a drawer. "Are you familiar with an area north of Colorado Springs, east of the interstate, in northern El Paso County. I'm looking at five miles northeast of the Black Forest area.

"As a matter of fact, we did surveys, ran soil samples and did some core drilling out there about a year ago. There's some rich land out there if someone had the bucks to develop it."

"Oil?" Matt asked.

"Natural gas. There's a pocket of that stuff big enough to hold Mount Evans."

"Do you know the exact location of the reservoir?"

"I have the surveys and maps at the center. How soon do you need them."

"Yesterday," Matt said. "Do you happen to know who owns the property, Bob?"

"I believe it belongs to an elderly lady in Texas. Someday, someone will inherit that land and get very rich."

"Is there a way I can get those copies right away? It's really important."

"I get back at six. I could have what you need tomorrow evening, say eight o'clock."

"I'll come by your house. Thanks, Bob. You're a life saver."

Four o'clock, Sunday afternoon, Victoria returned Mandy and Jessica to Matt's condo. They'd been shopping for school, but the subject of the wedding had overshadowed their time together. Jessica's attitude had soured the day. Victoria had told herself that Jessica would come around in time, but today confirmed that would never happen. Furthermore, Jessica was determined to make life miserable for everyone involved. Mandy, bless her, kept the peace, interceding between mother and obstinate daughter.

Victoria's head pounded and kinks compounded the kinks in her neck. Though she'd tried to avoid the wedding subject, the girls wouldn't let it rest. The more they argued and cajoled, the more she struggled with what to do. Her daughters were the primary purpose in her life. She couldn't disregard their needs for a business deal. As much as she loved Nick, she could not sacrifice her family. Nick would be the first to tell her to back out of the deal, even if she had given her word. Cleve might despise her for breaking the engagement, but eventually he would realize he'd narrowly escaped disaster. She fell far short of his ideal. And the contract to purchase INTECH was *not* contingent upon their marriage. She had accepted verbally. He could sue for breach of promise and would probably fire her. But he wouldn't have to. She would resign.

With all these thoughts weighing her down, now she had to face Matt. It was the last thing she wanted to do after four hours with Jessica, but he had asked to talk to her.

He sent the girls grocery shopping, then invited her to sit down. She hadn't been there since he'd moved in and decorated, and she was favorably impressed. If she'd felt more relaxed in Matt's presence, she would have requested a tour, but she wanted to get this conversation over with and leave. She sat on the edge of a chair cushion and declined a drink.

"What happened with Jase Tanner, Matt? Did you see him?"

The young man's name brought a scowl to Matt's face. "Yes, I talked to him. I don't think he'll bother anyone again."

"What did you do? Did you threaten him?"

Matt's grin held no humor. "More or less. I dropped a few names in Durango and at the college, and told him if I hear so much as a hint that he steps out of line, I'll nail his hide to the wall. I pretty much had him pinned against the wall as we discussed his options. I think he believed me."

"I've never seen you so angry. For a minute, I believed you were capable of real violence."

"I was, and I am. I've just learned that about myself. If anyone threatens my family, I'll do whatever it takes to keep them *all* safe."

She couldn't miss his implication. His vow included her. Once, the statement would have made her feel cherished. Right now it made her uncomfortable.

He sat across from her, leaning forward, his elbows propped on his knees, his expression earnest. "Victoria, I know you don't want to hear this, but I have confirmed that everything I'm about to tell you is the truth."

"If this is about Cleve having connections to the Sandoval Ranch, I already know."

"Did he tell you about it?"

"Nick told me. I think you're blowing this all out of proportion. So what if Cleve's mother, who is in a nursing home, owns the ranch?"

"Did he tell you he owned that land when you were showing him the Methergy plant."

"His mother," she corrected.

"All right, his mother," Matt said, his jaw becoming rigid. "Cleve Winslow manages his mother's estate. He controls everything that belongs to her. So, did he?"

"No, and I admit his not telling me looks like he covered it up, but I think it's just a coincidence. What difference does it make? So, he'll own INTECH. That just means twice as much property to develop. He can run cattle or buffalo or build research centers and industrial parks, which would be a lot more profitable."

"With you by his side to help him."

Victoria jumped to her feet. "What is this, an inquisition?" she demanded. "I work for INTECH. It's my job. Is there a law against doing my job?"

Matt stood, too, staring her down, just inches from her. "No. I'm not talking about you. Winslow is using you, which isn't against the law, either. Not a legal law, anyway. Maybe a moral one."

"Well, then I'm guilty too!" She refused to defend herself by telling him she intended to resign. Her reasons had nothing to do with illegal or immoral. Matt's inference slandered Cleve, who didn't deserve it. She had orchestrated the buy-out. For being the good guy, Cleve was getting nothing but grief. "I'm not going to listen to any more of your accusations, Mr. I'm-so-moral. You're trying to sabotage the sale, defame Cleve, and poison my friendship with Nick." She clenched her fist, wanting to swing at Matt or throw something through his big windows. "You're trying to ruin my life, *again*."

Matt's jaw clenched. "Theatrics don't become you, Victoria. Sit down." He put his hands on her shoulders and pressed her down into the chair.

She opened her mouth to object but couldn't think of an appropriate response, so she sat. Then he leaned over her, placing his hands on the chair arms. His eyes were dark and hard—angry, as he stared her down. His voice held an edge, tightly controlled.

"Sorry, but you sounded just like Jessica. Now listen. That property, controlled by Winslow, has a huge natural gas reservoir under it. And guess who owns the mineral rights?"

Confused, and a little frightened at this aggressive Matt Halstead, she stared at him. What was he talking about? Mineral rights?

"I'll tell you," he said. "INTECH owns the mineral rights to the Sandoval Ranch. Did you know that?"

She nodded, shook her head, felt like she was going in circles. "I guess I did. There's nothing of value to own. Nick checked, so, I didn't think too much about it."

"You can bet Winslow thought about those rights."

"What exactly are you implying, Matt?" she asked, her eyes wide, her mind reeling.

"Winslow discovered there's a huge reservoir of natural gas on that ranch, but INTECH owns the mineral rights. He checks out the company, finds out there are big debts. He digs deeper and learns that one Victoria Halstead has an in with the company owner, who is getting on in years and is badly in debt himself. Better still, Ms. Halstead is divorced and unattached. A lonely, beautiful, corporate executive, just ripe for the plucking."

"How dare you!" She started to jump up, but he held her down by her shoulders.

"Not me—Winslow. He dares anything to get what he wants, and he wants those mineral rights—cheap, without anyone finding out what he wants or why. Selfish brute, isn't he? He romances the lady, promises her the moon, gives her a flashy ring, sets a wedding date, and tightens a noose around the neck of an unsuspecting Nicholas Shrock, innocent bystander."

"That can't be. I talked—no—I begged Cleve to buy INTECH. You've taken a few coincidences and twisted them into a totally ridiculous conspiracy."

"I have proof."

"Show me, then."

"I can't. I don't have the documents right this minute."

Nick, then Jessica, and now Matt. Victoria felt battered, and all the animosity traced back to Matt. She had started to trust him again. Would she never learn? This time she pushed to her feet, resisting the pressure from his hands and forcing him to back up a step. "The only conspiracy I see comes from you. All the problems began when you arrived in town."

Illogical though that reasoning was, she grabbed at that thread. Matt was staring her down, his relentless gaze filled with disgust. She had loved him with all her heart, and he'd betrayed her. Then, when she'd gotten past the hurt, he'd come back and reopened all her wounds, promising love and trust, and she'd almost believed he meant it. "Walking out on me and virtually destroying my life didn't accomplish your revenge. No thanks to you, I got up and made a success of myself. So, back you come. You're the one with the questionable agenda, telling me you love me and you want to get back together. You've already turned the girls against me."

The pain cut straight to her heart. Hysteria rose in her throat. "Is that what's happened? Did you come back to finish what you couldn't destroy before?" Her fists balled, she pounded on his chest. He grabbed her wrists.

"Why, Matt? Why do you hate me so much?"

"Stop it!" he commanded. He might as well have slapped her across the face. She instantly went still and stared at him.

"I don't hate you, Tori. I love you." He let go of her wrists and wiped her tears with his thumbs. His voice became incredibly gentle. The hard look left his eyes; his gaze begged her to understand. "Don't you see? I can't let Winslow destroy you. Give me a chance. I'm supposed to pick up the proof at eight. Wait until tonight, and I'll bring you the documents."

Victoria felt so confused. Matt wanted her to trust him. He'd just told her she couldn't trust Cleve. Cleve said trust meant everything. She didn't know whom to trust. All she could do was nod. She sank to the chair and buried her face in her hands. Taking deep breaths, she wondered what had come over her. She'd lost control. Victoria Halstead never flew into a rage, never struck anyone, and never lost control.

The emotional storm ebbed, leaving her numb. Out of long practice, her composure slipped into place. "All right, Matt." She suddenly felt so tired, she could hardly get up. Her knees were shaking. "I'm going home now."

"Let me drive you."

"No. I'm fine, really." Her voice was flat—unemotional. Good. She'd regained at least the appearance of control. "Bring me your proof if you get it."

She got in her car and drove home, her mind on autopilot. She pulled into her garage, shut off the engine and sat, staring at the back wall, feeling empty inside. Confusion had taken over every aspect of her life, and this issue of trust—whom could she trust?

Cleve hadn't been forthright with her. Evidently he didn't trust her.

Matt had taken a few facts and developed his version of Cleve's motives, based on pure conjecture, colored by his personal agenda. What was truth? That depended on your perspective. She had to keep things in proper perspective. Matt claimed he'd left because of a mid-life crisis. Maybe his problem went deeper. She'd heard of perfectly sane people developing delusions and paranoia, like this elaborate scheme he'd imagined. Surely Cleve could explain.

Talking to Cleve suddenly became vital. Breaking their engagement would betray his trust. She knew how badly that hurt, especially since the engagement had been announced on network television, but she had to do it, and she didn't want him to believe her decision had anything to do with Matt's accusations. She needed to find out the truth, and she prayed it would exonerate Cleve. She couldn't have been that wrong.

Then the explanation occurred to her, so simple it made her laugh. Cleve didn't know about the gas. If he did, he would have bought INTECH and had the rights in the first place. All this convoluted mumbo-jumbo was too much trouble for a man with his clout. He was buying INTECH because of *her.* Matt couldn't seem to understand that anyone would care enough to do that for her. And Matt had inadvertently supplied her with the means to end the engagement without endangering the sale. Cleve would be buying assets far greater than his investment. She would tell him about the natural gas first. Maybe that knowledge would take the sting out of her announcement.

C H A P T E R T W E N T Y - T H R E E

VICTORIA DROVE TO Genessee, to the house that would have been her new home. She parked in the driveway and got out, stashing her keys in her pocket. Cleve came out and greeted her with a kiss.

"I expected you earlier," he said. "What took so long?"

"I took the girls out to lunch and school shopping."

"Come in. I'll fix us something to drink."

As she proceeded him into the house, she looked around at his beautiful home, trying to envision herself living inside the picture. Even with her artistic imagination, she couldn't see it. Instead, she saw Matt, holding her wrists, telling her he loved her and insisting Cleve had deceived her. She reached up to rub her shoulder and realized her hand was shaking. Breaking-up nerves. Cleve nerves. Matt nerves.

Accepting a cold drink, she set her purse down and wandered out to the sunroom. The lights of the large metropolis spread below them were blinking on in the encroaching twilight. Inside, the only illumination came from soft accent lights on the walls. Leaning against the back of a chair, she looked out toward the view, her face profiled to Cleve. Glancing sideways, she took in his large, imposing presence and became suddenly aware of her vulnerability. This man was not her enemy, she reminded herself. Matt's paranoia had infected her nerves. Cleve wanted to marry her, or so he claimed. He was smiling indulgently, and she hated to destroy his benevolent mood, but she couldn't continue her silence. First she needed to tell him about the natural gas. If he didn't know, maybe it would soften the blow she had to deal him.

But what was Cleve Winslow? Hero or villain? She couldn't tell by his gaze or his stance. Much as she thought she knew him, she now harbored doubts. The courage to question him fled, replaced by a sense of dread.

Something about this scene was out of focus. She didn't know what was off kilter, but the perspective seemed wrong.

"I was thinking about the ranch next to the Black Forest property," she said, trying to appear casual. "I wouldn't think raising buffalo would be that profitable. If INTECH owned it, we could expand the project to include an industrial park and a small jet airport. What do you think?"

His teeth gleamed white as he grinned. "Perhaps," he said, his eyes twinkling like he knew a secret. Was he keeping this secret to surprise her?

"We already own the water and mineral rights to the ranch," she added, watching him from the corners of her eyes.

"Really? I thought you said that property had deeded rights to your water."

"Deeded access and water usage. We own the rights. I thought we could contact the owner, maybe buy the land or lease it."

"Possibly. If it's important to you, I could find out."

"Oh, no, it's not important. I was just wondering," she said, trying to sound offhand, and hoping he couldn't see the nervous sheen developing above her lip. She could feel the beads of moisture. Why didn't he admit he controlled the land? Why the big secret?

"Nick mentioned that you might be related to the owner." She caught his sharp glance before he smiled.

"Really? Where did he get that idea?"

Victoria shrugged. "He knows lots of people. Someone must have said something that he misinterpreted." Now why was she covering up for Matt? Why hadn't she just said Matt had accused him of deception?

"I heard the most fantastic thing," she said injecting a note of gaiety in her voice and hoping he didn't realize that her insides were quivering like Jell-O in an earthquake.

He still smiled, watching her expectantly.

"What if I told you the ranch next to us had a huge natural gas deposit under it?"

His smile wavered for an instant. Suddenly, he didn't look quite so friendly. "Well, well," he said. "You're a wealth of interesting trivia. I don't suppose you know the name of the owner?"

She nodded. "We know it's The Sandoval Cattle Company, and the Sandoval brothers split the ranch. Seems like I heard the name Vargas, Isabelle Vargas. Does that ring any bells?"

He flashed her a grin she recognized as pure Winslow charm. He had used the same smile during the television interview. "How clever you are, Love. I knew when I met you that I'd found a treasure, and you've proved me right." He reached for her, but she stepped away, suddenly wary.

"Why the elaborate scheme, Cleve? Why didn't you just offer to buy the land?"

"A worthless hunk of real estate, so far in debt it would make your eyeballs float? Who would have believed I wanted that?"

"I imagine Nick would have been glad to unload it, actually."

"I wasn't about to pay twenty-six million dollars. Instead, I get INTECH cheap, sell some assets, for instance, the mineral and water rights, and then let the company go bankrupt. I'm hardly out anything. Come on, Ms. Financial Executive, my plan is brilliant."

The bottom dropped out of her world, giving her a glimpse of hell. A piece of her died inside. Matt had been right all along. "You deceived me, pure and simple."

"Don't be dramatic. Where's my smart businesswoman? There's nothing illegal in any of it."

That's what Matt had said. Cleve's deal did not break the law. *Not a legal law, anyway. Maybe a moral one.* She'd replied that made her guilty too. "What about Nick?"

"You keep harping on Nick. He's a big boy. He doesn't need your mothering. Shrock took a risk to build a dream. He failed. I had nothing to do with that. He knew it was a gamble, and this time he lost. I just happen to be holding the winning hand. Shrock will have his little ranch. And you, my dear, are going to be wealthy beyond your wildest dreams."

"He'd have been better off selling to Matsuko."

"Now, we couldn't let that happen, could we? Let all that gas potential fall into foreign hands? That would be un-American."

Foreign hands. She almost laughed. The research center idea was to promote international cooperation. But Cleve had no interest in research. How he must have laughed at their puny attempts to utilize a fuel source from a garbage dump while he sat on top of a sea of natural gas. And to think she'd hesitated to break their engagement and hurt his feelings. What a joke!

How could she have been so stupid? Just like her seventeen-year-old daughter, she'd walked into this scene with her eyes wide open and her head full of dreams. She wrenched the ring off her finger and handed it to him. "You can forget it all. The engagement, the sale—everything."

"You think you have that power?" He laughed, and the sound grated. "Don't be naïve! I warned you that I wasn't Mr. Clean, but you wouldn't believe me. I said you'd run at the first sign of reality, and look at you. You don't have the guts to grab the future. Well, go whine to your precious Nick. You're too late. We're closing on that sale Wednesday. If he backs out now, he's ruined."

"So sue us. I'll go to court and disclose everything," she threatened.

"You've forgotten one little thing. Remember the reason Shrock is selling INTECH in the first place? Who do you think holds his notes?"

"You? You're the one who bought his mortgages and has been pressuring him to pay up?"

"You don't think I'd play unless I held all the winning cards, do you?"

"I don't believe this, any of it," she said, staring at him in disbelief. "You're amazing."

"Thank you. I suppose I should be insulted by your reaction, but I take it as a compliment. Put the ring back on, Sweetheart, and we'll forget this conversation took place. Someday, your little display of indignation might even be a source of amusement."

"You're serious," she said, her voice rising with hysteria. "You deceived me, you're cheating Nick, and you think I'd still marry you?"

He grabbed her wrist and jerked her against him. "You promised to marry me. You gave me your loyalty. I trusted you." His hold tightened until she thought her wrist would break. When she realized how easily he could hurt her, fear crept into her heart.

Dear God, help me get out of here, she prayed. "What you're doing is wrong, Cleve. I can't be part of it."

"What kind of loyalty is that? You'll only stick by me if I'm doing things your way, is that right? The law is on my side, so what right have you got to judge me? The truth is, you don't care about me," he growled. "You never did. Take your scruples and get out of my sight."

Victoria stared at him, dumbfounded. He released her wrist and turned away from her in disgust. There was nothing more to say, nothing more to do but get out before she cried or raged or got sick. Without hesitation, she turned and ran.

It was dark. Victoria revved the engine of her car and peeled out in a squeal of rubber on asphalt. Braking, then powering into the curves, her sports car careened on the edge of control as she sped down the mountain road. When she pulled onto the interstate, her brain began to function. Rage, anguish, impotence assailed her. She struggled to throw off the useless, mind-blowing emotions, none of which would help her out of this mess. Her thoughts turned to God. She had called out to Him, and Cleve had let her go. Coincidence, maybe, but her escape gave her a glimmer of hope. Perhaps God hadn't totally abandoned her. And she was desperate. "Okay, Lord," she said out loud, "You've got my attention. Now what? What can I do?"

All down the interstate, she searched her mind for a solution. Matt promised to bring her proof of Cleve's deceit. What if he'd come and left already? She took her freeway exit and pulled to the side of the road. Removing her seat belt, she reached for her purse. She'd left it at Cleve's. She might never see it again, she thought dispassionately. Finding a pen and scrap of paper in the glove box, she called the operator on her cell phone, got Matt's number, called his condo, and reached Jessica.

"Quick, Honey, where's your father?"

"Isn't he with you? He said he was going to the house."

"I'm in my car, I may have missed him. What is his cell phone number?" Her fingers shook as she waited to write it down.

Jessica gave her the number, and she dialed. Her fingers got mixed up and she had to redial. "Be there, please be there . . . Matt? Thank goodness, where are you?"

"I'm headed north on C-470, towards town. Are you at home? I must have just missed you. I put a packet in your mailbox with copies of everything."

"I'm about twenty minutes from home. I need to talk to you. Can you come back?"

"Yes, I'll turn around at the next exit. Where have you been?"

For a second she closed her eyes. "I went to Cleve's," she said, nearly choking on her admission. "I confronted him, Matt. You were right. I'm sorry."

"Tori, you took a terrible chance. He's dangerous. I think he arranged the vandalism and the assault on your night watchman. Go home and lock your doors. When I get there, I'll flash my brights at the house three times so you'll know it's me. Pack a few things. You're coming home with me until this is cleared up, understand?"

"Yes, all right, Matt. Please hurry."

Hanging up, she pulled back onto the road. Her head throbbed. Her nerves were about to snap. Her hands trembled as she steered. She pressed harder on the accelerator.

Suddenly realizing she hadn't refastened her seat belt, she felt unreasonably insecure. Twisting, she reached for the shoulder buckle above the door.

A flash of light in her side mirror blinded her.

High beam headlights came alongside as a truck pulled out to pass her. *The stupid . . .* He must not know the road curved just ahead. Victoria took her foot off the gas to slow so the truck could get around her.

She heard the grinding, scraping crash of metal on metal at the same time the steering wheel wrenched out of her hand. Images flashed instantly through her mind. The curve, the steep drop, the rocks. She grabbed for the wheel just as her car launched into space.

"God!" she screamed. Everything spun. Air rushed past her, she heard a high pitched whistling sound. Then she hit the ground hard. All the air whooshed out of her lungs. A deafening explosion pierced her ears and a brilliant flash split the night like sudden daylight. Fireworks rained down on her. She watched live embers burn into her arm and thought with detachment how odd that the burning didn't hurt. She tried to scream. There was no sound except the roaring in her ears.

She tried to take a deep breath, but she couldn't draw air. Gasping, she pushed against the ground with her right hand, trying to rise up. Her hand buckled under her. She lifted her arm. In the blaze of flames lighting the darkness, she could barely make out her limp fingers, the odd angle of her wrist. She suspected it was broken, but she felt no pain.

She tried to roll onto her side to sit up, but her body wouldn't move. Her skin itched from the prickly grass. Good. Sensation. She was alive. She could turn her head part way, side to side, but couldn't lift it, couldn't move her back. She looked around, blinking.

An intense blaze burned about twenty feet away. She remembered that a truck had rammed into her, or maybe she had hit it. She'd been reaching for her seat belt. She remembered blinding light, the crash, and flying. She'd been thrown free.

All at once, reality dawned. Her car had hit the rocks and exploded. If she'd had on her seat belt . . . she began shaking violently and her stomach burned with acid.

A vehicle stopped. She thought to stand up and wave for help, but her body wouldn't move. Two people—men, she thought—got out and started walking towards her burning car. She heard them talking as if they spoke into megaphones. In the background, the fire crackled, but the roaring had stopped.

"No one could live through that wreck," one male voice said.

She wanted to yell, *I did, come help me,* but her throat felt plugged. Her shallow breaths were like sucking through several inches of felt. *Please help me,* she prayed silently. Some unseen hand had gotten her out of the car, surely not so she would be overlooked now.

"Better make sure. He was mad as a pit bull last time. Said we screwed up. Don't know what he expected. We burned the trailer. Beat the guard."

Victoria's eyes widened in horror. She tried to lie perfectly still, hoping they wouldn't hear her. Her hand started to throb.

"Yeah, man. You're lucky he didn't get a look at your face." The voice had an accent. Not southern, not Spanish, sort of a mix of both, she thought. They had nearly killed Otis, *had* killed the dogs. They wouldn't give a second thought to killing a helpless woman.

Something rustled in the grass near her. She imagined all kinds of crawly bugs, or snakes. Closing her eyes, she forced herself to be calm, be still. Maybe it was just a stray cat. The thing wiggled closer, making the grass move against her leg. *God, help me,* she prayed.

Then she thought of Matt. Dear Matt, she'd been so wrong, so blind. He had tried to warn her—to save her. She didn't deserve it, but he loved her. And she loved him. She'd never stopped loving him. She was flipping out. Reality was slipping from her grasp. Not an hour ago, she'd thought Cleve was innocent, in spite of Matt's claims of proof. And she'd accused Matt. She had placed her trust in the wrong hands. Hands that would destroy anything or anyone for gain. Cleve intended to destroy Nick. Nick. She had betrayed her friend. *Oh, God, what have I done? Matt, where are you?* she cried silently.

She saw headlights, then a car stopped. A door slammed. Muttering and cursing, the men turned and ran. She heard an engine gun, gears grind, then a screech of tires.

Another man came running, yelling frantically, calling her name. *Matt.*

"Matt, here!" she tried to yell, but barely squeaked. She began to sob, then broke into a frenetic laugh. What if he didn't find her. *Please God!* She tried again. "Over here, I'm here!"

He stopped, turned toward her. She pushed with her left hand, barely moving, but whatever was slithering through the grass darted away.

The next hour was a blur of sirens, lights, and people: doctors, nurses, and policemen. Through it, Matt never left her side. If the pain was an indicator, the shock had begun to wear off even as they strapped her to a board, lifted her onto a stretcher and into an ambulance. With each movement, the pain took her breath away.

Her teeth chattered, she shivered all over and talked and talked and talked. Matt tried to soothe her, but she desperately needed to make him understand. Cleve had to be stopped. She needed to tell Nick. And then she heard the crazy laughter. She wished whoever was laughing would stop. Her chest hurt unbearably. She looked around for the other woman, the one laughing, but there was no one else, only her. She clamped her teeth together, trying to stop it, but still the sound gurgled out.

The doctor, x-rays, a long hall—Matt stayed by her side, except in the x-ray room. They wouldn't let him in. Then back to the room. They waited, it seemed like hours. She kept falling asleep, but every time she closed her eyes, she saw fire, and panic would set in. The police came and Matt left with them. When he stepped out of the room, she panicked. He was gone so long, she thought he'd left for good, and she felt a deep sense of loss. She must have dozed, because he suddenly appeared, taking hold of her uninjured hand and promising to stay.

The doctor returned. She had a broken wrist, broken ribs, scrapes, bruises, burns and severe muscle spasms, but no neck or spine fractures. They gave her a shot, then set her wrist in a newfangled cast. As the pain began to recede, sleep clawed at her consciousness. She thrashed about. "Matt?"

"I'm here, Honey." He stood next to the gurney and held her hand. She tried to squeeze his hand, but her muscles didn't want to work. "Relax, now, and go to sleep. They're going to wheel you down to a room and put you in a bed," Matt said.

"No. Have to stop him. Help me get up."

His hand smoothed her hair back from her face. "Sweetheart, I'll take care of Winslow. You rest and get well. Your back is in the worst spasms I've ever seen. You have to let the medicine relax those muscles. If you fight it, you'll only drag out the time you'll have to stay here. Let the muscles relaxants work so I can take you home."

Her mind seemed like cotton wool, fuzzy and smushy. She heard him say "fight," but she was so incredibly tired. "Wrong battle . . . " she murmured. A tear worked its way down her face. She felt tiny stings when the saltiness soaked into open scratches, but the pain barely registered. She had to get up and stop Cleve. " . . . lost the war."

"No, Honey, we won't lose the war. You uncovered the enemy. Now you need to regroup while the cavalry takes over. My horse is right outside."

She pictured Matt, on a horse, twirling a lariat over his head as he chased Cleve. She cracked a little smile. It hurt, but it hurt good. "Matt." She felt herself slipping away and tugged at Matt's hand urgently. "Promise me," she insisted.

"I promise. I promise that I will protect you and the girls and Nick. We'll stop Cleve Winslow, with God's help. 'I can do all things through Christ who strengthens me.' Remember that, Tori."

"Trust . . . " His face came close. She felt his kiss on her forehead and closed her eyes. A sense of calm enveloped her, and she drifted.

A nurse woke her, took her vital signs, and gave her ice chips. Matt was there. He and the nurse helped her get up and shuffle to the bathroom. They moved slowly. The medication had dulled the pain. Still groggy, she could hear herself talking, and they answered, but she had no clue what was being said. Then blessed quiet.

She opened her eyes, squinted and blinked, disoriented. Looking around, she realized she was in a hospital—alone. Her heart started pounding. Her chest hurt. She hurt, all over. Every movement caused pain, brought images of the accident into her consciousness. She struggled to scoot up, but she couldn't seem to make her legs or hips function.

"Here, let me help you," Matt said from the doorway. Relief flooded her. He hadn't left after all. He told her to bend her knees, and he eased her up, effortlessly, it seemed.

"How do you feel?" he asked.

"Like I've been dragged a mile behind a horse." Her words dragged and slurred. "Mouth tastes like rotten eggs."

"That's probably the medication." He fished in his pocket. "This might help." He popped a peppermint into her mouth. She sucked on the hard candy for a few seconds.

"Better, thank you. How long did I sleep?"

"About six hours."

She started to lift her right arm. Pain shot up her arm and she felt the weight of the cast. She winced and laid her arm back down.

"Your wrist is broken. You have a couple of broken ribs. That's the worst." He pressed his lips together. For a minute, his eyes had a sheen, as if he was holding back pain, or painful emotions. "You could have been killed." He covered his mouth with his hand, shut his eyes, and took a deep breath. When he opened his eyes, she could still see pain or regret, and she knew she'd put it there. He took her good hand and held it tight.

"What happened, Matt? I remember the crash—losing control—the men. It wasn't an accident, was it?"

"No, though our only proof is what you overheard and what I saw. They found evidence of impact. Whether intentional or not, someone forced you off the road. Your car flipped, then hit the rocks and exploded. It was a miracle that you were thrown free. The two goons who were in the field when I arrived high-tailed it out of there. I couldn't see their faces. If they'd been trying to help, they would have stuck around."

"Will the police catch them?"

"I hope so. I gave them a description of the truck, although the license plate was too dirty to read. Hopefully I saw enough to identify it if they find it."

She shut her eyes and leaned back on the pillows. The question that hounded her thoughts seemed to stick on the roof of her mouth. She didn't want to face the answer, but she had to know. She opened her eyes and found Matt watching her, a worried frown knitting his brow. "It was Cleve, wasn't it?" she asked.

"Behind all the attacks and vandalism? I believe so, but we have no proof. Last night you said something about Nick's debts. Does Winslow hold those notes?"

"Yes. I said I would stop the sale, and he laughed." She shook her head. "He *laughed!* Then he told me about the notes. Said he'd ruin Nick if we backed out."

She closed her eyes and turned away from Matt's knowing gaze. She couldn't accept the sympathy in his eyes when her mind shouted *guilty, gullible fool* at her heart. She hadn't just fallen for a smooth line, she'd jumped in up to her neck and wallowed in the quicksand. The enormity of Cleve's deceit, the part she had played in his plan hit her with the velocity that her car had smashed into the rocks. Remorse and grief rained down on her like the sparks from the explosion. Nick's loss was her fault.

"I'm so sorry," she whispered. "I was so wrong."

"You're not to blame," Matt assured her, but she thought his voice lacked conviction.

Matt told her to rest, and he'd be back in the afternoon. Her body was tired, but her mind wouldn't disengage gears. Like a bad record, it replayed all that had happened the past couple of months over and over. Matt had been so sweet, staying with her all night, even after what she had done. He realized her guilt, even if he denied it. Cleve might have hatched the plot and deceived her, but he hadn't forced her to do anything against her will. She had made her own choices. And what disastrous choices they had been.

An aide came in to get her up and help her take a sponge bath. Her muscle spasms had eased enough to allow some motion. She brushed her teeth and hair and felt immensely better.

Mandy and Jessica arrived as the aide removed the wash basin. They looked worried, but relaxed visibly when she gave them a smile. They had wanted to come earlier, they said, but their father had told them to wait and let her rest.

They weren't aware of anything, except that she had been in an accident. Victoria left it at that. When she told them she'd broken her engagement, they showed such exuberant delight, she would have laughed if she hadn't been crying inside. Mandy announced she had enrolled in Metro State College in Denver for her first year. Mandy was facing her own disappointments and trying to make wise decisions, and Victoria's heart ached with love and sympathy for her eldest daughter.

"Mom, we've got to go. Dad gave Jessica the day off, and Tony is taking us out to the house to get some of your things so you can come to Dad's when they let you out of here. The doctor told Dad maybe this afternoon or tomorrow. He's giving you his room. I'm going to bunk with Jessica, and Dad will take my room. It'll be great, you'll see."

"Don't go to a lot of trouble for me," Victoria said.

"No trouble, Mom," Jessica said, speaking up to add her assurance. She'd been unusually quiet most of the morning. "You've got to get well," she said, then she burst into tears. "I love you, Mom. I'm sorry I've been such a brat. I didn't want you to get married, but I was wrong to act so bad." She wiped at her eyes. "If you change your mind and decide to get married after all, I promise I won't make any trouble."

Holding out her good arm, Victoria said, "Come give me a hug, Honey, but gently." Jessica carefully embraced her mother, and Victoria told her she understood and she promised not to change her mind.

After the girls left, Victoria counted her blessings. Her daughters topped the list. Mandy had stepped forward, taking charge, planning to care for her recovering mother, running her father's household, chauffeuring her sister, planning her own future. She hadn't made any references to her terrible experience with Jase or the canceled wedding, but Victoria had felt the waves of empathy coming from Mandy, directed to her, as if, even in her bid for independence, Mandy understood her mother's pain and grief.

Contrite and loving, Jessica had resolved to do her part to make life easier for her family.

Victoria blamed herself for the problems they'd faced over the summer. Her relationship with Cleve had been the root cause. Both girls had watched her fall—as wild and out of control as the roller coaster ride at Elitch's—into a relationship she'd pretended was love. That had been a lie. Love had not been the tie that bound them.

Victoria felt certain Cleve's presence in her hotel room had influenced Mandy's decision to go to Jase's apartment. Mandy had idealized her mother's romance, making her an easy mark for the same kind of desires and lies. Besides, her impressionable daughter would rationalize that if mom stayed overnight with Cleve, spending the night with a man couldn't be that wrong. Jessica's frustration and unhappiness at her mother's romance had made her do whatever she could to stop it, even ruining the summer camp she'd saved for all year. Victoria had responded to her younger daughter's pleas with anger and rejection.

A good, hard look at her motives shamed her. She'd felt so self-righteous. She'd helped the homeless, the battered, and the less fortunate.

Look what she'd done for Matt, for Nick, for INTECH. Even the mayor recognized her worthiness. *What a sham.* In truth, she'd done everything for approval and love. What did she have to show for her efforts? The bitter tears of her own betrayal and failure. Had she always been so self-centered? No wonder God had abandoned her.

By noon, she was deeply entrenched in a full-fledged pity party. She'd rehashed her transgressions over and over. Even in sin, she was an over-achiever. When Tina bounced into the room filled with her usual high spirits, Victoria's balloon of remorse had gotten big enough to burst.

"Hi, I brought lunch from the deli." Only the small, family-owned German sandwich shop near Tina's salon qualified as *the* deli to Victoria and Tina. Victoria managed a wan smile.

"What's wrong? You in pain?" Tina's concern made her guilt worse. Victoria shook her head. No pain could match the agony in her heart.

Setting the sack on the bedside table, Tina pulled up a chair and flopped down on it. "All right. Moment of truth time." She stared and waited.

Victoria looked away and tried not to cry, but her remorse ate through her self-control. Once the wall cracked, the tears poured forth.

"That slime-bag," Tina muttered. "Listen, kid, and listen good. Cleveland Winslow isn't worth a single tear. Consider him purged and forget him."

"I'm not crying about Cleve," Victoria wailed.

"Okay, spill it. Remember, you're talking to the general, here."

"I lost, Tina. The war's over. I walked right into an ambush with my eyes wide open."

"Come on, it's not that bad."

"Worse. Have you talked to Matt?"

"Yeah. You scared him so bad his hair turned white overnight."

"He knows I'm all right. He saved my life, you know."

"It's a good thing. He'd never have forgiven himself if anything had happened to you. He's upset enough without taking on more guilt."

"Well, he shouldn't be upset. I'm not worth it. All I've done is cause trouble, and now Nick is going to lose everything because I had to try to be the big hero."

"Don't be sappy, Victoria. I talked to Matt an hour ago, and he didn't sound discouraged. He was in a hurry, but I'd say he sounded pretty chipper. You know as well as I do that one battle does not win or lose a war."

"This one did. I'm through."

"What does *that* mean, 'I'm through'? You going to jump out the window or something?"

"I'm not fighting anymore, Tina. If the girls want to live with Matt, I'll let them. If I lose my house, I don't care. I'll never get another corporate job. When word gets around what I've done, I'll be lucky to get a job bussing tables. But I don't care anymore."

"You make me sick, you know? Matt begs you to take him back, and you're whining about quitting. I never figured you for a quitter. I mean, I've seen you crawling on your belly and you didn't give up. Do you remember what you told me about war, Victoria? Do you?"

Victoria shook her head as if it was too much effort to think.

"You told me to pick my battles, make sure the cause was worth fighting for, then go for the enemy with both guns blazing and don't stop till the dust settles."

"I thought *you* said that," Victoria objected, a tiny twitch working at the side of her mouth.

"Huh-uh. You said it first, I just repeat it back every time you want to cop out."

"I'm not copping out. I'm facing the truth. I went in with guns blazing, all right, but I picked the wrong battle and the wrong enemy." Any trace of humor fled as she told Tina the worst. "I refused to trust Matt and threw his defection in his face every chance I got. Then I trusted Cleve. He waved trust like it was the flag and he was George Washington, and I believed him. Look what happened? I betrayed Nick, the man I respect most in the whole world, and for what? Love? To save my job? Talk about trust. I can never trust my own judgment or motives again."

"Enough!" Tina stood over the bed and slammed her fists down on her hips as if she was afraid what she'd do with them otherwise. "I trust you. I'd trust you with my life and so would Nick and Matt and the girls. Quit beating yourself over the head. You're picking the wrong battle again. Instead of fighting yourself, get well, get off your duff, and help Nick get his life back together. Then grab a hold of Matt and Mandy and Jessica and hold on for dear life. Matt made a mistake, Nick's made mistakes, I've made my share, but Ms. Victoria has always been perfect. Well, you just fell off your pedestal, big time. But guess what? Nobody cares. You didn't belong up there anyway!"

With that impassioned speech over, Tina grabbed her purse and stormed out of the room, leaving the untouched lunch on the table, nearly knocking over the medication nurse who was bringing Victoria a pain pill. Victoria swallowed it without a single objection.

THE MEDICATION WORKED. Victoria was pain-free and drowsy when Nick came in carrying a large bouquet. In a gruff voice, he told her how scared he'd been when he heard about her accident and Cleve's involvement. She reached for his hand and felt his distress as his hand trembled in hers.

"Nick, I'm so sorry, please forgive me."

"Hey, you're the victim, here. There's nothing to forgive. You just work on getting well."

"How can you say that? I betrayed you."

"No, Victoria. If you'd betrayed me, you wouldn't be lying in that bed. You nearly got killed trying to save my bacon, which, I might add, I fried all by myself. I don't deserve such loyalty."

Victoria looked at the man who had given her a chance and encouraged her every step of the way the past four years. He had believed in her and placed his faith in her hands. A tremendous sense of grief settled over her. Why was everyone jumping to her defense? She didn't deserve their kindness.

She took a nap after Nick left. Sleep seemed to be the only escape from her thoughts. The doctor came and woke her. He checked her wrist, her ribs, her neck, her chart, and said she could go home if she had someone to take care of her. He wrote out a prescription for pain and signed a release order, and Matt and Mandy came to collect her. Mandy brought her a tunic dress that buttoned up the front, with loose sleeves so she could slip it over the cast.

At the condominium, they settled her on a couch, looking out at the patio. Large pots and planters dotted the rooftop garden filled with multitudes of colorful flowers. Matt said perhaps they would have dinner outside tomorrow if Victoria felt up to it.

Her family's solicitous behavior made her want to scream. She wasn't worthy of their attention or their kindness. Reclining against a pile of soft pillows, she listened while they bustled about getting supper and laughing and talking to each other in hushed voices, so as not to disturb her. They were a lovely family. She felt like a stranger in their midst.

After dinner, Victoria went to bed. The girls had changed the linens, but she caught a whiff of illusive fragrance that was uniquely Matt's, a scent that brought back a wave of memories. Sometimes when he'd be gone on business and she'd get lonely, she would hold his pillow and inhale the essence that belonged to him. Even now, the scent filled her with longing.

Soft voices come from the living room. Hearing the muted sounds of people loving and sharing each other's lives, seeing the pale, warm glow of lamplight from the living room, Victoria felt vulnerable and alone. She was an interloper in the home of the three people she loved more than life itself. Now that all pretense had been stripped away, she knew she had never stopped loving Matthew Halstead. The excitement and power Cleve had aroused proved to be lifeless, impotent particles of dust.

Mandy had gone to work. Matt had taken Jessica to her first day at the Christian school she had enrolled in near downtown. She had said she would live with her father, and she had carried out her threat, though she insisted she'd chosen the school because it had a great reputation, not because she was deserting her mother. How could Victoria object to that? Victoria decided after she sold her house, which seemed inevitable, she'd look for a place close to downtown and the girls.

Victoria had the entire day to herself. She longed to explore the upper rooms. The girls had described their choice of furnishings, but she'd only visualized the rooms in her mind. She remembered the gazebo on the rooftop and thought of that day, which seemed so long ago, when she'd stood up there holding on to Matt, gazing around at the magnificent view. The narrow stairs presented too much of a challenge, so she wandered aimlessly around the main floor.

Matt's bookshelves held a good selection of books; she picked a recent best-selling novel and settled on the couch. She couldn't concentrate. She worried about the sale. What was Matt doing? Even with Matt's brilliance in the field of corporate law, what could he do to extricate Nick from Cleve's intricate trap? She had tried to find out his plan, but he only smiled and told her not to worry. Not worry? How could she not worry? She saw Matt's Bible on the table next to the sofa. Picking it up, she opened it to a bookmarked page and read the passages he had underlined.

"I cry aloud to the LORD; I lift up my voice to the LORD for mercy. I pour out my complaint before him; before him I tell my trouble. When my spirit grows faint within me, it is you who know my way. . . . Listen to my cry, for I am in desperate need; rescue me from those who pursue me, for they are too strong for me. O LORD, hear my prayer; listen to my cry for mercy, in your faithfulness and righteousness come to my relief.

The words amazed Victoria. It could have been written about her, but King David, a mighty warrior, a man who had the world's riches and political power at his feet, wrote it, and yet he cried out to God for mercy and help and strength. And Matt. Matt had always been self-sufficient; in fact she had never felt she could live up to the example of her husband, and yet he had embraced God—had turned to Jesus for salvation—and, from the looks of his page-worn and underlined Bible, he poured over the Scriptures.

She turned to the page marked with the ribbon marker. Matt had underlined, *"righteousness from God comes through faith in Jesus Christ to all who believe. There is no difference, for all have sinned and fall short of the glory of God, and are justified freely by his grace, through redemption that came by Christ Jesus."*

Victoria knew that. She believed it. So where was the grace? Why didn't she have grace in her life? She read on. *"Where, then, is the boasting? It is excluded. On what principle? On that of observing the law? No, but on that of faith."* She didn't boast—in fact she tried to stay out of the limelight. Didn't she?

Whom do you rely on, my child? To whom do you turn when you are troubled? To whom do you give credit for your blessings? These strange, disquiet thoughts wouldn't leave her alone, but kept echoing through her mind.

Matt didn't come home for dinner. The girls fixed hamburgers and talked her into playing a game with them. They tried their best to keep her entertained, and she tried her best to comply. She went to bed at ten but still lay staring at the shadows from the light on the patio when the living room clock struck midnight. What if Cleve hurt Matt? He had to have figured out that Matt knew the truth. Despite the words of comfort and assurance she'd read earlier, her imagination took off into nightmare scenes of horror. She'd reached a state of panic when she finally heard Matt enter the loft and tiptoe across the outer room. Poor Matt, working late, trying to unravel her mess. She said a prayer for him, for Nick, for divine intervention against Cleve, hoping just maybe God would listen. She heard footsteps approach and knew Matt was peeking in on her. She shut her eyes and pretended sleep. The last thing he needed was to be concerned about her.

Victoria wandered around the condominium, listless and depressed on her third, and probably last day there.

Mandy had gone to register for classes and get books and supplies. Both girls had moved their belongings to Matt's. They planned to live with their father full-time, for convenience sake. The condo was a few blocks from the college, so Mandy would save time and money and be in the area for evening classes or events.

In an hour, Matt and Nick would face Cleve over a conference table. What would happen? Matt had seemed distracted, but not dejected, this morning at breakfast. He had spared her a smile and told her not to worry, "God is in control," before he left for the office.

Victoria paced and worried anyway. She looked for Matt's Bible, seeking some reassurance, but she couldn't find it.

Absolutely nothing she could do could fix the mess she'd made, and no way she could make up for what she'd already done. After today, she had no reason to stay at the condo. Cleve would no longer consider her a threat. She was sore, but healing well, and perfectly capable of caring for herself. So she'd go home, alone, to an empty house. Then she would apply for unemployment, list the house, and work on her résumé.

But what purpose did she have? No one needed her. That wasn't self-pity, just fact. She'd been traveling on a very long road, and she'd reached a dead-end. She couldn't see a direction to go. She didn't know which way to turn.

A need for perspective made her climb the stairs. She held the rail with her good hand and pulled. Her broken wrist and sore ribs made the ascent difficult. She reached the loft landing, then stood at the bottom of the steps to the roof, looking up, feeling a sudden fear. She hated heights. Thinking about standing on the rooftop by herself made her legs ache and her heart pound. Up there, at the top of the steps with Matt, she had felt an awe-inspiring presence. She hadn't wanted to acknowledge God, but the glorious beauty that had surrounded them had humbled her. Today, alone, she needed God—needed to find that intimacy with God that she saw in Matt. Her need overcame her fear. She took one step, then another, until she stepped out onto the rooftop. For an instant, she felt the overpowering urge that fed her fear, the urge to leap off the edge.

Clinging to the top of the stair rail, she looked out towards the mountains and saw the endless sky, the big, fluffy clouds and majestic mountains stretching as far as she could see north and south and layer upon layer to the west, reaching toward the heavens. And Victoria felt the presence of God.

On that roof, surrounded by glass, then nothing but openness, Victoria felt naked and exposed clear to her soul. No one could see her but God—the same God that she had denied—and He saw all. All her flaws. She felt ashamed and wanted to hide, but how could you hide from the

Creator? God knew everything she had ever done. Everything she had ever thought—the motives of her heart. Her heart beat hard in her chest, until she thought the whole world could hear it.

"Why didn't you answer my prayers?" she cried out loud, flinging her question to the skies.

She didn't expect an answer. When a cloud obscured the sun, a chill crept over her, even though the temperature was in the nineties, and she felt such a surrounding presence, she grabbed a chair with her cast-wrapped hand to keep her balance.

My God, my God, why have you forsaken me?

Her heart hammering, she looked around. There was no one, nowhere the words could have come from, but from her mind and her heart—the words Jesus had cried out on the Cross, just before He died. Just like her cry—why didn't you answer, God? And the answer came clear. *For you, Victoria, for you.* Jesus went to the Cross for her. God abandoned His own Son for her as the Son took upon himself all her sin. If He made such a supreme sacrifice for her, would God abandon her? No. Not ever. And then God raised Him up. Jesus conquered death—for her.

"But I turned my back on you," she sobbed. She waited for something, though she didn't know what. Lightning to strike, perhaps. Instead, the cloud passed and the sun shone so brilliantly, the light nearly blinded her for a moment, before another cloud softened its glare.

She remembered her flight down the mountain, fleeing from Cleve. She had cried out to God, then snatched her plea back, searching for her own answers. She had not trusted God, and yet He had saved her, miraculously throwing her from her car as it plunged off the highway.

How often had she grabbed the reins? Always.

A bird soared overhead, riding the currents with such joyous freedom, she wanted to take flight and join it. She thought of Matt's sentiments when he had shown her this spot. God was here, spreading this beauty around her, just as He had painted a sunset for her in Breckenridge and just as He'd brought Matt back into her life. God had answered her prayers. He hadn't deserted her, even when she rejected Him. He had always been with her, meeting her needs even while she gave nothing.

She looked for something of value to offer God and was dismayed to realize she had nothing.

She searched her heart to find something good, not only in the last few months, but the last five years, and the seventeen years before that, and back beyond her marriage. She could make a long list of accomplishments. But what were they worth and what difference, in the light of God, had they meant to anyone?

Nothing. Everything was God's, so whatever she offered was already His. As far back as she could remember, she had known God was the Creator of everything, the ultimate Artist. When she painted, she copied the true Master's handiwork. She had painted portraits of Mandy and Jessica, but God had created the originals, then He had given them to her to love as He loved.

As He loved. God loved her, just the way He created her. Not because she could do anything for Him, but only because she existed. She had never understood that before. She'd been trying to be good enough to deserve love. God didn't need her good deeds. All these years, she'd tried to show her love by doing good deeds. But loving God meant accepting *His* gift of perfect love—His Son. Instead, she had insisted on doing everything her way. And look where she'd gotten.

Any good she'd done, she had obliterated by her failures, with Matt, with Nick, with Mandy and Jessica. She'd put her trust in the wrong places. Matt, Cleve, herself. And everything she had done, she had done by her own choice and in her own strength.

The magnitude of her conceit and foolishness pressed down on her. Unable to stand, Victoria sank to her knees. *"Oh God, I've made such a mess of everything. I'm so sorry. Please forgive me."*

Burying her face in her hands, she knelt before God and cried her soul out, until she was empty. And when there were no more tears, she felt the warmth of the sun on her head, and she looked up to see the sun pouring through an opening in a cloud, with glorious rays shooting out in all directions. God had painted another masterpiece, like a gift, just for her to see. The heaviness lifted off her heart. As she stood, she thought about Matt, facing Cleve for her and for Nick. She started to grab the rail for support, then stopped. Truly trusting God meant letting go. Slowly, with shaky confidence, she lifted her hand and prayed for Matt and Nick and Mandy and Jessica, laying them at the foot of the cross and asking Jesus to help her believe and trust.

Five people milled around the room. An official looking document sat at each place at the conference table. Matt, Nick, and Linc conferred quietly in one corner. Charles, Cleve's lawyer, picked up and thumbed through a contract. Cleve stood apart at the opposite side of the room, looking smugly confident and impatient. The three men talking together seemed in no hurry to proceed. Finally Cleve spoke up.

"Come on, you're wasting my time. Let's get these papers signed."

Matt called his secretary on the intercom. While he waited for her to join them, he took a deep breath and silently muttered a prayer, remembering the verse he'd read that morning and asking Jesus to strengthen his faith and trust.

She entered the room, carrying several documents. "Is everything ready?" he asked her.

"Yes, sir."

"Good, thank you." Extending a hand toward the table, he said, "Have a seat."

They all took places at the table and Cleve picked up the contract in front of him.

"We won't be needing those," Matt said. He passed his to the secretary. Linc and Nick followed suit. Charles looked confused.

"What's going on, here?" Cleve demanded.

"My client has decided to cancel the contract," Matt explained calmly. "Louise, do you have the release?"

The secretary handed Matt the form.

"Thank you. I asked my partner, Lincoln Halverson, to witness these proceedings. I don't want any question as to the outcome of this meeting. This . . . " he said, sliding a paper over in front of Cleve, " . . . is a contract release. You need to sign it. INTECH and Matsuko Corporation signed a new contract yesterday afternoon."

"That's illegal," Charles declared. "My client will never sign your release."

Rage colored Cleve's face. For a second, Matt wondered if the man would oblige them by having a heart attack and dying right there. "I won't sign, and you can't renege on this contract. I'll sue you for every cent you have and every cent you'll ever make. INTECH, Shrock, Halstead, this law firm, every last one of you," he threatened.

"I don't believe you'll want to do that. We have enough evidence about your dealings in this contract to prove fraud, and we will if you take us to court."

"I drafted this contract personally," Charles objected. "It is perfectly . . . "

"Shut up, Charles. You're bluffing, Halstead," Cleve blustered. "I haven't done anything illegal, and you know it. Besides, that won't save Nicholas, here, from bankruptcy." He gave them a smug grin and opened his briefcase.

"You see these?" he asked, standing and holding up two documents. "Copies of loans, signed by Nicholas Shrock and due this week. I own these notes. Try to back out of the sale, and I'll foreclose tomorrow."

Rising to his feet, Matt held out his hand, and the secretary handed him two papers. "Sorry to spoil your game, Winslow, but I'm calling checkmate. These are loan releases, paid in full. You are holding worthless paper." Matt signaled his secretary, who left the room.

Cleve stared at Matt, then turned to Nick. "You are going to be very sorry for this day's work, I promise you. You'll pay for this."

Behind him, the door opened. Matt didn't flick an eyelash. Neither did Linc. Nick, at the end of the table, was intent on Cleve and didn't notice. Charles glanced around, looking bewildered and uncomfortable.

"What, exactly, are you threatening?" Matt asked. "Do you intend to beat us up, like you had Otis, INTECH's night watchman, beaten, or perhaps arrange an accident, like Victoria, who, by the way, is sore, but mending, no thanks to you?" Matt watched Cleve closely, but saw no shred of reaction. The man was totally amoral and devoid of feeling.

"You're blowing smoke. I had nothing to do with those incidents, and you can't prove I did."

"Cleveland Macy Winslow?" a voice said from the doorway.

Cleve tensed and slowly turned to face two policemen.

"Allow me to introduce Lieutenant Chandler and Sergeant Coffman of the Arapahoe County Sheriff's Department."

"Cleveland Winslow, you are under arrest for the attempted murder of Victoria Halstead." The sergeant produced handcuffs while the lieutenant read Cleve his rights.

"You are making a serious mistake, officers," Cleve said. "Ms. Halstead is my fiancée. We're getting married next week."

"Interesting that she disagrees, Winslow," Matt said. "In fact, she's staying with me at this very moment."

Cleve threw him such a look of cold hatred, Matt nearly stepped back, but he stood his ground, staring back.

"You can't prove anything," Cleve said. "I'll be free this afternoon. Charles, arrange it." The menace in his words was unmistakable.

"I doubt that will happen," Lieutenant Chandler said. "We have Rico Vargas, your half brother, in custody, and he has made a full confession." Winslow's face turned ashen, his gaze faltered—the first honest reaction Matt had ever seen from Cleveland Winslow.

The officers escorted Cleve out. Charles followed, looking nervous and shaken. Linc and the secretary went back to their work. Nick collapsed in a chair.

"Are you all right, Nick?" Matt asked, coming around the table.

"Did you see the look he gave you? It was deadly enough to kill. I hope they don't let him out on bail."

"I've spoken to the prosecutor. He won't be out for a long time."

"You know, I've never felt so angry I could kill a man before, but now I'm not so sure."

Matt poured Nick a glass of water. The older man seemed to have aged ten years as the meeting had unfolded. Matt felt decidedly shaky, himself. He sat down next to Nick and ran both hands through his hair.

"When I think of what he did to Victoria, I have to remind myself that vengeance is the Lord's prerogative. I have no doubt He will exercise it some day. Then I think, if I hadn't been such a colossal idiot, she would never have been in this position."

Nick placed a hand on Matt's shoulder. "You know, Matt, regret only serves one purpose. That's to bring us to our knees before God Almighty. I'm not much of a churchgoer, but I know about the Lord's forgiveness. My Sarah was one of God's own precious saints, and she prayed for my soul for a good many years. Took longer than it should have, in fact, but I'm a stubborn man. I'm thinking you know about that."

"You're right. I finally ran headlong into Jesus in Boston. That's when I knew I had to come home and make things right."

"Good. You're on the right road. But sometimes we forget that we've been forgiven, and we keep dredging up our mistakes. What's broke is broke. If you can fix it, do it. If you can't, let it go and handle your problems different the next time. Life's too short to dwell on what-ifs and should-haves. Victoria thinks she let me down, she thinks she let the girls and you down—yes, you too," he repeated at Matt's sharp look. "I tried to tell her different, but my say-so didn't do any good. I hope someone can convince her real soon. There's a proverb my Sarah used to quote to me all the time. *'Love covers over all wrongs.'* Pretty powerful stuff. I know it worked for Sarah."

Lumbering to his feet like a tired old man, Nick took his leave, saying he had lots to do before Matsuko took over, especially if they were going to get Methergy running again.

※

It was still early, for a working day, but the contract signing had been slated for eleven, hours before. Matt knew Victoria would be anxious about the outcome of the meeting. He'd almost called her, then decided he needed to tell her in person. He had no idea how she would react. As he unlocked the door, he prayed that she would understand and not be hurt by the news.

She'd been pacing. She always paced while she worried. Judging by her furrowed brow and the red teeth-marks on her lower lip, she'd been wearing a path around the loft for some time. He saw the questioning look in her eyes, but she didn't say anything—just stood there with doubt and fear making her seem more vulnerable than he could ever remember. He gave her a small smile.

She smiled back, but the strain remained. He understood her frustration, waiting, totally powerless to do anything. For Victoria, doing nothing was the hardest of all. For some, control meant power, but to her, it meant security. Losing it meant failure, and she'd lost all control of INTECH's fate. If only she would turn it all over to the Lord. She thought her whole future rode on the outcome of this meeting, but she was so wrong. Matt wanted to sweep her into his arms, but he resisted. They needed to talk.

"Hi." He brought his hand from where he'd been holding it behind his back, and held out a tissue-wrapped bouquet of flowers.

Her eyes registered surprise, then her gaze flew to his, wide and fearful. "Pink tulips." The hush in her voice and the questioning look in her eyes told him she remembered. When she'd had a miscarriage, he'd taken a bouquet of pink tulips to the hospital. She'd cried then, crushing the flowers against her chest. Then and now, he'd meant them to express love and understanding. He prayed she'd understand. She released her cast hand that she'd been holding to keep it from dangling down and accepted the flowers.

"Thank you." She took a deep breath. "What . . . what happened?"

He hesitated, unsure what to say or how she'd react. Her hair had been pushed back with nervous hands, making it lie in ridges. Her beautiful brown eyes held an incredible sadness that made him want to kill Cleve Winslow. Did she love Winslow still, even after what he'd done to her?

"Well, it's over," he said. Her eyes grew wary. "Nick signed an agreement with Matsuko."

"Matsuko! How? What? What about Nick's notes?"

He held up a hand. "Hold on. Let me get out of this suit and tie, and I'll tell you."

When he came out a few minutes later, she was pacing the living room. He noticed she'd put the tulips in a vase on the coffee table. She pivoted to face him. The afternoon sun glared through the window, making it hard to read her expression, but there were fresh tear-tracks on her cheeks. He wanted to hold her and soothe her, but she stood so straight and still, she looked untouchable.

"I got suspicious last week when I found out Winslow was Isabelle Vargas's son, and he had control of that ranch," Matt told her. "The proof I told you about Sunday, which you never saw, came from Bob Atkinson, who works at the Federal Center. He told me on the phone about the natural gas, but I didn't know until I saw his reports that Cleve had requested the surveys and reports over a year ago.

"To make a long story short, I was so certain we'd get proof, I reopened talks with Matsuko last Friday. The paperwork had already been done, so all we had to do was sign. We upped the ante by ten million and they agreed, contingent upon proof of the natural gas. They even gave Nick a generous advance in place of a down payment, so he could pay off the notes. When Winslow walked into my office today, he'd already lost the contract."

"But he said he'd sue for breach of contract. Can't he stop the sale?"

"I doubt he'll do anything." He stopped and looked at her, looking for anything that could give him hope. She'd concealed her feelings, leaving him operating on blind faith. He felt like he was sweating from the inside, out. "I'm sorry about Cleve. This can't be easy for you. I know you loved him."

She hung her head.

"Tori, tell me what you're feeling," he prompted.

"Foolish," she said, her voice muffled as her chin was lowered to her chest. "I talked myself into pretending love played a part in that relationship, but it never did." She fiddled with her hands, staring at them instead of at him.

"Partly, I was avoiding you," she said. "Every time I saw you, I remembered things I'd worked hard to forget. Cleve made me feel invincible, brilliant. He said I was beautiful. I lapped up his attention. I hadn't planned to marry him. He implied that the sale depended on our engagement, though he didn't come right out and say so. I didn't fight it. I feel like Mandy, only I'm old enough to know better."

She put her hands over her face, muffling her words. "At least Jase Tanner will think twice about repeating his behavior," she said, her tone bitter. "Cleve walks away scot-free. He'll find another victim."

"Cleve didn't walk away. The police arrested him at my office for attempted murder."

Her head jerked up. "Attempted murder? Otis?"

He shook his head, watching her closely. "You. They're also charging him with the beating, arson, and vandalism at the Methergy Project."

She closed her eyes, and her shoulders slumped. Matt went to her and put his hands on her shoulders.

"Tori, Nick told me you blame yourself for what happened."

A shudder ran through her. "I talked Cleve into making an offer for INTECH. I was so stupid; I fell right into his plan. I was so self-righteous about trust, I shoved it down your throat more that once, and I was so sure of myself. Mrs. Fix-it. I would solve all Nick's problems, and he'd be so grateful to me that . . . that he'd love me." Her eyes grew even wider with distress. "I can't believe I'm so petty. Nick trusted me, Matt. He believed in me and I . . . I betrayed him. And he doesn't even blame me." A tear trickled down her cheek. Matt gently wiped it away.

"The only things you're guilty of are trusting and loving. Those aren't bad things, though you've certainly found lousy men to trust, haven't you? First me, now Cleve."

"Don't lump yourself in the same category as him," she said.

"Thank you. Honey, I know you're feeling remorse and regret. Believe me, I'm very familiar with those emotions. I told Nick this was all my fault for leaving you. You know what he said?"

"Probably something about emotions being nonproductive."

"Close. He said that regret is to bring us to the Lord. He said if you can fix something, do it. If not, then let it go, thank God you have time left, and do better the next time. Victoria, I want that chance, to do better the next time, and I want it with you."

He saw the tremors in her hand, and he dared to hope. Her eyes searched his, and he prayed she could see how deeply he loved her.

"I went up to the roof this afternoon," she said.

"Were the girls here?"

"No. I was alone."

"You shouldn't use the stairs unless someone is here to help you. It isn't safe."

She laughed humorlessly. "Safe? With you three coddling me, I couldn't possibly get hurt. Do you know why I went to the roof?"

"The beauty up there is compelling, however, knowing how you feel about heights, I can't imagine. Why did you go?"

Her chin trembled when she smiled—a sad smile. "I needed to figure things out. I thought if I could see the mountains, I might get a perspective on my life. I was right. I finally figured it all out."

Matt felt a moment of alarm. Tori's figuring had gotten them into a lot of trouble lately. And she might have reasoned that she didn't need him at all. "What did you figure out?" he asked.

"That I'm an idiot," she said. Her gaze searched his. Matt returned her gaze, trying to figure out her thoughts.

"Matt?" She took hold of his hands. He could feel her shaking clear through to her fingertips. "Will you forgive me?"

"Me forgive you? For what?"

"For not listening to you. For insisting on doing everything my way, which brought on this disaster. I flaunted Cleve in your face. I've been despicable."

"Oh no, Honey. That's not true."

"Yes it is. I've made so many mistakes, I don't know how to do better. You talked about trusting God, and I realized today, I don't even have the strength to do that."

"Sweetheart, God doesn't expect us to be strong. That's His job. He just wants our love and obedience."

"I found that out today. Matt . . . ," She looked down at their hands. She was gripping his hands so tight, her fingernails were cutting into his flesh. When she looked up, he saw her fear and uncertainty.

"What's wrong, Honey? Just tell me. I'll take care of it. I'll do anything."

"No." She dropped his hand and took a step back. "Don't say that until you hear what I want. If you say no, it's all right. I can go back to my house now. With Cleve out of the picture, I'm safe and I can take care of myself."

"Stop it. I won't say no. What do you want me to do?"

"Marry me."

He stared at her, not believing his ears. It took him two seconds to recover from his shock before he pulled her into his embrace.

"Yes! Yes, I'll marry you, if you're sure. Oh Tori, say you mean it. Please, God, let me have heard right."

"I don't know if I can do it right this time. Matt, I'm so scared. What if I drive you away again?"

"Sweetheart, you didn't drive me away. I was looking for something that doesn't exist. But we both found what we've been searching for. I'm scared too. But this time we're not alone. With a lot of faith, and the Lord's help, we'll find the way."

ABOUT THE AUTHOR

Sunni lives with her husband, two dogs, two cats, and a herd of Scottish Highland cattle on a small ranch in NE Washington near the Idaho and Canadian borders. In a county with no stop lights, she enjoys the breathtaking beauty of the mountains, forests, abundant wildlife and the Pend Oreille River. In this inspiring setting, Sunni pursues her love of writing and reading, keeps busy with church activities and as treasurer of the local Habitat for Humanity affiliate, and entertains her girls—four young granddaughters and their moms—with fancy tea parties.

Sunni would love to hear from you and send you a personalized bookplate. Write her at PO Box 2018, Newport, WA 99156, or send an email to sunnijeffers@povn.com.

Additional copies of this book and other titles by
RiverOak Publishing are available from your local bookstore.

RIVER
OAK
PUBLISHING

If you have enjoyed this book, or if it has impacted your life,
we would like to hear from you.

Please contact us at:

RiverOak Publishing
Department E
P.O. Box 700143
Tulsa, Oklahoma 74170-0143
Or by e-mail at info@riveroakpublishing.com

RIVER
OAK
PUBLISHING